Daughter
OF DREAMS
AND DREAD

DAUGHTER OF DREAMS AND DREAD

Copyright © Clare Kae 2020

First edition: November 2020

For inquiries, please direct all mail correspondence to:

79 Ekibin Rd

Annerley, Queensland 4103

Australia

clarekae.com

Cover Design by germancreative

Edited by Katie Adams

Proofread by Katie Lindskog

ISBN: 978-0-6489708-1-1 (hardback)

ISBN: 978-0-6489708-0-4 (paperback)

ISBN: 978-0-6489708-2-8 (ebook)

❀ Created with Vellum

To Hailie

the one who believed

CONTENTS

CHAPTER 1
TIME

Blood welled beneath my broken fingernail. A drop wavered before it fell, winding down my arm like a snaking vine before dripping off my elbow. My eyes trailed its path until it splashed on a dry leaf with a wet sort of plunk.

I felt the sting—the pain. Impossible pain.

I shouldn't be able to feel pain here, let alone bleed.

Tears blurred my vision, but I didn't let them fall—didn't move a damned muscle besides glancing up from the ground, because the piercing eyes of a dozen wolves were trained on me.

They were nothing like the monsters of fairy tales, all teeth and claws and violent delights. Though, the sweet iron stench of the shredded elk carcass behind them begged a different calculation. Some were grey, others white, yet some I swore had glistening coats of silver and gold.

My feet were rooted to the soil while my lungs ceased to draw air. Ten of their pack returned to their meal, whilst two with bloodied maws took a step toward me—looked through me—before turning to join the rest in tearing chunks of flesh from the elk's shaggy hide. I couldn't take in air fast enough, but recognised my chance to escape becoming their next meal. With one final glance at the predators and their prey, I lurched and ran like stink.

I only stopped running when the small slivers of azure sky above turned purple and chafe burned the insides of my thighs raw. Pressing my back against a tree trunk, I eased myself to the ground between two roots, curling my legs into my chest as the image of the bloodied carcass pounded against my mind. I squeezed my eyes shut, though nothing eased the memory. The sight and the smell.

The way my stomach growled in hunger.

I smacked my forehead with the palm of my hand. Once—twice, before wrapping my arms around my knees.

I'm not sure how long I sat against the tree, my skin like ice and my eyes shut to the strange world around me. Lustrous green light flared beyond my eyelids, hovered a moment, then disappeared. Sometimes glimmers of colour seemed to swirl around my skin, whirling tendrils of warmth flowing behind them, but I never opened my eyes. Not until my head loped to the side and my limbs became heavy. Even if death lurked around the corner with red maws, just waiting for me to fall asleep.

Because maybe—just maybe—dying will wake me up.

As sleep lulled me into darkness, an image of my mother's free-spirited smile drowned away the fear. She tilted her head, mellow light from the hallway beyond my bedroom casting a golden halo around her frame.

The last time I saw her.

"Close your eyes," she whispered. "Close your eyes and think of something nice."

I DIDN'T DREAM. Not in a way that was ironic anyway.

I stood tall as a tear fell free, cascading down my cheek to line my lips with salt. The forest surrounding me becoming a viridian blur. I blinked away the burning, raised my gaze to the swaths of yellow light piercing the small rifts between the treetops, and scowled at the rising noise. Birds in the leafy canopy above had begun twilling a merry tune that made me truly hate the feathered twats.

Walking past a shrub of bright pink berries, hunger gnawed at my hollow stomach—I wasn't dumb enough to eat them. It had been days since I'd eaten, properly anyway. Though, nothing was proper about this place. There certainly was nothing proper about the nightdress skimming my thighs, nor the fact that I'd spent three days wandering around a fucking dreamscape. This forest, beautiful as it may be, was a goddamned nightmare.

A second wave of hunger rumbled and more tears threatened to fall. This wasn't a dreamscape. This was real. My arm had the countless divots of blood-inducing pinches to prove it. No wound deeper than the pinch I'd given myself yesterday in the face of those wolves.

My fingers flexed as I rotated my wrist, feeling the fresh sting on my forearm. The pinching had become more than routine. It was an obsession. Because no one in their right damned mind would believe they'd been snatched from their own bed in the night and dumped on their ass in the middle of an outlandish forest. So the pinching— which started harmlessly enough—had become a barbaric, blood-letting obsession, all in the hope that one time, just once, I'd wake up.

I stopped my mindless strides, pressing a hand across my abdomen —as if that could stop the rumbles and echoing hollowness, and focused my vision on the endless sprawl of trees. Like ancient sentinels, they stood proud in every direction. This forest would have been lovely, spectacular even, if it weren't so damned beautiful, because we didn't have forests like this in Australia. Everything had beauty in its own way there, but nothing like this. Not lush and old with gnarled limbs, serpentine roots and faraway roars entwined with the wind. Roars and whispers beneath the shadows and flashes of glimmering air.

A scream wrestled up my throat, so I clamped my mouth shut. My voice was hoarse enough from two nights of screaming into clenched hands. How I ended up in a different country was beyond me, and the logical parts of my mind wracked for an explanation. If I were somehow stolen from my home for the purpose of trafficking, I wouldn't have been transported overseas and left untouched and alone in a forest. That left the dream scenario, and that was where the pinching had come into play. Any other reason for my being here defied logic, and made my heart fracture just that little bit more each time I thought on it. Two nights of broken sleep and three days of walking headlong in the direction of the rising sun had almost run my sense of hope that I'd wake up from some convoluted nightmare, completely and utterly dry.

But I would not stop walking. I wanted to go home. I wanted to see my mother, my brother—and probably a psychiatrist. A rough chuckle rolled from my mouth. What a wonderful tale this will turn out to be. Though I'd have to survive it first. Leaving my thoughts behind, I ploughed on ahead.

One hundred steps, pinch. Two hundred, another pinch. Three hundred—this one finally drew blood. Five hundred steps—a bramble rustled to my right, but I saw nothing. Every movement, each snap of a twig or change in the wind would have sent me into a fit of panic two days ago. Hell, I was a trembling mess even yesterday. But now, with the bramble being too small for a wolf or anything bigger to hide in, I made my heart slow, stood firm and raised my fists.

A gun would have been nice, left fully loaded along with a basket of sandwiches from whoever dragged me here. Never mind the fact I'd never touched a gun in my life, but heroes in movies always had a decent weapon. *Heroes in movies didn't cry for three days straight either, or piss themselves when they'd first seen a squirrel launch onto a tree.*

My urge to smile disappeared.

I wasn't a hero, or brave. I was bloody terrified.

A sob broke free, a plea to everyone and no one. "Someone, help me. Please." My clammy hand scoured my face, erasing fresh tears and smearing old ones.

Focus, Estelle.

I parted my mouth and breathed in slow. The forest breeze dropped, stealing away its gentle caress, leaving gooseflesh in its wake.

It's just an animal…

Silence fell. My legs trembled as my heartbeat became the only living sound, drowning away this morning's birdsong. Or perhaps that had died ages ago. The thudding in my chest blurred and refocused my vision with its beat, as if the air around me quaked in time with each pulse. Its rhythm sent the tree limbs dancing—an ancient and dreadful melody pounding from within me. I tried to calm my racing heart, tried to make myself look strong, but my shaking fists gave me away.

It's just an animal...a small, fluffy animal.

What shot out of the bramble and darted towards the canopy was not, however, an animal. It was...a fairy. The air trailing behind it glimmered, fading like smoke off a candle. I froze, dumbfounded, as it settled on a branch mere meters above where I stood. The face was indiscernible, yet the body was distinctly humanoid. Just tiny—with dragonfly-like wings adorning its back.

I blinked once, then again, as an oddly familiar and hysterical lightness washed through me and I narrowed my eyes. I thought back on all of the inexplicable things I'd seen of late in the deepest throes of my despair—especially in those crazed two days filled with nothing but darkness and dread. Each oddity could have been a trick of the light, a hallucination at the very least. But here, this fairy was the first real piece of evidence that this place *was* a fabrication of my mind. A dream.

Hope ignited and I released a quaking breath muffled with stilted laughter. Despite myself, all the terror I'd clung to fell away as I stared at the fairy. As unfathomable joy exuded any lingering fear, this forest of nightmares turned into the stuff of dreams, so I tilted my head and smiled at her. For her.

This isn't real.

Taking a step towards little *Tinkerbell,* I squinted to study her closer, catching only a glimpse of colour before she darted from her perch and behind another twisted tree. I didn't mind, not at all. I sighed and let my curiosity free.

I inhaled the taste of damp earth entwined with the scent of wood and herbs and wild things. Archaic drumbeats pounded between the trees and my heart thundered in time. But now instead of the sense that faraway war drums heralded my ruin, I felt a part of the symphony—the song. A crucial fragment within millions.

The fairy flickered through the air like a tongue of fire, her iridescent trail flowing towards a large white oak tree. A cluster of stones encircled the trunk, interspersed between its roots.

Wonder was a funny thing...curiosity even more so. I strode forward and reached down to brush my fingers over one of those stones without a second thought. Black carvings dominated one side, ancient and primal. Powerful. At least, that's what I felt as I traced the rune. Something faraway screamed at me—its words and voice the smallest of whispers in the wind. I snatched my hand from the carving all the same.

I moved to the oak tree, marvelling at the soft moss swallowing up my pale, freckled hand. Clinging to the trunk, I leant back, peering up at its height, though the top was hidden within the canopy.

A flash of brown shot forward, sending me stumbling on a root and onto my ass.

At least I didn't piss myself.

This, at least, was an animal. Just not one I'd seen before. Squirrels were one thing, but this creature was something else entirely. Similar to an Australian possum, it nestled into the crook of a low-hanging bough, studying me as I studied it. Its face seemed lupine—yet its body was distinctly feline, with the fine paws of a house cat. The long furry tail dropped over the far side of the bough, curling back and forth like a villainous panther from a cartoon. The longer I looked, the less brown its colour appeared too. Instead, it was a patchwork of black, tan, and rusty red, its beady eyes a sunset orange.

It was the prettiest damn animal I'd ever seen, and my fear of the unknown had disappeared into something rapturous. I stood and smiled again, broader this time. In answer, it cocked its head to one side then back again. *It was playing with me.*

A cold zephyr bristled over my shoulder and another trail of glimmering mist shot past—close enough to scatter like glitter over the scabs on my arms. The fairy settled beside the possum-cat-thing in the tree. Closer than before, close enough I could see the air around her shimmer. I tried to peer into her face, small as it was—the entirety of her head was the size of an olive, and seeing the faintest flash of ivory I realised she was smiling at me too. Wide and without restraint.

The wind lifted the symphony amongst the dancing trees and brushed against my skin, lifting my silken nightdress to flare against my thighs. And I had no words to describe the joy that I felt, but pure, unrestrained euphoria seemed a good place to start. This wasn't real, or it was...but nothing had ever made me feel like this before. So, I did not squander it—did not think on the sour feeling rising in my gut. If it were a dream, I'd likely wake up and never feel this way again.

The creature clucked and whirled its tail as if agreeing with me. I stood on my toes, reaching out a hand to test its boundaries—and could have sworn it leant down to press its head to my fingertips. The fur was like velvet, exquisite beneath my skin. "Hello," I whispered after gaping like a fool a moment too long. "My name is Estelle." The fairy waved her tiny hand and the creature cocked its head.

Then, like the crack of a stock whip, the fairy shot from the branch. The glistening trail she left in her wake fissured like fracturing ice across my shoulder.

It all happened in a few heartbeats really. In one beat, we were blissfully unaware of any danger lurking in the shadows—the danger I'd been dreading for three long days. In the next, the creature's eyes snapped wide as a large black arrowhead plunged through its neck.

The music in the forest died. So did the wind.

A warm burst of blood splattered across my face, but the broken cry of agony from the dying creature was the worst part. I threw myself out to catch it, but the flailing body dropped through my hands and thudded onto the forest floor.

I sank to my knees.

I had to do something—but I knew—deep down I knew it'd died the moment it met the ground.

My gaze remained glued to the dead animal, the sticky warmth of its blood cascading down my face, as the forest did indeed grow dark again.

CHAPTER 2
BAD DREAM

"Hello, sweetling."

Hairs on my arm stood erect as the deep voice ground like gravel against my skin. I kept my eyes fixed on the wine-red blood pooling into a bed of dry leaves, not wanting to see if the owner of the voice matched the threat of his tone.

Three days I'd been here. I thought the sound of another person's voice would be my salvation. Yet, my shoulders stiffened and fear curdled in my gut. A worse kind of fear than any since this nightmare began. The heavy thud of the creature's fall onto the forest floor echoed through my mind and etched itself into my memory.

"She a dumb mute, eh?" A second voice, squeaky and high-pitched, like nails racking down a chalkboard. My stomach lurched and sweat pooled in every crevice of my body. I clutched at the hem of my nightdress, trying and failing to tug it further down my thighs.

The first voice ground out. "No need for that, sweetling, no need to be shy. We can be friends, yes?"

My skin crawled. I wrapped an arm around my chest as I tried to make myself small, as if I could sink down into my bones—but when his gravelly words cut through my daze, I furrowed my brows. His accent was thick and heavy...something close to Scottish. *Scotland?* I was in fucking Scotland?

"Look at me!"

I glared at the men, my attention fixed on the smaller of the two, the *Rat*, rubbing at his wrist with an unnatural vigour. He had an anxious, if not raving disposition—possibly conscious of the angry blotches marring his pasty face and hooked nose. My gaze wavered. The larger, balder man grinned at me with a mouth full of browning broken teeth. Scars defaced his stocky arms and neck, slicing into warped-brown skin. Where the Rat was a repulsive kind of adolescent, the other looked to be in his forties.

The elder spoke again, his grinding pitch making my limbs shudder. "I am Rooke, this lad here is my nephew." He gestured to the Rat with a wave. "Funny, that a sweet young thing like you would be all alone in the big, bad woods."

The Rat bent double with glee. "She sure is sweet, Uncle. Sure is sweet! We can make coin, sleep in a soft bed."

The coil in my gut tightened.

Rooke held his bow in one hand, an outlandish and primitive looking one at that, with an arrow already nocked. He followed my gaze and smirked. "Brought the furball down from a stone's throw, straight in the neck. Could bring you down from further I think."

I wasn't sure I was breathing anymore. Perhaps, if I sat still enough —I could disappear completely. I'd never used self-defence before, never had to think about it. The only things I knew were from movies or books. Nose, throat, balls—aim for those. If I tried to run, Rooke might actually intend to shoot. My heart hammered harder as each scenario played out through my head. *Hurry.*

But my limbs, they locked into place. I dragged the memory of the creature and fairy into the forefront of my mind, the inexplicable joy and wonder I'd felt. "This is a dream," I whispered. "This isn't real."

Not real.

Rooke's deep chortle shook something innate and sacred from within me. Something like innocence. "Oh no, sweetling, this is real."

He turned to the Rat and grinned his hideous grin. "She got hair like fire, eh lad?"

The Rat clapped. "Sure like fire, Uncle. Sell her to Okarc mines!"

"No," Rooke looked down at me over his nose. "Sweetling here has an unusual face, she will fetch a better price in Byram."

My gaze flicked back and forth between them, their words nonsensical. I'd never heard of an Okarc or Byram in Scotland—and why would a mine buy me?

Fuck.

I sprang up and went to turn on my heel before something hard shoved me back to the ground. The Rat knelt between my shoulder blades, cackling.

Rooke fiddled with a rope at his side. "Hold her ruddy wrists. Tighter!"

I squirmed and writhed beneath the Rat's grasp, but when his fingers closed around my wrists to the point it felt like they'd puncture skin, a hoarse scream tore from my throat. Ignoring what every single cell inside my body shouted at me to do, I started to cry, my voice already raw. "Please," I breathed between tears. "Let me go! I won't tell anyone, I won't call the police, just let me go!"

The words morphed into frantic and unintelligible rambling. Pathetic.

"Shut her up, lad. And tie her ruddy wrists together already!"

The Rat seemed to be struggling with my squirming. He spoke through gritted teeth. "She, won't, stop, moving!"

Rooke laughed as his weight joined his nephews on my back, squeezing the air from my lungs. "Perhaps she needs a lesson taught, eh? How to shut her mouth. Though come to think of it, headed for Byram, maybe there is another lesson needed to be taught with her mouth."

Something inside me snapped, and I spoke between heavy pants. "You put anything in my mouth, you're going to lose it."

Heavy laughter rumbled above me. "What if I shove my fist in your mouth, break some teeth. What then, lass?"

"Get your goddamn hands off me!"

"What was that, sweetling, I could not hear you." A solid fist connected with the center of my spine, hard enough to make my bones shake. A scream ripped free, morphed from rage to pain.

Not real—not real.

Pain, pain, pain.

Real. All of it.

My scream died as everything within me went hollow and dark. Both men laughed as I let up, finally winding that rope around my wrists—and I wasn't sure if I spoke or if it echoed off the trees around me, but a voice whispered, "Close your eyes and think of something nice."

"FUCK!"

"ROOKE!"

The Rat's squawk became guttural and gurgling, his rasping curses drowning as he begged for his Uncle. I heard heavy footfalls pounding away as the Rat's screams faded. A sound like air being sliced in two rushed past, and the footfalls ended with a crash onto the forest floor.

The impact hauled rational thought into my body, sending my eyes flying open. My wrists were no longer detained, the weight on my back lifted—so I turned. The Rat was kneeling in the dirt, but his head was sunk forward. Blood spilled from his mouth, splattering on the hilt of a knife embedded in the center of his chest. I whirled around to see Rooke, face down in the leaf litter not ten steps away, another knife lodged into the back of his skull.

A cloud of darkness engulfed me...no, not a cloud—a blanket. I did not try to see who'd thrown it as I knelt and untangled the rope, before wrapping the fabric soundly around myself, tucking it tightly beneath my arms. Close—they'd come so close to...

I didn't fight them.

"What kind of stupid whore goes into Galdurne Forest on their own?"

Another male, another thick accent. Yet this voice was much more, *pleasant*, if not slightly cocky. But what he'd just said...*he called me a what now?* Any feeling of gratitude swept away in an instant. "Excuse me?" I said, my tone dry.

"You are excused," the man shot back. I still hadn't faced him, adjusting the blanket tighter still, but there was a hint of amusement in his words. "Now tell me, lass, what are you doing out here by yourself?"

I snapped my head around, finally beholding the owner of that rolling, smug voice, squatting in the dirt. He was indeed young, though still older than I. Early twenties maybe. The man's head was angled to one side, his mid-length black hair spilling over a broad shoulder. My gaze returned to his face, where a lingering smirk seemed to be fixed upon his features. The bastard *was* amused.

At the scowl I didn't hide, a spark of mischief shone in the stranger's eyes. Turquoise eyes. Eyes that held a burning intensity within that made me think of living flames. But when the man blinked, the fire vanished. I pulled my blanket higher.

"Do not worry yourself," he said—voice gentler, "I do not do whores."

I wanted to say, *screw you asshole*, but I settled for a rasping scoff, my throat raw. "Why do you keep calling me that?"

"Well," he started, signalling with bright eyes to the blanket wrapped around me, though his gaze flickered to my brow, right between my eyes. "The garment you were wearing suggested so."

Before I could formulate any kind of response, he smirked and tossed me an old-style water skin. Glaring at him as I twisted it open, I gulped down water until it overflowed and spilled down my chin. I threw the skin back, albeit harder than he'd thrown it at me.

"You think because I'm wearing pyjamas, I'm a...prostitute?"

His eyebrows quirked in quiet surprise, though he chuckled at my tone before answering in light humour. "Apologies, *milady*, if I have given offence. I am simply offering an observation. Besides, it is a perfectly reasonable explanation as to why a young lass such as yourself is alone and so underdressed in the depths of Galdurne." His head straightened. "That, or a love affair gone bad," he added with a wink.

Bastard.

I couldn't think of a comeback witty enough, so I instead glanced toward Rooke, his face squashed in the blood-stained mud. Dead. Good.

The word jolted through me, making me flinch. He may have been evil and about to...yet to feel satisfaction at his *death* should have been unnatural. But there he was, a knife in his skull, and here I was. With no feelings of remorse or guilt. Just relief. I recaptured my senses—the *pain* that hummed through my limbs—if this wasn't a dreamscape, police would be here soon. I'd have to explain everything. I was a murder witness and the stranger who'd saved me, he was a murderer.

A pointed cough interrupted my whirling thoughts, so I twisted to face the man again. His thickset lips lifted, enhancing a small cleft in his chin. Faint freckles littered his broad nose, standing out against bronze skin. My attention snagged on his outfit, so unlike anything I'd ever seen. Lightly muscled arms exposed, brown leather clad the rest of his body. He cleared his throat and my gaze snapped to his face, now grinning from ear to ear—turquoise eyes sparking with playful light. "So long as I pass your inspection," he began, the cocky lilt back in full swing, "You are free to express your gratitude whenever you see fit."

The prick was teasing me now...so I dredged up a small scrap of courage and lifted my chin. "I'll thank you when the police get here."

A quick blink, then he quirked a brow. "What is a police?"

I gathered up the blanket and stood, narrowing my eyes at the stranger. "Very funny. Do you have a phone so I can call my family?" To that he didn't answer, but pushed up from the ground and gave me an incredulous look. "A phone, you knob!" I spat.

A beat of silence.

"Look," I added, calming the anger roiling within my veins, at him —at everything—and gestured around us with a hand. "I don't know how I got here. I woke up in this bloody forest days ago before coming across these two dickheads..." The memory of their leering faces and clammy hands seared through my blood. My curtness stumbled and I lowered my eyes. "Thank you, by the way."

I wasn't sure if telling this man I'd seen a fairy would help my chances of appearing sane, though when I peered up, he was staring as if he'd already made his mind up about that. After a moment, he swallowed and spoke again. "You talk funny."

"And you talk like a drunken leprechaun," I snapped before exhaling, transforming my voice soft and beseeching. "Can you please call the police?"

"Lass, I cannot understand a word you are saying, but I have gathered you are not a whore. You can call me Rose. This is your lucky day, I do not usually hunt in these parts—ain't nothing around for many a stone's throw."

I blinked. That he was a hunter at least explained his weapons and clothes...but— "Wait, your name is Rose?"

He lifted a brow again, his amusement gone. "And just what is wrong with my name?"

Despite myself, despite all that had happened and all that could have happened, I bit back a chuckle. "I got saved by a man named Rose."

He rolled his eyes and turned to stalk towards Rooke. Memories and common bloody sense came crashing back. This man—Rose—had just killed two people. And the way he swaggered to Rooke and tugged the knife from his skull without reservation, suggested he was indeed dangerous. *He's killed before*, a voice in my head yelled. Criminal. Murderer. Yet that coil in my stomach had not returned. Apart from a constant sense of annoyance, there was no instinctual feeling of danger with this man. Though, there *was* still sweat on me—covering me, dripping down my face. I reached to wipe it away, but when I pulled my hand down it was smeared in red. Yelping at the creature's blood, I stumbled away from the dead men.

This whole situation was a goddamn mess.

Lurching for a patch of grass, I dropped down to scrub the blood from my hands on the thicker bristles. Honestly, I must have looked insane. Hysterical. But I didn't care.

A warm hand nudged my shoulder and I screamed, backing away to shake it off. "Hey, come back to me, lass," a soft voice sounded. "It is just me. They cannot hurt you now." My shoulders sagged as the weight of his hand returned. "They are gone."

*Come back to me…*careful words, spoken as if knowing I'd gone to a darker, raving place. Full of storms and blood and fear. He held a scrap of cloth out and I snatched it away to wipe the smeared blood from my hands and face before tossing it aside and cradling my head in my hands. After what felt like a lifetime, Rose spoke again—any hint of that arrogance gone entirely. "Are you alright?"

"No! No I am not fucking *alright!*"

Shock at my swearing flashed in his features before he schooled them back to neutrality. "Just please," I breathed, *"Please* get me to a phone."

Rose pursed his lips, narrowed his eyes, then reached a hand down to help me stand. I let him pull me up, noting when I stood that I matched him in height. He took a deep breath and pushed a smile onto his face. "Listen, I do not know what a *prone* is, but I shall take you somewhere safe."

Maybe I wasn't the insane one here.

Whistling sharply over a shoulder, Rose signalled to a large bay horse hidden in the shadows between trees. "Are we riding that?" I asked, hesitation lacing my words. Ride together, have myself so close to a criminal…"Don't you have a car?"

He just shook his head, not to tell me no, I realised—but in quiet bewilderment. His mouth gaped open and closed, before he turned on his heel to stride for his horse, mounting in one graceful leap. I knew I shouldn't go anywhere with him—an actual killer at that. Stranger danger and all. But I also didn't think anyone else would be here soon enough to help me. Besides, I felt safe, stupid as it was, with him. I needed to get out of this forest before calling home. Between the wolves and those two men, Rose was probably my best bet at getting out alive.

Sunset orange eyes snapping open.

Blood spraying.

A thud to the forest floor.

"Wait!" I yelled, staggering back towards the stone-encircled white oak.

"What is it?"

I ignored the question, trudging to the fallen animal at the base of the tree. The arrowhead still protruded from its neck, but at least the blood had clotted now. Eyes burning, I knelt and brushed its velvet fur.

The ground between the roots was soft, so after twisting the sides of my blanket into a secure knot I plunged my hands into the soil and dug. The creature was only slightly bigger than a house cat, so the hole didn't take long. I didn't know any prayers, so I whispered an apology—murmuring my well wishes for a safe journey to wherever souls go. I took one of the stones encircling the tree and placed it upon the makeshift grave.

When I pushed myself upright with grubby hands, I whirled to see a bemused Rose, waiting patiently on his horse. "I have never seen someone bury a yole before."

So that's what it was called. I didn't deign to answer, but instead tried to rack my brain for mention of yoles in any books or documentaries.

"You know," he pressed on, "I have never heard a lass cuss as much as you either. Or speak in that strange accent. Where are you from?"

When I reached the horse, I raised my head to glare at him. "I'm from Australia, you drongo. And trust me, I *cuss* pretty damned modestly for my age."

Rose gave a jerking shake of his shoulders as he huffed a breath. "I still cannot understand half of the things you say."

Despite myself, my lips curled upwards. "Ditto."

I couldn't read the expression he gave in return to my half-smile, so I reached a hand out to grasp his. He hauled me up to sit behind him before I adjusted my legs around his, awkwardly at that. I wasn't a small girl, but Rose had lifted me so easily, a feeble part of me was thrilled.

The horse side-stepped and tossed its head, adapting to the new weight, and I shivered at the tremulous strength between my thighs.

Mum had paid for a riding lesson, once—when I was six. But I hadn't been on horseback since. I don't know why, I adored anything with four legs.

"So, where are we going? Glasgow?"

Rose peered over his shoulder. "Somewhere safe."

"That's enigmatic."

His lips stretched into a wide grin. "Lass, I pride myself on my ability to be both charming and mysterious."

I levelled a flat glare. Chuckling, he twisted forward and kicked the horse's sides, lurching us into an instant canter. I threw my hands out to grasp Rose's hips, but he only laughed harder as he urged the horse faster.

To my utmost relief, the knot in my blanket held firm.

I was a bloody classical damsel in distress.

CHAPTER 3
BETTER BE HOME SOON

I am not sure why I thought galloping on horseback through a forest would be majestic. The majority of the ride was spent with my face buried between Rose's shoulder blades, his hair whipping my skin with each bounding stride. A copper-coloured flag streamed behind us as my own hair flew in the wind. My hands had found their way to Rose's torso, clinging to his muscular frame.

Rose tugged at the reins to halt his horse, angling his head over a shoulder with an arched brow. "You are holding on a little tight there."

Heat bloomed my cheeks as I snatched my arms away. I had a choice here between embarrassment or indignation—I went for the latter. "For the last time, where are you taking me?" I'd asked here and there along the way, trying to raise my voice higher than the pounding hoofbeats, and each time Rose answered the same way—as he did now.

"And to answer you for the last time, somewhere safe."

"What the hell does that even mean?" I bit back, making sure to show my frustration. It seemed to have the desired effect—any lightness died from Rose's eyes, replaced with something more solemn. He lurched and swung a leg over the horse's neck, sliding off in one fluid motion. When he looked up at me, still astride his horse, the intensity in his glare kept my mouth shut.

"*It means* that there are things far more dangerous in this forest than those two pigs. And trust me, the less furry kind would relish in hurting a young lass—regardless of her foul mouth. It also means that though you are undeniably foreign, possibly dangerous yourself, I have brought you somewhere *safe*."

I fought the questions arising and made myself listen as Rose ploughed on further still.

"I do not know where or what *Australia* is. I have never heard of it and believe me—I am well versed in the nations of this world." Something small, in the back of my chest cracked at this. At the fact that there was no deceit in his features...his voice. "Whatever land you think you are in, with those police and *prones* you speak of, I suggest that you stop speaking of it."

"Why?" I breathed.

His turquoise eyes bore into mine as he frowned. "Because magic is forbidden. Any sign of it is forbidden. With your strange accent and words, you may as well march up to the pyre yourself."

Magic.

I definitely wasn't the insane one here.

Though Rose's voice and expression were deadly serious, hysterical fissures of laughter bubbled from within my throat. I clamped a hand over my mouth in an attempt to muffle it. The look of utter bafflement on Rose's face did nothing to help—in fact, his gaping mouth and wide eyes made it worse.

My humour ebbed, as Rose took hold of his features, pressed his lips into a thin line and scowled. Through the dying remnants of my giggles, I finally managed to speak again, trying in vain to match his glower. "Magic? You're a bloody tosser. This game you're playing—it's over now. Let me call someone. Now."

He just shook his head slowly, brows still creased. "Do me a favour, lass—"

"My *name* is Estelle."

"...Estelle." His tone remained hard, but quiet surprise at my name gnawed at his frown. "Do not spit your nonsense words around to anyone else. You hear me?"

Rose may have been out of patience, but now so was I. "No! I absolutely don't hear you—you're a goddamned criminal. You *killed* those men back there." I flung out an arm to encompass the trees at our backs. "I should never have gone anywhere with you in the first place. So take *your* nonsense magic bullcrap to somebody else and let me find someone who is actually going to help me."

The hues of blue in his eyes flared. "Criminal? I saved your sorry life back there, *Estelle*. Show a little bleedin' gratitude!"

I'd never yelled at anyone before. Not really. Nor had I fought with anyone—my brother Grayson aside, yet even then we'd never yelled at one another. Conflict was an unpleasant, sickly feeling. It felt like a stone plummeting in my gut while fire licked the skin at my nape. I wanted to wrench the feeling away, but it surged—and my limbs shook with the pressure beneath my skin. "You're a murderer! Take your gratitude and shove it up your ass, then leave me alone!"

I was flinging insults at a man I knew full well could hurt me if he wished—but the effect was instant. And bizarre. Any trace of anger vanished from Rose's face as he raised his eyebrows and huffed in pure male exasperation. "You are a right vix of a woman, you know that?"

His voice was softer now, edged with the same lightness from when we first met. Though that pressure was still whirling in my blood, the spark of humour in him soothed it slightly. And what he'd said...

"What is a vix?"

His crooked smile returned. "Demon-spawn...evil critters. Like fairies, but the size of a child. They will eat your innards without blinking and make you watch." Rose kept talking—some old tale about the harrowing creatures, but I stopped hearing his words. Although I barely knew him, I was certain Rose was not lying. I knew it in my bones—about vix...*fairies*...this world. I'd seen a fairy with my own damn eyes. I'd *felt* the cool zephyr around her skim my shoulder as she flew.

Felt.

I'd felt a great many things.

This was impossible.

But true. *Real.*

All of it.

No phones, no police...no cars.

How would I get home?

Where the hell am I?

Cold panic pulsated in my core as chills raced down my spine and my stomach contracted. I threw myself from the horse's back, somehow landing on two feet, and pushed past Rose to stumble for the closest tree to hurl behind.

"By the Maker, I was just teasing you. Vix have not been seen for near ten years now—"

Bent over my knees, I threw a hand out to silence him. Face down and panting, my words came out as a rambling slur. "It's not...not the vix."

Real.

"I fell asleep in my bed four days ago..." I wasn't sure telling him this was the most sensible thing to do, but I guess someone needed to know. It may as well be him. "I fell asleep in a different world—*my world*—and woke up, *here.*" I pushed up off my knees and turned. "I don't know why or how. There's no magic where I'm from. But...I believe you. It's insane, and terrifying, but I believe you." I wiped my mouth roughly, as if it could shake this off as a wild hallucination. A fantasy.

When I looked back at Rose, his brow was bunched and his gaze burned, as if he too was suffering some kind of existential crisis.

"I need to get home," I said, my voice just louder than a whisper. "I don't know how, but...will you help me?"

As I stared, Rose's face went from confusion to worry to fear. After a long moment, he offered a grim smile.

He drifted toward me, careful as a hunter approaching his quarry. "I will help you if I can, Estelle. But I do not want to make any promises I cannot keep."

Sincerity was there, in his face—entwined with concern and a sense of regret. The smirk returned—though it seemed more forced than before. "If you walk a stone's throw to your left..." Rose pointed with a stoic finger, "...You will find a small clearing with a cabin. The man who lives there will take you in. You have my word."

I bit down on my lip and glanced in the direction he'd gestured to. *Another strange man.*

Rose closed the distance between us and placed a hand on my shoulder. The touch was so different from Rooke's and his Rat nephew, and the fire in his eyes quelled my rising fear. "Worry not, he is an old friend. One my mother trusted above all others. No harm will come to you with him, I can promise you that much."

As calm eased the tension in my spine, Rose's shoulders and expression relaxed. "This is where I must leave you, wayfarer. If I do not make an appointment by sunset my contract is void."

"You're leaving me?" I clamoured—the calm I'd felt mere moments ago disappearing like smoke in the wind.

"Trust me. It will be less trouble for you if I am not there." I furrowed my brows, which he had the good sense to wince at before continuing. "Listen. Even the smallest trace of magic, anything *abnormal*, can get you killed. Many folk here are poor enough that they would hand over any sign of it for a few coppers. So promise me you will be careful."

Resigning myself to the fact I would be alone, *again*, I barely heard the quiet command in his voice. But for him to sound so worried, the better part of me couldn't leave him hanging on a thread. I've always wanted to make other people happy, I supposed Rose was no different. I met his gaze. "I promise."

As Rose studied me he relaxed, content with whatever he found. His mouth parted, then seemed to grapple with unspoken words. He blinked, twice, and schooled his features into that damned easy arrogance, tilting his head for good measure. "Estelle is a right weird name, you know? I will be back—you are far too interesting a commodity for me to not return to. Try not to miss me too much."

When the words settled in and I looked back at him with incredulous eyes, he winked before spinning on his heel to stride towards his horse. He mounted, looked me up and down, then smiled broadly before kicking the bay's sides, sending them shooting for the tree line, leaving me in a whirlwind of dust.

"Bastard," I muttered under my breath.

Well, I thought, gazing around the now eerily silent forest, the gnarled trees not as tightly packed as they were when I met that arrogant ass. I could either wait here in the dirt and scream about my misfortune, or I could swallow my fear and get myself to safety. To this cabin Rose spoke of. Gathering up the blanket, I re-checked the knot and set off in the direction Rose had pointed. To walk a *stone's throw* away.

Quite literally having walked the distance I could pelt a stone, I came across a small clearing, housing a very unostentatious log cabin. The sun had dropped low, telling me I'd spent another entire day inside this green labyrinth.

Galdurne, Rose had called it.

As I stared at the simple wooden structure, I couldn't help but think it was like something out of a child's storybook. Or a horror movie. I suppose it depended on how you'd describe it. A cottage in the forest sounded lovely, but a cabin in the woods…

I pressed a hand to my beating chest—I had to trust Rose. I *did* trust him, stupid as that was, so I steeled myself and stepped into the clearing.

I HAVE NEVER BEEN great at meeting strangers. I'd always relied on having my head in the clouds or music blasting in my ears, antisocialism being one of my many flaws—according to my best mate. I still hadn't fully processed my interactions with three strange men all in the space of a few hours, but there was time for that later.

Time to let myself be consumed by it, later.

For now…what would this man say? *What would he think?*

A lone girl wrapped in nothing but a nightdress and blanket

standing outside his door. Was he even home? Alas, the thoughts eddying my head and setting my teeth on edge were interrupted when the door snapped open wide.

He was huge.

Bigger than huge.

The man before me would put any professional footballer to shame. The muscles in his arms alone...*Jesus Christ.*

Not to mention this man's height, he had to be two feet taller than me—and I was six feet tall. Older than Rose but perhaps younger than Rooke, I couldn't tell. Whatever small confidence I'd found with Rose evaporated. The man had a wiry brown beard streaked with grey falling to his chest—ending in an intricate braided knot, entwined with silver beads adorned by runes. Chestnut hair was tied into a bun behind his head and both arms were covered in elaborate black tribalistic tattoos, vivid against fair skin.

In essence, the embodiment of an ancient Viking Warrior stood before me.

What the hell, Rose?

The man peered down at me with raised brows, bronze-coloured eyes brimming with scrutiny.

"Umm...hello. Rose sent me here. He—he said you could help me." Unfortunately my words, or my pathetic demeanour only seemed to displease this man more. He crossed solid arms over a barrelled chest, so I lowered my gaze to my feet. "I'm sorry if-"

My attempt at an apology was interrupted by a thunderous voice.

"If *Rose* wants something, he usually gets it. Are yeh going to cause me trouble, lass?"

His accent was thick like Rose's, deep and rolling, and truly did remind me of thunder as it vibrated off the very walls of the cabin. Rose said he was an old friend...but this man had practically spat his name.

"Did yeh hear me, lassie?"

Bloody idiot, I chided myself before snapping my stare to his face. "Yes sir. I mean, no sir. I won't cause any trouble, I promise. I just need..."

But I didn't know what I needed. A place to sleep? A meal? A way home? I shifted on my feet, still outside the threshold, and tightened the blanket around me.

"Stop being so scared of me, I ain't as mean as I look. The name is Tor." The thunder remained, yet his voice was gentler now, like a roiling storm in the distant sky. "From what I can tell, yer lost. Yer not from around here. And yeh..." His voice trailed as he grimaced at my tight hold of the blanket. "Did Rose find yeh in the woods then?"

Though his appearance suggested anything but, there was kindness in his face, and a strange sort of sorrow I couldn't discern. I nodded.

"Yeh can stay as long as yeh need, there is stew inside—clothes too, in the bottom drawers of the dresser." He retreated into the cabin, stepping aside to let me pass.

"Thank you," I said without going any further.

I wanted to be transparent with this man, upfront. The kindness I sensed in him only solidified that desire. Gentle giant indeed. "Yes, by the way, Rose saved me. There were two men and they—"

"No," Tor cut in. "I do not want to know." His interruption was clipped and swift. "I do not need to know."

"Oh, no," I said, my voice quickening. "Nothing happened, they wanted to capture and sell me, or something. They were talking about a mine and a place called Byram. Rose found me before anything happened."

"Did he kill them?"

I nodded again.

"Good."

Apparently, murder was deemed good in this world...but yes, *good.*

"I'm Estelle," I said, throwing out my right hand to shake his. "Estelle Verndari." He only frowned and peered at my outstretched hand, then back at my face.

"What am I s'posed to do with that?"

A nervous chuckle escaped me as an all-too familiar movie scene with an eerily similar scenario radiated in my mind. "You shake it, like this." I grasped his hand and firmly shook it, his hand dwarfing mine.

The fact that it could have been entirely impolite to do so only crossed my mind afterwards and I scrambled for an explanation. "It's what people do when they meet, where I'm from."

When I released his hand, Tor lifted it to his face for inspection—turning it over as if I'd passed along some horrible disease, before releasing a guffaw and stepping backwards further. "I would suggest that yeh be more careful with what yeh do and say around folk. I do not know what Rose told yeh, but most here are wary about anything different from 'em. While yeh cannot hide that strange accent, yeh can hide information that folk do not need knowing."

Shit. I'd already stuffed up. But Tor, I sensed I could trust to not report me. *To whom*, I didn't know.

"I will help yeh as best I can," he continued, voice raising as if that storm was rolling in. "There is a tub in the corner to wash yerself, I filled it not long ago. When yer done, there is fresh stew in the hearth. I will go outside for a while. Lock the door behind me and do not open it for anyone but me. Understand?"

I nodded again as I stepped around him and into the cabin.

It was cosy and rustic and there were enough blankets around the small home to indicate it did indeed get cold here. Tor seemed too big for the space, the entirety of it would have easily fitted into my lounge room at home. And my house on no accounts was considered large.

A small fireplace, or hearth as Tor had called, was situated midway against the far wall. Surrounding the hearth, which flickered with fire-light, sat three makeshift chairs carved from tree stumps and padded with furs pushed up against a large table. Above the hearth a ledge held a variety of pots, utensils and dishes, and as my eyes roamed I realised it alone served as Tor's kitchen. The far corner on my left was sectioned off with a stone wall and a large spotted pelt serving as a doorway—which is where I hoped my well-needed bath awaited.

To save myself appearing too rude as I gawked about this man's house, I twisted back to Tor, noting the single sized bed tucked into the dark corner closest to the bathing area, separate from the sprawling bed situated on the opposite end. "Thank you," I said softly, "For taking me in."

The man's beard twitched as he smiled.

"Yeh seem to have been through hell, lass, it is the least I can do. Maybe on the morrow, yeh can tell me where yeh came from and why yer here. For tonight, eat. And rest."

I returned his smile, let it fill my face. Tor started awkwardly away from the threshold, but halted. He turned and studied me, throwing out his right hand. I placed my hand in his, a smirk lifting as he shook it inelegantly—and a little too tightly. "It is nice to meet yeh, Estelle."

"And you, Tor."

With a sharp nod, Tor released me and spun away, stalking out of sight. Recalling the rumbling echo of his words, I rushed to close the door and pushed in a large metal latch to make it lock. I indulged in a deep breath to still my thoughts. When I took another, the heavy scent of sandalwood and clove overwrought my senses.

A pleasant place, this home. As serene as any storybook setting. The only thing amiss being the giant tattooed Viking living within it. I traipsed to Tor's enormous bed as a single bright blanket caught my gaze. Draped over a corner, it was made with the most beautiful sage coloured wool. I knelt and traced my fingertips over the soft chunky knit. The scent of cloves emanated from its folds, and a heavy, guilty suspicion plummeted through me. I snatched my hand away and stood, glancing through the windows to see sunlight retreating from the onslaught of night.

Another day gone.

Another day...*gone.*

What would Mum think?

My face screwed up before I could stop it. In the sanctuary of Tor's home, I crumbled. The blanket fell to the ground as I wiped tears from my eyes, but the stench of muck on my hands had me almost running for the bath.

AFTER SPONGE BATHING in a wooden tub half-filled with luke-warm water, and relieving myself into a damned chamber pot, I dried away the rivulets of water with Rose's blanket. Dropping the heavy fabric once again, I went towards the dressers Tor indicated earlier, ditching my soiled nightdress onto the floor. That leaden weight returned when I opened a drawer and women's clothes sat undisturbed; linen-type shifts and loose-fitting trousers in a range of colours.

I'd seen enough movies to know the long strip of soft cloth wrapped around one's breasts—so I pulled one out and enveloped mine as tightly as possible.

I tugged on a white shift along with a pair of loose pale-blue pants and fingered out the knots in my still-damp hair, shaking it out like a lion's mane. Stomach churning, I moved to the hearth to spoon stew into a bowl with a large ladle. To be frank, it tasted awful, but food was food and I was ravenous.

I devoured two and a half bowls before my belly protested.

Once I'd cleaned up after myself, I glanced towards the door. Tor still had not returned.

With nothing to do but dwell on my thoughts, the day's events plagued my mind. Memories flashed like a broken TV; blood streaming down my face, sunset-orange eyes snapping open, clammy hands grasping my thigh. Overwhelming and horrific—then there was Rose.

Weariness set into my bones, so I wrapped myself in furs and climbed into the smaller bed, clinging to the warmth as if were a living thing that could protect me from the world. From *this* world.

"Close your eyes," I whispered to myself in the silence of the night-dark cabin. "Close your eyes and think of something nice."

THREE LOUD KNOCKS woke me and for a moment, I thought I was back home. That my mother would burst in, demanding I dress for school.

The scent of sandalwood and the dull warmth of a dying fire greeted me instead. Three more knocks and a thunderous voice bellowing my name had me stumbling from bed to unlatch the lock.

Tor strode across the threshold, shrugging off a new fur from his shoulder onto the table. His glance caught me before darting towards the hearth.

A disapproving sigh sounded from his mouth. "Rule one, during the Heim, do not let the fire go out at night." His eyes shifted back to me, catching me mid-yawn.

Blinking away the drowsiness, I slurred, "What is a Heim?"

Tor crossed his arms and tilted his head. "The cold season."

"Oh," I nodded slowly. "We call it Winter...what do you call the other three seasons?"

He shook his head. "There are only two, Estelle. The Heim and the Kairi. The Heim can be deadly to those ill prepared. Or careless. Lucky for *yeh*," he gestured to the dying fire, "The cold season is near over."

"Yeah, see the thing is..." I drew out the words, reluctant to admit my ignorance, "I don't know how to keep a fire going." To that I earned a dubious look—as if I'd just declared myself to be a flying pig. Heat flooded my cheeks.

"Yeh do not know how to tend a fire?"

I shook my head. Refusing to look down just yet.

"I do not s'pose yeh know how to ride a bleedin' horse now, either?" The question was more of a scoff. A sarcastic joke. But with Tor, the truth. I wanted him to know the truth, no matter how rapidly embarrassment was rising.

"No, not really. I had a lesson once when I was little."

Tor seemed to be at a loss, his teasing backfired. "Do yeh know anything at all, lass? Do yeh have any kind of skill?"

A flare of indignation and stubborn offence surged—and disappeared faster than it came.

"No."

A sad statement—but the truth. I finally looked at my feet, my teeth clamping down on my bottom lip. What was a modern education when two men had held me down and almost...no. I didn't know how to defend myself, how to keep a fire going, or how to find my own goddamned food. I didn't know how to *survive*, without everything I'd taken for granted. Not that I'd ever intended on needing to know such skills, but all the same. Tor was right. Apart from my ability to make amazing pancakes, I couldn't *do* a damned thing.

"Well," Tor's voice boomed, distracting me from self-pity. "I will just have to teach yeh."

I knotted my brows and looked up. "Teach me what?"

He pursed his lips before answering, considering me. "Everything I can. I can tell yeh ain't stupid. Yeh will pick things up easy enough. I will teach yeh how to hunt, how to keep warm, and how to fight for yerself." Through his proclamation, I caught a tiny wince...small enough to be a shiver, but I caught it all the same before he continued. "And I will teach yeh how to ride a bleedin' horse."

I just stared at him. He was serious, utterly serious.

"Yeh came from another place entirely, Estelle. I ain't that smart, but I know that much. I might not be able to help yeh get back, but I can teach what yeh need knowing before finding a way. Whilst staying here though, I expect yeh to pull yer own weight. Hunting and finding food will be a good start."

Even if a small part of me quailed at the idea of hunting—of killing anything—I told myself it wasn't sport. Here, hunting was survival. Essential. I needed Tor. I needed to learn these things if I had any chance of finding my way home. Of surviving this world.

I would not wait to be saved.

Damn being a damsel in distress.

Determination soared beneath my skin, Tor's roiling voice unleashing a storm within my blood. I met his gaze. "Yes," I breathed. "Teach me. Teach me everything."

Tor smiled and strode for the hearth to poke at embers. He twisted to speak over his shoulder and I frowned when I caught his crooked grin. "First of all, lass, haul yer arse back to bed."

Seeing my confusion at the abrupt change, Tor's smile widened.

"Yer no good to me with a twitchy eye."

As I pulled the furs up to my chin and faced the wall, exhaustion coasted. No tears found me tonight. But memories did.

Faces.

My mum's. My brother Grayson's...even Dad's.

What would they all make of this? What would they say if they could see me now? Would they think me brave or weak?

Somewhere between envisioning a Sunday morning making breakfast with Grayson and wondering whether proper fire maintenance would be a topic in my school exams, I drifted away again.

A voice appeared in my dreams—unlike anything I'd heard before. I could not tell if she was old or young, but the woman's words soared as if carried by the wind. A prophecy. A story. A promise.

In the beginning, there was nothing but darkness. A darkness to devour, a darkness to kill. No life prevailed; there was nothing at all. For an age, that darkness was the sole being of the world. Alone.

But when that age turned into the next, the darkness became lonely, its desire to devour ceased and loneliness turned into desperate longing for companionship. So from the darkness light was born. It flooded into the world. Not in the way that monopolised, but like children sharing a womb, light so shared the world with the dark.

Their union created life and death. Stars formed in the likeness of light and the sky was shaped in the likeness of dark. Worlds were born, beings conceived, and civilisations forged and destroyed. Where there was life, there was death. A perfectly balanced unity of two equal souls.

But light grew greedy—it wanted too much, imagined too great, and longed for superiority. It shoved out the dark, tossed away its equanimity and worked in solidarity.

It created Gods—those to rule forever and to never die.

To restore balance, the darkness fashioned Gods of its own. To wield death to those who yearned for immortality. No longer united, their conflict fed into the world. Civilisations shattered, nature altered, and beings were annihilated.

Night and Day were born, and so too were the creatures that served them.

Another age passed and their quarrel festered, seeping into their children—the Gods.

On and on the battle between life and death ensued, until the Gods themselves sought harmony. Until the Gods sought Hope.

But there was one God, the first-born child of darkness—one who had inherited their creator's malice—who sought only to destroy Hope. In this, it created a being in its image to carry out its unholy desire.

It created man.

CHAPTER 4
FEAR ON FIRE

"Estelle!"

What the hell?

"Lass, wake up!"

A stormy voice cracked through my dreams like thunder. The darkness was here. *He* was here... *a darkness to devour the world.*

"What are yeh muttering about? Time for training, get yer arse up and we can go."

Training?

Reality brushed away fear. It was dark because dawn hadn't arrived yet. I was in a sandalwood scented cabin and Tor was waking me, with only the embers of the night's fire lighting the room.

"*Why* are we getting up so early?" I groaned.

Tor chuckled at my childlike whining. "Yer training with me now, lass. Yeh will not be waking with the sun again for a long time."

I untangled myself from the mass of furs with as much dramatic flair as a tortoise racing a hare. *That dream*—my actual dream—had seemed real. But this seemed real, or it was. I don't know.

Dreamception.

Wincing as my feet hit cold stones, I tucked away lingering questions about my dream for later. I might be growing fond of Tor, but I wasn't ready to ask him about light and dark and the creation of gods. Slowly shoving my *arse* out of bed, a hollow feeling uncurled in my gut —I hadn't woken up at home. I didn't let Tor see the welling tears, instead trudging towards the bucket of cool water in the corner to wash my face.

Heavy footfalls came to a stop behind me and I whirled to see Tor's giant frame, his hand outstretched with a large chunk of crusty bread.

"Eat. Then we hunt."

I mumbled my thanks and nibbled at the hard crust. Between mouthfuls I asked, "So what, exactly, am I learning this morning?"

A half smile. "To see, lass. To watch and see."

My brows creased, but Tor only nodded his head and moved towards the door. With no choice but to follow, I ran to keep up.

I FOLLOWED him not fifty meters into the dreary forest, where he had pointed to this thicket, bade me to wait and watch, then left.

Well past sunrise, I still squatted in the prickly foliage of a berry shrub. I had been picking one off intermittently and chewing whenever my muscles locked up. Tor had warned me not to eat too many as they were a strong anodyne—but they tasted too good to resist. Tzarberries, they were called, and were a vivid cerulean colour. The bright pink ones, I'd learned, were called Quietus. They were, indeed, *very* poisonous.

Stay hidden and stay quiet, Tor had ordered.

Well, if I was going to learn his way, I might as well do it right. So I stayed hidden and I didn't make a bloody sound. I tried to *see*, as Tor had put it, but there was nothing *to* see. The forest had been silent since I'd settled in the thicket. No yoles, no wolves—and certainly no fairies.

No horrific men for that matter either.

Should I have told Tor about the fairy? He most likely thinks me mad enough already. Both Tor and Rose were very clear about the danger of being different. I was pretty damn certain that seeing a fairy was different—fairies were magic.

Which was bad. Right—*magic bad.*

My thoughts drifted as I waited, alone in the shadows of the woods, and I found myself wondering what might have happened if Rose hadn't found me. What hellhole I would have been sold into for god knows what. Perhaps I could have found the nearest thing constituting law enforcement—or maybe they were the baddies. I'd have to be smarter now—not let anything slip if I met anyone else. I'd promised both Tor and Rose as much.

Limbs numb, with still nothing to *see*, I stared at the canopy. Huge tree limbs arched overhead, massive and centuries old. Older perhaps, unless trees grew differently here? For the millionth time this morning, my mind drifted back to the dream I had last night.

Creation. Life and death.

A difficult concept in any case, but to envision light and dark as beings, as souls—and humans were the children of darkness? *Well, that's depressing.*

Sure, there were some evil pricks in the world; every second day of the week some horrible thing appeared in the news. But created by the dark? Or at least the God of darkness? It was too much to try and sort through. And too early in the morning for it. Mind spinning, I tried to refocus on the forest.

See.

See? *All I can see are damned trees!*

Apart from this thicket, the grass, and a fallen branch beside me there was nothing. This exercise Tor set for me—utterly absurd.

This was some wax-on, wax-off bullshit.

As the temperature rose, my eyes grew heavy and I fantasised about home. If it were the weekend, we'd be packing the car with camper chairs, readying to watch my brother play footy. If his team won this time, they'd qualify for the finals. Such small worries...such small things. How much had I taken for granted?

I'd been gone for four days now. Surely the police would have been contacted. Heck, my town would get a wake-up call then. *Local teen missing!* The headlines would blare. Perhaps 'A Current Affair' had caught wind of it: *Did she run away? Or was she kidnapped? Find out after the break!*

Any small humour I found faltered.

They won't find me.

Grief barrelled straight to my heart with scalding intensity. I tried to blink away my tears, but they cascaded down my cheeks, my shoulders shaking with silent sobs. I wanted to go home.

Whatever *this* was, it wasn't fair.

A stick snapped to my right, as did my gaze.

Well, what do you know, another yole. This one was grey, almost blue-roan, with streaks of black framing its face.

Wherever you are Tor, stay the hell *away.*

The animal was gorgeous, almost as beautiful as the one yesterday. I didn't dare move. This was the first damned thing I'd *seen* for hours. I didn't breathe as tears cooled on my cheeks. I didn't shift a bloody muscle. They were all cramped and locked anyway.

The yole snuffled through the leaf litter, digging with its tiny nose for a morning meal. Completely unaware of the danger lurking above.

A shadow streaked across the sun— I watched it glide between the branches, light shining through membranous wings. It perched on a branch, pitch-black and grotesque, eyes fixed on its prey. Sharp talons hooked at the apex of each wing like a bat. And honestly, it seemed to have the body of a deformed monkey. From its pug-like face, razor sharp teeth protruded out over its bottom jaw, and clawed feet gripped the tree as it clambered down the trunk, winged arms scrabbling as it went. Directly above the yole.

It was a hideous thing that coiled fear in my stomach. The air stank with its presence. And this yole would die from talons and claws made for shredding.

No, it won't.

Whilst I was sure those talons could tear *me* to bloody ribbons, I shot my arm out to grasp the fallen branch and tore from the thicket. In the same heartbeat it leapt from the tree, I yelled at the beast. Its head swivelled. Black eyes met mine. Its prey forgotten, it spread its dark wings and soared towards me.

I had moments—less than.

For a split second I froze as the creature shifted, thrusting out both talons and claws, readying to strike. In the next my body reacted of its own accord, much better than it had with Rooke and the Rat. I parted my feet shoulder-width apart and assumed the position of a baseball strike with the branch.

Here batter-batter…

Black flashed before my face before I struck. Hard.

The monster crashed into the tree and slid to the ground with a thud—the branch was split in two and the creature wasn't moving. Planting fists on my knees, my body shook with…adrenaline? I sucked in cool air right to the base of my lungs. A blur of roan-grey snagged my eye. The bloody yole. The animal parked itself in front of me, sitting up on its hind legs, staring. "You're welcome," I gasped between shaking breaths.

In answer, the yole darted and leapt onto my leg in a flurry of motion. It scrambled up and around my body before finding my left shoulder, brushing its long tail against my cheek.

"Seems yeh made a friend, then," Tor's bemused voice thundered behind me, echoing off the tree trunks.

I straightened and spun to find him leaning cross-armed on a nearby tree, smirking down his nose at me. The ass had been watching. "I thought yeh said yeh had no skill," he said, surprise lining his words.

I frowned. "Strength isn't a skill."

"If yeh got strength, yeh can fight. Even if yeh don't know what to do with it. Now tell me, what did yeh see?"

"Okay…I saw the sun rise, then I saw lots of trees. Then I saw this pretty cool stick…" I held up both halves of my makeshift bat with a sheepish grin.

He rolled his eyes and pulled a bow from his back to swiftly shoot the mangled monkey in the eye. Even if the sound made me wince, I felt no sympathy for the creature.

My stomach unclenched with its death, the stench disintegrating from the air. "I saw this yole digging for food before I saw that thing try to kill it."

"So, what did yeh learn?"

I blinked, once, twice.

"I learnt that yoles forage for food during the day, that those monkey-things are carnivores—that they're swift and agile, but otherwise not so scary."

"What else?"

I released a long breath, trying to back-track my morning. Nothing. There was nothing else, unless he wanted something prophetic? "Natural selection," I said. When Tor's brows lifted, I amended. "The strong survive. The weak do not."

"Good," he grunted.

"But," I cut in as he turned away. "What if the strong protected the weak?"

Tor glanced at the yole then back at my face, and the corners of his mouth tugged upwards. "Then, the weak live to see another day."

I flashed a smile as he flipped the bow up around his shoulders.

"Yoles are one of the cleverer animals in the forest, though this one," his eyes narrowed at the animal on my shoulder, "Does not seem to be too smart to not notice a bleedin' jarrah above it. And I ain't never seen one get too close to someone before." He paused, seeming to ponder and soak in the forest. "Long ago, the forest was protected. Maker knows it has seen better days."

"Jarrah?" I asked.

Tor pointed to the corpse. I glanced at the mangled mess, then pursed my lips and squinted into the darker depths of the forest. I knew there were horses in this world, but *jarrahs* and *yoles*—I wondered how many other strange creatures lived in the dark between the trees.

"Anyway, while yeh did not exactly hunt it, yeh made a kill on your first day." Tor added, the slightest touch of pride in his words.

"You killed it."

"Yeh downed it?" He offered with a smile. At my scowl he pressed, "Yer in for a treat. Salted jarrah tastes just like chicken."

I scoffed and studied the dead jarrah, grimacing at the black blood pooling around its head. *"Tastes like chicken my ass."*

Chuckling, Tor strode past me—hauling the jarrah onto one broad shoulder. The yole darted from mine to scamper away into the forest, giving my cheek a final brush of its silken tail.

Tor winked and gestured for me to follow.

Silence fell between us as we walked the short distance back to the cabin, our feet crunching on dried leaves and sticks.

As we breached the tree line, I beheld the beauty of Tor's home in the full light of day. The clearing, wholly surrounded by towering white oak trees, was the size of a tennis court. A stream meandered like a gurgling azure serpent through lush green grass, while a quaint stable sat under the shade of the oaks along the easternmost side. A dirt path ran beside the house, winding away through the undergrowth beyond—I didn't know where that path led, nor did I ask, as I noticed a horse shifting within the stable.

I asked Tor if I could go and say hello, but was swiftly denied. "Kip will be sleeping, the bleedin' lump. Yeh got more to do inside." He pushed through the cabin threshold and threw the jarrah's corpse onto the bench before untangling the weapons from around his body. Two axes were strapped to either side of his hips and an assortment of knives were sheathed on a thigh brace. The bow used to kill the creature, he unhooked from his back and leant against the table.

Each knife was placed in a neat line on the surface beside the corpse, before Tor spun and quirked a brow. "Which one?"

"Which one, what?"

"Which knife do yeh use to skin the beast?"

Scrunching my nose, I stared at the jarrah. Like hell I'd know.

I scanned the set of knives—each was nicked, with worn brown handles. One was short and wide...made for *stabbing*? Another long and thin, made for...*poking*? Two others looked like usual kitchen knives, one for the usual slicing and the other with a serrated edge. The last had a broad blade that curved at the end like a scythe.

For boomeranging?

"The curved one?"

"Wrong," he barked. "Yeh need 'em all."

I rolled my eyes as he bent to retrieve the long-bladed one, but stopped short, twisted it mid-air and offered the hilt to me. I took the knife in trembling fingers.

"First things first. Hack off the wings."

At the cool frankness of his voice, I blinked up at him, mouth agape.

"Yeh need to slice through the membrane with this knife, then saw through the bone with the jagged one."

My eyes widened at the knife in my hand. I looked up to his face then back at the crumpled corpse again. "You want me to...you want *me* to do that?"

"Well, yeh said yeh wanted to learn," Tor grunted. "Yeh cannot learn without doing!"

Regathering from my gaudy rambling, I tried to articulate more. "I want to be clear, I don't *want* to do that."

Tor's demeanour hardened. "And let *me* be clear, lass. Yeh have to. Grow some bleedin' balls and skin the damned thing."

I opened my mouth to debate—but he was right. I bit my tongue. I had to learn, even this.

Crossing my arms, I feigned indignation to make sure he'd think I wasn't as much of a pushover as I was. Tor didn't speak another word, but mirrored me and crossed his arms—and with arms four times the size of mine, it was much more dramatic.

Ass.

Loosening a subdued sigh, I dropped my hands and ambled to the table, squeezing the hilt of the knife in my palm. Taking a readying breath, inhaling the scent of sandalwood entwined with blood, I lifted the knife and prodded the wing. My insides churned. Grasping one of the jarrah's talons, I pulled it taut and positioned the tip of the blade close to where the membrane met the fuzzy torso.

Before I could balk, I flicked my wrist up hard and fast, slicing an imperfect tear along the underside of the wing. Thick black blood flowed, rivulets pouring onto the stone floor beneath. The sweet smell of iron engulfed me. Ice spread through my limbs. My gut lurched and I twisted just in time to avoid hurling over the carcass.

Tor growled and wrenched the knife from my hand, spinning back to the carcass to finish, shooting an order for me to get outside and chop firewood instead. Wiping my face with the back of my hand, I scurried outside to escape that damned smell. Fresh air thawed the ice in my veins and swept away images of death and decay, mutilated bodies and rotting flesh, as I made a dash to the stream to wash away the blood and vomit from my face and hands. Grabbing a nearby bucket, I hurried back inside the cabin and busied myself with cleaning my mess off the floor—all the while ignoring the smell and sight of the skinning.

After ridding the contents of the bucket in a hole, I gazed at the stable. *Cut the wood.* Right then.

An erect stump stood beside the cabin, surrounded by a pile of roughly-cut logs. No doubt poor Kip had his work cut out bringing it here—or Tor himself.

By the time I'd hauled one of the smaller sections onto the stump, my upper body ached.

I squeezed the axe's hilt, trying to grasp a sense of the weight and balance. *Like I'd understand what to feel for, anyway...*but knowing I'd failed only the second of Tor's tasks—it was time to put whatever strength he saw in me to some damned use.

Lifting the heavy axe above my head, I brought it down on the stump, sending split logs thudding to the ground. Finally, I had done something right.

THE SUN WAS at its peak when Tor called for me to stop. My body felt broken, so utterly ruined it almost hurt more to stop—*almost.*

The axe slid from my sweat slickened hands, now blistered and raw. My knees buckled and I sank to the ground, as the sun burnt down on my face and neck. Tor watched from the door of the cabin, head tilted, his gaze cool and calculated.

Each drop of sweat and quake of limbs confirmed my weakness. Woodchips bit my palms as I forced myself back to my feet. Trying to hide my trembling legs, I squared on Tor with a glare inviting any snide comment.

Instead, his rough-hewn face softened and he jerked his head once. "Good job, lass."

He disappeared inside the cabin without another word, and I waited until the door latch clicked before I turned to the stream. Cold water beckoned with a cheerful babble.

Limbs wailing in protest, I half dragged myself to the stream and submerged—very unfemininely—into the water. I moaned as my body floated just below the surface. *Even my butt muscles were sore.*

I shouldn't feel in this world, but I did. Dark thoughts crept into my mind like oily vines, but I shoved them away—constructing instead a solid wall as if my mind were a house made of stone. If I let those thoughts in again, they'd suffocate me. But as I floated in the stream, I wondered how thick that wall really was. As if in answer, the wind carried a faraway howl into the clearing.

And the big bad wolf huffed, and he puffed...and he blew that house down.

CHAPTER 5
TELL ME

W ater pooled in the grass by my feet, dripping from sodden clothes as I waited by the cabin door for Tor to bring me a dry outfit. I dashed behind the stable to change. Each movement, no matter how small, sent waves of pain shrieking through me—my muscles screamed and my shirt scuffed against my sunburn.

Another howl, though distant and far away, made me hurry back inside.

The jarrah corpse was nowhere to be seen. The metallic smell of blood had vanished, an overwhelming scent of lavender in its place. Indeed, when I looked at the table, neat bundles of dried purple flowers tied with twine replaced any evidence of the skinning. The natural smell of the cabin entwined with the lavender soothed my nerves, and I smiled at the image of Tor picking lavender and tying them carefully to place around.

Tor was bent over the hearth, divvying up something resembling stew into two bowls. The concoction was a muddish brown, but the meat was blue. *Vibrant*, luminous blue. Tor handed me my bowl along with a huge chunk of warm bread. I raised the meal face-height for further inspection. It had to be the strangest thing I'd ever seen—and

I'd seen a fairy for God's sake. My reservation was met with a grin before Tor dug in. Swallowing hard, I braced myself and nibbled a miniscule portion of meat.

It was delicious. And just as Tor said, it tasted like chicken. But better. So much better.

After the hunting ordeal this morning and the few hours demolishing wood with only a slice of bread for fuel, I was famished. I devoured my bowl without so much as a word, and a second one, too.

Once both sufficiently full—Tor eating double more than me—I ambled to my bed, wincing as my muscles sank into the softness inch by inch. I rested my head against the wall before booming laughter rattled me straight.

"Yeh think that is it today, lass? Get yerself up." Tor laughed harder at my incredulous glare. "Yeh did good with the wood, but we ain't even started on yer training."

I stared him down. "You're not serious."

Tor flicked his brows up, his grin spreading wider. "Oh aye, I am deadly serious. Now get yer arse back up."

I made a show of slowly—loudly—shimmying to the edge of the mattress, groaning and cussing under my breath. Yet despite myself, Tor's mirth was infectious. I found myself smiling back. There was something about a ginormous, bearded, tattooed hulk of a man grinning unabashedly that I couldn't help but find joy in. Especially when I remembered the lavender.

"Thank you, Tor. For getting rid of the smell." I gestured at the table. "I'm sorry for making a mess all over your floor."

Tor licked his lips and crossed his arms over his chest, shaking his head. "I am sorry, Estelle, I should have thought on it...stupid bastard I was. I will not ask yeh to hunt anything yeh do not want to, nor do what yeh do not want neither. What yeh kill, or do not, is up to yeh." Tor lifted a hand, scratching his head before continuing. "And yer forest fairies I expect."

"How do you know-"

He raised a giant hand, silencing me.

"Yeh stood at my front door with bleedin' fairy dust all through yer hair, like a great sparkling buffoon."

I waited for the reprimand—or at least a warning—but instead, I was met with a warm smile. "It has been a long time since the forest had someone protecting it."

Inside me, an ember burst to life, a spark of fire against the dark.

I FAILED MISERABLY AT SWORDPLAY.

And really, I couldn't blame it on my aching body. Just my utter lack of grace and coordination, though I certainly did try. All humour disappeared from Tor's demeanour, honed into something harder. Something dangerous. He was masterfully skilled, even if he was taking it easy on me.

Tor had swords, great and small, a massive array of daggers and smaller knives, a selection of bows, and a great hoard of arrows. The moment I saw his collection, I tucked away any questions for another time. Because Tor seemed to be on a very important mission.

Me.

Any small joy I found in the first few minutes, when Tor had shown me how to grip the sword and arc it effectively—and I'd pictured myself as some heroic warrior queen—died quickly. He was brutal. Any attempt to block his swings was swiftly countered with a whack on the wrist. Albeit softly and with the flat side of his sword.

I was worse at hand to hand combat.

The skills he *tried* to teach me were self-defence, but I was scared of punching or kicking him too hard. Especially since each area he told me to aim for seemed...precious. He certainly had no such qualms. For each punch I pulled, he hit harder. Not enough to really hurt—in the short time I'd come to know him, I don't think Tor would be capable of that, but he wasn't soft. He got grumpier every time I threw a 'weak' or 'stroppy' punch, and eventually his temper got the better of him.

His brows furrowed, bronze eyes aflame. I balked and stumbled away. He'd been grouchy at me for most of the afternoon, but this anger was swift and brutal. "Do yeh think this is a game, lass? If yeh attacked again, they are gonna hit harder than me!"

"I've never had to do any of this before! I don't want to hurt you," I snapped back—but it sounded more like a whine once it was out.

Tor loosened a dark huff. "Yeh hurt me? What will make yeh understand, yeh gotta learn!"

"I. Am. Tired. And sore!" I flung my arms out wide. "How can you possibly expect me to do this properly?"

Tor's eyes sparked with fury, his face reddening. Gone was the man who had picked lavender and who laughed at my adolescent insolence. This man's voice boomed so loud it shook my bones. "Yeh got no excuse! If yeh are out there and some bastard finds yeh with no one to come to the rescue, yeh dead! Do yeh not get that?"

Right. Because I was a helpless girl, who needed rescuing. Irritation grated across my skin at his words...I didn't give a damn that he was right. "You think I don't get it? Of course I do—I could have been raped yesterday! What is the matter with you?"

Tor flinched, and a floodgate seemed to break open. "The matter with me?" His voice was quiet—infinitely more terrifying than his thunderous shouting. Wrath seeped from every inch of his ginormous frame, but I didn't care. First Rose treated me like an idiot, now Tor? I didn't care if this ridiculous new reality had made me into an intolerable git.

"Yeh do not know how to protect yerself, yer gonna be dead. Finished." Tor continued, voice dangerously quiet. "I did not teach her, but I will be damned if yeh do not know how to fight for yer bleedin' self! Yeh will not be weak. Hear me?"

And just like that, my anger dissipated. "Who, Tor? Who didn't you teach?"

His eyes blazed brighter, but his face—despair broke to the surface like a tidal wave. He remained silent for a moment which stretched into an eternity before his eyes limned silver, but his tears never quite breached.

"My daughter. Danii."

Oh, *gods*.

Tor's face twisted with grief and irrevocable pain. His hands balled into fists, so tight his knuckles went white as bone. Tears hung in his eyes, liquifying the deep bronze of his irises.

It broke my heart.

"Tor...I didn't...I'm so sorry." I didn't know what else to say. What else could I say?

His beard twitched, fighting back pain and fury and angry words. He un-balled his fists and crossed his arms, as if steeling himself. "She..." His voice broke and he took a great, shaking breath. "She asked me to teach her. All of it. How to fight, how to hunt. How to protect herself. I said no. I was a proud, pompous, arrogant fool who thought I was enough to protect her."

His voice shattered as he tightened his arms across his chest. I wondered if I should comfort him—try to do *anything*. I'd only known the man for a day, yet he was letting me into the most tragic part of himself. Perhaps my being here—challenging him—reminded him of her. Perhaps that's why he took me in. Why Rose knew he would.

I could not imagine the pain, the grief Tor must feel. All that fury, all that despair. "Would not have been much older than yeh—my Danii. Same stubborn attitude...she met some lad in the village a little while away and used to visit him every now and again. One night, she did not come home.

"I rode to the village to find the damned lad. He told me she had left the day before. A loyal young tyke he was. He jumped straight onto his own bleedin' horse and rode with me all day." Each word was strained, slow. Then the way he said the next few words crushed me completely.

"We found her."

Catching himself, his nostrils flared. "We found her chained and bloody in a cave a little ways off the path back to the cabin. The bastards...they were sloppy. Amateurs. She could have...she could have fought them, if she knew how."

Silent tears coated my face and my throat burned. Then Tor looked straight at me. "Past two days, I been thinking, it would be why that bleedin' Rose knew to send yeh here. Knew I would not turn away a young lass when she needed help." He raised his eyes to the sky. "Maker knows I never have. Never...except for the one that meant the most."

I took a heavy breath, unsure what to say. There were no words of comfort I could offer that would make this right. So I offered the only thing I could. "I'll be better. I'll do better. I promise."

Tor rubbed a fist across his face, and like a great weight had been lifted from his chest, the despair harrowing his features calmed...*just a little*. "I will too, Estelle. Yeh have my word, I will not let yeh down as well."

I smiled up at him. "I believe you, Tor."

With a grim smile of his own, a tear finally broke through and slid into his beard.

A FORTNIGHT PASSED. My days filled with a never-ending cycle of vigorous training leaving me exhausted by nightfall. Too exhausted to even contemplate a plan to return home, or cry over the fact that Mum wasn't tucking me in with a kiss on my cheek. But each day, I found myself waking a little less heartbroken than the morning before. Whilst I still hoped—more than anything—to wake up safely back home, for the first time in my life I was doing something. Something exceptional. Extraordinary. Dangerous even.

I was still hopeless at swordplay and hand to hand combat, but I discovered an affinity for archery. To Tor, the bow was a last resort. And we'd only begun training with one four days ago, due perhaps to my continuous lack of skill with a blade.

I loved the strained-muscle feel of pulling the bowstring taut, and the rush of power when I loosed the arrow. Whenever the bow was in my hands and I found my mark, a spark shot through my blood. At first, I couldn't figure out how to keep the bloody arrows nocked, earning me no small amount of snide comments from Tor. But once I'd nailed that aspect, I found pulling the bowstring far back enough to have a bit of force behind my shot easy.

I had even hit the target on my very first attempt—it didn't matter that it was a ginormous hay bale only ten feet away, I'd still jumped for joy. Tor seemed impressed too, and to me that mattered more than anything. Perhaps I'd found aiming easy because of all the late nights playing first-person shooter games with Grayson, or maybe I'd just discovered my first natural talent.

My favourite training was riding. Kip was a quiet horse, perfect for a beginner, if a little bit slow and lazy. He was large, much bigger than Rose's bay—I supposed anything smaller would have buckled or had a heart attack bearing Tor's weight. The gelding was white with brown blotches painted over his coat, and his hooves were covered with white shaggy hair that brushed the grass when he moved. The only struggle I had was actually mounting the damned thing. I was tall, but Kip was huge. More often than not, I would use the woodchopping stump whenever Tor wasn't watching.

We never went far, just around the small clearing, but on horseback I forgot Tor was training me. I whooped through bouncy canters and raised my arms to pretend I was flying. It was incredible. I felt free. Whenever we rode, I would look out into the forest and wonder what it would be like to soar on the back of a racing beast through the trees.

Most days, Tor and I were outside from dawn until dusk—always doing something, always learning something new. If it wasn't combat training or riding, it was chores. *Exercise*, as Tor liked to phrase it. Chopping wood, mucking out Kip's stable, carting heavy buckets of water around the place, all part of my days' work.

And Tor, after his confession about Danii, poured himself into my training. I guess the guilt he'd felt about not preparing her, he transferred onto me—I'd never seen such dedication from someone. He offered guidance about anything and everything. He was always quick to criticise too, but hey—no one's perfect.

But the *pain*.

After that first day, my muscles simply refused to move at all. I could not for the life of me rise from the bed the following day. At least, I couldn't until Tor threw an entire bucket of cold water over me.

My body still ached, but the pain was a constant reminder I was doing something useful. Improving myself. Only yesterday, I lifted a massive hay bale on my own—a feat I couldn't accomplish two weeks ago. I could also run an extra few hundred metres more by the passing of each day, even if I did usually throw up when I stopped.

If Tor was dedicated, then I would be too.

Once the sun dropped and night bloomed, Tor told me of the world —of the laws and customs and the societal expectations. Kiliac was a completely totalitarian and tyrannical place, where patriarchy suppressed lives with slavery and segregation of social classes. In essence, it was a completely shitty place. An exact replica of what historians and teachers told us the 'old times' were like.

Almost.

As both Tor and Rose had said, magic was outlawed—*magic*—by the great-great-grandfather of the current king, Horen. Magic-wielding races had viewed humans as little more than vermin throughout history. With their banishment, humans emerged from their hovels and scattered through the land like roaches, plaguing the realm within decades. Elves, fairies, iytmas, trecrann, vix, and dragons retreated into the heart of the forest. Horen, like his father before him, sent legions into Galdurne to extinguish anything deemed enchanted.

Magi, on the other hand, were a different matter. Rare humans gifted with abilities that were marked for death. Magic used to be diverse, from elemental to healing and necromancy, telepathy and telekinesis. But since magic was outlawed, no one was extraordinary. Anyone carrying signs of magic, even newborn babes, were slaughtered.

Once, Tor spoke of a great war between elves and men and my interest spiked—from the mythology I knew, elves were god-like beings. Tall, graceful, immortal and fair. I told Tor as much, but he just smiled sadly back at me, for they were the fiercest protectors of Galdurne and were the first to go to war with men.

"I ain't never seen 'em, no one in the past fifty years have, neither. Most likely they all died. But from the stories, they ain't graceful, or fair. They are more animal than human."

Maybe that's not such a bad thing, I'd said.

Solemnly, he agreed.

One night, Tor got rip-roaring drunk. Between bawdy songs of legends and *very* honest mocking of my lesser talents, he admitted that it would have been Danii's birthday and that his wife, Elara, would have been proud of me if she'd lived through childbirth. I knew he meant proud of Danii, but I didn't interrupt.

The next morning, when he woke me at dawn—smelling of ale and vomit—he did not remember it. And I did not mention it.

CHAPTER 6
LOOKING TOO CLOSELY

Every morning before sunrise, Tor woke me to hunt. Well, Tor would hunt, but only for jarrah and its ilk, never animals he assumed I would care about. I should care for all the denizens of the forest, but some just felt like poison—like they shouldn't be here. It was those that Tor brought home and skinned behind the stable where I couldn't see. Soon, I'd told him...soon I'd stomach learning to do it myself.

Some days he would ask me to follow, sniping at my clumsy footfalls. *Quiet* and *silence* becoming his new favourite words. Other times, he would send me to hide and study the comings and goings of the forest.

Yoles quickly became one of my favourite animals, and one or two sometimes accompanied me when I was supposed to keep a silent vigil. They'd curl up in my lap and nicker when I stroked their fur— their personalities akin to playful otters, wriggling their heads under my hands.

Jarrahs, through some small mercy, I only saw on a rare occasion. All pure black, all horrible. I didn't see the fairy—or any others— again, but the *creatures* of this world! The awe when I came across something new, was indescribable. Whilst there were familiar animals like squirrels, rabbits, foxes and deer, others were alien. One such creature, was a cioraun—something I was *bleedin' lucky didn't notice me.*

The gargantuan predator had features characteristic of an ancient saber-tooth tiger, with dagger-like fangs. His coat was ash-grey littered with pale blue spots that glowed luminescent. Muscled legs ended in massive paws with curved claws capable of ripping me limb from limb, and his eyes were the same glowing blue that dotted his coat. *Definitely alien.*

I could have sworn he looked my way as he passed by, as if he could see through the shrub I hid behind, and smell past the mud masking my scent.

I spotted another predator not a day later. No bigger than a lynx, incandescence sheened its snow-white fur. Its face was lupine, it stalked like a cat, but it was the tail that made this animal phenomenal. Well, *tails.* Six in total, all ending in a different colour—white fur blending perfectly into each hue. Long shimmering fur floated as if submerged in water, a fluttering rainbow with two colours I didn't know and couldn't name. Its beauty disguised its danger. It caught a rabbit in seconds, seemingly appearing behind it out of thin air. When I told Tor he was dumbfounded, he'd thought them monsters made of myth and legend—no more than ghosts, and made me swear not to speak of them—as they were creatures of *absolute* magic.

Right. Magic bad.

That night over dinner, Tor rambled about the legends surrounding the *yau*, how they could disappear and reappear like spirits in the wind. Perhaps it really did appear out of thin air behind the rabbit. A shiver crawled down my spine at the thought.

Apart from the yau, other lupine species stalked past my hiding spots. And, to my seemingly undying luck, none ever noticed me. Some were variances of wolves with two tails, horns protruding from their heads, or with wings and a scaled tail. Others were giant versions of a normal wolf—at least double the size of those from home.

This morning was much the same as any other—Tor woke me before first light, tossing me a piece of bread for breakfast and snickering at my steady stream of curses. Now, I was squatting on a tree branch, grouchy about an attack manoeuvre I couldn't for the life of me execute yesterday.

An inquisitive bark shook me from my thoughts, and I looked down to find a fantastical wolf staring up at me from the ground.

This was a two-tailed type, and absolutely beautiful. Its chest was charcoal black, and lustrous locks of pale gold fur sprouted from atop its neck, travelling down and blending seamlessly into the dark coat beneath. Its ears cocked forward as ice-blue eyes fixed on mine with unnerving intelligence.

"Well, you're a beauty, aren't you?"

At the sound of my voice, the wolf yipped and spun. She sat on her haunches, angling her head to one side and stuck out a lopsided tongue. I couldn't help but laugh. And I *really* wanted to pat her.

"If I come down, will you eat me?"

She sneezed, shaking her head. I bit my lip, but my inner adoration for fluffy things won over the little voice of caution in my head, which sounded a lot like Tor. I scrambled down the tree to straddle a lower branch, and reached down to let the wolf sniff the back of my hand.

Yipping again, she wagged both tails. Caution be damned—I leapt off the branch, landing on the ground and sending dried leaves scattering.

She pounced, nipping at my arms. Her snout nudged under my palms as I chuckled and wound my fingers through her silken-like golden fur. When my scratching slowed, she nudged her head against my hands to entice more thorough petting. "Needy," I scoffed.

I was playing with a two tailed wolf...

The air strung taut as the breeze died, and the wolf's head snapped up as fast as mine. She bared her teeth, letting loose a low snarl. My insides screamed to run—not away from, but towards the invisible threat.

A feral power uncoiled in my veins, a mighty beast hidden—biding its time—awoke, and I bared my teeth like the wolf.

She took a few stalking steps away, whipped her head around and bore her eyes into mine.

Let's go, she seemed to say.

You don't need to ask me twice.

For the beast inside had risen and come out to hunt.

~

I DON'T KNOW how far I ran beside the wolf, but soon we were joined by more. Wolves of all shapes and sizes—all headed in the same direction. None so much as looked sidelong at me. I was one of the pack, and something was pulling me forward like a chain.

I ran hard. Adrenaline coursed through my veins, pumping my legs, and when I let the beast take control it drove me faster still. My footfalls were sure and steady. I was a predator too.

Other animals, ones I recognised along with those I didn't, all charged—predators and prey alike. A yau ghosted through the trees, long tail flying like a rainbow flag. Yoles scattered amongst the forest floor and in the branches above, racing along with the rest. And I welcomed the cold, dark air twisting around my skin as we plunged into the forest's depths.

Two winged wolves leapt and flew over a fallen log blocking our path. The other creatures careened off to run around the sides, and the yau ghosted straight through it. I took a readying stride and jumped as high as I could—grappling for a hold in on the trunk. Fingers scream-ing, I hauled myself up and scrambled over the girth, my legs hardly giving way as I landed on the other side. My rational mind was in awe of this newfound prowess, but after a heartbeat, I tackled that beast and brought it to heel—because in my peripheral vision stood a snarling cioraun.

The big cat sniffed at the air and chuffed. My beast released a quiet snarl as the cioraun's luminous eyes searched mine, like it could see deep within me.

As much as I wanted to stay and marvel, that strange pull would not yield. My heart hammered inside my chest, each violent beat radiating through my bones. "We're wasting time," I breathed to the cioraun, darting into the steady stream of wildlife and insanely not caring there was a near ten-foot tall extra-terrestrial tiger at my back.

Not five paces further, the cioraun caught up and ran abreast mere inches from my side.

Right then.

The iron-clad chain's wrenching grew stronger with each stride, pulsed with each breath. I was getting closer. We all were. After another few hundred meters, I heard the guttural, unmistakable cries of men.

Fifty meters away now.

Twenty.

Ten.

I leapt up and over a boulder, and when I landed on the other side, chaos, in every sense of the word, had broken loose.

The forest yawned open into a clearing from a fairy-tale. In the middle, crystal-blue water surrounded a small island where a large violet coloured oak tree rested. But the scene was marred.

Brutalised.

And that crystal-blue water was stained red.

Bloody corpses of great white deer littered the clearing. Arrows and spears scattered across the grass and protruded from their sides. But the chaos was not the freshly slain creatures. Chaos rained down on the legion of armoured men—the legion who had killed and maimed and drawn blood from the creatures of the woods.

A yau ghosted from one man to the next, leaping and slicing through their necks as if carried by the wind. The cioraun...well, I was right about those claws. Soldiers were shredded into bloody ribbons before they could blink. My beast roared to join, to slash and claw and bite, but these were human. I wasn't a killer. And although the beast bellowed and raged at the herd's massacre, I forced it into submission.

So I stood and watched, trembling, and listened to screams of terror and pain.

ONCE THE BLOODSHED ENDED, I didn't know what scared me more: that I'd watched a hundred men slaughtered in a matter of minutes—their blood and fear burnt like a brand into my mind—or that I'd felt satisfaction at their deaths.

The pack of wolves I'd run with moved among the clearing, feasting upon dead.

The cioraun stalked amongst fallen deer, though it did not feed. Instead, the great cat leaned his head down and touched the brow of each deer and stag with his nose—*mourning them.*

Perhaps it was the shock—the sweet metallic scent and red wasteland—but I hardly noticed the iron-clad chain had remained until a harsh tug brought me back to my senses.

Something inside me purred.

I scanned the clearing for the source, the other end of the chain. But there was nothing. Nothing but death.

A roar drew my gaze to where the cioraun stood—it chuffed and shook its massive head, pawing at the ground. He stood between two fallen deer beside the water's edge, a tiny mass of white fur curled next to his paw.

That tiny ball of fur held the other end of my chain.

I darted towards the wounded fawn in the grass.

For large deer, their young were so small. So fragile. Blood poured freely from two long gashes marring its hindquarters. I pelted towards the mess of downed men, skipping past the wolves. There was no time for meekness, nor shock—that fawn held my chain for a reason.

He would not die.

There were no buckets strewn across the clearing, so a helmet would have to do. I removed one from a fallen soldier and ran to the small lake, filling the helmet to the brim. I took the water back to the fawn and knelt, setting the helmet between my thighs, and ripped strips of fabric from my shirt. I soaked one strip and pressed it against the wounds. The fawn bleated in pain, flailing delicate limbs, so the cioraun laid beside me and rested a huge paw on the little mound of white fur, holding the baby still while I worked. I glanced at the big cat as he dipped his head onto the blood-soaked grass. "Thank you."

His glowing eyes found mine and he blinked once, before I returned my attention to the fawn. The wounds were so deep, bleeding so freely, I wasn't sure it would survive. Tears welled, blurring the lower half of my vision as I gently peeled back the cloth to inspect what was beneath. In one moment, its wounds were gushing blood into and through the makeshift bandage, staining my hands crimson. In the next, when I took the sodden bandage away and placed my other hand on the flank to keep pressure, the blood clotted and the skin surrounding the raw flesh began to stitch back together.

My mouth fell open.

Whatever magic these deer possessed was powerful, for I felt it too.

An innate knowledge of glistening golden light reached through my hand, into my blood, searching for the iron-clad chain, fortifying the links with molten gold. Making it unbreakable. Light sank into my skin and every scratch or bruise was washed away beneath a tidal wave of power. I closed my eyes and leant into the warmth—it wrapped around me like the purest embrace of a summer's day sun, entwined with the coolness of a moon-kissed wind. The scents of the forest amplified, underlaid with wood and rain, fur and *life*.

The steady drumbeat from within the heart of Galdurne pounded.

The light and warmth vanished. I was free falling. Underground, surrounded by blood and mud, gasping for breath—suffocating.

Dirt morphed into smoke and billowed out, revealing a colossal dark shape charging towards me.

A great dappled white stag with a dark face and black legs shot through the smoke. Its antlers were mighty, curved and pointed like dragon wings about to take flight, and flaming molten gold eyes stared into mine.

I blinked and the vision was gone.

The fawn, now healed save for two long ivory scars tarnishing its dappled white flank, raised his darkening face and was looking up at me with golden eyes.

My smile stretched from ear to ear.

"You're mine."

CHAPTER 7
QUEENS

The fawn was heavier than he looked.

This majestic animal had a hell of a lot of growing up to do. If I let him down to walk, he bleated and cried and carried on. *Very majestic.*

The cioraun accompanied us to Tor's cabin, fussing over the fawn like a bloody mother hen. If the baby kicked and screamed at my feet, the feline grumbled and nudged him forwards with his snout. If the fawn was in my arms, looking unnaturally smug, the cioraun stopped me every few meters, sniffing to check if he was still there.

"He's alright, you great lug!" I snapped at the overgrown cat for the hundredth time.

With the mid-morning sun beating through the trees, the return trip to the cabin was arduous. Adrenaline and strength drained away, all that was left were shaking limbs and an inability to breathe properly. Not helped, of course, by the demanding ball of fluff in my arms. But Tor would be beside himself with worry—that alone kept me going.

The screams of those men…

There must have been fifty or more deer in that clearing…a massacre. Tor's stories swirled through my mind, of Kiliac's capital—

Ashbourne—sending legions into Galdurne to eradicate its magical denizens. Was that all it was? An extermination of that herd?

The soldiers got what was coming to them.

Images flashed relentlessly in my mind's eye of carnage, blood and bone. Each new memory made my heart hammer harder in my chest.

Those screams...

A loud bleat jolted me from whirling thoughts.

Little golden eyes met mine with an almost human-like warmth. More than human, probably. I felt for our gold-linked chain, took comfort in the pressure as it wrapped tighter around me. The light I'd felt in the clearing drifted through my body like summer rain—gone were the images of death and decay. "Thank you, little one," I whispered to the fawn. He nibbled at my fingers until I smiled again.

"Now, what should we call you? I've never had to name a deer before." I chuckled at his narrowed gaze. "*Outrageous*, I know. Hmm... how about Bambi?"

Both the fawn and the cioraun snorted, so I took that as a solid no.

"Maximus?"

That one earned a disgruntled bleat.

Grinning at the stubbornness, a mirror to my own, I thought about my favourite stories—fairy tales, history, myths and folklore. My mind meandered to a time when my brother and I were children, playing outside with sticks for swords, acting out our favourite movie, pretending to be heroes of the Trojan War. Even now I could hear the clanking of stick against stick as we struck, along with the ringing laughter...

"Achilles."

Those molten gold eyes found mine again, and though he'd been stubborn and unruly, little Achilles dipped his head in accord.

FOR THE UMPTEENTH TIME, the cioraun nudged my arm to get a better view of Achilles. "He's bloody fine, you drongo! Shove off!"

Shifting Achilles' weight to my right arm, I pushed the big cat's head away with my left as I scolded him. When the feline stumbled away and chuffed, rather indignantly at that, a roiling voice boomed.

"Maker's balls!"

Tor sat, dumbstuck, astride a panicking Kip—desperately trying to squirm away from the predator at my side. The cioraun rested back on his haunches and glanced between me and Tor. *Friend or food?* he seemed to say. I laughed and swatted him on the snout..

"I'm sorry, I didn't mean to take off. But something happened, I was waiting in the tree where you left me and then there was this *thing* pulling me into the forest, so I went...and I found him."

I lifted Achilles a fraction higher so Tor could see him properly, but he didn't have eyes for me, or the fawn. I wasn't even sure he heard. Tor's bronze eyes were fixed on the feline, one hand resting on the handle of the axe strapped to his hip—the cioraun just sat and stared right back.

"Tor!"

His gaze shot back to me, his mouth gaping open. I pressed my lips into a hard line to refrain from laughing. "Lass...what the bleedin' hell are yeh doing?"

I stood a little straighter. "It's fine, Tor, he's not going to hurt you." I looked at the cat and grimaced. "He's more of an annoying fusspot than anything else."

Wrong. I'd seen what his claws and fury had done.

"There was a legion deeper in the woods and they'd just—they had just killed an entire herd of white deer. The rest of the animals, well, they fought back. It was..." My words vanished as I tried and failed to swallow the lump in my throat.

Achilles nudged my arm, lending me strength.

"It was awful...it was the worst thing I've ever seen. There was so much blood..." I released a heavy breath, then shook my head as if it could rid the memories. "All the soldiers are dead. But this fawn, it was him pulling me there. I know it was. When I found him," I glanced around, dropping my voice to a whisper. "Some kind of magic flowed through us. I think I was meant to find him...I'm just not sure why."

Tor's attention rested on me now, his features tight. "So yeh are a magi, then."

Not a question, but…"No. I can't be—the fawn healed himself. I just felt it when he did."

"Yeh would have felt nothing if there was no magic of yer own. Besides, healing ain't something animals do. And that pull yeh were talking about," he pointed at Achilles, "That fawn right there is yer dyr."

I frowned and lowered my gaze to Achilles. "My dyr?"

"Soul bound," Tor said simply. "Like that legend I told yeh about with them iytmas and their bears…though humans do not usually find a soul bound. Them protectors of the forest, elves and other sorts, they find their dyr's easy enough, but I am telling yeh, that is what it is. And…" His tone hardened. "Yeh have magic, whether yeh like it or no. That puts us both in danger."

A well of horror deepened in my chest. I remembered the legends he referred to, the stories of the elves and iytmas who were tied to magical creatures for life, and couldn't face existence alone if their dyr died. And me? I had magic? *Healing* magic? That made me a magi, as Tor called it. An *abomination* to humankind. I'd been so sure it was Achilles…

I was in danger. Worse, I was putting Tor in danger. The gaping pit yawned open. Squeezing my eyes shut, I held Achilles close against me, his soft down a balm to my fear. "I can be gone by nightfall if you want me to leave."

My eyes opened in time to catch Tor's face soften to sympathy, his bronze gaze lit like a torch in the dark.

He swung down from Kip, closing the distance between us in three easy strides. "No, lass. I want yeh to stay. I know yeh want to find out why yer here and more than that, how to get home…" He swallowed hard and shook his head. "Estelle, I am just a grumpy old arse, not one for pondering, but I think yeh was brought here for a reason. It is bleedin' scary for yeh, Maker, today must have been terrifying, but it proves something. Yer here for them, to fight for them." He dipped his head towards the cioraun and spread an arm to encompass the whole forest.

"And I want to help. I been hiding in that cabin too long, cowering from that bastard of a king—cowering from everything. It is about time someone saved Galdurne, and I reckon that someone is yeh."

I held Tor's gaze, then glanced at the cioraun and Achilles. Find my way home...or stay and fight for them. Help liberate them.

I'm just one bloody girl. What the hell could I do?

Achilles' golden stare pierced straight my soul, molten gold ore rumbling within my chest like an awakening volcano. My heart tore in two. I wanted to go home, but that meant leaving Tor...leaving Achilles. I'd just found him, but I knew in my bones, breaking or abandoning our bond would undo me.

He was my soul-bound.

My dyr.

Achilles stared at me with such *hope*. And I knew my answer. It had taken something like this to realise it, I guess. Something extraordinary.

The life I had before—while I loved my family and friends, more than they'll ever know—was plain, safe and mundane.

The modern world was dull. Lifeless.

Go to school, have kids, work, and then die. That was my future. Some part of me had always screamed at the thought, at the prospect of an ordinary life.

Besides, I'd seen firsthand how brutal *this* world could be. How savage. I didn't stand a chance at getting home in the first place without knowing everything I could about it. And maybe there was no way to go home.

Perhaps this was it for me.

Perhaps this was my new home.

I had always put the ones I loved above me. Always been selfless. I owed it to my family to find my way back, but this world, these creatures...Tor. A fantasy. But all of it real.

I knew that now.

Maybe it was time for me to choose for myself, and not rely on the wants of others to make the decision for me. The forest needed me. My family didn't—not in the same way.

So I smiled at my dyr and turned to Tor. A strength I've never known rose to the surface. I could do something—I could heal in a world full of ruin.

"Yes. I'll stay. I'll fight."

The beast inside me roared.

"YOU REALLY ARE DIRTY, MATE."

Achilles and I had played away most of the day. More often than not he'd tumbled into the dirt as he bounded around the clearing—Tor having forgone my training, *just this once.*

My dyr was a speedy little thing and I smiled to myself when I envisioned how magnificent he'd be full grown. But right now, he was clumsy and graceless—and battling to escape my holding him down in the stream. He writhed as I tried to scrub away matted dirt and blood from his coat, splashing wave after wave of water over my already saturated clothes.

"It will be over soon, I promise. Look! You have white fur again!"

My pleas unheeded, I tried discipline. Apparently he responded more to *put a bloody sock in it* than any attempt at begging. Noted.

"First you bury a yole, now you are bathing a fawn. You really are odd, wayfarer."

I twisted at the familiar, cocky voice, to behold Rose squatting behind me, watching in cool amusement.

*Shit...*say something.

I forced indifference into my voice and features. "Didn't your mother ever tell you it's rude to sneak up on people?"

Nailed it.

Turquoise eyes glinting with a new game afoot, Rose smirked. "Nah, she told me to take small joys wherever I could find them." He nodded to my sodden clothes. "And right now, seeing you like this gives me more joy than you could ever know, lass."

I tried to be irritated. I even waited for shame...but humour sparked in his gaze, and I laughed at the cocky bastard.

The smile that spread across Rose's face sent chills along my spine.

"Hello, Estelle."

I answered with a wide grin.

"Do that more," he said quietly.

"Do what?"

"Smile."

The intensity in his eyes burned so bright that my skin heated.

Did he know? Did he know he was so intimidating? I'd met a few self-assured jackasses in my life, but he was different. Still in his brown leathers, he was cleaner than I saw him last. Ebony hair half-pulled up behind his head, bronze skin glowing in the late afternoon sun.

Achilles broke free and ran to him, saving me from further humiliation for gawking. Rose chuckled and caught the fawn before he barrelled into something precious. Amidst the picture-book scene, a loud voice boomed across the clearing. And Tor's tone was not one I'd heard since first meeting him.

"Rose!"

As he twisted up, Rose stumbled, balking at the giant stomping towards him. For the first time since I'd met Rose, he looked unsure of himself. Truthfully, he looked downright terrified—and to be honest, seeing Tor stomping towards *me*—if I didn't know him, I would run the other way. The gentle giant I laughed at, cowering from a fussy cioraun, was gone. Here was the man behind the rough-hewn persona.

I'd forgotten to ask about his *friendship* with Rose.

"Good evening, Tor." Rose said, standing tall. "You are looking very fine. I wanted to thank you personally, for taking in Estelle."

I glowered behind Rose's back. *As if I was his responsibility.*

"Yeh would think, *Rose*, that after saving the lass from 'em bastards that yeh'd at least walk her to my damned door. Not leave her to walk up to a stranger's home, alone."

Rose gulped down air, his air of nonchalance fading.

With a dangerous and knowing smirk, Tor continued, "But of course, yeh had very important places to be."

Entertaining as it was to watch Rose squirm a little, I remembered how safe he'd made me feel that day, and how thankful I was for what he'd done. I stepped between the men and planted my feet—and Achilles pranced forward to stand beside me.

"Tor, Rose saved my life. No, he didn't walk me to your door, but he made sure I got there safely enough. He trusted you."

"All the same," Tor snapped without shifting his focus. "He left yeh alone with a stranger."

"Yes, he left me, but you weren't a stranger were you? You two obviously know each other, so there's no reason to be a damned ass about it!"

A choking sound came from Rose, and I whirled to face him. His brows were raised in shock and strangled incredulity, but the twitch of his bottom lip suggested my profanity with Tor amused him.

Perhaps once, Tor commanded the kind of respect to not have an adolescent girl snap back at him. But he scoffed and finally noticed my sodden clothes. When I caught his eye he shrugged and faced Rose. "I suppose yeh be wanting to stay and make sure she has been well cared for?"

An honest question, but a sarcastic one. His words grated, especially as Rose replied. "Of course, my thanks, Tor. I would also ask your permission to return and see her, from time to time."

If my blood wasn't beginning to boil, I might have laughed at that.

Tor had no such qualms. He chuckled before answering. "No use asking me, lad, Estelle can make up her own bleedin' mind. But if she says yes and yeh do come back, if any harm comes to her, I will kill yeh."

"You bastards *do* know I'm standing right here, yeah?" Tor made his threat with such calm and earnest...I knew he had become protective, but I hadn't realised how much.

I backed away so I could see them both. Rose winked, but stood tall and lifted his chin when he faced Tor. "I believe you, Tor."

My eyes bolted to Tor's, and his locked into mine. Those words Rose spoke...it was the same thing I'd said after he told me of Danii.

Was Rose the boy she used to visit?

Tor read the question in my eyes. "No, lass, he was not." With that, he spun on his heel and retreated inside the cabin, shutting the door with a bang.

"I was not what?" Rose said into the quiet that followed the slam of the door.

I whirled on him. "What the hell happened between you two? You told me he was an old friend!"

Gone was the light humour we'd shared. I'd known him for a matter of hours. Tor, I'd lived and trained with for two weeks. I had no reservations about where my loyalties lay.

"He used to work for my father. It ended badly, something to do with his wife. He went over the edge and my father dismissed him."

I couldn't grasp Rose's tone, but if he was talking down about Tor —I placed my hands on my hips in the hope I'd sound bold. "I'll ask Tor about his version of events, thank you very much. And you can take whatever notion you have about me being your responsibility and choke on it. I'm not something you can summon, or check in on whenever you feel like it."

Rose just smiled that half smile of his, and damn him, he looked fine doing it. "I forgot, you know."

I snapped back. "Forgot what?"

"How much I enjoyed you."

Bugger me.

His smile, his eyes, I almost whimpered. But Tor didn't trust him, let alone like him—and I trusted Tor. "Look, it's been nice, but—"

He closed the distance between us, grasping my hand in his. The turquoise in his eyes flared a little before chilling to a cool smoulder, and I barely had time to process him holding my hand before his smile returned. "Give me a chance. Get to know me before sending me away."

I glanced down at our hands and back to his face. Was there

desperation there? Half of me felt I owed it to him to be nicer, he had saved me, but I snatched my hand away and crossed my arms.

"Hey," he started. "I did not mean to sound like an arse and speak as if you were mine. I did not intend to offend Tor either. He was the only man in my father's employ that my mother trusted, for that I will forever be indebted to him. I just had no idea where you two stood is all." He released a long sigh. "I am sorry, Estelle. Please, give me a chance."

Perhaps it was the desperation I saw in him, but I uncrossed my arms. I wanted to ask more about his and Tor's story, though I had a sense of some long-lost wound.

My voice wasn't quite as clipped as I meant it to be when I replied. "Fine."

And as the bastard caught it, his grin stretched from ear to ear.

SITTING in the grass on the bank of the stream, we talked until the sun hung low. I told Rose everything; about my training, my hopelessness with swords and hand to hand combat, learning how to hunt, and about some of the creatures I'd seen. I left parts out, such as this morning's events. When he asked about Achilles, I said I found him a few days ago, lost in the woods. I didn't tell him about the yau either, not wanting word to get out and another legion to be sent.

I answered his questions about my old life. About my family and my world. It probably wasn't wise, but Tor never wanted to hear about where I came from—I think he was scared of it. But Rose? His curiosity was intoxicating. I told him of history, democracy, technology —anything I thought necessary to summarise an entire civilisation in the space of a few hours.

Reliving things about home, I felt like a child reliving cherished memories, not recounting something I'd lost. Only when Rose asked if I'd figured out a way to get home did I stall—to say no wasn't a lie, in any sense. But shame lingered for not *wanting* to find a way home.

Silence fell between us. I filled it by tearing the grass from the bank and pelting it into the stream, as if it were the root of all my problems.

A soft nudge on the shoulder interrupted my wallowing, and I turned to see Rose's smiling eyes. "I am glad Tor decided to train you. It is a necessary skill, learning to fight. Though you are terrifying enough already, I would hate to take you on in a scrap."

"I'm not terrifying at all, you should see Tor when I pull a punch."

Rose laughed aloud—and forced or not, I was grateful. "Tor is training you in all skills? Not just swordplay and weaponless combat?"

"That, along with riding, archery, and Kiliac's history."

"Good," he said. "What about knife fighting?"

I shook my head and he frowned. "When nothing else is available, knives are your best chance; punching can only get you so far. I will train you—an extra skill will not go amiss."

His superior tone grated at my nerves. "And what makes you qualified to train me? You must think highly of yourself."

"Oh, aye, I am the best there is. I have proved it many a time in tavern games. But if you want to pass up an opportunity to learn from a master..."

I snorted and shoved his arm. "Fine, you can train me. Stop being so damned humble."

"Then it is settled. I know Tor, he is a hard master, you do well to stick with it when he pushes you to your limits. Most in your position would quit."

"Is that what you think of me?"

A knowing smile. "No, Estelle. I do not know what to think of you. You are infuriating."

Caught between flattery and irritation, I simply said, "There's a lot you don't know about me."

Is there, really? I wondered. My whole life, bar the strong and terrifying possibility I was a magi, had been summed up in such a short time. Truthfully, there wasn't much to know.

Mischief flared in Rose's eyes as he spoke. "Well, lass, there is plenty more about you I would like to know."

With that, he pushed up and angled his face to wink. "I must ask Tor something, alone, if you will excuse me." He bowed and turned on his heel to march into the cabin. Achilles, who'd been resting in Rose's shadow, snorted in his general direction and trotted to lay in my lap.

"What the hell does that mean?" I asked the fawn.

He just bleated nonchalantly and curled up in my shadow.

As the final remnants of sunlight shone through the clearing, I thought on the day. It had started with me rough-housing a two-tailed wolf, and ended here, explaining modern civilisation to the man who'd saved me a fortnight ago. It was endearing, I supposed, that he was so interested. Behind his obnoxious persona, Rose was incredibly astute.

I tried to relax, tried to take in the forest in all its sunset glory, but Rose disappearing into the cabin with Tor bugged me. They were talking about me and I wanted to know why.

A slam of the cabin door stole my attention. As Rose emerged, closing the distance between us with a swagger in his stride, I resolved to ask Tor later. I stood when he plastered a lazy grin across his face. "Estelle, I have truly enjoyed our afternoon together, but I must go now. Another appointment I am afraid."

"What—no. All I've done is talk about myself like a damned fool, we didn't talk about you at all."

Rose smirked. "You want to know more about me?"

"Of course I do."

"What do you want to know?"

I scrambled for an appropriate question, but nothing smart or witty came to mind, so I said, "Everything."

He tipped his head back and laughed. "Well, *that* would take much longer than a single afternoon to tell. But I will be back, if you will let me?"

I wanted to beg him to stay, but I remembered Tor's threat; he and I had a lot to talk about tonight.

"Yes," I said. "Please, come back." I only had one friend in this world, at least, one human friend. Another would be nice. Rose's turquoise eyes burned with an emotion I couldn't read as he considered my words with a smile drifting across his face. *That damned smile.*

"Of course, wayfarer. I am at your disposal."

He whistled and his bay trotted towards us from where she grazed near Kip's stable. Biting my bottom lip to hide the small smile at his answer, I stalked past Rose to stroke the mare's nose. "What's her name?" I asked without glancing at him as he stepped up beside me, close enough to touch. So close, the hair on his bare arm brushed against my own.

"Finn."

I moved to massage her neck. "She's gorgeous."

"Beautiful," he agreed, but he wasn't looking at the horse. He was staring at me, his face blank and unreadable.

My mouth went dry as warmth swirled through my core, but I forced myself to roll my eyes. Rose jerked his head and flicked the reins up over Finn's neck.

"What's wrong?" I scoffed. "Your ridiculous cliché didn't pan out as planned?"

His smirk returned. "I will miss you, is all."

"You haven't known me long enough to miss me."

Rose grinned, his skin and hair glowing in the twilight. "I will miss that smart mouth of yours."

I snorted and backed away so he could mount the mare. When he was seated, I gave Finn a final pat on the neck, only just catching a blood stain on his hands.

"Do I get a goodbye stroke?"

I tried and failed to keep my composure. My lips wobbled and scarlet flooded my cheeks. And in a voice half-way between a murmur and a gibe, I said, "You're a right proper dickhead."

Rose shook his head. "There is my foul-mouthed lass."

He scooped up my hand in his, leaning down to press a soft kiss to the back of it, and as night-kissed air seeped through the clearing, his stare all but paralysed me. His voice sinking to a low purr did something else entirely. "I will see you soon, Estelle Verndari."

I schooled my face into neutrality. "See you later."

He released my hand and pressed Finn into a trot. Looking back over his shoulder, Rose winked again before kicking her into a canter, then they were gone in a heartbeat.

Before I could stand too long gaping towards the forest like a love-struck teenager, Tor came crashing out of the cabin. "Swords, lass, now!"

I threw him an incredulous look. "It's almost nightfall!"

"Yer gonna have to learn how to fight when yeh cannot see, and it is gonna be now."

"How about *you* tell me what all that was with Rose?"

His bronze eyes darkened. "Lass, get yer self over there and pick up a sword. If yeh hit me, I will answer yer questions. If not, keep your bleedin' mouth shut."

"Challenge accepted," I shot, dropping my voice to a low snarl. "And don't speak to me like that. Ever."

A menacing smile spread across his face.

Challenge accepted indeed.

TOR HAD NEVER BEEN this voracious. He was angry. *Really* angry.

Any attempt of speaking was met with a gruff rumble or snide comment. His anger wasn't directed at me, but I hated it, and I made sure he knew it. Every remark he made—I sent one back. Each time he snarled, I roared.

Compared to training by day, I was a blundering fool in the dark. Tor's temper was made no better by Achilles charging to headbut him in the shins every time he yelled. When Tor bellowed at the fawn, I rushed to lock him in Kip's stable.

Tor's grumbly mood didn't improve, but his attitude softened a little each time he shoved me on my arse and I shot back to my feet, ready to go again.

Finally, a few hours past nightfall, I parried his onslaught, dove beneath an outstretched arm and wacked him in the back of the knee with my sparring sword.

Despite the mood of the evening, Tor smiled broadly at me. I guessed we were done, then.

Both drenched in sweat, we walked together to the stream to sit and soak our feet. Tor angled his face towards the forest and spoke, his voice rough, "I used to work for Rose's father. I was a general in the Ashbourne Militia, and the things I used to do for that man...after Elara, I could not do those things no more. See, Estelle, I used to lead 'em legions into Galdurne."

Every cell inside my body froze, but I waited silently for him to finish.

Tor lifted a fist to rub his eyes. "There came a time when Elara cried when I returned home. I think she hated me after a while, for the things I did. But I loved that woman—Maker, I loved her. So one day, I told Rose's father that I would not lead 'em again.

"I was sent away from my duties, to be part of the guard assigned to Rose's mother and her children when they travelled from place to place. It was during them more peaceful years, when Elara started loving me again, that she gave me Danii.

"When Elara died, Rose's mother steered her escort off course to bring me and Danii here, and I have not left since." He loosed a heavy sigh. Shame and anxiety lay in his eyes, like he was waiting for my forgiveness—or waiting for me to damn him.

He was either ashamed of his past, or frightened by it.

I steeled my burning heart. "I don't blame you, Tor. You were following orders. It's how you live now that matters. What *you* do to make it right." Tor dropped his head low, so I reached up and squeezed his shoulder. "You are a good man."

He turned to face me, cheeks glistening, but smiled the warmest smile I'd ever seen. I grappled with the fire inside me to lighten the weight on his shoulders. Light humour seemed the best course. "I'm glad you made Rose sweat earlier."

Tor chuckled, easing the tightness in my chest.

"I get his father's a bastard, but is Rose as bad?" I tried to ask lightly, but my gut clenched—I didn't want Rose to be the monster that made someone like Tor scared of what he'd done. I didn't want to be a fool for not seeing it and telling him everything about me.

Not everything, a small voice reminded me.

Tor grimaced. "I knew Rose as a spoilt lad, always running off and causing trouble on the road between towns. But no, he is not like his father. He takes after his mother, I see that now. I apologise for my actions today."

White-hot relief coursed through me. "There is nothing to be sorry for. It would be hard to not have prejudice."

Tor swayed his feet in the water. "What does *prejudice* mean?"

I fought back my amusement, biting my lip to stop smiling. "Prejudice is judging Rose by the actions of his father."

He stared at me in silence, and when he spoke again, my gentle giant had returned. "Yes, lass, I had *prejudice*. Rose is not like his father in the slightest. He never was as a lad neither, always more concerned with stealing jewels for his mother than anything else. And as long as yeh say so, he is welcome here."

I finally let my smile break through. "Thank you, Tor."

AFTER DEVOURING a healthy serving of stew and ransacking Tor's last reserves of goat milk for Achilles, I shuffled into bed and tucked the fawn into my side beneath the furs.

As I lay there, listening to Tor's heavy snores fill the cabin, I thought of the day—how I charged through the forest like a wildling, snarled down a cioraun, spent an afternoon with a very arrogant, yet endearing man, then finally—*finally*—got one back on Tor.

Pride swelled in my chest.

But other visions came. Screaming, blood, dismemberment of bodies. Tor's body lying amongst them.

Magic. My magic.

My choice.

Achilles wriggled to nestle into the crook of my neck, so I closed my arms around him and pulled him close. My soul-bound. My dyr. Our gold-linked chain rose and fell with each breath, and I wondered how I ever lived without it before today.

But the guilt of my decision to stay kept me from sleep. I shuddered beneath the furs and sobbed silently into my fists as Achilles pressed so tight against me that it hurt to draw air. Though the worst part of it all, was that after reliving the day over and over again, for the first time since arriving here, I didn't long to wake up home.

The realisation settled, and as if in answer, deep in the distance ancient drumbeats sounded and a voice entwined with the wind sang to me.

Close your eyes and think of something nice.

~ ROSE ~

ESTELLE. I had never heard a name such as hers.

I have never met a girl such as her.

Riding away was near impossible, a veritable pain I had to push through, plant a well-practised smirk on my face, and kick Finn into action to hide my wretchedness. For she was glorious, in every sense of the word.

Everything, from the fire in her hair, to her strong build and womanly curves, to her eyes—piercing emerald that sent a punch into my gut each time I looked into them. It was a colour that reflected the viridian wildness of Galdurne itself.

I had met a great many beautiful women, but now, almost all of them looked the same. Estelle was something more than that, something entirely different. She was resplendent.

It had been a long time since I had enjoyed killing.

After hearing her scream pierce through the trees that day, then rushing to find those piece of shit maggots holding her down, I knew what they were about to do, so I savoured *their* screams. Then despite her terror, Estelle had cursed and yelled and called me out. Now she was stronger, and not just physically.

I had intended to come to old Tor's cabin and tell the girl to lay low, stay hidden, that I would never see her again, that strange girl in the woods who buried a yole.

But there she was, soaking wet and struggling to bathe a fawn in a stream—her hair unbound, billowing around her in the wind. And when she spun to look at me, the emerald in her eyes was incandescent. I could not leave.

When she told me of her world, the one she came from, my heart broke. She did not notice and I did not stop her. Her voice was lovely and warm, and seemed to soothe the cracks that each of her words were forming. Shattering and healing all at once. For in the world she spoke of, men were not monsters. There was no magic, but the magic was in the way her civilisation had grown into something marvellous. This woman, this *girl*, had been taken from her own magnificent home and sent to this forsaken place. What kind of god would be so cruel?

I needed to help her, find out whatever I could about the old legends—perhaps there would be something salvageable in one of the libraries. All books and scrolls concerning magic had long since been destroyed, apart from any wholly ancient and priceless tomes spirited away and hidden, but folktales and children's stories, that is where I would look first. And then I would go back and tell Estelle anything I could find.

For I would go back to her, because I was a selfish prick and I wanted to see her again.

I told Tor not to mention anything more than necessary about me, and in exchange for his silence, I would seek a way to help her. I slit my palm open and let my blood fall to his feet as I said it.

Please come back.

Her voice drifted around me, as real as the smell of oakwood and wild plums in the air. Her emerald eyes seared in the forefront of my mind and hair like fire swayed in the wind each time I closed my eyes.

I would go back to her.

I could not stay away.

CHAPTER 8
NO ONE'S HERE TO SLEEP

"Hold your swords higher, lass!"

I rolled my eyes and raised my swords as Tor bellowed those same bloody words for the millionth time today. I was using two today, as I 'could not possibly be worse than with one'. We'd ridden Kip a fair way into the forest depths, Tor having deemed it necessary I started utilising Galdurne—using the roots, shadows, and uneven ground to my advantage. But I was more hopeless with swords in the forest then I was on the even grass of the clearing. Frankly, I'd thought it impossible to be worse.

My shoulders sagged, and when my arm wavered—shaking from overuse and a blooming bruise on my wrist—Tor charged past my block and thwacked my shoulder with his own sparring sword. He sighed at the easy target, closed his eyes and gestured to the west.

Loosing a moan of long suffering, I dropped my swords and broke into a jog. Achilles perked up his head and dashed from his spot between the roots to follow at my heels. I was to run and count a thousand paces, finding as many obstacles to leap over, climb, and use as leverage on my way as I could. Parkour, essentially. Thankfully, Tor stopped following me after the first few times, so I avoided most of the boulders, branches and low-hanging trees. Left them un-parkoured.

I inhaled as a sour smell wafted around me, carrying with it an image of scrubbing the day away in the stream, weightlessly floating beneath the clouds. Achilles bleated as he ran, as if he were imagining the same.

Since first arriving in Kiliac, I'd become markedly better with a sword—or two. Each day my skill improved and Tor went harder on me. It would make me better in the end, I told myself. After nearly three weeks of training, my skill with a bow had increased tenfold, so Tor ensured I focused on improving every other skill. Logical, but infuriating.

I counted one thousand paces—my footsteps beating against the forest floor in time with my heavy heartbeats—spun on my heels, and ran back. Making a lazy running leap up onto a boulder, I flipped and landed on the other side, a smile stretching across my face—I forgot, sometimes, that I could do these things now. Incredible things. Because it never occurred to me to take the easy road and half-ass the fitness Tor drilled into me day after day. I'd take it and be grateful.

When I returned to our training grounds for the day, Tor was sitting against a large tree, sharpening his hunting knife atop a knee. He gestured with a jolt of his head to the spot beside him. "Take a breather, lass."

Blowing a heavy gust of air from tight lungs, I snatched up the brown water skin Tor had made for me. I poured water down my spine to wash away the sweat pooling at the base, allowing droplets to cascade through the inside of my pants as I revelled in the cool caress upon my skin. But the water in my stomach gurgled, roiling like ocean waves in a storm.

"Yeh know, I am glad it was Rose that found yeh that day," Tor said after a time. "He really has turned out a good man."

The pain in my stomach twisted as I considered Tor's words. I hadn't the slightest clue where this was coming from, but by the way he wrung his hands and bunched his face, I suspected he'd been thinking on it for quite some time.

"Yes," I said back. "I think he is. I hope he is."

Tor blinked, cool amusement lining his gaze. "It is good yeh will have someone young to talk to, with only this old bastard and a graceless furball for company most of the time."

Pressing a hand across my abdomen, I replied with a smirk. "You're the best old bastard I know, Tor. I wouldn't have it any other way. Unless you keep giving me these shitty workouts."

His hearty chuckle bellowed around the woods. "I was not a general for nothing. Yeh know, once I led a company to Dragons Bay, and I swear, we was the only ones to find the—"

"Stop!"

Tor rose from the ground swifter than a man of his size should.

My stomach thrashed like a raging sea as the beast inside me uncoiled, preparing to strike. A sour smell filled the air. Vicious and all consuming.

I glanced at Achilles, whose eyes darted around the forest with an almost predatory focus. He pawed the dirt and arched his neck, side-stepping to stand before me. To shield me.

"Something's wrong," I whispered.

Tor unsheathed his two axes, spinning them in his hands. "What do yeh mean?"

I snapped my focus up, to where the stench radiated. "Something in the trees."

"Estelle." My name was a quiet, but rough command.

My gaze meeting his was instant, just as we'd practised. He threw me the real sword, one he'd strapped onto his back just in case. I caught it and firmed my grip on the hit, but my stomach whirled and raged, and cold panic set into my limbs. A single sword—I was near useless with one sword.

"Run, lass."

Panic subsided as I planted my feet. "I'm not going anywhere."

"Shit," Tor spat, rolling his shoulders, attention on the canopy, searching for the invisible threat. His head tilted towards me and with a voice like thunder he began, "Call for—"

"TOR!"

Three grey-scaled beasts dropped from the canopy.

Monstrous like the jarrah. Poisonous. Wrong. Reptilian bodies with serpentine faces, black feathers sprouting from their bodies, and tails slashing like scaled whips—spiked barbs flicking through the leaves. I froze, my next breath dying in my throat.

Tor's did not.

He hurled an axe into the skull of the one in the middle, impaling it against a tree trunk. The other two scurried towards him. Tor bounced on his heels and twirled to the left, drawing his second axe up and under the neck of the second. Blood spilled over scaled flesh and black feathers, and a guttural screech tore through the forest. The third leapt over its kin's flailing body, claws extended. Tor ducked as it approached, pushed up and plunged his knife into the underside of the beast's jaw with a sickening rip of membrane and tendon.

I stood, paralysed, my own sword trembling in my fingers. Tor spun my way. "Focus, lass! Behind yeh!"

Achilles planted himself between me and the beast gunning for us. I turned to see bright yellow eyes charging from the dark between the trees. I didn't know what to do. Tor had trained me against human attacks—sword against sword. But not this.

I was going to die.

The air beside my ear cleaved apart. A flash of metal had me diving to the side, dropping my sword in the dirt. A giant lizard crashed to the ground with a knife embedded in its eye. Its legs flailed as it clung to life.

Kill it.

I lurched and scrambled for my sword. Fingertips finding the leather hilt, I crawled towards the creature. The blade flashed above my head. I thrust it into its neck with a whimper. Bone crunched beneath my strike—my terrible, imperfect strike. The gushing wound flooded the dirt with blackened blood. I hadn't put enough force in it to behead the creature, but agony ignited its eyes and it gave its final flail.

I wanted to cry—to cry and scream and cower, but more screeching and Tor's strained grunt had me on my feet.

Yellow eyes flashed. Pain tore through my body—my entire being —excruciating and endless. Another lizard beast had my hip in its maw and I screeched as its teeth ground against bone.

The beast tore its teeth from my flesh with a jolt. Dappled white down appeared, and Achilles angled his head, preparing for another charge. Tor fended off another two on the other side of the clearing. He spun on light feet, slicing perfect arcs with axes into their hides, godlike in his dance of death.

The beast with my blood dripping from its maw fixed its glare on my dyr, so I limped to stand beside Achilles, sword dangling loosely at my side.

Tor's shout was thunder in a blackening sky. "Hold your sword higher!"

His words echoed at the edge of my blurring vision, snapping me to attention. I raised the sword as the creature charged, blindly bringing it down half a heartbeat later.

My arm jolted, the sword ripped from my grasp. I opened my eyes to see a glazed image of the lizard flinging my sword from between its teeth as it struck, fast as a viper.

Towards Achilles.

My body arched around the fawn.

Achilles bellowed. Red blood gushed from the monster's jaw, from where its teeth were clamped around my arm—my shredded arm.

There was no beginning or end to my scream.

Tor seized its jaw in both hands and cleaved it apart. The beast didn't have time to shriek as half its face bounced in the dirt.

Two yellow eyes appeared over Tor's shoulder and my scream became one of warning. Teeth clamped into his collarbone, legs wrapped around Tor's body, it ripped deep gashes across his torso and sides with sharp taloned feet.

Tor roared, in pain and in fury, as I cried out his name.

My cry echoed between the trees. The beast's head vanished in a flash of teeth and tawny fur before Tor slumped to the side, revealing a huge cioraun battling five more of the scaled monstrosities. And from the shadows, a familiar ash-grey cioraun leapt to face off another that dropped from the trees.

My breath hitched. Tears freefell down my cheeks. The world was upside down, it made no sense, and the pain of my gaping wounds vanished into nothing. A shadow engulfed me. Pulling me down into a darkness that would devour me.

A hard nudge at my back barely stole me from the dark. Achilles scrambled around to my front, planting his face before mine.

Such fierceness, such strength in his golden eyes.

Gold.

Molten gold—my gold.

My power.

Using my free hand to grasp Achilles' neck, I pressed my brow into his. I forced my breathing to slow, closed my eyes, and imagined incandescent light erupting from within me. As Achilles shoved his head even harder against mine, warmth grew in my chest and flooded my bloodstream. The shredded skin on my arm and hip knit back together like a time lapse film of fibres interweaving. The light inside me, inside Achilles and me, rained forth from my core. The colour inside Achilles' eyes whirled like a sun-kissed ocean hurricane, and when I tore my gaze from my dyr, both wounds were no more than shining white scars and smeared old blood.

At a roar behind me, I spun and beheld the chaos. Another cioraun had joined the fray, tearing through the swarm of monsters that had descended upon us. I didn't know how to fight these things the way Tor was, nor indeed, the way the ciorauns were.

But I had something else—I had my dyr.

And Tor needed me.

My lips twitched into a smile as I grasped my fallen sword from the ground.

One of the lizards angled for the ash-grey cioraun's flank. At my piercing whistle, my dyr charged the lizard's side, knocking it to the ground.

I was a step behind him.

I angled my blade straight and plunged it into the beast's neck.

Wrenching the sword up through the gore and tendon was swifter, easier than before, and I turned to follow Achilles. He ploughed into another and I ended its life. As Tor and the three ciorauns fought the monsters through brute force, Achilles and I picked off those who tried to flank them, until finally, the swarm retreated back into the shadows.

~

THE SIX OF US STOOD, limbs shaking, our breath a wet rasp. None uttered a word until I panted through a heavy exhale, "That was one hell of a training exercise, Tor."

Face awash in black blood, Tor grinned as he dropped his axes to the mud. "Well," he began, jutting his chin towards my newly scarred arm. "I told yeh to keep that bleedin' sword higher, did I not?"

Doubled over my knees, my heaving breaths bubbled into hysterical laughter. Tor's rumbling guffaws joined moments later. The ciorauns yawned and a wheezing noise came from their mouths, their large teeth bared in shared amusement. Old mate, the fussy grey feline, sported a deep gash behind his ear, and my mirth ceased as I lurched forward. The light inside was more familiar now, more controllable as I healed him. I stumbled out of the warm trance with the soft touch of his whiskers tickling my cheek.

When he turned to leave, I faced Tor again, only to see the tawny-coloured cioraun licking at the blood covering his arms. He seemed torn between awe and terror, and stood with an unnatural stillness. Eventually, to his credit and with great effort, Tor reached his free hand up to scratch the cat's forehead, and it too turned away with a low purr.

A small twitch lifted Tor's beard as he watched the cioraun bound into the tree line, but his expression changed as he ran an assessing eye over my body—my new scars.

"Yeh alright, Estelle?" he asked when he finished his inspection.

I nodded as I strode to him, casting my gaze over the mottled blood covering his arms and torso. Seizing his right hand, I allowed the warm, iridescent light to flow through me. Our gazes were caught by the shredded skin knitting back together, leaving a shining scar where open wounds once were.

"You have to teach me to fight other things now, I cannot rely on the chance I'll have enough time to heal myself as I cower," I said in a quiet yet firm voice. "I need you to teach me how to survive everything."

"Aye, I will."

Taking a long breath, I wiped the blood from my hands onto my shift, and balled them into fists at my sides. "What were they?"

"They are nothlings," he said, eyes roaming the canopy. "A parasite brought over from the Dealon Empire to help destroy the creatures of Kiliac. Seems they were out for their daily meal."

"Humans brought them here?"

"Yes, but they went rogue."

"Evidently," I said under my breath.

When Tor didn't answer, I rubbed at the sweat, or what I hoped was sweat on my brow. "I was scared, Tor. I froze."

"And do yeh think I did not shit myself during my first fight?"

A reluctant smile tugged at my lips. "I guess everyone would be scared in the beginning."

Tor's strong finger wrapped under my chin, tilting my face up. "I still get scared, lass."

If I didn't know Tor the way I was beginning to, I wouldn't have believed it, but I recalled the terror in his face when we were separated in the onslaught. He wasn't speaking about fear for himself. No. It was fear of losing me. Losing me as he'd lost his daughter.

"I suppose only fools would not be frightened. Fools, or those who had nothing to fight for."

Tor winked in agreement and, dropping his grip from my chin, he gestured in the direction of the cabin. I leant to scratch Achilles' muzzle and followed in Tor's footsteps, my pace quickening as I fought to keep up with his long strides. Forging ahead, Tor spoke over his shoulder. "Next time yeh get a feeling in yer gut, lass, call for yer forest friends right away, will yeh?" He pointed at my stomach. "I just thought yeh had wind needed passing."

I scoffed. "I promise."

"Thank the bleedin' Maker yeh decided to stay here."

"Why is that?"

"I need yeh to stay and protect me, too."

I didn't bother to try and hide my smile. "Always, Tor."

CHAPTER 9
WHATEVER IT TAKES

T he ground shuddered beneath my thundering footfalls.

The ancient drums pulsated in my head and heart, the forest flashing by in a maelstrom of shadow and light and colour. The young stag raced in a blur at my side—Achilles was stronger now. We both were.

We shot past a pack of wolves feasting on the remains of a large cave bear. They raised their heads as one and stared at the wild girl racing by, a bow at her back, uncaring of the predators within the forest.

She was one too.

As I ran, I felt the change in the air, like tendrils of oil seeping into water. I leapt and twisted, unsheathing my bow and pulling it around me as I sprang, my arrow already nocked.

The jarrah soared at me, talons at the apex of its wings stretched to strike. I let my arrow fly, tucked my head into my chest, and rolled onto my feet in one fluid motion. And when I saw the arrow protruding through the jarrah's right eye, I beamed. "Bloody oath, nice —right?"

Achilles snorted and pawed the ground with his darkening foreleg. He'd grown so much since I found him, six months ago to the day.

Now he stood roughly at the same height as a pony. My grin widened as I strode forward to tousle the crown of his head, pride swelling with the brush of my fingers over the two hard lumps about to break through, and swaggered to the jarrah corpse.

I'd seen vile things in the forest since arriving, but I hated jarrahs most. Perhaps it was an early memory, or maybe because I was vain and jarrahs were so ugly. Close after them came the riki, the car-sized arachnids. Because, of course, there had to be giant spiders. I scowled as I tugged the arrow from the jarrah's eye with a wet squelch and unsheathed a hunting knife from the strap around my thigh. My blade bit into the beast's throat, slicing a deep arc across it. A fountain of black blood soaked into the forest floor.

Always be sure, Tor's voice resounded in my head. Killing jarrahs did not feel like killing. Not anymore.

Once, a long time ago—in a different world, Dad had driven me somewhere and I remember the car hitting a bird. I cried for days afterwards with a sickening feeling, like bugs crawling underneath my skin. It was guilt. I hadn't known it then. And why should I have? I was eight at the time.

I didn't feel guilty when I killed a jarrah or a riki. Or any of the other foul creatures lurking in Galdurne for that matter. The forest, it seemed, was infected. Infested with jarrahs, riki, nothlings, wraiths, and humans

So, I made it my mission—on my days off from training with Tor— to *cleanse* the forest, so to speak. Through some small mercy, I hadn't seen anymore Ashbourne legions or soldiers since the massacre of the deer herd. I don't know whether I'd be able to fight them, kill them. But the other monsters? Well, I couldn't pass up the chance for moving target practise.

Jarrahs and riki were easy enough to hunt and slay, but wraiths— spirit-like creatures with smoky humanoid forms—were more difficult. Like the yau, they had the ability to ghost from one place to another. But I could sense their poison wafting through the air. All I had to do was shoot an arrow in the direction of their pungency.

I looked down at Achilles, now gnawing at my leather pants—black leather, made from all the jarrah skins I'd collected in my first few months. Tor had taught me how to clean and tan the hides, and how to make clothes from them.

Around a month ago, I'd saved a yau from an onslaught of wraiths. The memory still brought cold chills seeping down my spine. An image straight from a horror movie—the 'ghosts' fought against one another with shadows and wind and scraping claws. I'd learned to shoot blindly that day, to loosen my arrow in the direction my gut told me. There were five dead wraiths in seconds when I gave in to that instinct.

In return, the yau tugged out a tuft of iridescent fur from each of its six tails. I'd braided them through a section of hair on the right side of my head—just above my ear—and worn the never-fading colours ever since. Much to Tor's dismay.

"Ready to go, mate?"

Achilles bleated and pranced on the spot, brandishing his back with a proud arched neck so I could tie the jarrah onto it.

Smiling at the smugness alight in my dyr's eyes, I began the long slog back to Tor's cabin.

WHEN I MADE IT INSIDE, I chucked the carcass onto the table and called out to Tor. "Another jarrah! You'll have to teach me to make something other than clothes soon, you know! A new pack would be nice, aye?"

But it was not Tor that answered in a bewildered voice. "Maker's balls, lass, what happened to you?"

A dark-haired, handsome man lounged all-too-casually across my bed.

I glanced down, noticing the dirt and blood caked over my arms and torso. "What's wrong with the way I look?"

Rose laughed. "As always, Estelle, it is a wonder to see you."

I crinkled my nose. "And you, I guess." I ignored his feigned outrage as I shrugged off my bow, leaning it against a leg of the table whilst Achilles leapt forwards to nudge his way under Rose's arm. I strode after him to nestle beside them both.

"Do you have anything sweet for me?"

Rose's grin was as wild as the fire in his eyes. "Always."

He laughed and retrieved a small paper-wrapped package from his bag. In his last few visits Rose brought me sweets, after I'd admitted my weakness for anything with sugar—I adored Tor, but he couldn't cook anything other than stew to save himself. I snatched the package from Rose's outstretched hand and tore away the wrapping to reveal a divine looking apple pastry and ate it in two bites.

"You remain the most beautiful pig in all of Kiliac."

I released a sensual moan for dramatic effect, earning a hearty chuckle in response.

During his first few visits, I often speculated at Rose's intentions where I was concerned, but he never made any move, and I certainly didn't. Rose's flirtatious remarks were playful banter—a game with no real intent. And since I'd never been part of that game back home, I thoroughly enjoyed feigning cool indifference to wind him up.

"So, where is Tor?" I asked him a breath later.

"No idea. He was not here when I arrived."

"Then how did you get in?"

"I have my ways," he purred.

I shook my head. "Sneaky prick. Can you teach me? How to pick a lock?"

More feigned outrage spread across his features. "How *dare* you! Pick locks! Me? Do you truly think so low of me? I am a respectable, charming, attractive..." A muscle ticked in his jaw, and gods, I barely heard the rest. "...I am running out of words. Yes, I will teach you. We can forgo the knives for a day I suppose," he added with a sigh.

Pinching my own thigh, I beamed at him, then excused myself to wash and change from my leathers, throwing my middle finger up over my shoulder at his offer to help me bathe.

THE HOUR SPENT PRACTISING lock picking was deluged by bickering and swearing. Every time I tried to turn the pins the right way, they snapped, depleting the handful Rose had tucked away in his pocket. Narrowing my eyes, I twisted my tongue to the left, shimmied the pin as carefully as I would remove a fly's wing. The pin went rigid and fractured like ice.

"Goddamnit it!"

I threw down the tools and stomped towards the stream to squat on the bank. Rose gave me a minute to stew on my failure, and came to sit beside me, grinning.

I rolled my eyes. "Shut up. Arrogant ass."

He tsked at my curse, wrapping his arm around my shoulders. Any trace of annoyance vanished with the contact—we rarely touched.

"It is a delicate skill and will take some time to learn. Do not worry. Have patience, Estelle. It took years of practising almost daily to perfect it."

"Sure it did," I murmured.

His answering smile lacked its usual edge, and he glanced at his arm slung around me like he'd just now noticed it was there. For his sake, I changed the subject as he dropped his arm—keen to forgo my disappointment. "The last time you were here, you mentioned travelling north to Byram for work. Did you get there on time?"

"I did," he nodded, throwing a mask over his emotions. "And I managed to sneak into that old underground library after dark. The men attending the place are as blind as bats even if they do have Maker-blessed hearing." He chuckled to himself. "Luckily I have a Maker-blessed sense of smell. The wretched codgers carried the stench of piss and, well, the other unmentionable excretions that I am too gallant to mention, and I managed to remain undetected."

I snorted. "If you're talking about shit, I believe I've called you one multiple times."

Rose turned to me with impish expression and flicked his finger towards his crotch.

"Oh. *Oh*. Rose!"

I screwed up my nose as he laughed.

"Is Byram as awful as Tor says it is?" I asked, shaking my head at his mirth.

Rose's laughter died as he nodded. "As dirty and dangerous as a town can be. It is no small wonder the wealthy live beneath the ground. I never understood why Byram's sister was so well-off, whilst Byram is covered in shit and blood."

"Byram's sister town is Tusc right? On the other side of the bay?" I pursed my lips when he nodded again. "Then its wealth would come from it being the first place King Horus landed in Kiliac. It was his son, Horen, that moved the royal seat to Ashbourne. Tor said that when he was stationed in Tusc, they would quite literally ship their impoverished and dangerous people across the bay to Byram."

Rose blinked at me, many times with a deadpan expression. "Well, you are just a little know-it-all now, ain't you?"

I winked back at him. "Always. I listen when Tor tells me things. Most of the time."

Rose's face relaxed as he snorted.

"Speaking of dangerous and impoverished, why the hell would you go there for work?"

"It pays good coin to sell your sword for a Byram noble. Even if it is just to guard their way out of the tunnels to the docks.

"Fair enough." I stretched my feet towards the stream. Laying back to rest on my elbows, I took in the warmth of the Summer sun—*Kairi* sun. I enjoyed being with Rose, laughing with him and speaking to him. Sometimes we'd just sit together in silence, taking in the sound and smell of the life around us. As he laid down at my side, he seemed as content as I in enjoying the latter.

After that first conversation, many months ago, Rose and I had talked about a great many things.

The only subject he was quite uncomfortable discussing was his family.

Rose jabbed me lightly with his thumb as my vision glazed over the swaying trees. I glanced at his face, surprised to find him serious.

"You have not asked if I found anything in that library."

Licking my lips, I pushed myself up straight. It was a fine line, feigning eagerness and disappointment at the same time. "Should I have? Is it different to any other you've been to since you began?"

I felt dirty not telling him about that fateful decision I'd made, so many months ago. That I was not leaving—not yet. Not for a long while. But if he knew literally anything about what happened to me, I needed to hear it, so that when the time came I could go home.

Rose sighed. "No. Nothing, again. I am beginning to think you really did just drop out of the sky like a bag of bricks. I *have* managed to learn a lot about safe travelling routes around the realm. Sorry."

"It's ok." I crossed my legs, turning to face him square on. "I don't have high expectations after so long. I want to go with you, one day, and I'm still so grateful you're wasting your time on it...on me."

He shook his head and inched closer, eyes glittering. "No amount of time where you are concerned is wasted, lass."

My cheeks heated, so I wedged my head between my hands. "Still —you should use your spare moments to visit your family. Your mother and siblings, I mean."

Rose stared out over the stream without answering.

"How long has it been since you've seen them?"

"I do not want to talk about my family. I want you to tell me more about them *tele visions*."

"You never want to talk about your family."

He swallowed, once, twice, and clenched his jaw, looking to the sky as if he were fighting back words or searching for the right ones. "What do you think that looks like?" he asked, pointing to a large white cloud.

I breathed in, reining my curiosity and pushed a smile to my lips, following his finger's path. "A dragon."

"Me too."

At the sadness lingering in those two words, my brows furrowed. In all the stories and history Tor had told me, I'd never asked about the legendary, mythological beasts, because... "They've all been killed, haven't they?"

Rose loosened a long sigh. "Humans are a plague. We have destroyed everything. Dragons, they were magnificent. Truly magnificent. My mother took my brother and me to see one, once. An ancient Hydra off the coast near Fayr. It was her friend apparently. She did not know my father had followed us there. It is said that it was the last dragon. And that was the day I decided to not join my father's command of the Militia."

"It couldn't have been the last one," I said softly. "Nature finds a way."

Though if history had any story to tell about conquerors and the conquered, Rose was right. I just didn't say it, especially as he faced me with such a bright light in his eyes.

"You truly think so?"

"I know so," I lied.

He smiled again, a different way this time. Boyish and hopeful. My lips pressed into a thin line as I imagined him as a young boy, beaming with wonder at a magnificent water dragon—the horror that followed.

Rose twisted back to the sky and spoke again. "My brother and I used to play this game, finding shapes in the clouds." His eyes narrowed. "He had a much better imagination than me, coming up with stories of creatures in the sky flying down and taking us away to another place."

Another sad tidbit of information from his past—one I didn't get the impression he intended to tell. Hoping his openness might last, I kept my voice light. "What's your brother like?"

"A less attractive version of me."

Like he'd snapped, the sadness vanished and I was again speaking to cocky Rose. I frowned, but implanted the image of him looking up at the clouds imagining faraway places into my memory. No façade would take that away now.

Rose left at sunset, smiling his stupid smile and taking off with a cocky wink. I remained, sitting beside the stream with my thoughts to keep me company—Achilles had long since retired to Kip's empty stall to sleep on the hay.

After allowing me a fragment of a glimpse into his old life, Rose had reverted back to smirks and laughter, teasing me for just about everything. Flirting too, as was our way now. It was a game, but maybe Rose's arm around my shoulder and his candour was a manoeuvre? To see what I'd do and how I'd react? He told me a while ago that he was twenty-two-years-old—or as he'd put it, 'two and twenty seasons under the Kairi sun'—and after an immense amount of banter and prodding, he'd admitted that he certainly was not new to the game. I wasn't sure at the time whether the burning sensation in my chest and neck was wrought from jealousy at those past girls, or shame that I was so inexperienced by comparison.

When I'd told Rose I'd only ever kissed one boy before, when I was seven, he had laughed and offered to 'fix that problem' for me.

My old best mate, Tahnee, never had these issues. And she'd definitely kissed more boys since we were seven. She'd rival Rose, to be perfectly frank. Once, her boyfriend-at-the-time thought it'd be a grand idea to go on a double date to the cinema. His friend, Robbie-something, gave up trying to flirt with me because I didn't respond to a thing he said. In my defence, he was interrupting a decent movie. No, like Tahnee relished telling me, I was an introverted, prudish virgin.

A small, roiling part of me wished I hadn't chosen her to play with in the playground as children do, that I hadn't always been in her perfect shadow. Vain, pathetic, stupidly cliché, but it had always been there: jealousy, hidden in my mind. At least if I hadn't been in that shadow, I might have known how to play the game with Rose.

I'm glad Tahnee isn't here. He'd leave me high and dry in an instant.

A sudden thump to my spine whisked me back to the present and I twisted to see Achilles, golden eyes narrowed. I winced at the accusation in them.

"I'm sorry. That was wrong, wasn't it?"

In every sense.

The young buck grunted and forced his way into my lap—like one of those giant dogs who don't know they aren't lapdogs. I didn't mind,

I never did. My arms wrapped up and around his neck, cuddling him and welcoming the pressure.

"Estelle! Stop lounging about and come help with these bleedin' sacks!"

Tor's voice travelled across the clearing, jolting Achilles up in an instant. Scoffing at him, I jogged towards where Tor had dismounted Kip. Sacks of food had been tied behind the saddle.

"You went to the village again?" I asked, unstrapping one of the cloth sacks.

"I know what yer gonna say, lass, and the answer is still no."

I glowered. "Come *on* Tor! You and Rose are the only people I've talked to since I got here, I'm like a bloody prisoner!"

Immature and irrational, yes. But what good was being a teenager if I couldn't be unreasonable sometimes? Tor's face twisted with impatience and long suffering. This was an argument we had at least once a week. He usually rode to the village on days he knew I was out 'playing in the forest'.

"What's to make me not just follow you one day?"

"Because yer not stupid," Tor said. "Like I have told yeh before, those folk do not have two coppers to rub between their arse cheeks. If they notice anything off about yeh, they will report it in hope of a few coins. Or they will want to hurt yeh just for being cleaner and fuller than 'em."

All rational, completely plausible reasons. But still unfair. So I kept up my tantrum, adding in a stomped foot and widespread arms for good measure. "Tor, I'm not going to ride into the village on the back of a cioraun for heaven's sake. Do you think I'm a total idiot? I want to meet *people!*"

Tor's bronze eyes flared, probably with the memory of me, two months ago, astride a black and purple cioraun returning to the cabin after spraining my ankle in the forest. I could have healed it, but then I wouldn't have ridden a cioraun. He crossed his arms, most likely worn out by our long-running debate.

Consideration and sympathy lined his eyes as he spoke. "Estelle," he said through a long exhale. "If I take yeh to the village and something happens to yeh...yeh know what that would do to me."

Yes, I knew. Over the six months I'd been here, Rose had become my closest friend, but Tor—he'd become so much more. Protector and mentor didn't cover it. My own father never took much care in what I did, or where I went. I still loved him, as any pitiful, hopeful young girl would. But Tor had become more than my father ever was, showing a paternal devotion Dad never had to show in my twenty-first century world. And to Tor, with the deaths of both Elara and Danii weighing in his past, I'd become everything to him. I was his family now.

And he was mine.

"Tor..." I said, my tone low and beseeching. "I *promise*, if anything happens, if someone there so much as looks at me funny, I promise, I'll come straight home. Besides," I added with a shrug, "You'd be there with me the whole time anyway."

Home.

Tor caught the way I'd said it, and an emotion I couldn't read flashed through his eyes. He sighed again, then responded, albeit a little defeated. "The next time I go, yeh can come. And yeh will do everything I say. Yeh will not take off. Yeh will not speak to anyone unless I say yeh can. Understand?"

Grinning at my win, I nodded. "I promise."

I tossed one of the sacks up onto my shoulder, bending my knees to adjust to the weight. Tor pressed his lips together, then ruffled my hair, heaving three sacks over his shoulder and striding around me to haul them into the cabin. I beamed at Achilles, then took after Tor with my one heavy load.

CHAPTER 10
MUDDY WATERS

Five days passed before Tor needed to go back to the village. For more grain, he said. He didn't notice that I saw through his lie. I'd spotted a full bag of grain stashed in the underground chamber he kept his weapons in—but I wasn't going to waste his act of kindness for my ever-growing excitement to see the village.

To see other people.

A minute, yet annoying fear—that they would all be malicious, murderous brutes—hid beneath my excitement. At least I wouldn't be disappointed if I set my expectations low.

We mounted Kip before dawn, leaving Achilles tucked away in the stable. It took the better part of the sunrise for me to convince him to stay, reasoning that walking through the streets with a young white buck might look a tad strange, besides—who would stay behind to guard the place?

Eventually, Achilles yielded his grumbling, stomping to lay in the shadowed corner of the stall, not seeing me off nor responding when I called my farewell. But after riding a stone's throw away, I sensed that golden chain being pulled taut. I hadn't remembered the strength of that link, but then I hadn't been away from Achilles since first finding him. Each meter Kip strode away from the clearing it grew harder to breathe—my chest tightening with every step.

But *knowing* nothing bad would happen to either of us while I was gone, I focused on my breathing until the tightness in my chest dimmed to a low throbbing ache. A flock of butterflies replaced it, battering inside my stomach like a siege gate.

I was finally going to meet new people.

I just hoped they weren't as pathetic as Tor made them out to be.

GALDURNE WAS fantastical and the cabin had become home, but I'd forgotten there was a whole world outside of it all. And it stunk. Literally.

Riding into the village was like riding into a dodgy renaissance fair.

I'd truly hoped to be pleasantly surprised by a Disneyesque, wonderfully novel medieval town with flowers in the windows and the smell of baking bread wafting through the streets. Perhaps people breaking out into synchronised songs about lost princesses and reading books whilst the baker went past with bread and rolls to sell.

This was definitely not that.

Gaunt faces with sunken eyes barely looked up from the mud, so underfed and underdressed the place felt like a death camp. Starvation and sickness were painted over every beating heart. People slept on the roads and some just sat in the dirt staring at nothing at all, while ramshackle homes bordered a dried up fountain serving as a town center. I leaned forward to whisper in Tor's ear, "I never believed you. This place is horrible."

"Aye, lass," he murmured over his shoulder. "It is. Was pillaged over a year ago by bandits. Most of the homes were burned to the ground and any wealth was stolen. Ashbourne, of course, sent no aid. Most of the villagers left and them who stayed are now fading away. Sorry, I know yeh was excited and all...but I wanted yeh to see it how it is now, and then make up yer own mind."

"Thank you," I said, my voice flat. I didn't think I'd find any new friends here.

We rode through the town center, to the few structures which, for the most part, remained intact. The only place I'd seen so far that resembled a functioning town. A tiny bakery huddled on one corner, with an outdoor butcher set up outside next to another market-type stall selling grain and hay.

Tor nudged Kip towards a hitching post and dismounted, gesturing for me to follow. I'd worn a dark red shift, tied in a knot at my hip, and my black leather pants. Having taken the yau fur out of my hair, I'd tied it up in a haphazard bun atop my head and unruly strands dangled out around my face and neck. Compared to the people here, I was clean, well-fed, and entirely out of place. Not quite as dramatically as Tor—he really was a giant. The villagers stumbled out his path, leering at me with half lowered eyes as I followed in his shadow.

While Tor paid for another sack of grain, I studied the mud caked around my boots. There were only ten or so people around, but the heat of their glares sent fear trembling through my limbs. I shouldn't be scared, I'd ridden a damned giant saber-tooth tiger and taken on a swarm of nothlings, but the resentment pulsating off everyone had my knees quaking. With my eyes on my boots and thoughts askew, a tentative hand touching my shoulder jolted panic through me like an electric shock. I whirled to behold a girl, roughly my age, smiling.

She was blonde, or would be if it wasn't for the dirt and grease dulling her long hair. A huge scar marred her face, a tight red line running from her chin, over her mouth and up to her right temple. Blemishes pock-marked her copper skin and she was missing half her teeth. Her left arm was mutilated. Broken and maimed, then broken some more.

Amethyst eyes sparked with determination, shining like the sky at dusk. Her body might be brutalized beyond repair, but whoever hurt her had not broken her soul.

I smiled back at her.

"My name is Kiita," she rasped. "What is yours?"

The moment she spoke, I sensed it. Felt it. The rawness in her voice—this girl was sick. Terminally sick.

Kiita had survived torture and brutality, and she was dying.

"My name is Estelle," I said quietly.

Kiita grinned wider, revealing cracked, brown teeth, and reached out her right hand, palm upraised. Begging.

I fished coins from my pocket, ignoring Tor's warning squeeze on my elbow, and gave them all to her, trying my hardest to smile. Her eyes gleamed at the pile of silver in her hand, brows raised high. I'd given her enough to eat for a year—or, at least, the remainder of her life.

She shook her head and tried to give all but one coin back, but I gently closed her fingers around them. A tear slid down her cheek, drawing a line through the grime on her skin as she tucked the coins beneath her ruined dress. Tor tugged harder on my arm, but Kiita grasped my hand in hers, rasping out her thanks.

I'd never been more out of control than I was in that moment.

With my hand in Kiita's, the golden light flickered and erupted. It soared out, snaking up Kiita's skin, wrapping her body until she was encased in a veil of gold only I could see. I felt the sickness deep in her lungs.

My light uncoiled into her mouth and she inhaled it, obliterating the damage to her airways. The sickness burst and scattered like smoke in the wind. It slipped from my grasp, pulsing through her bloodstream to cool her fever, healing any small hurt. I scrambled for control, I couldn't heal her surface wounds, but the bones in her left arm straightened and strengthened.

It had lasted only seconds and Tor's massive frame blocked us from the other villagers, but, *oh gods*, I'd healed her. I'd used magic. And she knew. Of course she knew—her face was smudged and streaked with tears.

What have I done?

I stared at Kiita and she stared straight back at me. With a single blink, she tucked her left arm into the folds of her dress.

"Please," I whispered.

Kiita didn't respond. Her eyes flashed as she grabbed my hand and pulled. She started rambling, feigning a rasp into her voice, forcing it to be low and croaky. "Thank you, miss. Thank you. Please, let me show you my talent. I stitch dresses, come, come. I make a dress for you."

She tugged me away and Tor followed close behind. I dared a glance at the surrounding villagers who scowled, resentful at my generosity towards a fellow beggar on the street. They didn't know. They hadn't seen.

Kiita led me out of the small marketplace and into a ramshackle house with gaping holes in the walls. A pile of grubby blankets lay in the corner, and a boy, not half my age, huddled beneath them. Kiita released my hand and crouched down beside him, her eyes, fierce and unyielding, bore into mine. And her voice—devoid of the rasp, was hard as steel. "This is Col, my brother. He is dying."

I read the request in her words, the ultimatum: heal him and she won't tell.

Tor spoke in a gentle rumble, moving to block the door. "Lass, if Estelle does this..." He broke off. His demand drifting away as Col convulsed, barely conscious.

"Please," she said, the steel in her voice melting. "He is my brother."

I looked into Kiita's face. So much desperation, so much hurt. I knelt and placed my hands on Col's arms. For a heartbeat, nothing happened, and I was terrified I wouldn't be able to do it. But then Col looked up at me, his eyes a duller shade of amethyst than his sister, lifeless. He had already given up.

The golden light erupted.

❧

"VISIT US, SOON," Kiita pulled me into a warm embrace. Col was standing, apparently for the first time in months, clinging onto my leg. I wrapped both siblings in my arms.

Away from the villagers, my power encased them both, erasing any external wounds from their bodies. I couldn't touch Kiita's scars—no matter how hard I tried.

"As soon as I can," I promised.

"Why do yeh two not move on, aye?" Tor said from where he stood, gaze darting around for witnesses. "Yer both healthy now, yeh can leave this place."

His voice was gentle, but I read the truth behind them. He wanted them to leave so they couldn't speak about me to anyone.

Steel hardened Kiita's reply. "This is our home. My father died defending it. I need to stay and help the others."

I nodded at her. "If you or Col ever need me, come straight away, through that old path between the knotted trees. Do not hesitate."

Kiita's eyes locked on mine. "I will."

TOR and I rode back to the cabin in silence. He was furious—furious but proud.

Once Kip was untacked and locked in the stable, Tor turned to me. Recognising the lecture about to come, I spoke before he could. "I think it's about time someone helped those people. How can I possess a gift like this and not use it? How can I decide to not heal those who need it?"

His face twisted, and when he spoke, it was in a surprisingly gentle tone. "You are right. Just...we will have to be careful."

I frowned at his words. "We?"

The corners of Tor's mouth lifted as he quirked a brow. "Yeh think I would let yeh save the world all on yer own?" He raised a giant hand to scruff my hair. "Someone needs to be there to make sure yer head does not get too big."

Tilting my head to the side, I let a smirk bloom. "When am I not careful?"

He chuckled. "Yeh know," Tor said as we made for the cabin, "Yer magic, I thought it was human, but even when I was young some of them rebel magi—they were different. Yer magic ain't human magic, that is for sure."

"Then what kind is it?"

"I do not know," he said. "Something more. Something extraordinary."

~

KIITA CAME to the cabin that night, bringing a family from the village with her.

She carted them on a makeshift wagon, pulled by an old mule and led by Col. The whole family was near death. I healed them, one by one, and they cried at my feet—worshipping me like some damned saviour. Each took a knife and slashed two lines across their palms, the children as well. A blood debt and a promise. To never tell my secret—old magic, apparently.

Fear shining in his eyes, Tor ordered Kiita to be cautious with who she brought to our home. Both she and Col made the blood promise to Tor then and there.

They came again the next night with two more families on the wagon. The night after, they brought three wagon loads of people.

Every single person made the blood promise to Tor and me, kneeling and vowing their silence.

Tor hardly slept and took to patrolling the clearing each evening. He was terrified of someone reporting me. And if someone told, I'd be executed on the spot. The risk was high, but the smiles and life on the faces of the people were worth it.

Within a week, I'd healed everyone in the village.

CHAPTER 11
HUMAN

In recent days, Tor needed to be treated like a minesweeper game. One wrong move and *kaboom*.

He'd pledged to aid the village, voicing his support of me healing its people, but he was paranoid. In the beginning, I'd smiled and rolled my eyes when he jumped at a noise and scurried to the windows, searching for shadows of soldiers hidden among the trees. After three days without sleep, I was beginning to worry.

Head in his hands, purple circles beneath his eyes, Tor slouched over the end of his bed.

"Did you sleep at all, Tor?"

He dragged his stare up to meet mine. "Not a donkey's arse."

I grimaced, both at the jibe and his state. "Let me find you some fresh tzarberries, at least." I spooned mint leaves into a mug and handed it to him.

He took a long sip and sighed through his nose. "And be out cold when an attack comes? I do not think so. And yeh are not going anywhere."

I crossed my arms. "So, the comfort of home becomes a prison?"

"Just give me the peace of mind. Stay inside the cabin."

"For how long? A day? A week? A month?"

Tor eyelids fluttered as he fought to stay upright. "If someone told—"

"I'd be dead already. But they haven't. No one is coming to get me, because the villagers made the blood promise to us. You told me it was binding magic."

Sipping his tea, he answered in a soft voice, so soft, it grated against the best of me. "Promises can be broken."

I crossed to his bed and sat beside him. "I know they can, and I know I'm in danger. But every time I breathe here I'm in danger...life is about more than survival."

His eyes found mine again, bronze liquifying in the firelight. "Yeh gotta survive to live, lass."

I broke the hold of his gaze, glancing out at the clearing as the first hues of sunlight graced the air. Dawn was near, the dawn of another day cooped inside. For someone who had lived and breathed running through a forest with all of the wild and untamed things, every minute inside was harder than the last.

"Let me go into the forest. I'll go west not east, where it's deeper. I'll be safe there. That way you can get some sleep and I can get out of here for a few hours."

Tor sighed again, dropping his head back into his hands. "Yeh take Kip. Yeh take your bow and a sword, and yeh be back before dark."

I bit my lip to hide a smile. I was faster than Kip within the trees, but I wasn't about to argue. Not when Tor was this far over the edge of dreariness that he was loosening the curfew I'd been under for days.

"And you need to sleep. You're no good to me with a twitchy eye."

Tor's rolling guffaws filled the cabin. "Oh aye, lass. Sleep is what I need. Go on, get out of here. Be sensible. And Estelle," he added, catching my shoulder. "Stop talking yerself into things. Yer too cunning for yer own bleedin' good, and I am too soft on yeh."

I whirled and planted a smacking kiss on his cheek. "Sleep well, old man."

I ran from the cabin, lest he change his mind. Gods, how beautiful the open air tasted on my lips! If all went well today, Tor's paralysing fear might ease—*if all went well.*

Achilles bolted for me across the clearing he'd shared with Kip overnight. Some nights he slept inside, others he preferred to see the stars. I grinned at my dyr, took his head between my hands, and leant down to press my brow into his in greeting. "Ready to go running?"

Tacking Kip was quick, and within minutes we trotted into the damp air of Galdurne—the untamed air and archaic aura of the forest coated me like a second skin. When Tor's cabin faded out of sight behind the tree line, I leant forward and urged Kip into a bounding gallop. With each wide uneven stride of Kip's hooves upon the earth, my heart raced, and this beautiful forest of mine welcomed me home.

Achilles raced beside me, sure and steady between the roots of the trees. A wolf howled on the wind, and I grinned, throwing my head back. Freedom lived between the trees, this was my place. Mine. I'd missed the peace these last few days. But my peace was interrupted when an arrogant voice broke the quiet. "And where in the Maker's skies are you heading, lass?"

Kip shied and cried out, shying back into a high rear. I laughed, tugging on the reins as he pig-rooted and turned, pawing indignantly at the dirt. "Getting out of dodge. Care to join me?"

Rose brought Finn to a halt beside Kip. His bay mare was shorter and finer-boned than Tor's old gelding—prettier, too. "Oh, aye. Just rode in from the deadlands near Kona, through all that shite and sand, and thought to myself, I want nothing more than to go riding with a stubborn red-head through a deadly wood." He levelled a flat glare.

Oh, he was moody today.

"Hello to you, too. What stick shoved itself up your ass?"

A muscle ticked in his jaw. "None, but do you think maybe we can retire to the stream near Tor's place? I need to rest my bleedin' legs."

"Go ahead and rest. I haven't been out of that cabin in days."

Rose's eyes flashed as the muscle ticked again. "And why, pray tell? Are you sickly?"

I gnawed at my lower lip. I couldn't tell Rose about Tor's house arrest without questions—questions I didn't want to answer. "Yes," I started, making the lie sound real. "I was suffering the nasty afteref-fects of my crimson tide, as you so phrase it." A half-truth.

The first time I'd bled here, I'd been embarrassed. The only two people I knew were men. But it was a natural part of life, both told me with a shrug—blood was blood. Tor had made multiple hide liners and Rose brought large handfuls of dried tzarberries for the cramps. If I didn't love them both before, that sealed the deal.

Rose's eyes softened with his laugh. "Fair enough. Can we not just go back to the clearing, though? It is not safe out here."

"I don't know what your problem is. We won't be seen. We always sit and talk. I want to do something else for a change."

Tension strung between us. My cheeks flushed as Rose's shoulders shook and a wicked grin bloomed. "What exactly did you have in mind?"

"Something that will get us both hot and sweaty. Maybe something dangerous."

His smile turned roguish. "How about a game, then?"

"I'm listening."

"How often have you been practising with those knives?"

"Enough."

I GLARED at the cross Rose made on a tree trunk ten meters away. The winner would be whoever got closest to the target with ten throws of a knife.

"What are the stakes?" I asked.

"Thinking of pulling out, lass?"

"Not as much as you are."

A choking sound brushed against my hair as he stepped closer, so close heat radiated from his arm against mine. "What do you want the stakes to be?"

I tilted my head to one side, as if thinking about the stakes—about anything but how damned close he was. "More of those apple pastries?"

"Aye. That can be done."

"And what do you want?"

He turned to face me, turquoise eyes flaring. "A kiss."

I turned away, hiding the widening of my eyes and the gentle suck of my lip between my teeth. Damn him. Damn him to the centre of Galdurne and back again. "Fine. But you're going to lose."

"Oh, I beg to differ. My stakes are higher."

Rose unsheathed a throwing-knife from his thigh and tucked an unruly strand of hair behind his ear. With a well-practised stance and a flick of his arm, the knife lodged into the tree, inches below his cross. His arrogant glance had me swallowing any smart remark. I'd watched him make similar throws many times, learnt how his body angled and moved, how his arm aimed towards its target.

I stepped up to the line in the dirt, shoved him away with my hip, and slid my knife from my boot. Assuming the same stance, I narrowed my eyes on the target, grasped the knife lightly, and threw it at the tree. The blade lodged itself an inch above Rose's. Nearer to the mark than he'd been.

His face creased into a deep frown. "You have been practising."

"Every day," I said with a grin. Indeed, I practised throwing knives each day after training with Tor, purely so one day I could wipe that condescending smile from Rose's face. That day was today.

I readied myself for his banter, but his brows raised high. "Impressive," he said.

Rose's next throw was closer than mine. His carefree demeanour shifted into something harder, more focused, a reminder that he'd lived in this world his entire life.

My second throw was off, barely skimming the tree. But then, perhaps I'd intentionally missed. Maybe I wanted him to win this silly bargain. His third throw was dead-center, and when he turned towards me with a wink, I rolled my eyes.

"I've still got eight more throws, jackass. One point each so far."

"You do not have a chance, wayfarer. You want that kiss."

My laughter rang through the forest. And stilled with a nagging coil in my stomach.

The air turned sour as two rumbling chortles joined mine.

Panic jolted through me. Rose stepped in front of me, squaring his shoulders, a lethal stillness to him that stole the air from my lungs.

Two figures, a man and a woman, rode out from the shadows beneath the trees.

"Oh aye, lass," the man jibed, eyeing the trunk where our knives had struck. "He has you well-beat here. Fancy a round with me, too? Our game did not put up much of a fight today."

Half a dozen yoles were strung over his saddle, and two wolf pelts hung on the flank of the woman's horse. A maelstrom of hatred coursed through my blood. As I stared at the couple, their eyes lingered on the yau fur shining bright in my hair. Achilles grunted as he came to stand beside me.

"And what a strange looking lot yeh three make," the woman purred, idly stroking the golden wolf pelt at her back.

Golden. The wolf I ran with the day I found Achilles...

Rose stepped forward with raised palms. "Greetings, friends. It seems you have caught quality game. Where did you find such a quarry? We found nothing all day." Casual, cocky grace spread across Rose's features, reminding me of the day I'd met him. Lies spilled from his lips easy and natural. Well-practised.

Either the hunters caught Rose's lie, or didn't care to hear him in the first place.

The man raised an eyebrow. "I know you."

Rose chuckled lightly. "Small chance, friend. I am not from around here."

The woman's gaze darted to Rose. "Yeh been in Ashbourne recently, lad?"

A vein in Rose's neck flexed. "Ain't been in Ashbourne for months."

The male spoke again. "Your father has offered a price to find you. Did you know that?"

The bastard father in command of Kiliac's Militia. Were these hunters stupid enough to think they could capture Rose and take him north to Meriden? I spoke in a flat, hard tone. "You need to leave. Tell no one you saw him."

Rose met my gaze, turquoise eyes burning. The woman laughed, angling toward her partner. "This itty-bitty baby is threatening us, Soren." She turned her leer to me. "Fuck off, child. We do what we want. Good coin is good coin."

In a flurry of motion, she had a bow aimed between Achilles's eyes.

Rose sprang in front of him, sword drawn.

The man grasped his partner's bow, pushing it down. "Easy, Gillian. These kids are having a bit of fun is all, leave 'em be." His attention pinned on the sword in Rose's hand. "We will not tell anyone we saw you."

The woman began to protest, but he shook his head. He looked at Rose, at me. "Good day to you. The game is rich a few stone's throws west of here." And with that, the man tugged on his horse's reins and steered east. The woman sneered down at me and pushed her horse to follow.

Goosebumps broke out down my arms as the forest swallowed them. My forest. I hugged myself tight, letting loose a steadying breath to ease my temper. Rose turned me to face him, his hands gentle on my shoulders, concern etched across his brow. "Are you alright?"

I nodded, resting my hand on Achilles' head—by the way he was shaking, he was as full of rage as me. The hunters had killed those I'd vowed to protect. Why hadn't they hunted jarrah and riki? Why the yoles and wolves?

Rose grasped my face lightly. "I have to follow them. And you need to get back to the cabin."

My brow creased. *Why?*

Rose read the question. "They know."

"They know what?" I couldn't draw enough air with anger writhing inside me.

Something strange etched into his face. He was about to lie again, but right now I didn't care. "Well, look at you. You ain't exactly invisible, especially with Achilles in tow. Give it a day and soldiers will be swarming these woods."

I nodded. "So we kill them?"

"I kill them. You go home."

"No." My frown deepened. "I'm coming with you."

"The last time I killed someone for you, you did not much like it. I would prefer you to not look at me that way again."

As he turned to walk away, I grabbed his hand, forcing him to face me. "I'm coming with you. I want to help."

I released a shuddering gasp when he nodded.

ROSE TRACKED the hunters for an hour, their voices carrying enough to follow after. They travelled dead east, likely towards Ashbourne, making camp, barely on the outskirts of Galdurne.

Rose and I pressed together, backs against a wide oak trunk. Ever-changing shadows graced us with cover, making us little more than shadows ourselves. Rose's thumb brushed over my hand and I returned the gesture with a tight squeeze.

When Rose whispered the plan, I'd nodded. Now, faced with the task in front of me, it was far less simple.

To kill a human.

With my head pressed into the trunk so hard my scalp scraped bark, I peered into the shadows. Achilles, Kip, and Finn were hitched a fair distance away and for once, Achilles had made no argument at being tied up.

"Ready?" Rose whispered into my ear.

I jerked a nod, unable to respond. My throwing knife stung my palm as I squeezed it too hard, my pinky wrapping around the blade, leaking drops of scarlet blood to the forest floor.

The hunters bent over a fire, roasting meat off a freshly slain yole on sticks. Rose tapped my shoulder and left me alone, slinking from tree to tree around to the opposite side of the camp. I leaned out, just an inch, to see the couple look at each other and smile, and my heart froze inside my chest.

There was love in their faces.

My mouth moved into a small 'o', about to whistle a birdsong to call off our attack, before flashing metal whirred through the air and struck the side of the man's neck.

Blood sprayed red. The woman released a guttural scream, lurching from her seat by the fire. Not towards her fallen lover, but towards me —to escape the same fate. Exactly as Rose had planned.

Now it was my turn.

I stepped out, knife in hand, and the woman stopped short. Her scream turned feral as she reached for her bow mid-stride. I wrenched my arm back, about to throw, but a ringing beat pounded beneath my ribs.

Not yet.

My arm dropped, just a fraction, as the woman loosed her arrow.

It lodged in the tree beside my head, her aim ajar. Her scream ripped the world out from beneath me and her body came crashing down, a knife embedded in the nape of her neck.

Fear rushed through me and I swallowed it, set it aside, and lifted my gaze to Rose running at me. I opened my mouth to apologise—to explain myself, but his arms wrapped around me and held on tight. "It is okay, lass."

Rough hands folded around my arms, brushing soothing strokes down to my hands as I trembled. Biting back my tears, I leant my head into the hollow place between his neck and shoulder. And as Rose held me, my eyes fixed on the blood seeping from the two hunters.

The man still had love etched onto his face, even in death.

Soren. His name was Soren.

WE RODE TOGETHER, both astride Kip, back to the clearing. Barely a word passed between us. Rose's arm held tight around my middle, keeping me upright as numbness weighed my limbs. A soft nose nuzzled my knee, chewing the leather of my tights, and I brushed my fingertips over Achilles's forehead.

Soren. The name of the hunter rang through my mind.

In no time, or after a long time, I wasn't sure, Rose dismounted and reached to help me down. We were safe, back within the sanctuary of Tor's clearing. The stream gurgled its soft lullaby, lush green grass swayed in the wind—a beautiful mockery. We could have been here, watching the clouds and laughing at one another's jokes.

Rose stepped into my line of sight. "Are you going to be alright?"

I plastered a smile onto my face and shook away the quivering pulses from my veins. "Of course. Why wouldn't I be?" I had to lie. If Tor found out about today he'd never let me out again. I would not live in fear.

Rose shook his head. "Be strong for Tor, but you do not have to do that with me. I understand." I met his gaze. There was such sorrow and concern haunting his eyes that my own burned. Lifting my hands, I rubbed at my face—pretending I could scrub away the guilt and fear and sorrow.

"I know it's a part of life here. I know it's something I need to deal with. But I didn't think it'd be so hard." Raw vulnerability—it wasn't something I ever wanted Rose to see.

"I would be more concerned if you did not think it hard. Never let your heart go, Estelle. Keep it hidden, but do not let it go."

I nodded and kicked a stone with my toe. "You won, by the way." When I glanced up again, Rose's brow quirked, so I pushed a tentative smile to my lips. "The game. You won."

The huff of breath that left Rose's lips might have been humour or relief. "I always do." He was still tightly wound, still ready to catch me if I needed to fall.

I stepped up and kissed his cheek. "There's your prize. Can we sit by the stream? I think I've had enough danger for today."

I turned, breathless, and strode for the water, keeping my face hidden from both Rose and the cabin where I had no doubt Tor was watching. From Rose's light-hearted snicker at my back, I knew I'd done my job well.

And as the afternoon turned into evening, Rose and I talked and laughed—pretending we hadn't just killed two lovers in the woods. A shared pretence that tore apart my heart.

But as I eyed Galdurne, heard the unmistakable howling and dancing leaves through the air, I knew that those hunters had deserved it. They killed innocent creatures. And they knew who Rose was, maybe my abnormalities too.

They would have told.

At least, that's what I would tell myself.

CHAPTER 12
I LIKE ME BETTER

The birds, I decided, were not so bad. They trilled a cheerful tune as I strolled beneath the branches, the early morning sun breaking through the canopy in dazzling rays, ever-so-delicately warming my skin.

I'd gone for a better reflection of myself, on this second journey to the village. Opting for my usual jarrah halter top, brown leather pants, and a high braided ponytail—my yau braid shining behind my ear. A twinge of guilt pierced my heart, as I wondered if that braid was the reason for two deaths not days past.

No, it wasn't. I sucked on my teeth and banished the thoughts. I'd spent too long already wrapped up within them.

Achilles left my side, gallivanting in and around the oak trees. Smug, of course, that I'd let him come today. When we broke free of the forest, stepping out and into the open field, I stared down the sloping hill to the plumes of smoke rising from behind the rooftops. My first instinct was panic, but the villagers ambled around the buildings as if nothing were amiss.

I began my descent down the slope—Achilles ploughing ahead in leaps and bounds, never having had such an open space to do so. With a smile, I walked after him, down into the village where people had stopped to stare.

A comely girl broke from the crowd, pushing between the bodies. A scar marred the skin on her face, but she was dazzling all the same. Shining flaxen hair fell to her waist and her skin was a wondrous shade of glowing copper. Yet it was not the beauty in her hair or lithe body that would make men tremble. It was her amethyst eyes. My smile grew wider as Kiita closed the distance between us and embraced me.

"Maker! Where have you been?"

"Tor's had me under house arrest because of you."

A man's voice sounded out, a northern accent thick in his words. "That old badger should know better than to distrust the blood promise we made."

"*That old badger*," I snapped back, "Is spending his day finding food for all of you."

Kiita's lips pulled into a smirk as her hand clapped my shoulder.

"Bjorn, do you not have enough shit to shovel? Get back to work," she said to the stone-faced bloke. "That goes for all of you," she said with a jut of her chin to the crowd. "Quit lollygagging."

To my surprise, the villagers jolted to her command, young and old, without so much as a question. I tried my best to mimic Tor's look of cynicism, etching a side-long glance towards Kiita.

She shrugged, utterly unfazed. "If this lot were left to fend for themselves, they would be sick again within the week."

"So, what are you going to do?"

Kiita loosened a long breath and planted fists on her hips, staring at her village— still in ruins. "I am going to finish what you started." Her gaze landed on Col, laughing aloud as he attempted to tie a length of rope around Achilles' neck.

"I am going to heal this place."

MORNING DRIFTED AND FADED, giving way to the midday heat. As the Kairi sun rose higher, sweat poured in tendrils along my arms and neck, turning the grime on my skin to muck. I'd long since bunched my hair into a haphazard bun, trying to salvage it from the mud and sweat. Because, we were indeed shovelling shit.

The streets were full of it. Shit and mud piled in mounds outside every doorway. Col and Achilles were hard at work, dragging away rotting skeletons of old homes with a small taskforce.

A young yellow-haired lad worked with me, wheeling away loads of muck as I shovelled, which he dumped into a massive hole a stone's throw away. Iro was his name, the son of the only stone mason in the village. The stone mason who was now recovering what he could from the floors of the old homes. The bakery, the butcher, and the grain seller carried on their work, offering food in return for manual labour instead of coin. Incessant sawing and hammering echoed from their side of the village.

I wiped my face with the inside of my bicep, sighed, and leaned on the shovel's handle. "We've been going for ages and there's still mountains left."

Kiita stopped, dropping her shovel as she turned. When she opened her mouth, I raised my palm. "If you're about to give me some inspirational bullcrap about enduring mountains, forget it."

She pressed her lips together. "When you said you wanted to help me, I never once glorified this job."

I chuckled, the salty taste of sweat making me cringe as I wiped muck off my tongue.

"Once this is done," she continued, "We can make some kind of *plan* about how we are going to rebuild."

A hill rose west of the village towards Galdurne, reaching right to the forest. "You should use the slope," I said.

"What do you mean?"

"Build your mess hall, or long hall—whatever you call it—so it's backed up against the forest. You'll have the protection of Galdurne behind you and a good view out front." I stepped away from my shovel and pointed with my hand. "Build a path to it, with homes on either side for extra defence."

Kiita stepped beside me, turning towards the slope. "We cannot build on such uneven ground."

"Yes you can," I said simply. "It will help with disease as well."

She turned to me in silent question.

"Your sewage, your *waste*," I amended at her frown, "Will flow downhill, away from the homes. Build everything else down here, stables, farms, stores. But build the homes on the hill."

Kiita stared at me, thoughts swirling behind her eyes. She nodded slowly and pointed. "We can build watchtowers on either side of the longhouse, so that we can see a raid coming from the south if it ever does." She stopped and considered me. "The forest will not always protect our backs. Soldiers and bandits have gone through unseen before."

"It's better than nothing."

"True."

A child's cackling snagged my attention and I turned to see Achilles, up to his head in muck, struggling to heave a heavy log through the deep mud. Col threw himself into helping push the young stag along.

"He is your dyr, is he not?" Kiita asked softly as Achilles's golden eyes met mine.

I nodded. Kiita and the others here had seen me perform magic, had promised by their own blood to keep me and my location secret— I didn't see the harm in admitting to Kiita that I had found my dyr.

"My mother was killed by a plague when my brother was just a babe, barely past the breast. After the bandits...after my father and many others fell, this place sank into ruin. Col was one of the first to get sick again. I do not remember the time before he was, I barely remember the time before he could not walk. You gave that time back to us. To him. Thank you."

A wide smile bloomed across my face at her candour. Kiita glanced at me beneath lowered brows, letting a wry grin show in return.

"So," she raised her chin, "I told you something about me, tell me something about you."

"Is that an order, Chieftain Kiita?"

Kiita's laughter held a freedom reminding me of my brother's easy humour when we danced together on the kitchen tiles. "It might be. I have never heard that word. If it means leader, I like it. If it means bitch, well, I like that too."

"The former," I said with a grin.

"Chieftain Kiita," she mused.

I flicked her shoulder. "My Chieftain is covered in shit."

"You are changing the subject."

I loosed a heavy breath and shrugged. "I only discovered I was a magi six months ago."

As much as I was beginning to like Kiita, the less people knew about me, about where I'd come from, the better. Better to be a simple magi than a traveller of worlds.

Her brows knotted. "How old are you?"

"Almost nineteen years under the Kairi sun."

"Ahh. Magic does not come to most until they are older and stronger. Or, until one has no choice but to be strong."

I chewed on my lip and frowned. "That actually makes a whole lot of sense." I thought back to the day I found Achilles, how close to death he could have been—how much strength I'd harnessed to save him.

"How old are you?"

"I am twenty years under the Kairi sun. And everything I say makes sense—tell me something new."

Rolling my eyes a little I smiled again. "I like sweet things."

"Then you will love me. I am as sweet as they come."

"Not when you smell like that, you're not." I gestured to her skin.

Another bright laugh. "I like you, Estelle Verndari."

I bent to grasp my shovel. "Friendships have been built on less."

Kiita didn't respond, but she flashed a warm smile. One that flick- ered for the remainder of the afternoon with each snide comment about the vigour of work the other was doing. Or about each other's smell.

It seems I was wrong when I'd first come here.

I had found a new friend after all.

"Have some water, aye? You look as if you have one foot in the grave."

I registered the heavy accent and glanced up beneath sweaty brows at the young man. Shorter than me, I remembered the broad face and brown hair. Bjorn, his name was. The one who'd called Tor an old badger.

Well, he wasn't exactly wrong.

I crinkled my nose and strode towards him, grasping the skin of water he held out, thanking him before guzzling every last drop. Kiita stalked to my side and snatched the skin out of my hands—only to snarl at the lack of water I'd left. Bjorn snickered, pulling an extra skin out to toss at her. We were filthy. Utterly filthy. Bjorn as well, he'd stopped shovelling to aid construction of the new bakery—wood shavings and sawdust covered him like a second skin.

As the sun sank in the sky, people downed tools to amble through the darkening streets and stretch out their limbs. Kiita and I silently surveyed our work. A twinge of pride settled through me as I realised it'd made a massive difference. The mounds had been carted away, and only flattened dirt remained.

Bjorn patted my arm. "Well done, ladies. I can finally smell fresh air." At my sidelong glare, he thinned his lips. "And *you*, of course."

"You truly know how to compliment a lass, Bjorn," Kiita sniped.

"Can you blame a lad for speaking truths?" Another voice piped up from behind us. I turned to see Iro slouching against his cart.

I scoffed. "I think you're both forgetting that you're equally as foul."

"No," Bjorn said, shaking his head and crossing his arms. "Not even close. I thought women would care so much more about their stench."

"You keep running your mouth, Bjorn," Kiita snarled, glancing pointedly between his legs. "And I will take away something you care very deeply about."

I grinned in wicked delight as both men looked to their feet.

Achilles pranced into our midst, Col tagging close behind. It was only when my dyr halted a few paces shy of me, snorted loudly, and turned to trot away that I dropped my shovel and grasped Kiita's arm.

"Come on. Let's go clean ourselves for the sake of the delicate men-folk."

Neither Bjorn nor Iro hid their grins.

As Kiita and I stalked for a stream hidden just behind the first line of trees, she gave a sharp tug on my arm. I stopped and twisted, frowning at the sudden hesitation overtaking her features.

"Bathe..." She glanced towards the forest. "Together?"

I blinked in the direction of the trees, returned my gaze to her. "Is there a problem?"

She sighed, dropping her arm from mine. "You said we were friends, and friends should not lie. At least I do not think they should?"

"Kiita," I interrupted, "It's okay."

I may have been naïve in a past life, but that person was gone. She'd grown in more ways than one. I shrugged my shoulders and gave her a half smile. "So you like women. As long as you know I don't," I shrugged again, "I can't see a problem."

A frown was the only surprise Kiita showed before she smoothed her brows. "Agreed." She turned for the trees but hesitated again, whirling back a second time. "I like both."

I snorted. "I find that to be the very *opposite* of a problem. There's twice as many options."

"You have no idea," she huffed under her breath.

I followed in her tracks, unravelling my hair from the knot and braid. "Is it illegal here, in Kiliac I mean? I come from across the sea."

Untying her own hair, Kiita's cutting gaze darted over me as if she were trying to solve a riddle. "No. As long as you are not a slave, your body and heart are your own. I hear the king himself prefers lads."

Tor hadn't mentioned it, nor anything about the royal family apart from Horen's supposed malice. "Does he have any children—heirs I mean?"

"Yes," she replied, her shoulders relaxing. "Three. He took a wife to pass on his seed, as is the way."

"I guess they're all abhorrent, pampered pricks."

Kiita's answering grin was nothing short of wicked.

"Indeed."

WHEN KIITA and I returned to the village, having scrubbed our skin raw, the sun had dropped low over the western horizon, just like it did back home. I tried hard to not associate everything in this world with mine, but I supposed it was as good of a coping mechanism as any. I hadn't, for instance, thought too deeply about why these people spoke English. But I was thankful for it, forever thankful to whatever divine intervention made it so.

A small group of people gathered around a bonfire in the old town square, and a figure stood in the middle of the cluster, easily a few heads above everyone else. Smiling, I angled towards Tor, Kiita quickening her pace to stride beside me. A new affection had arisen between us, or at least a sense of growing trust.

I'd never met anyone like her, someone that voiced her thoughts so openly. Rose, he was just straight up cocky most of the time, but there was always something hidden within him. With Kiita, everything was laid bare. It was not a quality I'd seen enough, especially in my old life. I envied her candour and boldness. Perhaps one day, I might learn to be forward like she was, to speak my mind and not apologise for it.

Tor seemed about as comfortable as a chicken in a fox's den in the midst of the villagers, and when he spied me pushing through the crowd his shoulders sagged noticeably with relief. Roasting on the bonfire were jarrahs which Tor had caught and prepared, and something else—

"Tor, tell me that's not a nothling."

A chagrined grimace fell across his features. "A small group came upon me. Only five, not a swarm of 'em like the last time."

I grasped his shoulder tightly, forcing him to face me. The gaping faces of the villagers be damned. "You could have died!"

He frowned and glanced around at the staring eyes, leaning down to pick up a slab of meat, angling his face so he could whisper in my ear. "I whistled."

"They came?" I asked under my breath. He nodded, hooking the meat to an iron rod over the fire.

Kiita noticed my face and without missing a beat, turned to the gathered crowd and pronounced, "We have a plan for the village."

Her speech went off on a tangent, others questioning and making suggestions I didn't listen to.

"It seems I'm not the only protector Galdurne has chosen," I whispered to Tor.

Tor's reddening face and barely contained smile warmed my heart. "Aye, lass, it seems yer not."

EVEN ATOP the hill looking down over the village, the smell of sawn wood, smoke, and sweat stained the air. Six days later and the progress was unbelievable. For people with limited technology, everything happened so rapidly. Apparently, I knew more than I gave myself credit for, without realising I had such knowledge in the first place.

The idea of carving out a level plinth on a slope rather than just using stilted foundations was unheard of, but Kiita had shrugged at my suggestion and ordered it done. After that, I guided the construction of retaining walls against the soil whilst others laid foundations. Tor and Bjorn had both been with me, the latter having scoffed at almost every direction I gave. By the end, Bjorn had just stood with his hands on his hips, nodding in the way a man nods at a job well done. After marvelling at our handy work, he had clapped me on the shoulder and asked for his next assignment. Since then, neither he, nor any other villagers, questioned any suggestion I made.

Iro's father, the stone mason, barely challenged my idea of constructing a barrel-sized receptacle made of rock and mortared with mud beside each home. I confided in him *my idea* of having a drainpipe running rainwater from the roofs into the container for drinkable water storage.

I gave a slight smile at the long, thin mounds of upturned earth. That had been my first project, or order from the village magi, as Kiita called it—designing a proper sewage system.

I'd drawn out plans for every home to have its own privy, each connected to an underground stone drain which used the natural flow of the slope and eventually led out and away from the village. Everyone stopped their tasks to help and it was done in a day.

I demonstrated how to 'flush' the waste in their privies with a bucket of water, and how it would travel down and away from their homes to help prevent disease. The look on the faces of the people when I was done, well, bewilderment didn't quite seem to cover it.

Congratulations, Estelle, you invented the toilet.

As I ambled down and into the village, my chest grew heavy. Everything had changed. Not just the reconstruction of the buildings, or the clean-up of the streets, but the villagers themselves. Cleansed of their sicknesses, they had purpose. It was as if a spell cast over them was broken—and I had broken it with magic I barely understood.

When Kiita announced the village needed a new name, folk were in the middle of planting tree saplings I'd brought from inside Galdurne around the new town square, laughing and talking light-heartedly as they did. I smiled at Kiita, nothing but magic could have caused such a change.

My magic.

Sorcery...*witchcraft.*

"Salem," I said with a secret smile.

The name had stuck.

Bjorn stepped up to my side. "Kiita will have your skin for lolly-gagging."

I snorted. "I don't see you breaking your back with a shovel."

He tilted his head towards the sky. "Thanks to you lovely women-folk, all the muck was shovelled on the first day."

I glanced at the brown-haired lad. This growing mateship between Bjorn and I was vastly different from my relationship with Rose. Once, Kiita jibed at our friendship, and he simply stated I was too tall for him, and that had been that.

"I heard you killed another nothling this morning, or was that old Tor again?"

I elbowed him in the arm, earning a satisfying yelp in return. "I can hunt, I'll have you know."

"I thought you was some jaunty forest fighter," he said, jutting his chin towards Galdurne.

"The nothlings, the jarrah and riki, they're different. They're not natural."

"At least they taste good."

A taut voice cut off my reply. "What tastes good?"

Iro strode towards us, a forced smile plastered on his face as his gaze darted between Bjorn and me.

"My arse," Bjorn muttered.

Pointedly ignoring Bjorn, Iro said, "Your idea with the privies, Estelle. It is ingenious."

I grinned. "Have you used one?"

Bjorn choked, but Iro just nodded pleasantly. He opened his mouth to say something more, but his father called out his name. Iro glared towards the stone mason, bowed his head and stalked away, muttering to himself.

Kiita's voice piqued from behind me. "He is smitten. Poor bastard."

Thankfully, Tor bellowed from across the square, Achilles and Col standing by his side, my dyr having hauled an entire log by himself and looking mighty smug about it. I grinned when I saw Kip dragging at least four behind him.

When I reached Achilles, I held his head to my chest. I didn't mind sharing him, especially since Col had become so attached, but I missed him when he wasn't at my side. Which was most of the time with the children of Salem around.

"What do you make of all of this?" I met Achilles' golden eyes as he snorted, then followed his gaze when he looked at Kiita and Col. I pressed my lips together and blinked to rid the sting behind my own eyes. "Me too, mate. Me too."

"CUT OFF THAT EDGE, WOULD YEH?" Tor gestured to the splintered end of the log at my feet. I wiped the sweat from my neck and grasped the axe without so much as a sigh. I'd learnt long ago not to backchat.

Kiita scoffed. *"Lass, do this. Lass, do that.* Is barking orders all you are good for, old man?"

I fought to suppress my grin, biting my lip between my teeth.

Tor crossed his arms over his chest, narrowing his bronze eyes at my friend. "Yeh come to the cabin and we will see if yeh can run anything other than yer mouth."

"Why would I even—"

The sound of my strike on the wood cut off her retort. "He's offering to train you, dipshit."

Her mouth hung open. "Are you really?"

Tor grasped my axe's hilt. "Everyone needs to know how to defend themselves."

Kiita nodded, but I saw the lingering simmer of pain behind Tor's eyes, I squeezed his arm lightly as I passed.

I backed away as he raised the axe and brought it down, cleaving the log clean in two. He whirled around with raised brows, amusement and challenge lighting his features. I smirked at our familiar game, and when I snatched the axe from him, I shoved his thigh with my hip. A chortle rumbled from deep in his chest as I threw my weight into the swing.

I spent longer than I cared to admit trying to cleave a thorough strike through the wood in one swing—snarling half-heartedly at the comments offered up by both Tor and Kiita. Eventually, I curtailed the log enough that Tor nodded, hauling it up onto his shoulder. Kiita and I exchanged an animated look before attempting to pick up a second log, but we had to call Bjorn and Iro for help. I scowled at the smugness in Tor's face when he strode past for another.

Villagers poured into the longhouse, bearing vines of ivy and thicket branches. Kiita and I both stared with creased brows at their wide grins, while Iro came to stand between us. "We are dining in here tonight, all of us. To celebrate."

Kiita beamed and strode forward to help with the beams, but Iro stepped a foot closer to me, leaning down to murmur into my ear. "To celebrate you, Estelle."

I grimaced at the comment—the unspoken pass.

While Rose had helped me build a backbone, it felt strange to receive flattery from someone else.

"Doubtful, all I did was a bit of light magic. Kiita pushed your butts into gear."

Iro huffed. "I have no idea what a gear is, but I understand well enough. But yes, you certainly did your magic—and more."

The skin at my nape prickled. Iro raised a hand to rake through his thick yellow hair, shifting on his feet. "Estelle... would you save a dance for me tonight?"

Pity roiled through my stomach, but I pushed warmth into my smile. "Of course, Iro."

The blood in his cheeks rose like a piking storm.

A beat of silence resounded as I shifted my weight through my toes, excusing myself to join Kiita ahead. When I stepped away, I caught Bjorn's knowing smirk and tossed him an inconspicuous middle finger. It was not as subtle as I'd hoped, because I was caught and met with a slap on the wrist by the baker's wife.

Numerous voices lifted in laughter.

Tor's thundering tenor was the loudest of them all.

~

EVERY VILLAGER in Salem dropped tools to finish the longhouse in time for dinner, and that night, a feast unlike anything I'd ever seen, celebrated the rebuilding of the town.

Villagers sat cross-legged on the floor, eating roast jarrah, honeyed vegetables, and freshly baked bread. The alehouse had gone to work—and delivered. Barrels were stacked by the door—most already drained to the dregs.

Tor drank an entire barrel on his own, if his loud guffaws and singing were anything to go by. The villagers piped up to chant along-side my gentle giant's songs. Even Kiita joined a bawdy voice to the chorus.

A voice trilled in my ear, and I whirled to find an older woman with pale skin and black hair beaming at me. "Are you wed, dear?"

I partially choked on my ale. "No. *Gods* no."

The woman's face tightened into a frown. "There is only one God, girl, and it would please him to see a healthy young woman wedded and with child. But you *are* a renegade magi. Unnatural to your own kind. Perhaps that is why you have not found a husband?"

I blinked, head spinning from the ale, and curled my lip. "Perhaps."

She tsked as if this was a perfectly normal conversation and picked at a spot on my sleeve. "You are not the comeliest girl I have seen. Not anything like the beautiful girls I used to know in the capital, with your unseemly red hair and freckles. And you are so *tall*." She shrugged, more to herself than anyone else. "You speak in the oddest timbre. But you are smart, *very* smart. Finding a husband should not be too hard. Maybe Tor would take you as a second wife? While your children would be monstrously large..."

I actually choked then, ale spluttering from my mouth.

"Ack!" The woman spat. "That is highly unbecoming!"

"I'm sorry," I said when I'd regained my breath, scrunching my nose up for emphasis. "I'm just terribly allergic to bullshit."

Confusion flashed through her hazel eyes. "Dear, I meant no offense, it is just—"

"Tor is my father," I said matter-of-factly.

And there it was.

The woman's mouth gaped open and closed. She offered up some apology I chose not to hear, because my eyes had found Tor again.

I must have stood there like a drunken fool for some time, because a delicate hand grasped my shoulder from behind and gave it a reassuring squeeze. I heard her tell the old codger to bugger off, and lifted a hand to grasp Kiita's fingers when she leaned in to whisper, "Try not to let these simpletons see you cry."

My eyes were lined with tears, my face hot. I sculled the rest of my drink to wash away the lump in my throat. "These simpletons are your people."

"Aye," she said, dropping her hand from my shoulder. "I am Kiita, Chieftain of simpletons."

I snorted. "At least they're happy."

She crossed her arms and smiled at her people. "That they are. Thanks to you."

"No, Kiita," I shook my head and gestured to the crowd. "You did what you said you'd do. You healed them."

Kiita's eyes lined with silver. "We. *We* healed them."

As Kiita looked out at the people of Salem with pride and joy, I glanced back towards Tor, and wondered if I had healed him, too.

CHAPTER 13
ALL I WANT

R esting on my haunches, I tilted my head back—my curls cascading down my spine, shining in the midmorning Kairi sun. Memories of Kiita, Bjorn, and the other villagers swirled through my mind—memories of their courage, commitment, and newfound passion for life. Though, my head was a damned blur after last night.

I'd awoken well past sunrise—and Tor hadn't even made it home yet.

He was probably still slumped over that same table in the long-house he'd fallen on last night. In hindsight, I shouldn't have left him alone, but I'd discovered last night that drunk Estelle was particularly fond of going on late night adventures with friends. Kiita, Bjorn, and I had the bruises to prove it. How I'd returned to the cabin was a mystery I don't think I'd ever solve, and Achilles was still cross with me, for what I wasn't sure.

"And just what has made you so happy?" Rose asked, his voice clipped.

He'd appeared out of the blue this morning, as was his way. We squatted by the front door of the cabin together, him trying in vain to teach me the art of lock-picking. He was nothing if not patient.

"Nothing," I answered in my best attempt at nonchalance.

A twinge of guilt surged in my throat. Rose was the closest thing to a best friend I had in this world, and I kept lying to him. He knew nothing of my affiliation with the forest, nor my healing power. But whenever I felt I should tell him, the thought of him being angry at not being told sooner, or worse—repulsion—threatened to throttle me dry. It was a stupid worry. I knew that. Rose knew my oddities best of all, he knew not only that I was a traveller of worlds, but also about the world I was from. Yet, I could not tell him those other things about me. The ones closest to my heart.

You're a damned coward.

I *wanted* to tell him today what I'd done to save the villagers—that is until he looked at me, turquoise eyes ablaze. No. I wouldn't tell him. I wouldn't chance ruining the friendship between us. Because telling him about my part in Salem meant telling him about my power.

As the sun crept higher, sweat dripped down my nape. It formed beads just above Rose's upper lip, too. One drop slid from his temple, over his hard, lined jaw, and trailed down his neck as he explained how to hold the pin at an angle where it wouldn't break. He lifted one corded arm to wipe the sweat off his forehead, and ran his fingers through his dark hair, ebony strands parting like silk. I swallowed down a surge of warmth, forcing my heart to slow its thundering beat, and wiped at my own face.

"You are hot," he said coolly, head cocked.

Oh, he was smooth and so damned self-assured.

Me? Not so much.

"Come again?"

The bastard smirked. "You are soaked with sweat. Let us go for a swim, lass." With a sharp jilt of his head, he gestured to where the stream ran into the forest, shaded and cool. I scrambled for a blasé retort, something provocative—to try and throw *him* off balance.

Tilting my chin, I glanced at him beneath lowered brows. I attempted to look seductive, but I probably looked like a stunned alpaca. "It's going to take a lot more than that for you to get me wet."

Oh gods! You're insane...bury me in a pit.

I straightened my posture and glared at the lock in the door—focusing on not glancing at Rose. Any attempt at banter vanished and I didn't breathe.

For a long while, I don't think Rose did either.

In my peripheral, I sensed his eyes on me, fighting for control, bottom lip quivering. Slowly, so slowly, his face twisted—his smile growing wider and wider until he exploded. His head tipped back as he roared towards the sky.

Like children, we curled on the grass by the cabin door, howling with laughter. When I laughed so hard I snorted, Rose cracked into hysterics. We only stopped when Achilles galloped over and rolled himself over us both, quite possibly thinking to exorcise the invisible demon possessing us. As the laughter ceased and Achilles was sure we were safe, my dyr squirmed off and trotted back towards Finn with his head held high.

Rose laid back upon the grass, red-faced and hair wild, resting on his elbows, holding his breath to fend off the remnants of his outburst. His eyes flashed as he lunged, reaching his arms out to wrap around me. In one swift movement, he had me ass-up over his shoulder, shooting for the stream.

I shrieked and kicked and battered his back as he carried me to the water, and he cackled harder at each feeble and somewhat half-hearted strike. The stream wasn't deep, but Rose leapt the last few meters into the water and dunked me under. Thrashing and twisting until he lost his grip, I planted a foot and grasped his shoulders to leap onto his back. Still laughing, he spun and ensconced me in his arms as he fell.

As we went under, I subconsciously wrapped around him, straddling his waist with my legs—and when we emerged, Rose held us both upright. His hands beneath my thighs, holding me in place.

The playful humour died. White-hot tension replaced it.

His eyes fixed on mine with an intensity that shook me to the core, and even the trees seemed to hold their breath. That soft mouth parted as he slid one hand against the underside of my thigh, pulling me closer against him. Rational thought deserted me. I tightened my legs and moved my hips forward, closing the space between us.

Rose loosed a small, breathless noise, his hand sliding along my thigh, a gentle path ending on my ass. A soft, lazy circle his thumb made across my backside sent sparks through my bloodstream, and all the while, we stared at each other. He was so damned close, the heat of his face warmed mine.

I could taste what it might be like to kiss him, my pulse pounding in time with his heartbeat against my ribs. My reservations stripped away, and I tilted my head so all it would take from him was the slightest fragment of a movement to have our lips meet. I wanted to kiss him...I was going to kiss him.

"Can I join you?" A bright, sing-song voice echoed across the clearing. Bright, yet underlined in a jibing tone I knew too damned well.

Rose released me and twisted toward the noise, dropping me into the water with a splash. Kiita was practically skipping towards us, face half-twisted in glee, flaxen hair billowing in the wind. Her purple eyes shone with roguish delight.

For once, Rose was at a loss for words, his face flushed red—in anger or embarrassment, I wasn't sure. Water cascaded over his taut skin and travelling leathers, my gaze marking its path.

A pointed cough from Kiita wrenched my focus from the heat in my core. I glared at her from behind Rose's shoulder—it earned me a wink in response. But when she gave her full attention to Rose, my breath caught in my throat. Kiita possessed a will of steel and an overwhelming allure. The scar running across her face was anything but a flaw, it only made her all the more exquisite. A strange sort of tightness washed through me as Kiita's twilight eyes fixated on Rose—never mind the possibility that she could tell him about my magic. No, that didn't matter right now.

"I do not believe we have met, nor have I heard about you," Kiita said with a cutting glance at me. My friend's voice lilted, and while it was void of the clanging tremor that usually graced her words, the feigned brightness was a force of its own. "I am Kiita."

Rose regathered his composure, his cocksure expression returning.

With the slightest glimpse at me, he spoke to Kiita with a smirk. "Nor I you, blondie. Rose. It is a pleasure."

Kiita lifted her brows at his name, her eyes filled with silly amusement. "*Rose?*"

"Easy, Kiita. He doesn't appreciate having fun poked at his name."

Kiita threw me an incredulous look, underlined with an impish gleam. "You think I would poke fun?"

My glare cracked her façade and she chuckled as she glanced between Rose and I knee deep in the stream.

Kiita flashed me another wink. "I will wait inside for you, wildling." Flicking her long hair over her shoulder, she gave Rose a cocky smirk of her own. "See you around...*Rose.*"

She spun on her heel and made her way towards the cabin; I counted her steps toward the door, and counted the seconds after the door clicked shut behind her—anything to avoid looking at Rose and allowing him to sense the heat simmering inside me.

"Estelle..."

His voice lacked its normal edge. I bit my lip and wrapped my arms around my chest, my shift clung to every curve, light fabric transparent and sheer. And Rose's gaze traced each line of me. The rational part of me wanted to distract him, or to call him out. But the irrational part...

I could still feel his body between my legs.

Rose broke eye contact and clambered out of the stream. He turned back to offer a hand, and I didn't take it. I dropped my arms to my sides, laying myself all but bare before him.

This game we played—it had gone on long enough.

Even if Kiita was here.

I strode to him, lifted my hands to his face, and inched my own forward. Only to have him grasp my wrists and pull back faster than I could comprehend.

Pull back...as if repulsed by the very idea.

I flinched and stepped back. Rose shook his head, his face twisting as he schooled into a smile. He *smiled* as he let go of my wrists. "Well."

His eyebrow quirked in a ridiculous mockery of normal. "It seems I have made you wet after all."

I furrowed my brows, curled my fingers, and clung to the feeling of his hands around my arms. Stinging tears filled my eyes and I didn't blink them away, nor did I look away from him. At least he had the good sense to drop his goddamned front. His hard swallow was audible and the citrus smell of him engulfed me as he stepped in close. But rather than voicing any kind of explanation, apology or excuse, he shot his hand up and flicked me on the nose. "I have to get to a contract by sunset. Say goodbye to your friend for me."

Kiita.

I dropped my eyes. He saw her and no longer wanted me. Well, at least as a plaything anyway. Beside her, I was no longer desirable—maybe I never was.

"Estelle."

I shot my gaze up, eyes burning.

Guilt flickered behind his smile. A smile I hadn't seen in months. One that softened into warmth and kindness. The finger he used to flick my nose, brushed away a fallen tear. "That is not it, lass."

I suppose after six months, I was as easy to read as an open book. Rose leant his head in to press his lips to my forehead. When he broke away, I opened my mouth to ask him to stay, to explain it all to me—explain my failure. But he planted that kind smile again and no words came.

"I will come back to see you, soon."

I blinked away my tears, breathed deeply, tried to calm myself and regain some sense of composure. "Stay safe."

When he turned to leave and Achilles trotted over from undergrowth of the trees, I stood and wondered what I'd done wrong.

Rose mounted Finn and took off without so much as a backwards glance.

He doesn't want you.

He probably never did.

I'd played the game—but I'd played wrong.

I never should have played in the first place.

~

"So, are you going to tell me who that was, or is he to remain mysterious?"

Kiita's demand brimmed with light humour, but I was irrationally upset. And angry. Besides, it was Kiita who had interrupted us.

"He told you. His name is Rose."

I sat on one of the stumped logs in a huff and crossed my arms, but a sudden jolt to my head had me tumbling off onto my ass. Kiita had thrown a pillow at me. Hard. I snarled at her like a wolf.

Her eyes narrowed. "Do not give me that wildling shit."

I'll show you a wildling.

Rolling up and grabbing the pillow, I twisted and leapt to pelt it at her face. She blocked with one arm, grasping another of Tor's cushions to vault at my legs. Jumping over it I lurched towards her.

Like a bullfighter flying a flag, Kiita grinned, coaxing me in. I leapt with outstretched arms, and landed face first on Tor's large bed when she twirled aside.

Kiita's full weight landed on me, her legs straddling my waist. "Do you yield, bitch?"

My anger morphed into humility as wracking giggles tore through me. Kiita planted a smacking kiss on my upturned cheek and rolled to the side. I smiled at her, but I was mortified. I'd acted out in anger— I'd never done such a thing. In words, yes, when Tor or Rose, or even Kiita herself pissed me off, but violence? No.

Not that a pillow fight was particularly violent. Yet, she hadn't minded. She knew what I needed, had damn-well coaxed me in—had not thought twice about my reaction. "I'm sorry, Kiita."

She smiled wider—and the brightness almost consumed me. "I know you are. Besides, it is good to know I can kick your arse."

"Oh, pull the wool over your eyes, would you?"

Kiita pursed her lips, turning onto her back. "I am here for my first day of training, but there is no burly, tattooed barbarian teacher, only a cocky little boy with his hands all over you."

I pressed my lips into a thin line. "Tor asked you to come here last night?"

"Yes, dumb-dumb, that is why I am here. Bjorn and the others wanted me to oversee the construction of the clothier, but I told him I was busy for the day."

"Tor won't remember a damned thing from last night. He's probably still passed out in the hall."

A sly smile slipped across Kiita's lips. "Bjorn does not know that."

I chuckled. "Well, in any case, you deserve a day off."

"Is that not the truth! *Look*, my hands are hideous from all that lifting!" She thrust her calloused hands into my face. They were indeed blistered and raw, so I took her two hands between mine as I turned further towards her.

"Rose isn't that little," I said, a tad too casually to be feigning indifference.

"He is rather attractive, I will give you that much." She chuckled. "Maker, Iro has his work cut out for him."

I released her hands—the golden warmth ensconcing them lingering on my skin—and rolled my eyes. "Shut up."

"The poor lad. One of these days I might put him out of his misery, but it is so much fun watching you torture him."

"I do nothing of the sort! When have I ever been mean to him?"

"That is just it, Estelle, you are too nice about his advances. He thinks he has a chance."

I considered her words, and released a sigh. "You're right."

Kiita wriggled further into the bed. "I am always right."

When I didn't respond, Kiita's face became serious once more. "Would you like me to do it for you? Tell him he has no chance."

"Gods no. What a coward I would be then."

"Indeed."

"Can we speak of something else?" I asked, staring fixedly at the ceiling.

After a beat of silence, I glanced down at her.

Kiita picked her nail, angst building, her shoulders tight. "I will tell you about how my arm got shattered, and what I witnessed that night."

Like a blanket thrown over a fire, the warmth stole from the room.

"Kiita," I murmured, "You don't have to."

"No. But I want to. I want someone to know, all of it, I want to get it out. You said yourself that we healed Salem together. I want you to help heal me now. *All of me.* If that is alright with you."

Kiita was like no one I'd ever known. How could someone be so forward? To have such a fierce candour, I wondered why she wasn't Queen of Kiliac herself. For a while after, she did not speak. Did not so much as move. I was about to tell her not to, that it was alright—but then I recalled what she'd said. She'd wanted me to listen, this was what *she* needed.

She took a great, steadying breath. "Have you ever felt helpless, Estelle? Truly helpless?"

"Yes."

Kiita's eyes filled as she looked me up and down. "Well, since you do not walk around like you are a broken toy, I can only assume you were saved by someone. My bet is on the boy."

I nodded softly.

"The bandits came to the village over a year ago, they came in the night. Their weapons were good steel. Soldier's steel. Our people were already sick, already starving, but my father told us we had to stay and defend our own. He was the last man standing, until he was not."

Incendiary heat filled the space as her chest rose and fell like waves rolling upon a shoreline.

"I did not do anything. I hid beneath a cart and watched my father stabbed nine times in the chest by three different women, who *laughed* as he died." Kiita closed her eyes and huffed something close to a chuckle. "Nine! I counted every single one. Stab, stab, stab. I do not think that sound will ever go away. I do not remember the sound of my father's voice, or what my mother looked like. But I remember those women. I will carry their faces to the grave.

"They must have heard me crying, I cannot quite remember. I do remember the pain, though. They laughed as they broke me, too.

"I did not fight. I did not fight for my father or for my people. And I know now, that helplessness is the worst kind of nightmare in this realm." Kiita rubbed her face with a fist and clenched her lip between her teeth, and the way she looked at me crashed a freight train into my chest.

"I wish I had the right words, Kiita," I whispered. "I don't think I ever will, so I won't try. Just know that I will be here beside you."

She nodded. "I never want to feel helpless again. I never want to be weak like I was that night. I want to be a fighter."

"You're not weak. When I first saw your face in the market, I felt your pain, but I knew you were not afraid."

Kiita smiled softly through the tears cascading down her face. "I am not," she said. "I set my fear on fire a long time ago." She took another steadying breath and closed her eyes. "I see their faces when my eyes are closed, I see their faces in my dreams. Laughing faces leering down at me. But just once, before I die, I want to see those women. One last time."

My brows bunched. "Why would you want that?"

Kiita's eyes flew open, twilight stars in an amethyst sky imploded, and only an everlasting night remained. "Because I want to look upon their corpses and smile."

CHAPTER 14
YOU MEAN THE WORLD TO ME

Every day since I'd offered my assistance to Salem's recovery, the villagers had worked themselves into the ground to rebuild it. Countless injuries came to me for me healing—cuts, bruises, and broken bones.

Healing became muscle memory. I would touch an injury and translucent golden light flowed as if it were alive. I liked testing its strength, seeing how far I could push it. Gaping wounds and burns were easy, broken bones simply a matter of setting back into place, and inner ailments could be snatched out of a body and disintegrated. However, I could not replace missing limbs, nor erase scars entirely. I'd tried on Kiita's arm once or twice, but the scar tissue on her skin remained brazen as ever.

It'd been four days since Kiita and Rose had met near the stream, and since that day, Kiita held herself—almost impossibly—higher and sturdier than ever. As if an invisible weight had been lifted from her shoulders and set her free.

But she wasn't. She said it herself. She would not be free until she saw those bandits again.

Saw them dead.

Out of every person in Salem who poured their blood and

sweat into rebuilding, Kiita poured the most. After a few days, I'd asked her to take a real break from the work and relax. So, we spent a night in Tor's cabin, just us with Tor and Col, but apparently a break to Kiita was spending a day sparring with me.

She was good. But I was better.

"Pay attention to yer opponent," Tor grunted, arms folded. I threw Tor a cutting glare. Kiita's hair and skin were soaked in sweat, her breath haggard, but her eyes glinted with steel.

As she lunged, I feinted right and dove left, swinging one sparring sword sideways and the other slashing up like a whip. Kiita blocked my higher thrust with her own sword but caught my lower strike in the hip and went down cursing.

"Stop cussing, sissy!" Col trilled, lopsidedly slung across Achilles' back, prancing through the water.

Kiita pushed herself up to kneel and beat the dirt from her legs. "Sorry, little man!" she shot back, still grounded, looking for all the world she was content to stay there. I reached a hand down and she eyed my palm. I knew how she felt. I couldn't count the times I felt as if I'd failed. But Tor never pulled his punches so I could win. I had to earn it. Kiita would as well.

She looked shattered. I could have gone hours longer—Tor had drilled endurance into me in the first few weeks I lived here, but I didn't want Kiita to pass out, nor feel lesser, so I feigned exhaustion. "Call it quits?" I asked between well-timed pants.

"Yeah, fine," she breathed. "You are not too bad, you know."

I smirked. I was awful at swordplay when I'd first arrived, and still total rubbish against Tor, though was adequately skilled with a blade now. Archery was my strongest skill, but I knew how to protect myself. How to fight.

It was all Tor had ever wanted for me.

"You're not too bad yourself," I said with a smile.

"Not bad," Tor's voice thundered across the clearing, "But could be better, Kiita. When yer not barking orders at the villagers, I want yeh here. Practising."

Kiita bristled, the need to bite back and resume her usual authority blazing in her eyes, but facing Tor, she just nodded.

"And that goes for the rest of 'em," Tor continued, jerking his head towards the east. Towards Salem. "Not here, I will begin training 'em all so they can defend that village."

"Thank you, Tor," Kitta said with a growing beam. "I will bark at them to let them know."

Tor crossed his arms and gave Kiita a mocking smile. "I sometimes wonder if yer not the most stubborn, exasperating tyke I have ever known, but then I remember that I live with this one." He gestured to me with a thumb.

"Hey!" I rounded on them both. "What did I do?"

"Yeh!" Tor scoffed. "Yeh started all this by speaking to this she-demon in the first place."

Kiita's chuckle sounded out. "Yeah, well this she-demon just happens to be the best Chieftain Kiliac has seen."

Tor looked back at her flatly. "She is the only Chieftain Kiliac has ever seen."

"True. And you are right, none of it would have happened without this one." Kiita grasped my shoulder and shook me harshly. "Speaking to me that day. The filthy buzzard I was."

I quirked a smile. "You still are a filthy buzzard. Not even flies dancing on horseshit would buzz near you."

"And I am proud of it." She released my shoulders and wrapped me in her arms, sweat gluing her skin to mine. I slid my hands around her and held her close.

"Once yer finished coddling, why do yeh not make yerselves useful and chop up that pile of wood, aye?" Tor pointed towards the ever-growing wood pile. A chore I'd neglected since we'd begun visiting Salem. "There are enough jobs here that need doing."

"Tor," I said with a long-winded sigh, clutching Kiita so our cheeks pressed together. "Today's our day off. Can't we rest?"

Unfazed, Tor raised a brow, glancing towards our dropped sparring swords. "Yeh have been resting."

"You call this resting?" Kiita quipped.

"Unfortunately," I muttered under my breath, "He would."

Tor chuckled. I stuck out my tongue, but Kiita's laughter cut short.

An all too familiar, arrogant voice echoed across the clearing. "The women folk causing you trouble, Tor?"

Rose dismounted his mare, patting her on the neck and untangling the reins from his hands. The memory of his complete and almost offhand rejection burned through me—and it hurt. What was he doing here so soon? He never visited so close to his last.

I could either let him see just how much his rejection hurt me, or I could just be downright pissed off. Seeing his obnoxious face, that bullshit half-smile, I went with anger.

Unfortunately, any snarky retort was interrupted by Achilles, prancing and unceremoniously grunting his way over to annoy Finn, passing directly between Rose and me. I had to hand it to my dyr, he made a mighty good show of it too.

"Twice in one week, lad? I should begin charging rent for this place." Tor shook his head, setting the beads and trinkets in his beard clinking softly. He looked as if he might say something else, but dropped his arms and made towards his cabin. His grumbles drifted with him, mumbles about how peaceful it was before all of us children showed up.

Kiita stared at me with a half-twisted smirk, arms crossed, the kind of glint in her eyes that meant trouble. She spun to Rose, head held high, and assumed that bright sing-song voice. "I heard you rescued our Estelle from a couple of brutes."

Rose inclined his head. "Aye, I did, lass. I have since asked our Estelle to promise she be more careful in her travels."

He spoke with his usual honeyed tone, but emphasised that word. Promise. An echo of his earliest warnings to not speak of my past...my wayfaring.

Kiita cut into the silence. "I did not notice the other day, but you speak with the finer Ashbourne tongue, sir."

"I do. My worst quality."

"I'd say pig-headedness is your worst," I snapped.

Kiita didn't waste a beat, her laughter echoed around the clearing, bouncing off the trees. Rose joined her half a heartbeat later, and if I wasn't studying his face—the way his lips didn't quiver as they did when he was lost in laughter, I might have thought he'd assume my comment was nothing more than our usual banter.

He knew I was pissed.

Good.

When their laughter died, Kiita grasped my elbow. "I assume you are here to see the red-head?"

"Aye, blondie. Meaning no offence, of course."

"Oh, and I was just about to take offence. But you are in luck." She pinched the underside of my arm. "Tor just offered to walk me and Col home."

"And where is that?" Rose asked.

"The village nearby," I answered for Kiita, shrugging out of her grip and scowling. "And don't lie, even he can see through it."

Rose laced his fingers together and smiled, winking at Kiita.

Kiita shrugged. "Was worth a shot. Besides, it seems he wants to speak to you more than I do. I will tell Iro you said hello."

"Bitch," I said under my breath.

Rose had the good sense to keep his damned mouth shut, even if the now-present quiver in his bottom lip told me he was enjoying this too much. Kiita clapped me on the shoulder on her way toward the cabin, grabbing Col from where he was trying to mount Finn. I made a point to stare after her, to not look at those too-familiar turquoise eyes.

When the silence dragged on too long, I spoke plainly. "Whatever you came here to say, say it now."

Rose stepped closer, hands still locked together. "How much does blondie know?"

"Her name is Kiita," I snapped. "And she knows more than you ever will."

For the first time in a long time, Rose balanced on the edge of impatience with me. With a heavy sigh, he asked again, "How much does she know about you?"

"Like I said, more than you."

It wasn't true—not in the slightest. Rose stepped into my line of sight. "You think I cannot see past your lies, too? You need to try better than that."

I rolled my eyes. "She knows nothing about where I came from."

"That is good, because you—"

"Why are you here?"

Shock and hurt sparked in Rose's eyes. He folded his arms over his chest and lifted a brow. "Do you truly not want me here, lass?"

No.

Yes.

Prick.

I didn't respond.

"You know," Rose started, smirk rising. "You look good when you are pissed off. Perhaps I should anger you more often. Next time, I will be sure to do it in the stream with the shift you wore last time."

He knew how I was feeling and he was joking about it. How do I tell the man I want that I'm angry because he doesn't want me back?

What did that make me?

I crossed my arms, mirroring his stance. "Your visits are never this close together."

"My business was nearby and I wanted to spend another day with my closest friend. Come on, admit you are happy to see me."

And there it was. Friend.

I truly was pathetic. Every damned fibre inside me screamed to not be petty, to accept and be grateful for his friendship—not be scorned. But something else was screaming louder, so I shook my head and my voice was colder than I'd originally intended. "I have to help Tor and Kiita today, I told them I would."

"Help with what?"

"Something."

"Ahh," he said lightly. "That does sound important."

I spoke as I spun on my heel. "It is. I guess I'll see you the next time you deign to grace me with your—"

Rose stepped around me, his face barely a foot from mine. "You and me," he said quickly. "Best of three." He gestured towards the swords I'd dropped not five feet away in the grass. "You win, I will leave. I win, you spend the day with me instead of doing your important something."

I scoffed, but it only lifted his smirk into a grin. "Scared, Estelle?"

Damn him. He knew I wouldn't back down from this. From him. Never had we even tried sparring together, nor had we mentioned that day in the woods, simply pretended it didn't exist, but he knew how damned competitive I was with Tor. After seven months of dancing around each other's moods, he knew how to manipulate me.

Tor had become family and Kiita a close friend, but Rose knew me best in this world. The realisation terrified me and set my blood aflame.

My animosity rose to the surface. "Fine. Challenge accepted."

I reached down and grasped my two swords, swinging them as I stalked off to the side—leaving Kiita's for him in the dirt. He removed his leathered tunic, leaving a close-fitting black shirt, and reached up to pull his hair into a tail. When he bent down to retrieve the blades, I prowled up and slapped the back of his legs with the broad side of my sword.

Rose lurched up and twisted, eyes ablaze. "Now, lass! That is not on."

"One point to me. And my name isn't lass."

His astonishment chilled into cold, calculating poise. He twisted both swords in his hands and bent his knees into a well-practised stance.

Well, shit.

The corner of his mouth angled up, not into his usual, crooked half-smile, but just enough. Just enough to drive me over the edge. I lunged.

I tried the feinted side-step manoeuvre that had sent Kiita onto her ass a few times, but Rose saw straight through it. He twisted to the side and underneath my swing to come up behind me. Two sharp whacks on my backside were followed by an obnoxious snipe.

"One to me."

Bastard. Bloody bastard.

I tried another lunge, feinting directly toward his torso. He lifted a sword straight up to parry mine and I whirled to the left, planting my footing to land a hard shoulder into his side. Rose stumbled, throwing out a leg to trip me.

He snorted as I fell to the ground, and tapped me lightly on the shoulder. "Two to me."

I pushed up and snarled. Fury rose—fury at his skill dwarfing mine. I stepped forward again, not bothering to feint in any direction. He flashed me a grin, spinning to the left, and a red haze consumed me. I bared my teeth.

Spreading my arms, I swung the swords in imperfect arcs and charged. Rose laughed, effortlessly dodging each maniacal swing. His swords flashed in the sunlight as he brought them down and used both to smack me on the backside again.

Rage melted into feral infuriation and I threw one of my sparring swords at his face. He blocked it with his own, so I threw the other. He ducked under the second—grinning like a damned fool. Angry tears blurred my eyes as I forgot about the swords, along with the challenge, and threw myself at him.

Rose dropped his swords and leapt, angling backwards at the last moment to catch me mid-air and hold me to his chest as we fell. The ground hit us, hard. His breath dislodged with a whoosh against my ear lobe. Red tinted rage disintegrated, and I tried to push away, only to be grasped around the waist. He rolled me onto my back and pinned me in the dirt. His hands held me still, his turquoise eyes held my heart.

"You are a bastard."

"I might be, but you just lost," he said with a wink. When I didn't respond, his brows furrowed.

"He is right, Estelle, you lost. And badly, you bleedin' wild zealot." Kiita stood not two meters away, wearing a fierce grin. As Rose rolled off me, I sent her a beseeching look, but she simply shrugged. "What does he win?"

"A day with me," Rose said, brushing his hair back with one hand. He hadn't even broken a sweat.

Kiita snickered. "Oh, what a lucky lass she is."

"Indeed, though sorrowful she had to resort to such savagery to try and win the fight," Rose added, tsking a few times for good measure.

"I hate the both of you." I muttered, pushing myself to stand.

At the deep nicker of the draft horse I knew so well, I turned to see Kip, already tacked up with Col on his back. Tor was waiting by the gelding, watching Rose with a searing glower.

"We'll have the firewood chopped before you get back, Tor," I called out.

"We will?" Rose whispered.

Tor called back, "Aye, yeh will. Or yeh will be sleeping in the stable with a cold stew tonight."

I flung a middle finger his way.

Achilles danced on his hooves beside Kip, much to Col's delight. He reared and galloped towards me, touched his muzzle to my chest, and took back off again, keen to join the party leaving me alone with Rose. "Goodbye to you, too," I muttered.

Kiita chuckled and planted a kiss on my cheek, ruffling my braided hair. "Bye, wildling. I will see you soon." I hoped the dirty look I gave in return was enough to convey my feelings on the matter.

I stared after them as they rode away, even as the intensity of Rose's gaze snapped my back ramrod straight. He was still on the ground.

"I think blondie likes me."

"Good for you."

I was being, well, a complete and utter bitch, but I didn't care. He'd pushed me away before, I didn't think I could handle it again. Hurt flashed through Rose's eyes, swiftly replaced with something else. Something colder. Without another word, I whirled and stalked to the stream.

Rose remained where he was, back facing me, and as I neared the water, blood near boiling, I concocted a wicked scheme.

I'd spent over half a year dancing around him and allowing him to play with me. I was not an ugly girl. I never have been, and I was stronger now. More beautiful than ever before.

Let him realise it.

~ ROSE ~

MAKERS BALLS, she was pissed.

What did I expect?

After leaving her so recently, I had fought with myself over and over about coming back so soon, but I had left her crying. It was as Estelle said, I truly was a bastard.

Her fury was nothing I had ever seen before. In our sparring match, a lesser man would have balked, but I knew her. And she looked too bleedin' delightful, snarling and baring her teeth, like that of a wild cat. There was no doubt she was skilled—Tor had taught her well. But she was livid. That was never a good way to approach a fight, so I played her like a fiddle.

Tor, blondie, and the little boy had left in a hurry, probably blondie's idea. Smiling at the image of Estelle's flushed face beneath me, I twisted my head around to look for her—shit.

Shit.

She was standing beside the stream, glorious in her wrath, feet shoulder-width apart and solidly planted on the bank—without her shift and without her pants. All that was left was a truly improper undergarment, along with tight fabric bound around her chest.

The way I had seen her body through her shift had not done it justice—it was a blurred image. Now, the veil had been lifted and all I knew was her. She stood tall, sunlight contouring finely corded arms and legs—delicate lines brushing the muscles across her abdomen. Her skin, once pale, now glowing with the slightest of gold, was peppered with tiny ivory scars. The bright emerald of her eyes shone as hair the colour of fire drifted around her in the breeze.

She was incandescent.

Estelle lifted a hand and slowly unravelled the strip of fabric at her chest down to the last furl, then removed it completely. My body hardened. Her breasts—Maker, they were perfect, well-formed and tight. My gaze lingered before I dragged it to her face. Rage and sadness hung there, but so did desire; warm and unruly. Had she done this to get a rise? She had succeeded if she had.

But I did not want it, any of it, to be this way. With her standing naked before me out of anger. So I forced my gaze to unpeel from her perfect body, and twisted around to stare at the grass between my knees, waiting with my head hung low for her to finish.

I would have to put a stop to this. One way or another.

What a bastard I would be then.

~ ESTELLE ~

REJECTION. Again.

I didn't truly expect anything different. But it still cut deep. I laid everything bare for him—literally. And still, rejection.

I took my time washing in the stream. Whatever he came here to say, it could wait. But I watched him. The whole time I bathed, I watched him, wishing he would turn around. He did not.

He did want me, that much was obvious from the way he'd looked at me. I'd be a fool to deny it. So why did he do nothing? Why did he turn away?

Of course, a physical attraction was different than feeling something for someone. So, he did not like me in that way, then. Point taken.

After bathing for what felt like the better part of an hour, I gave up and pushed out of the stream. With torrents of water descending over my skin, I decided I still didn't want to talk to him. Not yet. I tore away my undergarment—a new design of mine, better suited to my workouts and similar to what I wore before. I glanced Rose's way, but his head hung low. Sighing, I dropped to the grass onto my back to let the air dry my naked skin.

Still, he did not look.

Only when each droplet of water had evaporated from my body did I stand. Scowling at his back, I replaced the fabric wrap around my chest, then my shift and black leather pants. It was only when I stalked by him, on my way inside the cabin, that Rose stirred.

He surged up and I bristled at his footsteps scraping in the dirt behind me. Feigning indifference, I breezed through the door and shrugged the shift off again, throwing it roughly to the floor. Reaching for the chest beneath my bed I retrieved a leather halter, tugging it on before grabbing a thin scrap of brown leather to pull my hair into a loose ponytail.

"I found something." Rose's voice startled me, like firelight igniting in a darkened room. I jumped and struck the corner post of my bed with my knee.

"What?" I snapped. Half in pain, half in irritation.

"An old children's story," he continued, utterly unfazed as he sat on a wooden stump-chair. "Of people who can travel between worlds through a gate of sorts. Using some stone blessed by the ancient gods of light. It is not much to go on, though it is the most we have gotten so far. I will continue reading what I can about the stone and where I can find it."

At my narrowed eyes, he raised his palms and shrugged. "I know, not much of anything. The book was illegal, stashed safely away in an untouched nook within Ashbourne's library." His voice resumed its usual confidence—usual surety. "I truly enjoyed sneaking in past them slimy gits guarding—"

"You went to Ashbourne?"

"Yes." He frowned. "I told you, I want to help you. I have always wanted to help you."

I stared at him, bewildered, hoping at least some animosity shone through my glare. What he'd just told me, what he'd done! Ashbourne for goodness sake. Our eyes locked—a battle of will. He caved first.

"Estelle..."

"Don't," I breathed. "Please, don't."

There was too much heat inside these four walls, too much of him. Of us both. I was angrier at myself more than him, truth be told. I made for the door, leaving him on the stool, and rushed for the stable before I remembered Tor had taken Kip and stopped short.

"Now, I won that match fairly. My prize is a day with you. You cannot leave." Desperation underlaid his words as he caught up to me.

"And why would you want to spend a day with me?"

He snickered. "Where else would I want to be? Perhaps we could get each other wet again?"

Silence. My heart beat so hard he must have heard it. "What the hell is wrong with you?"

A muscle ticked in his jaw as he frowned. "Is it not funny when I say it?"

My voice broke. "You are the biggest fucking asshole I have ever met."

At the worry in his face, the quiet concern and guilt smouldering in his features, something fractured inside me. Tears welled as my face flushed. Tears. Again.

Rose reached for my hand, but I snatched it out of reach. My rejection finally stripped away his mask and shame dulled his eyes. "Would it help if I told you that it was not you?"

I took a deep breath. "It's not me, it's you, right?"

He nodded.

"Are you with someone?" I whispered.

The question had always been there. Always festered at the back of my mind. I'd never asked, because I was too much of a coward to hear the answer.

"No. No, I do not have a woman."

"Do you prefer men?"

"No."

A single tear slipped free and blazed hot down my cheek. "Then what is it? What is so wrong with me?"

Rose blinked and looked at his feet. The man I knew as strong, cocky, and arrogant, looked at his feet as he spoke. "I do not want to hurt you."

"You've already done that," I said quietly.

He nodded again.

"Then why the hell would you care about hurting me more? How could you hurt me more?" Insecurities which had built since I'd met him—the intensity of my attraction, my childish adoration for the first person to show me a shred of affection, and his rejection—it all spilled out in tears I couldn't halt.

A lifetime passed in silence. A lifetime more before he showed any sign of responding. But his eyes met mine, and cool calculation blazed there. My stomach dropped to my feet.

"Because I would rather not waste my time with a little girl so desperate and naïve to mistake my actions as true signs of affection. One who so willingly reveals herself wholly and thinks it striking." His words hardened, fists clenching so tightly his knuckles turned white. But still, he did not stop. And I listened, numb and silent. "If I wanted a whore, Estelle, I would attend a brothel. You are wild, unruly, and unnatural. Entirely not what men in this world would deem desirable. Find some other lonely man to leech on to."

I waited for him to finish. But he'd said his piece.

His words hit home, broke me. My stomach caved inwards and humiliation writhed through my blood. Fight or flight, they say. Well, I'd already fought today.

Now I'd fly.

I took off for the only other sanctuary I had in this world, and sprinted headlong for the depths of the forest.

Hooves pounded behind me, too light to be Finn's.

Achilles appeared at my side, and I hadn't the heart nor the mind to wonder how he knew to return to me. My dyr ran abreast and watched my face with molten gold eyes. He knew what I needed, just quiet comfort in his company. He ran with me as my feet pounded the forest floor—pounded in time to my fracturing heart.

I didn't know where I was going, I just knew I had to get away.

Desperate.

Naïve.

Wild, unruly, and unnatural.

Of course that was how he saw me. I was a damned desperate fool to think otherwise. Just an intriguing, otherworldly plaything. Sobs entwined with rasping breaths as I pushed my legs harder and faster. The trees did not dance and the drums did not sound.

Soon, too soon, heavier hooves beat against the forest floor. I ran faster still. How could I ever come back from this? How could I come back from being cut to the bone? Someone I thought meant the world to me had just shattered everything.

A horse's scream and a man's bellowing cry echoed through the trees behind me, followed by an almighty roar.

In that moment, when my feelings were wrenched away and only cold emptiness remained, I understood how much a heart could truly break.

~ ROSE ~

"THEN WHY THE HELL would you care about hurting me more? How could you hurt me more?"

Estelle was crying now. The emotions she always tried to hide breaking. I did not answer, pausing before I landed the blow. I had to become the prick I was too good at pretending to be. The alternative was my confession to her. About everything. About how I was so, so unequivocally in love with her, and the danger she would be in if I gave into that love.

How could you hurt me more?

This is how.

I finally met her eyes.

"Because I would rather not waste my time with a little girl so desperate and naïve to mistake my actions as true signs of affection."

Liar. Maker's soul and blooded liar.

I almost shattered then and there. Almost dropped to my knees and begged for her forgiveness. But I was too far gone now, and the pain I could see in her eyes—I may as well twist the dagger I had plunged into her heart.

"Because I would rather not waste my time with a little girl so desperate and naïve to mistake my actions as true signs of affection. One who so willingly reveals herself wholly and thinks it striking. If I wanted a whore, Estelle, I would attend a brothel. You are wild, unruly, and unnatural. Entirely not what men in this world would deem desirable. Find some other lonely man to leech on to."

You fucking bastard.

Estelle's face—there were no words to describe the depth of betrayal and hurt. Her tears fell freely and I knew she would not forgive me. Neither would I. She took off into the forest and I let her go.

I crossed the line—had to.

A flash of gold and dappled white caught my eye and her young stag raced from wherever he had been to follow her, kicking up a maelstrom of leaves and dust in his wake.

All of those months, of teasing and flirting, of course she fell for me as well. Finally some light comes into my life and I squander it. Break it.

Broken, like my heart.

My heart—where was she going? Not in the direction of the village she frequented, but into the forest—into Galdurne. By herself.

Where was she going?

Panic overwhelmed me. Estelle was upset and frantic and I let her run into the forest on her own, save the stag. I ran and leapt onto Finn, kicking her sides, and hissing into her ear—she knew what was expected, had never failed me before. The trees engulfed us and within a few heartbeats the shadows pressed in and the sky disappeared above the canopy.

A stone's throw, two. Still no sight of the flaming hair I dreamt of each night. Three more stone's throws, still nothing.

How far has she gone?

It is not possible.

No one was that fast. Finn was one of the swiftest horses in all of Kiliac.

Finally, within the darkness, the familiar glint of fire-red hair flashed as if a small flame had been ignited within the night. I kicked Finn again, harder. Not noticing the giant beast lurking in the shadows. Not until it leapt towards us.

The cioraun struck me in the shoulder and arm with its front claws, throwing me off Finn as I cried out. My mare halted her chase, bucking and screaming. Black spots clouded my vision as I hit the hard surface of the forest floor, and from the pain and nothingness all at once, I knew without looking that my shoulder was shredded to the bone. A blurred tawny-brown mass inched closer.

The snarling feline was a horse-length from my face. The luminescence within its mouth glowing as it snarled. Its front legs dropped low, readying to pounce.

I love you, Estelle.

Estelle.

Fire erupted in the shadows, red hair billowed in the dark, and Estelle jumped into the path of the beast.

The wild cat leapt.

I screamed.

It twisted mid-air and landed at her feet, rearing up with an earth-shattering roar. The young stag rammed into the cioraun without a shred of fear, and the cioraun ceased his bellowing to drop his enormous head towards Estelle and purr.

My eyes closed, a bleak kind of relief welling in my gut, and when I opened them again the cioraun was gone. Finn bucked and screamed, but Achilles was with her, grunting and comforting.

And Estelle? Where was she?

What was she?

When I found her terrified green eyes, her face lined with tears and wisps of hair stuck to her face, I thought I had already died. The cioraun had killed me. The shadows grew darker and Estelle's face swam in the air like a castaway mist. I was only aware of the smell of her, sandalwood and clove, as darkness consumed me.

A delicate touch on my hand lulled me into a deeper sleep, a soft warmth drifted through my bloodstream—warm light binding skin and bone.

I opened my eyes, thinking it would be the last time, just to see her once more, but my head cleared and my vision unblurred. A dull numbness pulsated through my arm, and I had the sense that thick scars stretched around my shoulder. But I did not look, for before me was her.

Estelle was here. Her face still tear-stricken, her hair still wild. Maker, I loved her hair.

Realisation sunk in. This was impossible. Estelle had healed me. Estelle was a magi.

The realisation must have shown on my face. She pushed up and stumbled away, crossing her arms in front of her chest. Protecting herself. From me.

"I wanted to tell you," she choked out. "But I didn't know how. I'm a part of the forest and it's a part of me. The reason I haven't tried to leave—tried to find a way to leave—is because I'm staying. Someone needs to stay and defend it. I lied about Achilles, he's my dyr and I found him after an Ashbourne raid."

Her voice shook and the tears began anew. She was afraid. Afraid of me. But still she carried on.

"I only found out I could heal when I found Achilles, he was nearly dead. I healed Kiita too, and the others at the village. I couldn't tell you. I didn't know what you'd think, or what you'd do."

When I stood, Estelle stumbled back another step, then another. I walked towards her, pulled to her as the tide is pulled by the moon.

Her face flushed scarlet, her eyes burnt. "It was my secret! Mine! You knew everything else about me. You knew how I felt about you! You knew I was falling for you and you played me anyway! You're a bastard! You're a cold, heartless piece of shit! How was I supposed to know you wouldn't sell me out?"

As I stepped closer she paced backward, staying out of reach. Her emerald eyes were aflame with anger, passion…magic. I loved her with every inch of my being.

"Say something!" she shot at me, hands curled in fists. "Say something you goddamned bastard!" She screamed the last words and planted her feet solidly beneath her. Waiting to hear my words, steeling herself for them. The long battle I had fought, the promise I had made to myself time and time again…

Fuck it.

"I love you. I have always loved you."

I strode the few steps between us, grasped her face between my hands and kissed her.

~ ESTELLE ~

I COULDN'T TAKE THIS. I couldn't stand the way he was looking at me. I had no clue what he was thinking. "Say something! Say something you goddamned bastard!"

The blaze in his eyes—it exploded into wildfire.

"I love you. I have always loved you."

Before I could move an inch, before my body registered his words, Rose closed the small space between us, grasped my face between his hands and kissed me.

The forest drums exploded into my ears and echoed into my heart. His searing kiss coursed through my veins, sending tendrils of new life into my bloodstream. Like leashing the beast inside me, I leashed the heat threatening to melt my core. I broke away and stumbled to the side, trying to regain my breath.

Rose blinked his surprise, before I whipped my hand back and slapped his cheek. Hard.

He stared at me, dumbfounded.

I lowered my voice, praying I matched Kiita's steel. "You're a prick."

Red lines bloomed into a handprint on Rose's cheek. "I am, lass."

I frowned. "You were lying to me. Before. Trying to push me away. Why?"

There was no mask now. Nothing for him to hide behind. "I was trying to protect you."

"That's bullshit," I snapped. "A shitty excuse for men to push away people that care about them. I don't need protection."

"I know. I know that now." He gestured to the surrounding forest. "I just thought, my father, he is the worst of them. If he found out I truly cared for someone, loved someone, he would hurt her for sport."

My face tightened into a scowl. "I understand why you thought you were right, but you're a damned idiot all the same."

"I know that, too."

"Your father can kiss my ass. If he ever tries to hurt me, I'll kill him. Then Tor can have what's left. And if he ever tries to hurt you, I'll kill him for that, too."

Rose made a choking sound before speaking. "I would very much like to see that."

I shook my head. "So, everything you said, was it all a lie?"

Rose dropped his shoulders and released a breath. He smirked, the expression lighting up his face, not a forced thing anymore. "Well, to be fair, you are wild, unruly, and unnatural. But that is what I adore about you. And a magi nonetheless, though I am unsurprised, to be true. You have always been different. More."

My rage and pain simmered away like smoke. I rolled my eyes and stared up at the canopy, placing my hands on my hips before sighing. "I did reveal myself wholly to you rather rashly."

Rose laughed. "Aye, rashly indeed. If I were not trying to act noble I would have watched you all day and been bleedin' happy about it."

"And you love me," I said. It wasn't a question.

"Yes," he said back, equally as plainly. "More than you know."

My heart thundered. "Then kiss me again."

A full-blown smile stretched from ear to ear. "Aye, I want to, but I am scared you might strike me again."

I released a low laugh and stepped forward. I ran my thumb over his bottom lip as his smile deepened—so at odds with his usual arrogant grin.

He'd always loved me.

Every comment he'd made, every intense glance, he had loved me. His reasons for keeping me at arm's length were dense, cliché even— but I did not share his fear. Tor would protect me. *I* would protect me. Though my heart ached to know that he wanted to protect me too.

He wouldn't kiss me again, I realised. He was waiting for me— would let me make that choice and accept the outcome either way. In his eyes I saw the world staring back at me and it was beautiful. So I leaned in and took it for myself, the drums echoing in my ears once more.

His lips were soft and warm, as I always imagined they'd be. We stayed quiet for a moment, taking in the feel of one another, until

Rose sighed and deepened the kiss. His smell, citrus and leather, engulfed everything. My hands found their way to the back of his neck, combing through silken hair to pull him closer. His tongue traced delicate lines across my bottom lip, so I let him in.

When Rose broke away, turquoise met emerald for a fleeting, intimate moment—he loved me and I loved him. His face dropped as a shaky breath left him and a single tear escaped his eye, rolling down his cheek. I smiled at him—for him—and lifted my hand up to brush it away. As I did he whispered into my ear, "You are wild and unruly. You are all I desire and more. I love you. I love every piece of you."

I threaded my fingers through his hair, pulled him in again, and our lips resumed their rhythm—more fierce and wild and unruly than before. His hands found my back and tugged me close, then dropped to cup my backside. Lifting me in one fluid motion, he wrapped my legs around his waist before walking us to a nearby tree, pinning me firmly against it.

As our tongues danced, his fingers traced my jaw, his hand slid behind my neck. I arched for him and into him.

The kiss seemed to never end. I didn't want it to.

CHAPTER 15
KEEP THE STREETS EMPTY
FOR ME

Kiita sat cross-legged in the grass, quivering in silent joy. "I do hope you made an ithyphallic out of that boy in any case."

"What is an ith-ee-falic?" I asked, drawing out the syllables.

Kiita tilted her head back and smiled towards the clouds. "It is an ancient word, carried to the empire by the northern slaves...and it is for me to know and for you to find out."

Shaking my head at her devilish grin, I murmured back, "I don't even want to know."

Kiita chuckled. "So, is he a fine kisser?"

She was enjoying this. Far too much.

Rose left me at Tor's door the previous evening and I'd made my way to Salem at first light. The moment Kiita saw me, she'd whisked me away to the shadows of Galdurne. Now, she shifted to stare at me, still grinning. "Oh, come on, Estelle! Speaking of it is the best part of all. It may well not have happened if you do not speak it!"

Laughter broke from my lips, rich as woodland thunder. *I guess some things don't change wherever you are, friends need to know all intimate details even here.* "There's not much to tell," I said. "I took him to that island with the purple oak and when I asked if we could...you know—"

"Fuck," she quipped.

"Yes. But he refused, spitting some bull about how chivalrous he was and how he'd like to take his time with me."

At the memory of Rose's stupid face when he said it...I smiled. Stinging struck my cheek, Kiita's thrown stick bouncing into my lap. "Ow!"

I glared at her with incredulous eyes. "Fine!" I threw my hands up. "He's a damned great kisser, not that I have anything to compare it with, but it was good. Better than good."

"I cannot believe you did not take a tumble. After seven months of dancing around one another that is all I would want to do."

"Don't make me regret telling you about the past half a year."

Of course, my origins—where I'd come from—I'd left mostly to interpretation. I trusted Kiita, more than trusted her, but I didn't want her thinking poorly of me. The people of Kiliac were deeply superstitious and I wouldn't risk my safety—or Tor's.

We sat in the grass a while, sharing in the glorious morning sun and our joy. She gently held my hand in hers, her light humour evaporating, making way for something softer. "Are you happy, Estelle?"

I smiled at her again, squeezing her hand. "More than I've ever been."

And it was true. *Gods*, was it true.

"Then I am happy too."

I wiped away the burning in my eyes and lunged into Kiita's lap, wrapping my arms around her and leaning my head into her shoulder. She hugged me close and I basked in a warmth that had nothing to do with the rising sun.

"Hurry up, sissy! Elle! They are about to show it!" Col's voice echoed off the trees behind us as he called from Salem's outskirts. He had nearly mastered the art of mounting my dyr and was riding towards us proudly on a prancing Achilles.

The children loved my stag dearly and most looked at the bond between us with longing. But Col loved him the most. Watching my friend's brother, I couldn't help but be jealous. I was too big to ride

Achilles just yet, but I couldn't wait until the day I could. He'd grow larger than a draft horse, and he'd certainly be faster than Kip.

"Coming!" Kiita yelled back, smacking her lips together as she glanced at me. The village had organised another celebration tonight, to honour the dead and celebrate Salem's new life. Kiita had sent riders to Ashbourne with a small piece of Tor's fortune for food and drink. They would not return before dusk.

Kiita shoved me off her lap and stood, patting the dirt from her thighs, and seemed to almost shake off the immaturity we'd just shared to bring forth the leader her people saw her as. I stuck out my leg as she started towards the village so that she fell flat on her face.

With a few more cackles of laughter and jabs in the ribs, we made our way back to the town center, where a large stone fountain was about to be unveiled by the stone mason. It had been kept under a large blanket throughout the past few days, the mason keeping his secrets until now. I hoped it was a statue in the likeness of Kiita.

Or Tor.

They had poured their heart and souls into the reconstruction of Salem, working tirelessly to ensure every person had a roof over their heads and food in their bellies.

I found a place within the gathering crowd, and a delicately steadfast hand reached for mine and held tight. I held my breath as the stone mason climbed the ladder. Eyes roaming, I noticed that every single person was holding the hand of someone else. This day of peace and celebration was a long time coming for these people. I squeezed Kiita's hand a little tighter, spotting a comely brunette woman holding Tor's hand across the square. His cheeks flushed red when she looked up at him and smiled.

I hoped he pursued it.

Cheers sounded throughout the square and Kiita's hand clutched mine almost painfully. The blanket lay on the ground beside the fountain.

It was not in the likeness of Kiita, or Tor.

It was a stag.

My vision blurred as I tried and failed to blink away the floodgates near bursting inside me. And when I looked back down at the people, they beamed back. They'd all known. Even Tor, who clapped the loudest, smiling at me with tears in his eyes.

Achilles nestled his muzzle underneath my elbow. I released Kiita's hand to wrap my arms around his neck, leaning in to press my cheek against his dappled coat. The golden chain between us seemed to glow as bright as the sun itself, and I knew then—the answer to a question that had been festering within me for seven long months. A question of whether, after I performed my duty to Galdurne, I might try to get back to my old world.

I wanted to stay, in this world.

Indefinitely.

"WANT ANOTHER?" Bjorn slurred with heavy-lidded eyes.

He slumped unceremoniously over three large barrels of ale, trying to figure out how to pour himself another drink.

"Not if it means I'll look the way you do just now," I snickered.

The celebrations had begun as soon as the sun had set, and the village was filled with laughing and shouting and music—archaic drumbeats and drunken songs sung with words I didn't understand, but I'd never heard anything so lovely. I looked out upon the village square, watching the people dancing—freedom flowing through their limbs like wind. Flowers braided through long ribbons were twisted around wooden columns and recently planted trees, couples beneath them, so wrapped in one another it was as if they were the only two people alive.

Tor had been one of those people, hours ago. He'd stolen away with the comely brunette from before. A dance or two ago he'd said he was taking Col and Achilles back to the cabin for a good night's rest; her name was Agnes, and that was all I needed to know.

Not to matter, I'd make him tell me more tomorrow. Even thinking on it, I couldn't help but smile.

Nearly a whole song after I rejected Bjorn's offered drink, he turned and pointed at me. "Just because you cannot handle your ale."

I pursed my lips to contain my laughter. "No, Bjorn, I do not handle it so well as you."

He just thrust his hand at me with his thumb in the air.

"You truly should have another, Estelle. This is after all, for you."

I turned to Iro, rolling my eyes. "Don't be daft. It is for everyone."

Bjorn released a hearty cheer from his place on the barrels. Iro shook his head, smiling, and pointed over his shoulder at the statue. "My father did just unveil a statue in your honour, no?" He narrowed his eyes, leaning down to level our gazes. "Or have you drunk too much to not see?"

Grimacing, I flicked his shoulder, lowering my voice. "All I can see is a stag. Are you calling me an animal?"

Iro grasped my fingers before I could pull my hand back. "Aye, lass, more animal than woman."

Bjorn held his horn of ale high in the air in salute. "Iro, you know the way to a lass's heart."

Snatching my hand from Iro's, I furrowed my brows. "Bold of you to assume I would take that as an insult."

"I knew you would take it as anything but."

At his unusually smug face, I offered a smile of my own and sipped from my horn. Focusing on the dozens of bodies swaying leaf-like to the rhythm of the music, I thought back on my previous day, of turquoise eyes and warm lips. I watched as a man took his lover's hips and pressed them close, seizing the moment to caress her neck with his brow. My own nape tingled as I recalled the feel of Rose's tongue tracing lines across my jaw. But the heat emanating from my core flushed away when Iro wrapped his hand around my arm. "Are you alright, Estelle?"

Regarding the genuine concern plastered across his features, I opened my mouth to speak the truth I should have made clear long ago.

The air flew out of me as something hard knocked me forwards. Fingers dug into my shoulder as Kiita wrapped both arms around my neck, nestling her head into the crook of my right shoulder. She, like Bjorn, was legless. "She is simply thinking about the lad she wishes was burrowed between her thighs. Can you not see how she watches them dance?"

Iro shifted around Kiita with raised brows and wide eyes. "You have a man?"

"His name is..." Kiita released her grip from around my collarbone but rested her arms on my shoulders, palms raised. "Wait for it...his name is Rose."

My lungs and limbs bristled.

"Wait!" Kiita barked. "Was I meant to tell folk?"

"Probably not," I said, taking another large swig of ale. I didn't dare meet Iro's eyes, but my skin burned with the heat of his gaze. As the three of us stood in heavy silence, I almost jumped when Iro flicked me on the shoulder—a mirror to my playful gesture from before this stiff conversation.

He drew my eyes and I let out my held breath as I beheld a kind smile. "He is a lucky man...but, where is he now? He should be dancing with you."

"Aye," I said. "He should be."

Iro chuckled and cocked his head. "Well, Estelle, if you would like someone to take his place for a night, come and find me." He dipped his chin once before stalking into the midst of the dancing crowd, yet the way he wrung his hands suggested anything but nonchalance.

"I am sorry," Kiita whispered, hanging over my shoulders.

I turned my head to peck her cheek. "Don't be, apparently it was easier this way."

With a loud crash, Bjorn stumbled out from his stupor behind the barrels—barely able to stand, he swayed beside us. "Kiita! Have you seen the sellsword that just arrived? Two knicks says she will like me better than you."

Kiita straightened at the prospect, jerking sideways to round on Bjorn. "Where?"

He grinned like a fool and pointed to the other side of the square. I followed the direction of his finger and beheld a striking woman with brown skin and a shaved head. She was dressed in dark armour, armed to the teeth, swigging a large horn of ale against a tree.

Kiita slapped Bjorn on the shoulder. "You have got yourself a wager, lad." Bjorn shot me wagging brows and took Kiita's hand to plunge toward the new arrival. Standing alone, I giggled, watching Kiita jump over Bjorn to launch herself at the stunned swordswoman, pulling her without a word into the circle of dancers.

Strong arms snaked around my waist, pulling me into a solid chest. I jolted—for a split second convinced Iro had returned to try another approach—until I smelled him. Soft lips grazed my neck up to my ear, leaving goose flesh in their wake.

A soft moan flew from me as Rose seized the tip of my ear between his teeth, his breath sending hues of heat through me. I jabbed his ribs lightly with my elbow as he unwrapped his arms, tugging me around to face him. "It's about time you got here," I said.

He kissed me, winked, and gave a lopsided grin. "I promised, did I not?"

I smiled. "You did. Even if you acted like an infant when I told you to meet me here tonight."

He released his hold to raise his palms. "Is it a crime for a man to want to spend an entire day with his woman? Not just be sent on his way and told to come back the next night for another tumble in the grass?"

"I think you and Kiita need to confer and define the term tumble."

A wicked glint flashed across his eyes. "Aye, I would be disconcerted to know it was her that showed you how to tumble, but only if I knew you had not invited me to attend said tumbling."

With a playful jab to his arm, Rose snorted and quirked a brow before running an eye over me. "Nice dress, Tor is more talented than I thought."

"Kiita made it, smartass."

I was indeed wearing one—simply made, with pretty sleeves and a flowing skirt. When I first donned it, I recoiled at how impeding it was to my every move. After months of living and breathing the soaring freedom of a forest as wild as the animals I ran with, a dress was more than uncomfortable. But Kiita had put great effort into making it, so I smiled and played the pretty doll as she squealed with delight. My hair was unbound and brushed out properly for once, and Col had braided a thin wreath of flowers around my head.

I pushed some of that unbound hair behind my ear. "Would you like a drink?"

"Hmm, I would rather like something else first," he purred.

"Brute."

Rose huffed a low laugh before pressing his brow against mine. "You look beautiful."

The corners of my lips quaked as I tried to hold back the emotions threatening to escape with each shallow breath. I tipped my head up to close the small space between us, basking in the tingle of each hair rising on my skin as our lips met. Rose broke the kiss faster than I'd anticipated, but before I could voice my displeasure, he tugged me by the hand away from the music and revelling figures silhouetted by the firelight. I followed his lead through deepening shadows between buildings until we came to an almost blackened niche.

He wasted no time, spinning back and pressing me against the wooden panelling, resuming our kiss within half a heartbeat, deeper than before. His hands trailed my ribs, before starting again at my neck, drawing circles with his thumb, skimming downwards over my collarbone, then finally tracing over my chest.

Electricity jolted through my core. I gasped, a sharp inhale against his lips. Rose smiled through the kiss and palmed my breast wholly. Through the thin fabric of my dress, I felt everything—every touch and spark from his fingers. I was untried and inexperienced, though through the lenses of my old world I had seen enough and read enough to know how to show him I wanted more. Wanted him. Lifting a hand to cup his nape, I pulled him in and trailed my other hand across his chest, down his muscled abdomen, and lightly placed it over the hardened bulge between his thighs. Rose moaned and pulled away, his eyes ablaze with desire.

"You said you wanted us to wait," I began, with as much sensuality as I could muster, my voice low and husky. "We've waited."

A shaky laugh. "We have all the time in the world, lass, why the rush?"

"Because I love you. And I want every piece of you."

He smiled and pressed his lips to my forehead. "Not tonight. I want to do everything right when it comes to you. A village celebration seems hardly the time."

I leaned my head against the panelling and sighed. The heat inside threatened to burn me alive, and judging by his knowing smirk, the bastard could see it. He leaned in, planting a hand on the wall at either side of my head. "But of course, I cannot allow my woman to be left wanting. That just would not be right, would it now?"

His breath sent new flames flushing down my core, and as he slowly descended to his knees, smirking all the way, my legs weakened. Those turquoise eyes that shone like a beacon in the night—the ones I saw in my dreams—were locked on mine as he moved a hand to my ankle, trailing it up and under the hem of the dress against the skin of my calves.

His gaze remained on mine, his fingers grazing my knee, then my thigh, then the soft fabric of my undergarment. He lifted another hand up and under my dress to tear the fabric apart.

I was going to shatter entirely.

Rose only tore his eyes from mine when he lifted the hem of my dress and bunched the material around my thighs. The beating music, laughter and bawdy cheering from the village square pulsated through me. I didn't care. Not now. I wouldn't have cared if the entire village was watching us in broad daylight.

The first touch of his mouth to my core ruined me. My legs buckled, and he held me upright with hard hands on my hips.

I didn't last long. Electricity thrashed as my pleasure reached its peak and I soared over the edge.

His tongue did not stop dancing through it all.

~

I DON'T KNOW how long we stayed hidden in our place amongst the shadows, but when we both remastered the ability to speak, we snuck back into the revelry. Rose pulled a hood up to obscure his face and held me close.

Hours or lifetimes later, strewn across the dirt with Kiita, Bjorn, and the sell sword, I prodded him for the umpteenth time for distinctly and conspicuously tracing idle circles over my ass whenever Iro walked by. The stonemason's son had not taken Rose's presence well and threw scalding looks every chance he got.

Bjorn lost the bet he'd made—the second of the night—and was now in a comatose state, face down in the dirt with a blanket atop him. He'd been that way for a while, since challenging Rose to a duel to ensure he was fit enough to be my man. Kiita and I had rolled our eyes as Bjorn proposed that if Rose could 'knock him down in one hit', only then would he be deserving of me. He was now suffering the consequences of that game. I'd have to tell him that it was Rose who had tucked the blanket firmly around him after he'd fallen.

Kiita and her new friend sat close by, the latter holding the former's legs over her lap. Rumi was her name, and she was utterly smitten with the striking blonde currently planting soft kisses over her shoulder.

As I leaned back into Rose's chest, his arms tightened around me and I looked up to the night sky through the smoke of the festival fire.

I wanted this moment to last forever.

If I woke up tomorrow, safe and sound in a four-poster bed...I think that would be the true nightmare.

So, I begged the stars to let me stay.

CHAPTER 16
WITH OR WITHOUT YOU

I'd awoken to an empty space beside me. Empty, but for a single red rose in his stead. I smiled at the idea of him doing it, how he must have laughed.

Nestled amongst the furs Rose and I shared under Kiita's roof, I stared at the ceiling and recalled every word and every touch of the night. Rose's fingers and lips—and tongue. I'd loved every second. Feathers battering the insides of my gut told me I wanted more—I wanted it all, I wanted him, and I never wanted it to end.

Kiita and her new friend stirred around midday, having shared a space in the second room. Not long after, Rumi bid us farewell as she continued her journey to Kona, the City of Wings, named for the large falcons inhabiting the steep sea cliffs surrounding it. Rumi had saved for five years, apparently, to purchase one of the falcons the pioneers of Kona tamed. She left with a promise to return to Salem and a long kiss upon Kiita's forehead.

"So," I began when Rumi had ridden out of sight. "Is she a fine kisser?"

Kiita didn't answer. Instead, she pinned me in a headlock, ruffling my hair.

Both heavy limbed and slow of thought, we took a mule and rode back to Tor's cabin—taking three stops along the way to expel the results of our excess, heaving horribly behind a tree. Tor took one look at our misery and ordered us to run through the woods. Apparently sweat was the only way to deal with a hangover. We objected at first, but ended up running anyway.

As the sun dropped, Tor and Col brought out food while Kiita and I soaked our feet in the stream. Our supper was peaceful—beautiful, even. Achilles came to lay beside me and planted his head on my lap, and I smiled as I massaged the inch-long antlers that had finally broken through.

Sitting amongst the grass with my newfound family, memories of Rose only further instilled peace and happiness for my new life.

When dusk neared, Kiita excused herself and Col to help clean the mess of last night's revelries. I offered to go as well, but Tor was quick to remind me about my lack of *proper* training these days past. Which was fine, I wanted to hear more about this *Agnes*.

~ ROSE ~

THE INN WAS PACKED to the brim, full of Ashbourne soldiers. I kept my hood low and stalked to a familiar bench in the far corner of the hall.

"You are getting fat, brother." My brother's voice was a warm embrace. I had not seen him in over seven months. Yet, when I woke in Kiita's home with Estelle sleeping soundly in my arms, I found a crumpled note hidden in my pocket. If he had seen me with her—there is nothing I would not do to keep Estelle safe. My fingers found the hilt of my knife.

"Was it you?" I snarled, throwing the note at him with my free hand. He stared for a moment, before leaning to retrieve the note that had floated onto the wooden floor. Straightening, he flattened the crumpled paper over the table, reading the words requesting I meet him here at midday today.

He scratched his head. "No, a Shadow I hired. I am surprised you did not notice, little brother. I apologise, I did not know how else to find you."

I bristled. Shadows were the worst shits in Kiliac. Assassins that excelled in remaining true to their name. It was a rarity indeed to see one before they slit your throat.

My slap on the table echoed through the inn like thunder. "Does he answer to you or father?"

Hurt flashed through my brother's eyes at the accusation. "I just wanted to see you, Rose. Why such animosity?"

"Do you know?"

Genuine confusion lined his face. My brother was not much older than I, but he already had a hard kind of maturity thrust upon him—it showed beneath his rough features. He was the most honest man I had ever met, so if his assassin had seen me with Estelle, my brother would have known, and he would have told me.

"Know what?"

I breathed out my relief. The sneaky prick must have dropped the note in some time yesterday before I had gotten to the village. The village newly named Salem, its people had so proudly told me. The people who, that drunken idiot Bjorn told me more than once, had been saved by Estelle. Healed by her. Each and every one.

I had never had anything in my life to be proud of, but I was so proud of her.

My brother's gaze was piercing, calculating every fleck of emotion showing in my face—he was too astute, so I forced an easy smirk. "That I am still more attractive than you?"

He roared a hearty laugh and ordered two ales from a passing bar maid.

As I stared at the person who knew me best in this world, I felt ashamed. I wanted to tell him of the wild, exquisite girl I had grown to love so deeply. I wanted to tell him everything about her—how lovely and kind and fierce she was. Most of all, I wanted to tell my brother how extraordinarily happy I was. But I did not.

We feasted on roast meat and bread, drinking ale until our stomachs were swollen and sore, and the soldiers around us grew drunk and raucous. When he told me of home, or spoke of visiting our sister and watching her play in the gardens by the sea, I used memories of Estelle to keep my smile from fracturing. He told me of Mother and we laughed together at the idea of her learning to bake after all these years, reminiscing on nearly choking to death on her cooking as lads. He never once mentioned father.

When he inquired into my life, I threw a swaggering grin and spun tales of roaming from town to town, bedding women and selling my sword to rich employers. It had been true. That had been my life. Yet it had changed forever when I met that strange lass in the woods. Now, I spent my time travelling from town to town, searching in vain for tales on how to return her home. It had always been the truth that I searched reluctantly, and now, I am not sure I even wanted to keep looking.

"Rose!"

His usually calm and stoic voice raised. It jolted me from my thoughts, and I tore my gaze from the empty plate to meet his eyes. "Sorry brother, what did you say?"

"I said that the hour is late, I need to return home. I truly wish you would come with me this time."

"I am not coming home, you know this. I am not facing him again."

My brother shook his head before gazing downcast. "I know."

I reached across the table, placed my hand atop his, and our eyes met for a fleeting moment of farewell. I did miss him.

A small cloaked man burst through the door amidst bawdy cheering from the other patrons. The stranger ran straight for my brother, halted at his side, panting with ragged breath. He snatched a letter from his pocket and offered it up. My brother ripped apart the seal to unravel the paper and I stayed only because the air between us went stale the moment we recognised the seal on that letter.

After some moments reading what was inked with furrowed brows, he looked at me. "I am so sorry, Rose."

"What does it say?" I stammered. Though I already knew.

"He knows about the girl. It is Meriden or her head."

Each word clawed at my heart until it was torn out entirely.

~ ESTELLE ~

"ADMIT IT!" I barked through heaving pants, chuckling with what was left of my breath, "I'm almost as good as you now!"

"I will not admit anything of the sort, lass," Tor said, his exhaustion equalling mine. We'd been sparring hand-to-hand and I'd even gotten a few good hits on him.

I lunged, twisting as I did. He swung a miss-hit over my head, and I punched a blow to his stomach. It barely phased him. He seized the underside of my knee with a large hand and pulled so I was knocked straight down—the air thrust from my lungs as I hit the ground.

When I reclaimed the ability to breath, I released a shaky laugh. "Ass."

Tor's rumbling chuckle sounded as he reached down to help me up. "Next time that happens, yeh got to—"

But whatever new lesson Tor was about to give was cut short by a tumultuous crashing of broken branches from the forest to the east.

With a well-practised glance between us, Tor and I both started towards the weapon stash. I stalled when Finn plunged from the darkening shade beneath the forest, an almost crazed looking Rose on her back.

I'd never seen that look before.

My blood froze cold in my veins.

With his frantic eyes locked onto mine, Rose stumbled off Finn. Heart sinking, I opened my mouth to speak, but no words came out. Tor was not so dumbstruck. "He knows, does he not, lad?" Tor's words were less of a question and more of a demand.

He. Rose's father.

The reason Rose had tried to lie and turn me away three days past —the person he'd thought I needed protection from. I had spoken to Rose further afterwards, breathlessly sniggering and asking how dangerous one man could possibly be. By the disconsolate expression on Tor's face when Rose nodded, I knew my answer.

"What is it to be then, lad?" Tor said into the silence, his voice resuming its usual roiling thunder.

Rose's eyes—they were no longer that brilliant shade of turquoise I had come to know. As he stared at Tor, then dragged his gaze back to me, the colour inside them was darker. Much darker. "Meriden."

Meriden—the Militia base in Kiliac's north-eastern mountains. Where Rose's home was. The one place he'd been running from for years.

"It doesn't matter," I snapped. "He cannot hold this over you. He cannot hold *me* over you. I won't let him."

Rose squeezed his eyes shut, dropped his shoulders then choked on a sob. I had not realised he'd been crying.

"This is unnecessary," I said, rounding on both men. "Just because your father knows about me does *not* mean I am in danger. He is one man. I have the forest."

"No, lass," Tor said, his voice stern. "He is not just one man. And yeh only have the depths of the forest to call on, they could come from the east."

"Then we will be prepared," I said, crossing my arms and steeling myself, turning on Rose. "He cannot make you leave me."

Rose rubbed a hand over his face. "If it keeps you safe, I will do what needs to be done."

Before I could answer, Tor strode to him and reached a hand up to squeeze Rose's shoulder. An unnaturally tender look passed between them and Tor nodded once, spinning away to the cabin, leaving us alone. I watched after him, rising heat, anger and hopelessness flooding my throat like bile. They'd made the decision, without me, with one fucking look. "No," I said when I looked back to Rose.

Rose's expression tightened. "Estelle, I—"

"No."

He stepped towards me, but I lunged away.

"N-*no!*" My voice cracked. "Last night was perfect. Today was so damned perfect. You do not have my permission to ruin it."

"I am going to Meriden. I will do what I must to protect you from that monster."

I looked up at the twilight sky, releasing the air slowly from my lungs. "How long until I see you?" He didn't answer, his hands trembled, the eyes staring back at me were not his. Squeezing my lips together, I nodded with a jerk. "You really are a bloody bastard."

He had come to say goodbye. A true goodbye.

I would not allow it.

Rose stepped forward, but I lurched away before he reached me. "I am not saying goodbye to you," I said with every dreg of Kiita's steel I could muster.

"Please," he said softly, desperately. "I am so, so sorry my love."

"I don't care. I am not saying goodbye."

I didn't know where this doggedness came from, this hardness. I did not have a heart of stone, the white-hot fire consuming it proved that. But somehow, *something* was keeping me from breaking right now. He closed his eyes and nodded, twisted on his heel and leapt onto Finn.

"I love you. I have always loved you," he said.

"No," was all that came from my mouth.

He stared down at me as the ghost of a smile lifted his lips, before he kicked Finn's sides. She reared onto her hind legs with a loud cry and spun to take off, shooting back into the forest towards the north.

I STOOD in the clearing for who knows how long.

Empty.

Numb.

My heart, though burning, still beat. And no tears found their way through. It only scared and confused me more—so unlike my usual emotions.

One night, Rose and I were sharing kisses under the stars. The next, he was leaving me.

Leaving me.

Rose was leaving.

I had not said goodbye, only watched his face fall further each time he tried. My heart cracked. I did not say it back. He told me he loved me and I had not said it back.

He was leaving for you and you threw it in his face.

He'd been crying and all I'd said was *no*.

What have I done?

Kip was too slow, Achilles too small. My stag remained frozen beside the stream, watching my every move. I glanced at him—took comfort in his golden eyes. "Stay here."

He cried out, but did not move from where he stood.

I bolted into the forest where Rose had disappeared. That inner beast of mine was slumbering so I begged it to rise, to help me run faster, but it did not stir. So I whistled, as loud as I could. For too long, I got no answer. I whistled again, but still nothing. Each ten steps I ran I whistled out to the darkness, until finally, *finally*, I heard an answering roar.

Not fifty paces away, a blur of ash-grey flashed. I scrambled onto a fallen log to run along it to the end, where I leapt as far as I could, roughly landing on the cioraun's furry back, the bones in my hips pounding at the impact. I angled my body down low and pressed my legs against his sides as he charged into the direction I needed. I'd never ridden this fast before. My chest floated and the wind hammered at my face, pulling my long braid to soar behind me.

My first ride like this should have been glorious.

But right now, I didn't care.

~ ROSE ~

WITH EACH LEAPING BOUND Finn made, a fresh tear fell.

I had not cried like this since leaving my mother.

No, Estelle had said. *I am not saying goodbye to you.*

I knew why she had been like that, and I did not blame her. I loved her more for it, that fire inside her she did not realise was ever-present. But with each pace away from Tor's cabin, I wished she had said she loved me too—that I could have kissed her goodbye. She was wrong. She did not know it, but she was so wrong. I had seen my father hurt people, been forced to watch it. I would not have her harmed like that. I should never have gone to Salem to see her. It was too public. But after that day we spent together, she told me to meet her there and I dared not refuse her.

I could not bring myself to fear what lay ahead. Meriden was a terrible place, full of the worst kind of men—and I would be punished, for my insolence in neglecting my former duty. My father would make sure of it, though I held no fear for my future. Only for her.

As I neared Galdurne's outskirts, close to the encampment I had been ordered to attend, Finn tossed her head and loosened a scream.

She had only once balked from anything. Only once. Three days ago.

A cioraun.

Straightening in my saddle, I twisted as an ash-grey smear soared from my left side and leapt into the path I had taken. Estelle was astride it, face wild, looking like the incarnation of a goddess I had always thought her to be. Any human reservations abandoned me as I dove from Finn's back and ran towards the giant feline. Towards her.

Estelle was already sliding off its side and made a leap into my arms. As I held her close, she cried into my neck, clinging to my shoulders.

"I love you," I said into her hair, time and time again.

Her body wracked with sobs as she choked out her words. "I have loved you more than I can bear. And I will see you again, whether you think it or not. Because I have not finished loving you yet, Rose."

I pressed my brow to hers. "Aye, lass. I will dream of you until then."

Then that farewell kiss I had hoped for—wished for—I claimed it. Deep and true.

~ ESTELLE ~

I WALKED WITH ROSE to the tree line, and watched after him in the darkness as he rode down a hill and into the encampment in a wide field where the forest ended and civilisation began.

If my beast were awake, she'd want me to call for every damned creature in Galdurne to rain hell down upon the legion of soldiers below. But she was not, and I did not. Instead, I watched the man I loved walk away and out of my life.

When Rose disappeared between the rows of tents and men the size of ants scrambled around the fires, I continued to watch.

It was only as first light's glow began to flush the horizon in warm hues that I rubbed my face and moved to climb onto the cioraun's back. He had stayed with me, remained at my side in silence.

The cioraun got me to Tor's cabin. My numbness and Achilles' prodding got me to my bed.

After staring at the wall for an age, an extra fur was gently placed over me as a large hand stroked my hair once, before the fire was extinguished and I was left with nothing but silent tears.

CHAPTER 17

DAUÐALOGN

I was still staring at the wall as the sun came up for another day, filling the cabin with light. Tor hadn't made me rise before it, nor had he bothered me the day before. I listened to the sounds of him rising from bed, getting ready for the day, and eventually leaving. I didn't dare ask how long he'd been sitting and waiting for me to turn around, but I did know he'd awoken hours ago.

As the changing light flowed in through the windows with the ascending sun, I still did not move. It wasn't fair. Neither Tor nor Rose even tried. They hadn't allowed me the freedom to protect myself from whatever mysterious force they were both so afraid of. When I'd first arrived in Kiliac, I was warned of its brutality, and for a time, I believed it. Even when I saw the hunter's lifeblood flow from his veins and knew I had a part to play in his death. But as I grew stronger under Tor's guidance and met people I'd come to love, I did not think it so brutal.

I may have dozed off once or twice, because the cabin door opening almost sent me sprawling off the bed. From the massive thump shortly after, I could tell Achilles had been sleeping as well and had knocked his head on my bedframe. A heavy wave of ice-cold water was thrown over me, soaking both the furs and I head to toe, causing Achilles to roar in indignation and bolt from the cabin.

I suppose my father's compassion was at its end. I tried to yell as I choked on the chilly water. "What the—Tor?"

He stood over me, his eyes narrowed. "Just because some young love romance goes sour does not mean yeh stop living."

"Oh!" I started, wiping the water from my face and projecting venom into my words. "And I suppose you didn't stop living when Elara died?"

Low blow, Estelle.

Not nearly in the same damned ballpark.

I cooled the hollow burning inside. "Bloody hell. I—I'm sorry, Tor."

He lowered himself onto the bed, soaking as it was, exhaling harshly. "I know yeh are, lass." Bunching his hands into his lap, he turned to me with a solemn expression. "But yer right. When she died, I thought that nothing in the world could fill that black hole she left behind. But Danii...Danii was my salvation then." He sucked in a great gulp of air, a strange expression twisting his face. "Just as yeh are my salvation now."

Hot tears escaped and rolled down my cheeks as I choked on a sob. "And you are mine."

He smiled and pulled me into his arms. After minutes or hours, Tor released me and thumped the wall behind us once with his fist. I sat up as the door opened, my stomach lurching. For a split second, I thought turquoise eyes and a cocky grin would greet me—but smiled all the same for my twilight-eyed friend as she breezed through and leapt onto me.

She sent us both sprawling over the wet furs, Tor twisting away and off the bed to avoid us. As he moved to the far side of the cabin, Kiita lifted her head and stared down from where she had me pinned. "You okay?"

I pressed my cheek against hers. "I am now."

She leant down to whisper, "That is horse shit, but you will be. Soon. I promise."

I'D TRIED to remain astute on our ride to Salem.

Not long after Kiita arrived, she asked—well, demanded, really—that we see the new stock of horses that had arrived in the village. She babbled on and on about a jet-black mare she had her eye on. Neither Tor or Kiita mentioned Rose, and I was both thankful, yet not at the same time. At least they didn't treat me like I was broken.

I nodded along through Kiita's recount of Rumi's life, from slavery to saving her master from near-death, ensuring her own freedom. Kiita was excited to see her again—as Rumi had promised—and was anticipating beholding one of those legendary falcons.

For Kiita's sake, I hoped Rumi was a good woman. My friend deserved the world.

My thoughts swam through the air like silk in water and I was daydreaming again. Studying how the breeze made the leaves dance in the shafts of mellow sunlight, the mention of my name dragged me back to Tor and Kiita's conversation.

"—of course she was useless when I first met her, but she has developed into quite the swordswoman."

"Swords are not everything, big man," I interrupted, nestled behind him on Kip. "Archery is just as fine a skill."

"Not if yer fighting someone who is a foot away from yeh," he said back matter-of-factly.

"I doubt a sword would be much use then, either, perhaps a toothpick?"

"Or nails." Kiita piped up from beside us on her mule.

The two continued deliberating what weapon would indeed be best in such circumstances, whilst I glanced at Achilles trotting beside us. In one heartbeat, his head was high and his ears stood erect, the next, they flattened faster than a lightning bolt. He was the first to notice the change in the air—that poison. I was the second, through our bond and the sour smell leeching into the breeze. I'd already slid off Kip's flank and had an arrow nocked before Tor and Kiita halted their conversation.

Tor didn't ask questions, he thumbed out his axe and threw a hunting knife towards Kiita. The mule panicked, but Kip straightened firm.

I felt through the air for that poison, tried to narrow my senses to it. There, to my left in a thicket—convinced she was concealed—was a primitive and savage looking woman with matted black hair and tattered furs, eyes locked on Tor. Both he and Kiita desperately scanned the surrounding forest to get a visual on the threat. The strange woman had a bow aimed right at them. She didn't know I could sense her, sense the poison lingering in her blood. The same, I realised, as the soldiers I'd seen so many months past. The same as those lovers, along with the jarrah and riki I hunted.

I pulled my bow taut, but that voice rang out.

Not yet.

I tried to drown my hesitation, that voice, but my moment of mercy could have cost me everything. She fired her arrow towards Tor, but her aim was ajar and instead hit Kiita's mule in the neck. It went down squealing. Achilles lurched from my side and knocked the woman to the ground. He reared and brought his hooves down, striking her face as she shrieked. He reared a second time and drove down to hit her again.

Then again.

Until there was nothing left of her face.

In the stunned silence that followed, Tor slid from Kip's back and jogged to the fallen woman, Achilles bounding to the side. In his trembling body I felt the pure red rage I had tucked away. Tor or Kiita could have been killed and it would have been my fault.

Tor bent towards the mauled face. I turned to look at Kiita, her face set in stone, crouched low over the mule. She'd put it out of its pain—something I could have done in a different way, yet here I'd stood like a frozen fool. When Tor twisted up and looked at us both with flushed red cheeks and an ire in his eyes deep as an ocean storm, my knees trembled. "Bandits," he growled.

Salem.

Kiita roared and sprinted for the village.

Tor glanced at me and nodded once, gesturing for me to follow as he whirled and went after her. We were near enough to the tree line that it wouldn't take us long to reach the cleared slope on foot. I pushed myself into action to run in his footsteps, joined by Achilles running abreast to me. Blood stained his forelegs up to his knees.

Another bandit, a large dirt-covered man, dove at us from behind a tree, balking mid-air as he beheld Tor, but it was already too late. Tor swung his axe. To my right, Kiita cleared the tree line and angled towards another man pelting headlong down the slope. As Kiita unleashed a shrieking battle cry, the bandit noticed us and turned to face my friend.

Their fight lasted longer. Pure terror flushed through me when the man landed a punch across Kiita's face, but Kiita used the shift of his weight to angle behind and slice the knife across the back of his knees. The bandit's guttural scream wracked my bones as I ran.

He was still screaming as Kiita pounced up and away from him, but they died, cut short as Achilles trampled over his dying body.

I tried to stir my beast, or even find a damned shred of courage, but everything inside me was void of bravery. I was a scared little girl in the face of this danger. I'd faced creatures resembling demons and ghosts and trolls, yet what I faced now seemed the most terrifying of all. Worse even than those two lovers in the woods, because now there was more than just my life at stake.

Tor and Kiita seemed to be driven by inner beasts of their own, reaching the first line of buildings before I shook myself from my stupor. I'd only cleared half the slope by the time they both threw themselves into the assailants within the square.

When I reached the village, the attack was over. Bjorn and a few other men were standing guard outside the ale house. Iro was there too, blood-stained sword in hand, ribs heaving, face distant.

From Kiita's urgent questioning, I discerned there were no casualties on Salem's part. They attacked too quickly for anyone to find refuge in the mess hall, so the people acted swiftly, seeking shelter elsewhere whilst a brave few stood and fought. The villagers were thanking the Maker that these 'bandits' were no more than gutter rats—not the fearsome group that had decimated their village in the past.

Col bolted out from the ale house and Kiita released a quaking wail, dropping to her knees to catch her brother as he flung himself into her arms, and the woman I knew as Agnes trotted into Tor's open arms to fold into his chest. So many people fought, so many people who had never fought before, yet had everything to lose if they didn't. I couldn't bear to look at them, any of them, nor join in their relief and sombre celebration.

I hadn't helped a goddamned bit.

I'd almost gotten Tor killed.

What use was I?

WHEN THE VILLAGERS threw themselves into removing the bodies, or cleaning away the splattered blood, I stood numbly in the shadows and watched. No one bothered to move me.

I glanced up at the stone stag atop the fountain at some stage and asked myself where that wild girl had gone—the one who'd saved a village of illness and charged towards a veritable legion of soldiers abreast fearsome beasts.

Perhaps she had walked blindly into an encampment of Meriden soldiers in the night.

The arrow that was aimed and meant for Tor replayed in my head, over and over. In my thoughts, I was stuck either in mud, ice, or just my own goddamned cowardice.

That arrow would haunt my fucking dreams.

I told my dyr to stay in Salem, for Col did not stop wailing every time we made to leave. And whilst I mentioned that we should stay, Tor took one look at me and shook his head. Apparently, he and I needed to talk. Alone. So I knelt down next to Col and promised that nothing would happen tonight as long as Achilles was with him, then asked the boy to protect my dyr if any bad came upon them again. Col ceased his tears and promised me he would be brave.

It was more than I could say for myself.

Kiita pulled me in for a tender hug before we left, whispering it was okay for me to be scared—it only meant I was human. She didn't know that I was not scared, just disgraced.

Tor and I rode Kip in silence back to his cabin in the late evening, guilt and shame crushing me from the inside out. He hadn't spoken to me since the attack and whilst I knew he wasn't angry, I was afraid of what was going on in his head. Disappointment would probably cut the deepest.

Standing to the side while he stabled Kip, I couldn't take the silence between us any longer. "I'm sorry, Tor... I can't... I couldn't..." The words did not come, breaking away into the wind.

Tor's head tilted as he studied me. He didn't say a word, just stared with eyes I couldn't read, so I continued, trying to dig down for that golden light to heal my fracturing heart and grant me strength. "I am not cut out for this life after all. I'm too soft, too weak. I probably always will be. I'm sorry I let you down." My voice cracked and my eyes burned. I lowered my gaze to the ground and let the tears fall.

Enveloping warmth overcame me as Tor closed the distance between us, grabbing my face between his hands, angling it up to look at him. So much love shone in his silver-lined eyes that I whimpered.

"Estelle, having a soft heart in a hard world is courage, not weakness."

His skin and hair glowed softly in the afternoon light, his beard runes swayed in the cool wind, and that bronze in his gaze settled over me like a veil. I realised then, that in this world—in this strange, mysterious world—it was not Rose who had changed my life forever. Nor was it Kiita. It was this man before me.

My father.

In more ways I thought possible.

In all ways that mattered.

He had told me, time and time again, yet I hadn't listened. I was strong. I had courage—and I'd be able to fight when it mattered. I believed in myself to do that much. And, it seemed, so did he. In his face I saw the world—my world—and I recalled my mother's voice telling me that love was, and always would be, the greatest gift of all.

I had already given it to one and had more to give.

"I love you, Tor."

A single tear escaped his eye as he dropped his hands to my shoulders and pulled me in for a tight embrace, ensconcing me with his massive arms. "And I yeh, my daughter. Always."

My shoulders trembled as I cried into his barrelled chest. We stood there for a while, my father and I. Stealing precious moments from the world. Pretending that such a thing was allowed in such a place.

That was our mistake.

Tor stiffened, his arms tightening as he turned to stone. His voice was a low murmur at my ear, lest a ghost in the wind hear him. "Lass, listen to me. There is an archer behind yeh."

My tears of joy froze on my cheeks.

How had I not sensed this?

Distraction was dangerous. It was one of the first lessons Tor had taught me.

"Yeh run to the stable," he began. "Yeh do not look back. Get the weapons."

His arms locked around me, his head didn't move an inch, but tension built inside him. And rage. There was pure, undiluted rage inside him too. "Tor..."

"Go, Estelle."

With those words, I did not hesitate.

The moment I made to move, Tor spun me in his arms and launched me through the air. Landing smoothly, I took off at a sprint. The air split, followed by a low thud and a grunt behind me, but I did not look back.

I trust you, Tor.

Reaching the stable in seconds, having leapt the last few meters past a panicking Kip to land beside the hatch near the hay, I wrenched it open with enough force to break the hinges. I grabbed Tor's heavy Warhammer first, needing to use both hands and all my strength to lift and throw it in his direction, and dropped back down to retrieve more arrows.

I was best with a bow and I would not falter again.

I could not. Not now.

Another thud sounded and my eyes snagged on a quivering arrow embedded in the wooden wall of the stable, not inches from my arm.

This archer, like the bandit, was sloppy. I was not.

I rolled to my right and lifted my bow, already nocked, in the direction the arrow had come from, the direction I could finally smell that tang of blood and oil. But when my eyes caught up to my aim, Tor already stood over the small man—small soldier. He'd crushed his chest with the hammer. The soldier's torso was a jagged mess of metal, flesh and bone.

Tor looked up, ordering me to come to his side with a well-practised flick of his wrist. Whatever force had stopped me from acting before and protecting Salem from its assailants—it was not present now. Pure adrenaline rushed through my veins and made each split-second last a lifetime.

As I closed the distance between us, another arrow cleaved the air over my shoulder and soared into Tor's chest, joining one I hadn't noticed until now. His face contorting in wrath and pain, as he reached a hand up to rip them away. When he looked back at me, tears lined his face.

"TOR!"

Now.

In a move I'd performed a hundred times in the forest, I leapt and spun as I ran to fire a shot, allowing my instincts to take aim. After letting loose and landing on the hard earth, I rolled to push onto my feet, closing the five-meter distance between my father and I—not looking to see where I'd shot. From the guttural sigh and loud pounding of limbs crashing down, I knew my arrow had hit home.

My first human kill.

When I reached my father, he spun on his heels with his weapon held high to strike another armoured soldier. The splintering thunderclap of his hammer splitting the man's head was the loudest thing I'd ever heard.

I'll never forget that sound.

Nor would I ever forget the sight of his head exploding from the impact.

Tor faced me, bronze eyes flaring at something over my shoulder. Two soldiers rushed at us. Ducking as one swung his arm, not his sword, to swipe at my head—I shoulder charged him from a low crouch. The other had gone for Tor.

This was a fucking ambush.

The soldier who'd attacked me was on the ground, dumbfounded and heaving from the impact. I used his floundering to bring my bow up and strike him across the temple. I didn't know if it was hard enough to kill him, I just knew I had to keep fighting, for Tor.

Tor.

The clanging of steel had halted behind me.

Whirling as my breath released, Tor was meters away. Again, he had his back to me, already having downed the soldier, but he'd stilled.

Slowly, so goddamned slowly, Tor turned towards me.

And the world stopped.

Six arrows protruded from his chest, all sticking out at different angles, shot from different directions, and blood coated his body like a scarlet robe.

Stinging warmth glazed the skin of my legs as Tor sunk to his knees. I lunged, but fingers tangled in my hair and wrenched me back. Clammy hands grasped my shoulders and wrapped around my neck, holding me still—keeping me from Tor.

I could heal him.

I had to get to him.

"Stop! Let me go!"

I used every move Tor had taught me, gaining a meter or two on the soldiers before more leapt in to hold me down. When tortured bronze eyes met mine, panic seared fierce and blinding. "Please! I need to help him! Help him! HELP HIM!" I screamed. Again and again. But no one listened. My words became imperceptible sobbing as tears streamed down my cheeks.

Tor's limbs dropped and the life in his eyes guttered. Mouth gaping, he tried to form words, holding my gaze to his as if it were the last tenure he had to the world. The words he was trying to speak were meant for me, and though I was a mountain away, I finally made them out. Finally understood.

Elara.

Danii.

"NO!"

My arms were being crushed, my hair ripped from my skull, though none of it took weight in my mind or my soul. I watched through clouded eyes, as one final word formed on Tor's lips.

Estelle.

A towering presence overshadowed Tor's kneeling body. A soldier dressed in obsidian armour grasped a raised spear.

I closed my eyes, but saw without seeing, the spear plunge through the back of my father's neck.

Beneath my useless legs, the grass floated away. I looked to the sky as the trees and clearing swayed in the wind, and a deafening throbbing pounded through my mind's eye before the gut-wrenching sound of a dying horse echoed into my bones.

Do not come for me, Achilles. I am already lost.

Close your eyes and think of something nice.

I closed my eyes and collapsed in the soldier's grip.

CHAPTER 18
LULLABY

I woke to the sun searing directly above where I lay, broken and useless. Staring into it, I hoped the blinding light would ignite the rest of me into flame and send me to oblivion.

Tor.

Tor was dead.

My father was dead.

Like boulders crashing down, the weight of my grief ruptured for the hundredth time since I'd awoken on this rickety carriage. Each bump and sway sent a new wave of agony through my spine and nausea consumed me from the inside out as heaving sobs left me breathless.

My face was crusted with old tears, burnt away by the heat of the sun. It was so damned itchy, but I couldn't move a hand to scratch it. My wrists were bound above me and tied to the wooden platform. At least a dozen soldiers accompanied the carriage, but they didn't need to tie me down. I wouldn't have moved.

Tor would be ashamed.

I had no idea where they were carting me off to. My only memory of the landscape before I stared into the sun was of dead trees and bare cliffs. A tangible force tugged on the golden chain inside me, as if

Achilles had taken hold of my rib cage with his teeth and was trying to wrench me back. He'd been trying for longer than I could remember, so I forced the same message down the bond I had time and time again, begging him to stay away.

Do your job. Protect Col.

Protect Kiita.

Stay away from me.

The raid yesterday. The ambush. It couldn't have been a coincidence. Everything happened too fast. Tor died too fast. The heart that Kiita and Tor pieced back together after Rose's departure was shattered beyond repair.

I only began crying again when night fell, the solace of the blinding light was stolen, and I was left with myself.

A WARM GLOW on the crown of my head woke me from a sleep I didn't recall falling into. The night had stripped away my blindness, so from the way the shadows lay, I knew we were heading into the direction of the sunrise. The only human settlement east of Salem was Ashbourne.

They were taking me to the bloody capital.

The seat of King Horen. As evil as they came, according to Tor and any villager courageous or drunk enough to whisper it. Throughout Earth's history there had been many cruel dictators. They were all the same. This one didn't scare me. At least, that was what I told myself.

With each soul-trembling sway in the carriage bringing me closer to the city, the smell of shit, body odour, and alcohol grew more pungent. And by the time the sun rose, I could make out the distinct babble of human voices. There was no green here. Everything was dusty, gritty, including the buildings—made solely from sand and rock. I tried to associate the place with something familiar. Perhaps this city could be one within the Mediterranean.

And perhaps I was not a captive tied down to a carriage.

And Tor had not just been murdered...

No.

I could not break. Not now. Not again.

While the outskirts of the city—along with its people—were filthy, the homes and shopfronts were relatively new. New, but shabby, like they'd been built in too much of a hurry. I supposed that indeed, Kiliac was the youngest nation in the Daelon Empire, but I'd truly expected something grander from its capital. As I was hauled through the streets, I made a point of not meeting anyone's eyes, fearing I'd see a familiar shade of bronze. Or turquoise. But every head was downturned as the carriage went by.

After too long, we came before a place that seemed worthy of a capital. Like it was the first thing built here and the city had been clumsily sprawled around it, which was probably exactly what happened. The castle was enormous. Dark, elaborate, and terrible—fashioned from stone as black as coal. The building itself would easily fit a football field or two inside, and the grounds spanned hectares out to the rocky cliffside. Out here, the smell of ocean salt overwrought the shit and odour from the city. A small reprieve from the stench.

From the wide road, the castle grounds dominated everything to the east. On the west was a row of houses much larger and less ramshackle than those I first saw—no doubt owned by Ashbourne's wealthier citizens. The most impressive sight, however, was the gate to the grounds, made entirely from pure gold. Gold. My colour. It made me feel dirty. Tainted. My blood soured beneath my skin and I closed my eyes, biting back my fear fuelled rage.

We stopped outside those gargantuan gates and my bonds were untied.

Fuck.

What was so important about me to warrant a royal visit?

Could it perhaps be that you are a magi? Or was it simply the fact that you fell from the sky?

Surely...Surely neither would make me so special. A simple execution should have sufficed.

My legs refused to work, so the soldiers pulled me from the carriage and beneath those golden gates, and under a second set of gates built into the outer wall. I stared at my dragging feet as they hauled me past stable hands and guards, launderers and...my eyes snagged on a body being whipped bloody on the ground. He was a young man, haggard and pale, with a brown metal collar around his neck.

I snapped my eyes back to my feet.

When I passed through the threshold of the dark castle, I sent a prayer to the gods I never believed in. Any damned god.

MY BODY LANDED on the hard stone ground before a large door, heavy set and forged from gold. Then the crack of a whip across my spine sent my head reeling.

A tongue of flame seared across my skin, but I did not scream.

I would not scream for them.

"Stand up!"

Another slash across my lower back had me growling like a feral beast towards the set of boots beside me. The brown leather of the whip coiled around those boots, and as it raised up like a snake rising to strike, then lunged, I threw my hand out and caught it. The pain was like grasping a boiling pot, yet it felt good to use some of the rage that'd festered inside.

I snapped up my head, teeth-bared, and wrenched the whip into my chest. The soldier holding its handle came down too—just as I'd intended. As he fell, the legs I'd feigned weak shoved up and I head-butted the bastard under the jawline. I smiled down at the man now sprawled on the ground, at the damage I'd done to his face.

Good luck using your jaw again, you stupid prick.

Honestly, the satisfaction was worth each of the next five lashes flaming across my shoulders. The soldiers dragged me to my feet and pushed me through the golden doors and into a throne room.

In my mind, I'd imagined the king as some fat, pompous prat, with a permanent sneer set into his face. But Horen was a beast of a man. He would have matched Tor for muscle, if not height. The only difference in physique, was that Horen looked to be at least sixty years old, with grey hair bound in a knot atop his head. His skin was a dried leather kind of brown, and violet scars peppered almost every visible inch. Past his intimidating exterior, he was not attractive. Not in any sense of the word. His nose had been broken one too many times and his eyes were as navy blue as the deep churning sea. Even from where I stood they felt like storm waves, crashing down to drown me. No crown sat upon his head, but even the air around him trembled in his presence.

There were few in the room, some fat old men and women I assumed were their pretty young wives, draped over their arms like folds of brightly coloured fabric adorning their stout figures. The majority of the crowd within the room were obsidian plated soldiers. Knights, I supposed. I counted sixteen, eight on either side of the throne.

One of those men had killed Tor.

Every inch of my skin burned.

To Horen's right hand, stood an equally tall, equally muscular younger man with long black hair, tied into a braid and slung over a broad shoulder. I snatched my gaze and returned it to the king, only to see him smirking at me—it rattled me more than I cared to admit. If I was brought here, this man must have ordered the ambush, and not only that, but the motley group that had attacked Salem as well.

Horen's voice echoed across the cavernous room, bouncing off the cold stone floor beneath me. "It is customary for one to bow before their king."

Unleashing as much venom into my words as I could, I held my head high. "Fuck off. You are no king of mine."

Horen tilted his head back and roared with laughter. No one else said a word. I don't think anyone else was even breathing. This maniac could go to the depths of hell for all I cared. I hoped he'd kill me first. I'd just have to bank on the idea that dying here would send me back to Earth—I did not want this world if Tor was no longer in it. If Rose wasn't in it. So, I forced a snake-like smile and said, "You know, for an all-mighty, all so powerful...king...you sure are one fugly ass bastard."

I felt it in my bones, everyone's heart stopping.

Good.

I held that serpentine smile as Horen rose from the throne. He chuckled to himself and strode to his nearest black knight. He wrenched a crossbow from the soldier, and when he aimed it at me, I was not afraid.

I hoped it was quick.

Close your eyes and think of something nice.

I closed my eyes and thought of home. My old home—of Grayson's laughter and awful cooking. Of my mother, singing brightly through her chores. I did not think of my father.

My father was dead.

Horen stretched the lever back until it clicked.

I was not afraid.

I was not afraid.

When the crossbow clicked again, my traitorous body flinched. But what I did not expect, was the brutalising agony that struck my left thigh. My whole body lit aflame as my leg ignited.

I screamed.

I was not supposed to scream.

But I'd never imagined pain to be like this.

Never this.

Another bolt skewered my right thigh. My knees gave way as my scream heightened, morphing into shrill wails.

As I knelt there, unsure of whether to touch the bolts crudely protruding from my legs and leaking tendrils of blood, Horen's voice boomed through the throne room. "That is how one bows before their king."

CHAPTER 19
ALONE

I passed out soon after my knees hit the stones. When I woke, the pain was worse. Much worse.

The pulsating ache in my arms suggested I'd been dragged down here. From the look of *this* place, or at least from the infinite darkness, I knew I was underground. A dungeon, I assumed. Whoever tossed me in here had done so roughly onto my back. The bolts still skewered my legs, stiff wooden shafts grinding against my bones with each wheezing breath.

I imagined myself removing them and healing the wounds, but I couldn't move a bloody muscle.

I think I began screaming again. I'd hoped my death in this world would be painless. Easy. I was so, so wrong.

I SHOOK MY LEG, forcing the pain to shatter through my mind. Blackness sucked me under and rocked me with silent arms.

When I woke, I did it again.

Being awake hurt too much to bear.

"MILADY? *MILADY?*"

A soft nudge on my arm and gentle fingers stroking my face coaxed me from another dreamless stupor. The tiny candle in the girl's hand blinded me when I pried my eyes open. Whoever she was, her voice was like silk. I tried to ask her name, but I couldn't force words to form.

"Do not speak, milady."

I raised hazed eyes to find the girl's face, half hidden in shadow. She was young. Very young. Brown-haired and doll-faced with a golden collar around her neck. "My name is Peeta, milady, I am Prince Taryn's. He sent me to tend to you."

I tried, for minutes on end I tried to form words. Eventually, all I could muster was, "Prince?" My voice was broken shards of glass.

"Yes. That is what you call the son of a king."

If I could have, I would have smiled at her.

"Drink this," she murmured, holding a cup full of a blue milky substance. Medicine or poison? Either would do.

When Peeta brought the cup to my lips, lifting the back of my head, I did not hesitate to swallow as she tipped the contents down my throat. The milk stuck against my insides like glue, cascading through my hollow chest and stomach.

Sleep stole me.

WHEN I WOKE AGAIN, the bolts had been removed and bandages were secured around both legs. Peeta was in the midst of cleaning my feet and I noticed with no small amount of gratitude, that she'd cleaned every inch of me, as well as the floor where I lay. The milky glue in my throat lingered, sealing what had been torn. While my words still felt like grinding sandpaper, I rasped out my thanks.

The pain in my thighs was tolerable now, though the smallest of movements sent the room spinning. Or, what I could see of it in the dull candlelight. I was indeed in a dungeon, and the movies had just about gotten it right. Straw littered the filthy, damp floor, and the mouldy stone walls surrounding me were only a metre or so in height. I could reach a hand up and touch the ceiling with my arm stretched wide, figuratively speaking.

Peeta hunched over me as she worked, this cell had obviously not been made with two people in mind. When the girl heard my voice, she lifted her petite face and smiled. My mouth dropped open, as I saw her right eye was missing. All that was left was a large puffy pink scar.

"What happened?" I croaked, pointing towards her face. It took all my damned strength just to do that.

She understood and her smile turned sad. "When one offends their master, they take an eye for insolence."

I squirmed and shuddered at the images racing through my mind. Of this girl, younger than she was, being mutilated in such a way. I didn't ask more questions, my empty stomach roiled, pulsating waves of nausea shoving up my throat.

Peeta worked in silence until she gathered her supplies and made towards the rusted gate. She stopped short and twisted to look at me with steel in her eyes. A familiar steel I knew all too well. She pulled out more bottles of that blue milk hidden under her robes and placed them beside my face, four in total.

"You should have let me bleed to death," I wheezed.

Through the dim candlelight, I could just make out Peeta's grim face. "I am sorry, milady, you are the king's property now. You do not have his permission to die yet."

THE DAYS BECAME PERPETUAL, or rather, my life became so.

I didn't bother trying to track the times Peeta brought me food.

I tried to be strong. I tried to starve myself. But Peeta stopped talking to me, through no fault of her own. She wore a leather muzzle each time I saw her, like a damned dog. So food was the only thing that brought me pleasure. I discovered the milk she'd left me was akin to morphine, usually one sip was enough to drown the pain in my legs and the ever-nagging ache in my muscles from lethargy.

Peeta always brought a new bottle whenever she changed the bindings around my legs, and sneaked another under my shoulder when a guard came to escort her away.

But I learnt to savour the pain.

Without it, I'd think of Tor and the way his bronze eyes had guttered. How he had crashed so heavily down to the grass in the clearing. The sound of the spear being plunged through his neck.

Or I'd think of Rose, riding away on Finn into a dark camp of Meriden soldiers. Or Kiita, falling from a dying mule.

My healing light flared occasionally at my fingertips, but I didn't use it. I didn't want to be healed. Within this cell, I could not feel Achilles. The bond between me and my dyr—I hadn't felt it since being carted into the streets of Ashbourne, and I didn't dare to dwell on what that meant.

He is not dead, I told myself time and time again, a prayer uttered before every drug induced sleep whisked me away.

"He is not dead," I said to the ceiling.

It did not reply.

It never did.

CHAPTER 20
FOR THE BLEEDING HEART

T he welt on my arm leaked a drop of blood as I pinched it between two fingernails. "Again," I chided myself.

I'd taken to skip counting up to one thousand and back down again. If I made an error, I'd lose a point, pinch my arm, and start over. If I made it the whole way, well, I won a point. Sometimes I wasn't a good sport and would try to cheat—until I remembered I was literally playing myself.

The gut-wrenching sound of a rusted gate opening pulled me from my game, and I squinted at the bright candlelight, ready to greet Peeta, looking forward to talking to her muzzled face with only varied expressions in her eye as answer. But it was not Peeta that held the candle.

It was King Horen.

Squirming, I bunched against the far wall of the cell. Realising as pain barked through my muscles, that it was the first time I'd really moved for however long I'd been in here.

Horen leered at my bandaged legs and smirked.

He turned and nodded once. One of his guards reached through the open gate and grasped my ankle, metal fingers digging deep into my flesh. I writhed and yelped, unleashing a snarl as the bastard tugged me out of the cell all too easily, feverish exhaustion had me slinking to the ground in defeat.

"Get her cleaned up," Horen spat. "We auction at dusk."

Auction.

They were going to auction me? Sell me like a...like a slave.

You are the king's property now.

Peeta's words burned into my mind like a brand. Joke's on them. I'd find the quickest way to a painless death the moment they let go of me. But—joke's on me. They did not let go.

The guard carried me from the dungeons, up an interminable stairwell, and threw me into a foggy room smelling of soap and oil. Condensation liquified against my skin, pooling sweat at my nape. Two collared women padded towards me as another snarl rose from my throat. I squirmed as they neared, harder when they tried to remove my clothes. The guard, still with his vice-like grip on my arm, struck me across the side of the head and the room spun, crumbling into nothing.

I CAME TO, throbbing and groggy, my body naked and being scrubbed raw. The guard holding my arm stared at my exposed chest, a leer in his eyes. So I twisted and bit his ear.

With a jolted grunt of pain, his closed fist punched me low in the stomach.

Bent double over my knees, my gaze travelled to the twin wounds on my thighs—they were no more than ugly coin-sized scabs now, with new, thinner scars cobwebbing out from the edges. Probably from Peeta carving out the bolt heads.

How long was I in that dungeon?

Large hands tangled in my hair, wrenching me upright, and moved to my biceps, locking my arms in place behind my back. Finally I stilled, squeezing my eyes shut in an effort to ignore the slaves bathing me.

I was dressed like a prized pig in an almost transparent white dress, my hair combed into heavy waves that tickled my skin through the thin fabric at my hips. I barely registered the rooms they led me through, keeping my gaze downcast. But when a flicker of golden light caught the corner of my eye, I gave my attention to the brightness of large golden doors.

The throne room.

Horen.

Another heavy-footed guard bound his hand around my elbow and I was taken to the centre of the cavernous room, towards the dais— and towards the twat sitting on the throne. The muttering crowd parted to let me pass.

An echoing voice resounded on the stones beneath my feet. "Bow, girl."

I glowered at the king, idly stroking a crossbow in his lap. A rogue tear falling, I bent my knees and knelt on the cold floor, bowing my head towards the throne.

"Better. Easier to tame than a filly."

My cheeks burned. I wanted to stand. Gods, how I wanted to stand and spit in his face, but the guards had their hands on my shoulders, pushing down with such force even breathing hurt.

"Surely the girl is worth at least ten thousand silvers. An apostate healer, and a queer sort of beauty at that! Lord Ulfwren, could she perhaps cure the hideous boil that ails your fine face?"

Laughter followed the jest, tense and almost feigned from the crowd, but it was there. My blood simmered, but I glanced to where the laughter was directed—to where a short, portly, and balding man smiled a thin smile. He did indeed have a boil the size of a golf ball protruding from his nose, but I looked past that to the fleck of kindness behind the shame in his eyes.

Something tight in my chest—something old and foreign—panged for Lord Ulfwren. For another prisoner trapped in this hell hole. A prisoner in fancy clothes and no fucking chains. He could leave.

I screwed up my nose. Lord Ulfwren was weak.

The death of the laughter in the room didn't register until a fist struck my lower spine, sending forth a new rush of pain. A tall obsidian knight appeared behind me and roughly gripped the back of my neck in his metal-plated hand. The three bastards lifted me from my knees and held me to the spot.

It took all of my will to stop and think on what Horen had said.

A healer.

So, he did know. If the king of Kiliac knew about my magic, why was I not dead already? A sickening chill that had nothing to do with the metal hand at my nape or my thin dress licked down my front.

I should be dead.

"Twenty thousand silvers!" spat a gruff voice to my right, adding another tongue of discomfort.

I should be dead.

I dropped my eyes to the floor. I had no power here. None at all. And that, perhaps, was as near to death as I could be.

"Thirty thousand!" another voice to my left sounded.

I should be dead.

"Fifty thousand silvers!"

"Eighty thousand!"

Horen laughed harder at each new price thrown at him. If my sense of value in Kiliac was anything to go by, I was making Horen very rich.

At least I was worth a lot.

"One hundred golden ingots." a loud, yet steady voice rang from the dais.

Silence seized the room. Indignity pressed down on me, hard as the weight of water on an ocean floor, but I raised my gaze to find the bearer of that steadfast voice.

A month ago, or however bloody long I was trapped in that hole in the ground, I had seen him and dismissed him as a bodyguard of Horen's. The frame of his bronze-skinned body fit the description. He carried the tell-tale features of a warrior, a sizeable scar running from above his right brow down to his jaw, broken in two by the skin around his eye. But he could not be a simple bodyguard, nor even a soldier—not for one hundred damned ingots of gold.

Horen's voice cut through my thoughts. "Surely, my son, you can spend that much gold elsewhere."

Son.

Horen's son.

This was Prince Taryn. The one who'd sent Peeta.

A loose lock of black hair fell over his shoulder to his abdomen. For a fragmented moment, the prince flicked his gaze to me. A forced smile fixed to his face as he turned back to his father. "My King, where else would I find a lass as striking to look upon as this? Besides, as the general of your armies, sire, having a magi healer at my disposal would be favourable to your cause, would it not?"

Horen leaned over his legs, resting his head upon a fist. The air in the room strung taut and the lords held their breath as they waited for the king's response. Taryn appeared stoic, but the small fleck in his jaw gave him away.

With the slightest tilt of his mouth, Horen sat upright and waved his hand towards me. "Indeed. So be it, unless there is another offer." He eyed the silent room, challenging anyone to outbid his son. "She is yours. I expect the ingots by sunset. You know my condition of sale, you will receive her in the morning."

Tendrils of ice coiled in my gut at Horen's last words, but a roar resounded in my ears—I had just been sold. Sold. The moment the word solidified and echoed through my head and heart like a bell toll, a cold metal collar snapped around my neck. My skin burned and froze all at once at the new tightness as another tear fell, unbidden, down my cheek.

At my throat was a metal ring I'd seen often enough at Peeta's. One of the guards unravelled a chain, hooking it into my clasp. I did not fight it—did not fight when they led me to the back of the room, to the left of the dais. At the far wall, shambling along as I was, a collarless, beautiful woman with black braids approached, a leather muzzle in her hands. Two more tears fell as she fastened the muzzle around my face. I only just caught a word from her lips, a mere whisper, as I smelled spearmint in her breath. "Bar."

I didn't know what she meant, so I dropped my gaze.

When the woman stepped away, stealing with her the sweet-smelling air, my chain was fastened to a hook in the wall. I looked up, flinching when I caught sight of my reflection in the mirror-like stone, glowing from the warm light of the torches.

I stared at myself.

Alone, silenced, and chained.

I played the counting game. The rule now, each time the fire flickered, I had to start again. I clung to my game, wrapped it around me in a shield against reality. I could not break. I wouldn't give these bastards the satisfaction of watching me crumble.

I STOOD, muzzled and collared, shaking in the king's chamber.

Large windows stood open to allow in the cool sea breeze. The wind caressed my skin, but it didn't ease the tremors raking me from the inside out.

Horen sat, nonchalant, at the edge of a colossal bed surrounded by four black-stone pillars, a wine goblet in hand. If it wasn't for the three guards holding me still, the leer on Horen's face would have sent me leaping through those open windows.

I released a strangled whimper when the king stood and sauntered forward. He reached for my face and I winced as strands of my hair were ripped away with his unclasping my muzzle to tug it off. I moved, quick as a whip, and just barely tasted his skin as I took his fingers between my teeth. But he was quicker. I snapped down on my own tongue and grimaced on the taste of blood. Horen smirked, thrusting his goblet towards me.

Scowling at the swirling wine, I bared my teeth.

He shrugged, drained his drink in one breath, and threw his goblet against the stones, smashing it into tiny fragments. A collared boy ran into the room to gather up the broken pieces, and bile rose in my throat at what I remembered of Horen's preferred lovers.

His voice speared through my thoughts. "You are going to heal me, girl."

My breath snared, cold dark humour washing through me. I'd been trying to prepare myself during the hours I'd stood in that throne room for what was to come tonight, but I hadn't expected this. Horen caught the change in my face and his smirk lifted. "I have a lump on my hip. I do not know what it is, but it is inhibiting my ability to move freely and without pain."

I lifted my chin and grinned. "You think I'm going to save your pathetic life? Think again, weasel shit. I wouldn't touch you with a ten-foot pole."

Horen's answering smile was terrifying. He crossed his arms. "Oh, I expected no less, magi, but I do so take pleasure in your resentment. Weasel shit, was it? I enjoy that one. Perhaps you will scream it at me in my dreams." His eyes squeezed shut and he rolled his shoulders back in emphasis as I scowled. "Unfortunately, defying me is not so easily done. Especially by a ruddy woman. None have tried. Well, they have tried, but not very successfully." He finished with a wink.

I shook my head. "You think you—"

My retort was stifled by his hand darting over my mouth. He pinched my nose between his fingers, blocking my airways, holding firm as my lungs lurched and my back arched. Then as suddenly as he cut me off, he stole his hand away. "I know what you are going to say," he sniped. "Something about me thinking I will never lose, but one day I will, and *mark your words*, you will find a way to kill me, even if it kills you." He nodded thoughtfully. "But my darling, I just keep winning."

The door behind me creaked open, but I couldn't tear my eyes from the king. His words whispered against my cheek. "And one day, I will smile as you are ripped apart, piece by piece." His lips brushed my ear, his knuckles grazed my neck. "But until then, I will show you, I always get my way."

He breezed past. I didn't move—until a familiar, shuddering voice cut so deep tears burst free. Spinning on my heel, I heaved. Horen ripped away Kiita's shirt.

Held by the hair, angry tears marred her face. A muzzle muffled her scream of rage.

"You bloody bastard! Let her go!"

Horen froze, a mocking smile alighting his features, eyes igniting and widening with pleasure. "If you say so, girl, I am a gentleman, after all. I will even remove that collar of yours to make you more comfortable." He flicked his wrist at a soldier who lurched forward to unclasp the metal around my neck. A surge of lightness soared in my core, but I remained where I was, staring at Horen.

The joy in Horen's voice jolted through me. "But these men! They are straight from the ruddy depths of Galdurne and deserve a reward for their brave service under the king's command, no?"

Kiita closed her eyes, trying and failing to writhe out of the soldier's grasp.

I was slower, dumber, as I continued to stare.

Horen smiled. "Surely, magi, you would not deny them such pleasure?"

The soldier holding Kiita laughed and leant forward to inhale the scent of her hair. Two guards snapped their hands around my biceps.

Hopelessness. It was what Kiita feared most.

The king had won. "I'll do anything," I whispered. "Anything you want. I'll heal you—I'll heal your whole damned army."

The king pursed his lips and frowned. "Ahh, but see child, you insulted me. Called me names." He swung his arms out wide. "Consider my feelings hurt."

The monstrous crack of bone echoed off the very stones I stood upon, but I didn't realise where it had come from—not until I saw Kiita, staring down at her limp left arm. When her amethyst eyes rose to meet mine, and the soldier seized her other arm as the hold on my own tightened past the point of bruising, I matched her ear-splitting shrieks of horror and pain.

The second break was worse. Louder.

I fought so hard to get to her.

Watching as Kiita's bones were broken was an agony I never could have imagined in my darkest dreams. I forgot why we were here, who ordered this, until a shadow loomed over my friend.

The soldiers backed away, letting Kiita fall to her knees, broken arms dangling at her sides.

Horen took Kiita's face between his hands, tugged it up to face him, and unclasped the muzzle. "I hope you know this is your friend's fault. She did this to you. And this next part is because she was careless enough to not realise insolence has consequences."

Kiita's mouth closed as silent tears fell. I screamed at her, begged her to look at me. My harried pleas turned to guttural cries when the king brandished a knife at his side.

His thumb traced a line over Kiita's scar and I gulped back my scream to hear what he'd say.

"Beautiful."

I don't know when I screamed again, nor when Kiita finally broke from the steely strength she fought so hard to retain. It might have been the first stroke, when Horen's blade sliced through her cheek's soft skin, or when the arc of his blade threw a scarlet curtain down her jaw and neck. At some point, Kiita's consciousness fell away, but I did not stop watching as Horen cut open her face. A scar not to mirror, but to rival the one she'd already bore.

Darkness consumed the air when Horen turned to look at me with a carefree smile, bloody knife held loosely at his side. "Am I done here?"

I nodded through a daze as I stared at Kiita, lying in a mess of blood and shattered bone. My tongue was thick, my mouth full with bile, but I forced the words out.

"If I heal you, you will let me heal her." It wasn't a question.

"Of course, my dear. I will even promise," the king replied, bowing.

I nodded again. Horen grinned as he unstrung his pants and dropped them, striding towards his bed, tossing the knife to the ground as he walked. A guard shoved me forward and I lost my footing, still fixated on Kiita's unconscious body. My knees stung with the impact of the stones, but I scrambled up and rushed towards Horen, sending out my golden power to find his fucking tumour. My power battled, squirming back into my own skin as I worked on Horen's hip, but I pushed through it, pushed with all of my pathetic strength to heal the king. I erased the tumour, along with any other aches and pains he carried. I did not dare leave anything untouched.

When his body was healed, I stumbled back, my light whipping back into my fingertips, and lurched for Kiita. A harsh tug on my hair sent me sprawling backwards onto my spine. I squinted up through blinding lights to see Horen standing above me—my collar in his grasp as he bent to reclasp it.

I couldn't speak or breathe through the shock to my lungs, so I just pointed toward my friend on the floor. She lay so close the blood pooling around her warmed my toes. Horen bent low and smiled, teeth white, skin glowing in perfect health. "I promise you, girl, you will obey." His smirk was what I imagined evil to be...to look like. My blood whirled. "I am a king. Do not ever ask me for anything again."

Horen stood, turning his attention to the soldiers. "Clean up this mess. Throw it back into that sorry excuse of a village. Burn it down before you leave."

I had nothing left to give. No tears. No cries of pain or terror.

Close your eyes and think of something nice.

I closed them, but no matter how hard I tried, there was nothing nice left to think about.

CHAPTER 21
WAY DOWN WE GO

"Watch what you are doing, woman!"

A sharp slap to the back of my neck rocked my head forward, the jug of wine nearly slipping from between my hands. I'd come too close to a lord, insulting him with my nearness. Chin pressed to my chest, I backed away from the table on silent feet, lest I insult all the lords and ladies with the noise I made, though I indulged a few silent words.

A month.

I'd served in this godforsaken castle for a month.

Tonight, I poured plum scented wine from a bejewelled jug for a table full of haughty lords and beautiful, conniving ladies. I had not heard a whisper of Salem, nor the welfare of its people. Apparently, it was not important enough to hold any kind of recognition in Ashbourne. Kiita—she could very well be dead. I wouldn't know. I'd made a brittle sort of peace with it weeks ago. It was the only way to stop the memories eating away at my soul bit by bit. The idea of her dead and at rest was better than the image of her in unrelenting pain in the ashes of the village we'd loved and remade.

In the month since Prince Taryn bought me, I hadn't seen him. Through gossip and whispers I'd pieced together that he had gone to

Okarc—Kiliac's official slave-labour camp. Or, as anyone without a collar called it, Kiliac's pride and joy, the settlement nestled above a veritable sea of gold ore.

I had always thought gold was my colour. Lately, it served as a sordid reminder of the collar clasped around my neck.

As Kiliac's militant general, Prince Taryn oversaw the small nation's powerful army, including the slaves mining for the wealth of said army. And as a result of my owner's absence, I was left to the mercy of the king and his court of bitches and bastards. Beatings and lashings were my new normal, though by whatever small mercy, fists and whips were the extent of my punishment. Apart from that, no man, or woman for that matter, touched me.

Including Horen.

I hadn't spoken a word to the king, nor he to me, apart from nonchalant commands to pour wine, since that night in his chambers.

Peeta had taken me under her wing—we talked in hand gestures by firelight. She was six years younger than I. I think. Thirteen, she signed. I gestured back that I was nineteen, but I wasn't sure if my birthday had passed.

I didn't even know how old I was.

Peeta taught me, or at least tried to, everything she knew about being a royal slave. Which essentially boiled down to: do whatever the hell you were told. Right now, I was to serve wine into raised goblets and look pretty. I and four other girls, not including Peeta, thankfully, were dressed in ridiculous scanty dresses with shimmering black fabric barely covering the bits and pieces, leaving nothing to the imagination.

Hail be to the patriarchy.

A slim, satirical smile stretched across my face. *Praise be.*

My hair was elaborately braided into sections twisted together, falling like a heavy rope to the small of my back. Dark kohl smudged around my eyes and my lips were painted a deep ochre. The girl I was before—she would have been mortified.

Tor would have been mortified.

Emptiness hollowed out my insides, threatening to devour me. I took a heavy breath, releasing a small, audacious sigh. *Please hit me. Whip me. Make it go away.*

A scowl ruptured my face. No one at the table heard.

Clicking my tongue, I waited for pain to come from any side, but all that came was the resentful glares of the other slave girls. Of course, any of them could be punished on my behalf. It wouldn't be the first time. But sometimes the pain was enough to blur out the rest.

I was pathetic.

After all my talk a month prior, I still clung to a feeble intrinsic desire for survival. Not that my existence was one worth clinging to— I hadn't even attempted escape. Though to be fair, I was escorted by a guard or two wherever I went.

I was worth one hundred gold ingots after all.

"More wine, lass!" The order came from a particularly nasty looking lady, holding her glass high above her head without a glance towards me. I stepped forward, keeping an appropriate distance, and filled her glass. Imagining tipping the liquor over her head, my smile reformed.

When her glass was full, I stepped back, almost tripping over my own feet when the door to my right flew open with a crash.

As soon as he breezed across the threshold, every lord rose from their seats.

Even the king.

Prince Taryn prowled straight by me, taking his place at the opposite end to his father—closest to me of them all. The prince raised his silver goblet in my direction without a word or glance. I lurched forward, almost knocking the cup from his hand.

Whilst no one else witnessed my error as they made their way back into their seats, I watched the corner of the prince's mouth lift.

"My son!" Horen beamed. "You are back earlier than anticipated. I take that as a sign all is in order?" The king stood, waited for his son's nod of confirmation before continuing, turning to his nobles. "Three hundred new workers will have all of your coffers overflowing with gold in no time! A celebration seems appropriate, no? To thank Taryn for his work."

The lords and ladies cheered, saluting their prince and general. The clatter dissipated with the raise of Taryn's hand. "Please, father, this munificent dinner," he gestured towards the ostentatious greased and honeyed food on the colossal table, "Is all I require."

Horen, half-cut, slammed his hand on the table. "Nonsense, you stoic oaf." He clicked his fingers at an older slave. "Go! Inform the kitchens to ready the wine and ale for dusk tomorrow, then scurry to the brothel and send for the whores."

The lords raised their goblets with another bawdy cheer, their wives pretending to be shocked yet delighted behind their hands. Like I said...hail be to the idiot who put these men in charge.

"You honour me, father," the prince proclaimed, raising his goblet in salute. "To the Maker—God of fine fucks and good ale!" His steadfast voice fuelled the tomfoolery, liquor flew, the men cheered louder still.

Through all the raucous jeering and dick-measuring along the table, no one noticed the prince release an exasperated sigh and slump into his chair. As if he too, thought this was some kind of elaborate, horrible dream.

Screw him.

I was the daughter of dreams and dread.

THE COURT'S celebration for their prince was an alcohol and smoke induced maelstrom of debauchery and indecency.

No matter where I turned, the view was not pleasant. In all corners of the throne-room-turned-brothel, young men and women serviced the older and uglier lords of the court. The ladies, of course, dispersed respectfully after the feast. My stomach roiled each time one of the pleasure workers were snatched up and pulled onto a lap—they were dressed only in delicate, intricate chains that clattered whenever they moved, and in the middle of their brow, each bore a small tattoo of an upturned heart.

The palace girls and I were on call for fill-ups, but all the alcohol had been consumed about two hours ago and we were left to stand against the walls like limp fish. My eyes found Horen, a young man and woman perched on his lap—both near naked in those rattling chains. He traced his fingertips up the woman's arm, while he spoke into the ear of the man.

I hated him. I hated this fucking place. But worst of all, I hated that I had not been touched like that in so long. I was a damned idiot for wanting it, but what I missed most in life was affection. Connection.

Though I'd live a life without being touched if that meant I could have Tor back.

"It is revolting, is it not?" Prince Taryn appeared seemingly out of thin air like a yau, his eyes fixed on the king and his whores. Not confident I was supposed to respond, I glanced around to ensure there was no one else he was speaking to.

I took a shuddering breath. This man owned me, so I supposed I should answer him. Whether he wanted truth or approval was unclear, so I went for both and spoke beneath my breath, lest I wasn't actually meant to talk back. "Indeed."

The prince's gaze flicked to mine and travelled to the collar around my neck. His eyes were vibrant burnished-orange, lingering on the skin around my collarbone. Some glimmer, some shadow of indignance flared at that damned stare. Without lifting his gaze, he leaned in to speak softly. "I am Taryn, prince in this court of reprobates and barbarians. What is your name? I do not think anyone here has bothered to ask, for no one knows."

Bastard. Prick. Self-entitled ass.

Before I could stop it, before realising that not only was he was being somewhat kind, but that I could land in a whirlwind of shit for back chatting, I scoffed at him. "G'day Taryn, prince of reprobates, barbarians and mangy, wanton, degenerates. I am your damned property. You may call me Estelle, if it pleases," I said with quiet venom and a mocking curtsy. "Though, girl will do just fine. Maybe wench? Whatever your royal ass decides, I don't give a shit."

If silence had a sound, it would be blaring right now.

My ear drums pounded in time with each thunderous beat of my heart. The awkward shuffle of my guard's feet on stone made me contain my hate-filled glower. I looked down at the empty jug I held between my thighs.

The prince.

I was dead. I was really, truly dead.

Finally.

With a warm exhale of breath beside my ear, Taryn laughed. Not in a sinister, nor malicious way, but a true laugh. A real laugh.

Despite myself, I chuckled too.

And it felt, good.

He rubbed his eyes and looked at me with an almost innocent, boyish humour. "I think I will use Estelle, if it pleases?"

"It does." I shook my head. "Please me, I mean." I wiped at my mouth, as if it might erase the sudden and strange spark of joy.

"I am glad to see your spirit has not been broken in my absence."

Oh. He couldn't be more wrong. But it was not what had happened in his absence that had broken me. It was piercing screams and the smell of scarlet blood.

To extinguish my thoughts, I opened my mouth, to ask about his prolonged time away—but realised it was no matter to me. Nor my place to ask, so I snapped my mouth shut and held my tongue. After waiting politely and expectantly for a response, Prince Taryn simply shrugged and changed the topic. "Have you been touched in the month you have been here?"

I frowned as another rebuke escaped quicker than I could think on it. "Can you not see the bruises?"

My response seemed to invite his gaze to travel over my bare skin, over the scanty dress I wore, revealing the entirety of my sides, legs, cleavage and navel. His attention caught on each blemish and graze, and he scowled, as if he had indeed just only noticed them.

"Aye, lass, I can. But I was meaning the other way. Touched, against your will."

"Are you asking if I've been assaulted?"

"Yes," he said, his gaze intense and unyielding. "That is what I am asking."

I blinked once, twice. Was he intentionally trying to unnerve me? Shame me? Parading around this castle near naked, any sense of propriety had all but winked out. All but, apparently.

Perhaps this prince of reprobates and barbarians did in fact, care.

When I didn't answer, he shook his head. "I made it a crime punishable by death for any man to violate another man's slave without his direct permission the night I bought you. My father included." Taryn gestured again towards Horen. "He did not care, he had just received one hundred golden ingots," he added with a hesitant smile.

So that was it. No small mercies for me. It was the prince's written law. Whilst I would be eternally grateful to him, that rising fragment of my old stubborn sense of self flared. "Do you expect me to thank you?"

He grimaced. "No, but I do expect you to realise that things could have been much worse, if it was not I who purchased you that night."

The flare became an inferno. "Screw you."

The metallic shuffle of feet behind me was louder now, closer.

But my words—my anger—only seemed to amuse the prince. His eyes burned like smouldering coal as he grinned, the expression making him look younger. My breath caught as I studied him closer than before, black stubble coated his jaw, and a brutal caramel scar parted his eyebrow, widening as it crept near his temple. He was attractive, in a hardened kind of way. And it felt nice, really nice, to appreciate something as vain as the prince's looks after such a long time of nothing. Of emptiness. Even being cranky and irritable towards him felt good.

My face smoothed at my realisation and I found myself smiling. Taryn's grin stretched wider as he cocked his head to the side. "Would you like a drink, Estelle?" His question was so gentle, warm, and earnest, my pulse skipped a beat. The heat of his breath lingered on my skin, and honestly, I think he was as shocked as I was when my head nodded of its own accord.

~

AS IT TURNED OUT, Taryn was easy to speak to. Too easy, in fact.

Though after so long without a decent conversation, a brick wall would be easy to speak to. I guess I was desperate for anything. The son of the one person I hated most in the world—worlds—he was all I had.

He sent a small team of servants to Ashbourne's brothels to retrieve more caskets of wine and slipped them a few coins to keep them concealed from the rest of the party. Everyone else was too drunk to notice anyhow. The wine tasted like honey-coated menthol as it slipped down my throat, but then, I was not drinking it for the taste.

Tucked away together on a lavishly decorated ruby couch in a corner of the room, screened off by vibrant-coloured tapestries and potted date palms, Taryn created a game of imagining terrible outcomes for each and every pompous lord in the room. My personal favourite was a story about old Lord Iyden having a heart attack as he tried to get it up tonight. These games, this childish giggling in a dark corner, had me forgetting how I came to be here in the first place. I found happiness where it wasn't supposed to be, however fleeting.

With each new drink silently slipped to us, the room became more fun to be a part of. Especially as the edges of my vision blurred and the wine began to taste decent. It was what I could be doing if it were not for fate deciding to dump me on my sorry ass in this world. I found myself imagining what my life would have been like, had I remained in my old one. Safe and ordinary.

Schoolies would have been fun, at least.

My speculation was short-lived, interrupted by a warm hand placed on my bare knee. I dragged a heavy stare from the dregs of my wine to his hand, then up to the prince sprawled on the couch beside me.

"You are doing it again," he murmured. "Going someplace else."

I tried to smile, it had been so easy until now. Now, each movement was like slugging through mud. "Wouldn't you?"

The prince considered me, watching my eyes as they wavered. He pursed his lips and looked at the ceiling, as if he could see the clouds and stars through it. "Yes," he finally said, still looking upwards. "Yes, I would."

I pushed through my roiling emotions and raised my goblet to drink away the burning. My head spun with the movement, but cleared with the tender brush of Taryn's thumb atop my knee. I studied his hand, his fingers—bronze against ivory tracing soft idle circles over my skin.

Sparks flew at the touch, electricity shooting to my core. I jolted and knocked the goblet from his grasp, spilling blood-red liquor all over his white tunic. "Bloody hell...I'm so sorry."

A soft chuckle in response. "Ah, not to worry, I will fetch another."

He made to push up from the couch but I beat him to it, shooting upwards. I almost fell straight back on my ass as the room spun. "I'll get it for you."

Taryn huffed another snicker. "Do you even know where my chambers are?"

I stood there like a stunned mullet. After all this time working in this damned castle, I'd either never noticed what room I was in, or been to his chamber. "No. But I'll find it."

He grinned from ear to ear and stretched out a hand. "Come on, I will show you where they are."

I was drunk, but I wasn't stupid. I knew where this went.

And perhaps it was the wine, or my own pent up loneliness, but I nodded and took his hand.

We walked out of the throne room together, leaving behind my guard with a casual wave from the prince. Once we'd crossed the threshold of those damned golden doors, Taryn pulled me into the wall. Everything stilled, the air around me and inside my lungs, until he lifted his hands to my collar, brandishing a key I never saw him retrieve.

He took my head in his warm palm and tilted it to the side,

exposing my neck. The key slid into the small lock at my throat and clicked, that golden collar clattered to the ground, and the Prince of Kiliac smiled broadly as he held my hand to lead me down the hall.

My collar was left on the stone-cold floor.

THE PRINCE'S chambers were enormous. We passed through a well-lit foyer sporting a marble table, bedecked in an assortment of coloured roses. Ahead was a sitting area with elegant white leather couches and a golden fireplace, windows adorned the black stone on either side of it. Taryn pulling me gently by the hand, I glimpsed an ostentatious bathing room containing an obscenely large tub.

He led me into his bedroom. An ornate bed dominated the centre, dressed in red and gold, and the entirety of the eastern wall was glass, allowing a view straight out over the ocean lit up by a starry sky. Opposite was an open door that, at a glance, looked to accommodate a study and small library. The rest of the stone wall held an assortment of dressers and locked chests.

Remembering my part in this farce, I released the prince's hand and hurried to the largest dresser. Tugging open the first drawer, I scowled when I came across furs and black leather. The next drawer held only a variety of boots, so I flung a curse at it. I rifled through at least ten drawers amidst Taryn's hearty laughter, before finding one full of finely folded tunics. I pulled the topmost one out and threw it at him over my shoulder, somehow forgetting, as I had done all night, that we were master and slave.

When I turned, my breath caught in my throat. He was in the midst of tugging his wine-soaked tunic over his head, revealing a perfect mass of sculpted muscle.

A feeble part of me swooned at the sight. No one, no real person, looked like that. With each miniscule movement, the muscles in his arms and shoulders shifted and rolled. Sweat beaded in the small of my back, and I forced my gaze to rip away from his bare torso to his face.

I released a shuddering breath when I found him considering my own body with the same blistering intensity.

With the rising heat, sickening guilt overwhelmed me. It had been some time since I last saw him, but I was still in love with another man. He'd left me, but I still felt so much for him. Perhaps soon I would be able to touch another, think of another. But not now. Not yet. I bowed my head and made to walk towards the door, but the prince took a step and easily blocked my path, still bare chested.

"I should go," I whispered.

Taryn moved forward another step, close enough that his body heat surrounded me. I lifted my face to survey his broad chest at eye-level —he was so tall, and so extraordinarily intimidating. Another half step, and his arm encased my waist.

"I—" My words broke away.

His hand reached for my chin and a finger lifted it towards his face.

A moan escaped me in a rush. At the hunger I found in his gaze, my limbs and lips began to quiver. It was all he needed.

In a dizzying blur, sweltering lips crashed into mine.

CHAPTER 22
SEVEN DEVILS

I broke off the kiss, stumbling blindly into the dresser.

A sharp pain met my shoulder blades at the impact, my attention solely on the prince. His arms caged me in, clutching the edge of the dresser at my sides.

"Taryn, please."

"Please, what?" he murmured, craning his neck to graze his lips over my jaw. Damn me to hell, I exposed my neck. "Tell me to stop, Estelle."

Kisses traced over my throat, my collarbone, as he released the dresser to brush a calloused hand against my exposed waist. Every inch of skin he touched sent raging fire burning through me. His other hand fingered the clasp on my shoulder holding my dress in place.

"Tell me to stop."

No words spilled from my lips, my body slackening under his touch. He released a soft groan and unpinned the clasp, leaning back to watch the thin fabric fall. I shuddered, my bare breasts meeting the heat radiating off him as Taryn leaned forward, resuming his teasing. Bending his knees, the prince dropped his head to take my breast in his mouth. A rush of blood flooded from the touch of his lips, the flick of his tongue hypnotising, sending my heartbeat thundering in time to the spin of the room. Freezing and burning and undoing me completely. But...*but.*

"Taryn," I started, but the word was a hoarse murmur of his name. Not stopping him. Igniting him.

Lurching upright, he ripped the rest of my dress away, leaving me wholly naked before him. His hands moved to my backside and yanked my legs up to wrap around him, his touch and presence more than I could comprehend, he was everywhere, he consumed me. He carried me slowly, so damned slowly to the nearest stretch of bare wall, his breath against my neck as he pinned me against it.

The jolt of my back against the wall stiffened my spine. A memory flashed in my mind—the tree. Rose. My legs wrapped around *him.* Taryn was not the man I wanted to lose myself to—it was Rose. It had always been Rose.

I opened my mouth to stop Taryn, *scream* at him, but his mouth covered mine. Taking me for his own, he kissed me deeper, his tongue seeking and tracing. Heat and electricity surged, pulsated. I sighed into his lips and opened myself to him, wrapping my hands around his shoulders tighter.

A hand writhed between my legs, fiddling with his belt.

No...*No. He is not Rose.*

I forced my lips away from his. At my movement Taryn froze. He looked up at me, waiting. Our breath rasped, hard and heavy. His exhale matching mine, he pressed his brow to my forehead. "Tell me to stop," he breathed. And he would. If I told him to, he would stop.

But an inferno blazed in my core. Taryn has set me ablaze and I was tired of being cold. I took his face in my hands and kissed him.

His hand brushed under my thigh, seeking the warmth between my legs. His finger slipped inside me. I yelped at the abruptness and he groaned, finding me wanting. I squeezed my eyes shut as his teeth closed on my shoulder, and I emptied my mind.

Nothing of me was left.

Nothing except fierce and primal desire.

His lips brushed my jaw, nibbling and teasing my skin. I forgot the name of the man I loved. The only name I knew was the name of the man before me.

Feral lust throbbed—every touch was searing. Every inch of me wanted him, and when Taryn added a second finger to my core, I tilted my head back, closed my eyes and moaned.

I did not see it happen. I did not see him enter me.

But it hurt.

And he was not gentle.

Desire shredded away. My lust-driven shudders morphed into cries of pain as he thrust in. He was larger than I ever imagined, tears filled my eyes and flowed down my face. A whimper slipped from my lips. Taryn just kept his gaze locked into mine, unflinching, and thrust deeper, harder, tearing into me inch by inch. I sobbed his name, over and over again, until my voice was caught in another clamorous kiss. He still did not yield. He would have stopped before, but he would not now.

A hand grazed my ribcage before moving to my breast, tracing circles over the peak. His mouth left mine to brush my skin, licking the supple skin beneath my jaw. Another rush went through me and noticing it, or at least my lack of shuddering whimpers, his hands and pelvis moved faster, and my hips moved unbidden in rhythm with his.

I called out his name, squeezed my legs tighter, and in answer, Taryn tipped his head back and roared his release. His body quivered with each new pulse. Wrapping his hair up in my hands, I trembled as I felt every spasm.

Finished, Taryn leant his head against mine, panting, and rested his considerable weight onto me. I pressed myself into the stone wall, trying to use its touch to cool myself. As the fervour faded, while we caught our breaths, I remembered who I was and who I loved.

Rose. His name was Rose.

I'd just lost my virginity to a man I didn't love.

Taryn pushed up from the wall, releasing my legs. They quaked under the pressure of my own weight, but strong and steady arms caught me as I fell. I was lifted and carried to the giant bed, gently set down on my back. I couldn't move—my entire body shivered with pain, guilt, and unfulfilled desire.

The heat of Taryn's body engulfed everything as he clambered over me, his hand resuming its roving on my breasts, and his lips shattered against mine. As he roamed, the guilt and pain faded, and the prince coaxed another maelstrom of heat through my core, the callouses of his hands, the softness of his mouth, grazing lower. I kept my head on the soft pillow and watched him nip the skin inside my thighs. My hands found his head and I entwined my fingers through the silken hair curtaining his face.

Sturdy hands seized my quivering legs and spread them apart. He planted kisses closer to my core. Another memory flickered and captured my soul, but then his mouth seized me and I lost all reason.

Taryn's tongue plunged deep. Higher, like a storm building, pleasure eradicated my mind and being. A tidal wave plummeted and he chuckled from deep within his throat at my rising moans and jerking hips. He held me still, teased and licked until the storm broke and release found me like the thrashing of lightning.

I screamed when a second storm rose and broke, too.

After the third, Taryn lurched up, grasping my hips and flipping me onto my stomach, pulling my backside up. His thrusts now were deeper, harder, the position allowing it, and when his release made him roar, my own thrashed in response.

The groan that slipped free was not at all one of pain as he pulled out and collapsed onto the bed, drawing me into his broad chest. My core still throbbed, still pulsated. I lifted my head and saw my legs stained red with blood.

I felt my heartbeat quicken as the realisation shot through me again, at what I'd just done. Because it was me. It was my fault.

I did not tell him to stop. I wanted him just as much as he wanted me.

Sensing my growing unease, Taryn grasped my face to tug it back to his, kissing me softly, the fervour now gone. "Do not worry yourself, Estelle, most bleed when they lose their maidenhead. I am honoured you gave yours to me." His voice was calm and steadfast, but tender. So at odds with his love making.

The prince kissed me again and I lost myself in the rhythm and taste of his lips, eventually teasing and building that ferocity back up within him, and in myself, with my lips and calculated touches. To lose myself in this, in *him*, was better than facing the damning thoughts in my head. He took me again, not minutes later.

Then again.

All through the night Taryn had me, in new and sometimes painful ways, but I welcomed it and screamed his name through it all.

His name. No one else's.

I withered away a little more inside each time.

CHAPTER 23

TO THE SEA

Through the vast glass wall, I had an unparalleled view of the sun rising over the ocean. Orange hues of growing light ignited the horizon with mighty streaks of crimson and kissed the clouds with cerise. The glow washed over the water, glistening like polished pearl. It was so serene. So beautiful.

I wished Rose were here to see it.

Not the man currently sleeping behind me, a heavy arm draped over my waist, the weight of it crushing my pathetically thin body.

Staring at the purity of the sunrise, I relived the previous night and allowed silent tears to fall. Not for the first time since Taryn drifted off. What we'd done, *what I'd done*, repeatedly—being drunk on alcohol and affection was no excuse. Especially as the man that lay beside me was the son of the only person I had ever hated in my life. And I did hate Horen, with everything I am.

But his son? I did not hate him. And of it all, that was quite possibly the worst part.

I stared and stared as the sun rose higher and Taryn's deep breaths grew lighter, until the shifting of his arm told me he was indeed awake.

Something happened to me last night, some lick of a flame of passion and rage. Those feelings were far away now, as far away as the rising sun. The drunken girl laughing and making love to a prince had vanished. The timid, obedient slave they made me become was all that remained when Taryn spoke, his voice groggy with sleep. "How did you sleep, pet?"

Pet.

Once upon a time, I may have roared at that. Perhaps last night, I would have. "Fine. Thank you, my Prince."

Lifting his lips to my neck, a low rumble sounded from his throat, warm breath spread over my skin, flushing memories through me. I didn't react, didn't curl into him as I'd done the night before, so he pushed up, rocking me onto my back to look into my face. "Your Prince? Not your royal arse?" he challenged, boyish charm accentuated by his sleepy demeanour.

My lips twitched. He lifted a hand to cup my cheek, wiping an old tear away with his thumb. "Are you hurting, lass?"

I shook my head and forced a sweet smile to my face, my features smooth.

Liar.

He studied me for a moment more before a relaxed grin spread across his lips. He dipped his head low, mingling our breaths together to press tender lips against mine. I moved to his rhythm, his pace already natural and familiar.

When glints of turquoise and easy laughter flashed through my mind, I pulled Taryn's mouth closer, deeper. He responded, wrapping me up in strong arms.

Despite it all—the shame and sorrow in my withered heart—my body yearned for his again, so I ground my hips and spread my legs.

Liar.

Liar.

Liar.

~

STEAM POURED FORTH from the door leading to the bathing room where Taryn had disappeared a while ago. We hadn't spoken after our latest bout, the prince merely finishing and striding from the bedroom. The only thought that came to mind was...*what the hell do I do now?*

I needed something to cover me. Whilst I'd gotten used to the scanty clothes, and although the prince thoroughly explored every inch of my body last night, being naked with him without rutting felt too personal. Too intimate.

Throwing my legs over the side of the bed, I stood and scurried for the remnants of last night's shimmering black dress, but streams of torn fabric fell through my hands like cascading water. I swore softly, dropping it to the floor, and padded to his dresser, retrieving the first tunic I found. It was white with decent sleeves and when I tugged it over my head, the damned thing fell to my knees—the sleeves past my hands. Rolling my shoulders, I marvelled at how large this man was. This man I'd had sex with.

Did sex make me feel any more of a woman? No. It felt good, for the most part, although pain lingered in my legs and vagina, but I felt much the same as yesterday—yesterday *before* the party. Before Taryn.

I wonder if Rose would have been different, more tender and loving.

Perhaps I shouldn't complain, from what I'd read and seen back home, a lot of men lacked in the art of pleasure giving. Taryn certainly hadn't any trouble on that account.

Patting the fabric down around my body, I frowned at myself. I was the bloody embodiment of the girl next door, wearing the boyfriend's shirt. Yet this was the most modestly dressed I'd been in over a month. At least the fabric wasn't transparent.

I stood on the spot, quietly smacking my hands together in front of me, waiting for Taryn to finish washing. I didn't know whether he wanted me to leave or stay, because in the end, it was up to him. The thought made me stiffen, made me want to scream and claw out my heart and cry until the rivers overflowed—but no tears fell, and I did not move.

"You are a vision, lass." Taryn's voice sounded from the threshold. I raised my eyes to meet his.

Goddamn him.

In broad daylight, Taryn's body—still wet—was ludicrous. Leaning casually against the doorframe, utterly naked, his arms loosely crossed over a sculpted chest, his damp hair clung to every line of muscle over his shoulders. I'd never actually *looked* at one properly before, but Taryn's was huge. *About as huge as it felt, in any case.*

I wanted to go to him. Seek comfort in his towering frame, in his chest I knew full well felt like silken wrapped steel. But right now, I'd value peace and quiet, time to sort through the mess inside me.

"Thank you, Prince," I said with a hefty gulp of air to cool my senses—bowing my head in a queer curtsy for good measure.

"Come now, Estelle." He laughed. "Bring back to me that fierce temperament I so adore." He pushed off from the doorframe and sauntered to a small table set against the wall of glass. I squinted at it and creased my brow, I hadn't realised food had been laid out. *When did they come in?*

Whoever brought Taryn's breakfast had seen me, in his bed.

"I must attend to my duties, Prince Taryn."

"Nonsense," he said. "Your only duty is what I ask of you. Right now, it is to come and eat with me. And stop calling me Prince." He slid into a chair by the table and held his arm out to me, his face warm. I couldn't refuse, and I don't think I wanted to. I walked to him, allowed him to grasp my hip and tug me onto his lap. He reached around me to grab a handful of grapes.

I felt so—awkward. So unsure of what to do with my body and hands. I slowly reached for a grape too, waiting for the reprimand of grabbing what didn't belong to me. Instead, he massaged my spine with his free hand. Loosening an audible sigh, I relaxed and sank further into his lap.

Breakfast was incredible. It was the best damned food I'd eaten in a long time. We ate silently, feasting on fruit, cheese and bread— famished from our exertions in the night. When I'd eaten my fill— something that hadn't taken long, my body used to one sorry excuse for a meal per day of late—Taryn spoke again. "Was it good for you? Last night. I know it was your first."

Such a complex, hard question. One I hadn't expected from him. It should have been easy to answer. Yet, I had to keep him happy, keep him pleased. "Yes."

But my answer did not please him at all. His hand dropped from my back and he slumped into his seat with an exasperated huff of air. I twisted, lest he force me out on bad terms, plastering a tender smile to my face. It earned me an upraised brow, so I threw depth into my words when I spoke again. "I just, it hurt slightly, sometimes, but when I became accustomed to it," I lowered my lashes and tried for a sweet glance, "Everything was magnificent. I'm sorry I'm so lacklustre, I just have a lot to think about."

A half-truth.

Taryn's mouth tugged upwards, satisfaction smoothing his features. He sat tall and leaned forward, pressing a soft kiss to my lips. "Would you prefer me to be more gentle next time?"

Next time...

I dredged up the most sultry look I could before replying. "No, Taryn. No I would not."

He chuckled, stretching around me to grab another chunk of bread. "If you agree, I will not have you working as a castle servant any longer. The only servitude I would ask of you would be to warm my bed, for I would like none other than you."

My ears and throat burned, then that old fierceness sparked. "So I'm to be your whore? I'm to wait in your bed for you to fuck whenever you want?" I said the words with contempt, but Taryn grinned through his chewing. I straightened my back and bristled.

"That is not how I intended it, lass," he said through more bites of food, grinning all the while. "But, if you so desire that as the definition, then that is your right." His hand moved to a flagon of juice; he sculled it and retrieved another handful of grapes. He chucked them into his mouth, one by one. "However, know that if you do accept, you will enjoy the many benefits of being a mistress to a Prince of Kiliac."

He finished the grapes and brushed crumbs from his hands before grasping my waist, irate as I was. His expression turned infinitely more serious, the burnished colour in his eyes brightening like the sunrise I'd woken to. "Stay with me, Estelle. Warm my bed, yes, but be *with* me. Belittle me, so that I may stay humble. Pleasure me, so that I may do the same for you in return."

This offer, this ridiculous offer, to be his *mistress*...

My true desire was to leave. Leave Ashbourne and never look back. But this—it might be the best option for me in a maelstrom of terrible circumstances. Though, to be a mistress you had to be free. I was not —he owned me. Yet if he wanted this so much, he could just force me to accept and obey. He was asking me as if I had a choice. As if he would respect my refusal.

Two options before me; to remain at the lords and ladies beck and call, or worse, at the king's, or stay with Taryn. The only thing I had to do was sleep with him. *Well, I'd already done that.* I could do it again, perhaps gladly. He'd been kind, and apart from the ravenous moments, warm. Would this be so bad?

It could be easy to be with him. Talk to him, sleep with him. Nice, even. Maybe in time, I would be able to look to the sea and not think of the man I loved, but think instead of the man whose arms I was enveloped in. But this man was asking me to be his whore.

"Can I think on it?" I asked, my voice already gentler than before.

I could use this—use *him*—to get the hell out of Ashbourne. I'd make him trust me, or simply learn if I could trust him enough to help me. I'd have a better chance with Taryn than I would alone.

One way or another, I would get out of here.

Taryn crooked his mouth into a half-smile, lifting a hand to brush the long strands of hair from his shoulders. "Of course, lass, take all the time you need."

I nodded, looking out over the ocean, not entirely noticing the hand on my leg. I drew my eyes from the sea to study it, watching it glide upwards, sliding beneath the fabric of the tunic. By the time his hand reached the supple skin of my inner thigh, my whole body kindled, hot rushes flowed through me and I fell back against his chest.

Just as my pleasure climbed its peak, Taryn's lips grazed my ear. "Say yes, Estelle."

I moaned as his touch became insatiable. His other calloused hand snaked down through the top of the tunic, pawing my breasts. "Say yes," he said again, louder. His rumbling voice crashed into me like the waves upon the cliff. I soared off that peak, the thunderstorm unleashing within me, and screamed. Not an inaudible yell, or his name as I had many times before, but that word. Over and over again.

Yes.

I may have just sold my soul to the devil, but right now, I didn't care.

CHAPTER 24

WHERE THE WILD ROSES GROW

I stood naked in the sea breeze, hair wild, skin prickling as sweat dried. I could bathe later, but for now, I wanted to taste the salt-kissed air through the open foyer window.

Taryn had left moments ago and, for the first time in a long time, I had nothing to do. My agreement with him meant I no longer served as part of the royal staff, well, royal slaves. No more jewelled jugs for ugly, pompous courtiers, no more floors to scrub or hearths to tend, and no more chamber pots to empty. Now, my only task was to wait for an all too muscular, all too charming prince to return.

A classical fantasy.

Except in this fantasy, I was the prince's damn property.

The wind picked up and the ocean it sped across brought colder chills. Gooseflesh rose on my skin. Standing on my toes, I grasped the window frame to lean out and look down. This side of the castle dropped directly into the waves crashing against the stones. *Poor design choice.* In a few years, erosion would eat away at the foundations and destroy it. Not that I would tell them that. They should have stayed in the desert.

The waves broke wildly, the noise like gunfire as it struck the rocky cliffs.

It would be so easy.

I closed my eyes, but nothing nice came. All I could see of the people I loved were the bad things. Kiita, kicking and screaming, her face torn open from chin to scalp. Rose, riding away from me with tears in his eyes and my heart in his hands.

And Tor.

Tor's body drenched in blood and littered with arrows—the spearhead being thrust through his neck...

Even Achilles, who I hadn't felt for far too long.

He was probably dead, too. They were *all* most likely dead. Well, Tor *was*. Tor was definitely dead.

I don't even remember my mother's or brother's face anymore.

The emptiness inside me expanded, creating a chasm of its own. I was going to step into it. I wanted to. My foot moved forward.

No.

My eyes flew open at the voice in the wind, and before me, with air shimmering all around her, was a fairy.

After all this time.

"Why?" I cried out.

You have a responsibility. It is not done.

Disgrace shot through me like a bullet and my stomach coiled in shame. Through the constriction in my throat, my words were barely audible. "All you're saying is that I've failed."

You have, and you will again, the wind replied. *Become more than you are. Protect us.*

As suddenly as she appeared, the fairy flew away, leaving an iridescent shimmer in her wake. Pain and fury and something stronger, broke through me like the waves upon the cliffs.

She was right.

I had to keep trying. I had to protect Galdurne...I just didn't know how.

Screw it, said the kindling flame in my gut.

You'll figure it out.

I slammed the window shut and marched through the foyer to the bathing room to clean my ruddy ass up.

SCOURED CLEAN, with red skin and brushed out hair, I sat on Taryn's bed. Then I walked to the window again. Then I sat at the table.

Gods, I was bored.

Remembering Taryn's small library, hidden behind a heavy oakwood door, I lurched off my chair, only to be thwarted by a locked door. "Fuck me dead! Can't even pick a lock to save yourself, you bloody wanker!" I kicked the door. Not, I realised with an unholy amount of pain in my foot, the smartest of moves whilst naked.

I wasn't about the leave the prince's chambers, in case anyone didn't believe I was not supposed to be cleaning floors anymore and whip me for it. With my hands on my hips, I pressed my hurting foot behind the other ankle and looked around. Apart from the library and Taryn, there was nothing to *do* in here. No one had been in to clean the room—pillows scattered the floor, so I went to retrieve them and return them to their proper places. Stretching out my frail arm, I was struck near-dumb. I was weak and skinny—there was something I could do after all. I ate every damned morsel of breakfast remaining on the table. My stomach was beyond full, but I shoved the food down my throat anyway.

Then, I ran. From the glass wall to the far corner in the bathing room and back again. The distance was no more than twenty meters, so I did it in suicide sprints. I played the counting game, reaching one thousand in counts of five before I stopped.

Even as my muscles ached, I channelled Tor's dedication and grit until I was drenched in sweat head to toe. Lying on the cold stone floor I sucked in air and calmed my racing heart. The front door creaked open and I straightened to see Peeta walk through. I didn't care that I was naked, but my lungs ceased as I imagined Taryn finding me in this state.

The girl's eyes widened at my dishevelled appearance, but she wasn't surprised to find me here, unclothed no less. Better yet, she came unmuzzled. I stood on shaking legs, almost falling straight back down again. "Peeta!"

"Hello, milady," she said, dipping her head into an elegant bow.

"Why are we back to milady?"

She offered a tentative smile. "You are the prince's mistress, milady, I will address you as such."

"No, you won't. I'm Estelle, please don't call me anything different."

She raised her petite brows at my beseeching tone, but nodded.

I made Peeta stay with me for the day, wanting to allow her the freedom of enjoying life as a child should—but I wanted company more violently than I could bear. I braided her hair, awfully, and found bits of charcoal and paper in one of Taryn's bedside drawers. We drew to our hearts content and I taught her how to play games like dots and boxes and tic-tac-toe. When an older woman, golden-collared, burst through the chamber yelling and demanding Peeta come with her at once, I pushed her out and slammed the door in her face, using my ridiculous authority as the *Prince's Mistress* to make her bugger off.

After a few heartbeats, I wrenched the door open and said that if she laid a hand on Peeta, she'd have the prince himself to deal with. It took a long time for Peeta to stop smiling after that. Perhaps, if I forced myself to be normal, to at least pretend to be happy, it would be so.

As the moon chased the sun out of the sky, Peeta sprang up from the beginning of our first reading lesson. 'Not many in Kiliac possess such a talent', Tor had told me. Horen was smart. He kept his people blind, deaf and dumb to the ways of the world. Kept them ignorant. Maybe I could remedy that, one person at a time.

"It is almost nightfall, Estelle," she said as she stood. "If I do not get to the kitchens there really will be trouble."

"Not true. Taryn will know what happened today, that I kept you here."

"Thank you, truly, but I should go before the prince returns."

Sighing, I nodded and got up to walk her to the door. I was about to open it for her, but she spun on the spot and looked up at me, a hand on her forehead, mouth agape. "Estelle, I forgot to bring you the milk! I will not forget tomorrow, I promise."

I narrowed my eyes, thinking on her words for a moment too long. I hadn't drunk the blue milk since being locked in that dungeon.

"Why would I need it?"

"For the pain," she said matter-of-factly, gesturing to my genitals like it was a given and I'd asked something dumb. Heat flooded my cheeks. "It's not too bad anymore."

"It will get worse."

My breath froze in my throat.

At the horror consuming my features, Peeta startled and tried to quietly excuse herself, stepping towards the door once more.

"Peeta," I raised my voice, "Did he, did Taryn..." But I could not finish that question.

The girl dropped her gaze and chewed her lip, obviously not wanting to let whatever it was she meant slip.

Please, no...

"Not me," she said before scurrying away.

I looked after her for a long while, puzzling it over in my head.

Not me...then who?

The pain.

Perhaps I was reading too much into it, perhaps Peeta just knew of other mistresses or lovers who could not take Taryn's size. Or perhaps I had indeed sold my soul to the devil.

SITTING cross-legged on the prince's bed, I chewed on my nails with a furrowed brow as the night sky floated through the bedroom and Taryn returned. Snapping my eyes up, I studied the Heir of Kiliac striding through the open doorway, a carefree grin alighting his face, a platter of food in hand.

Not me.

I stood beside the bed while Taryn set the platter on the table. He turned and crossed the distance between us to kiss me soundly. At first I let him, let the feel of him wash through me.

Not me.

When I pushed away he smirked—thinking it was some kind of game. Before he caught my hand, I put a palm to his chest. "Have you hurt women before me?"

His eyes flickered as he contemplated me, my hard expression. "What do you mean?"

My gaze hardened. "You know exactly what I mean."

Taryn cocked his head. "If you are worried I am going to break your heart, pet, let me tell you now that you will never be anything more than my mistress. I cannot marry a slave."

I stood taller. Stronger. "Tell me the truth, Taryn. What kind of man are you?"

At my voice, my resoluteness, a shadow clouded his handsome face. His grin morphed into a grimace, his eyes darkening like a violent storm. "I am a prince. And I do not answer to you."

This...this was the voice I expected him to have. Hard and cruel and frightening. I lifted my chin. "I thought you wanted me to *stay with you,* belittle you, *Prince.*"

Those eyes almost turned black. "There is a difference between playing and outright insolence. Do *not* push me, girl."

Girl.

Suddenly it was not Taryn I was talking to, but Horen.

I shook my head as memories of blood and screams surged. "I'm not doing this. Find someone else to warm your bloody bed."

Ducking under his towering frame, I moved for the foyer. All of my senses ignited at once and I quickened my pace as heavy footsteps rang behind me. But I was not quick enough.

Rough hands seized my hair and threw my head into the wall beside the doorway.

My brow connected with the stone first—the blow wracking my bones, sending waves of black through my bloodstream. Before I could release a strangled cry, a solid weight pressed against my back. Taryn pinned me to the wall with his chest, his voice low as he hissed into my ear. "I will remind you, that I *own* you. You do not walk away from me."

A solid knee came up behind me, separating my legs.

I swung an elbow back, connecting squarely with his nose.

In the fleeting moment of stunned silence, I lurched again towards the door, but Taryn grabbed my arm and wrenched me back into the wall, shoving my spine against the stone.

He struck my jaw with a back-handed blow.

Sent to the side, I doubled down over my knees, but used it, just as Tor taught me. With all the force I could muster, I swung back up and punched the side of his face.

The bastard didn't even blink.

He growled and grabbed my throat with one hand, delivering a brutal punch to my stomach with the other. My eyes watered, tears streamed down my cheeks. Then he punched me again, and again, and again. He knew what he was doing. He could have killed me, but he pulled each punch, just enough to keep me alive.

But I couldn't breathe. I couldn't think. I needed it to stop, needed *him* to stop. I rasped, wheezing through the blows. Only when my nails ceased trying to gouge bloody ribbons on the arm grasping my throat did he stop punching me. I slumped to the floor in a gasping heap when he released my neck. There was a fragmented moment of grace, until I was lifted by my underarms and spun to have my face shoved back into the wall.

I didn't fight back this time.

CHAPTER 25
I WAS JUST TRYING TO BE BRAVE

The days that followed were hell. I tried to crawl away on the third night, silent as a mouse whilst he slept, getting so far as the door to the hallway...but the obsidian armoured guards I didn't know he had stationed there were not as forgiving as my prince.

When I finally screamed from the fire raining down with the crack of their whip, Taryn shot from the foyer and smashed one of their skulls against the wall. Blood and bone smeared down black stone. The sound was like splitting wood—or a war hammer swung at a charging soldier.

After lifting and carrying me to the bed to tend to my wounds himself, Taryn declared—as he would publicly—that only *he* had the right to touch me. In any manner. I thought he might yield then. Sympathise. I cried and begged him to let me go if he cared, but the shadow veiled his features and I knew I'd made a mistake.

I couldn't move for two days afterwards.

I hadn't dared to heal myself, fearing my body was like a blank canvas to a painter. The more pain I was in, the more wounds I bore, the less aggressive he would be. But pain was a part of me now.

SUNRISE BECAME my new favourite thing.

I wished it lasted for hours. *Days.* Because once the red and pink streaks settled and the sun rose high above the sparkling sea, Taryn would wake.

I think I'd been here for nineteen days now.

Nineteen stunning sunrises. Nineteen brutal days. Nineteen nefarious nights.

I had to get out of here.

The only way—the *only* way—I could survive this, was if I stopped cowering and wearing disdain on my face. I started speaking nicely and accepted his advances rather than scream at him for them. The worst times only came after he returned at the end of a long day, exhausted or downright angry. With anger came violence. When he hit me, it felt like my bones might snap in two. Pleading with him was no use—it only made things worse.

No, the best way was to take it in silence. Causing me outright pain did nothing to ease his rage—there was only one way to do that.

At least that didn't hurt anymore.

The mattress shifted as the Prince of Kiliac rose from bed and prowled out of the room. He returned minutes later, piling fruit from the table onto a plate to set before me in bed. I straightened, taking wins where I could. I reached for a piece of melon, and Taryn shot his hand out to catch my swollen wrist.

Don't flinch.

He hated when I did that.

I allowed him to turn my arm around, studying the purple bruises littering my hand and forearm. I glanced at his face in time to see him shudder—as if he couldn't quite believe that he'd done it.

The only mood I hadn't been able to figure out was this one, when he was in another place, somewhere dark and solemn. But if I were to guess, perhaps my markings reminded him of his childhood, another man, another woman.

Lest the shadows darken, I reached to turn his face towards me, brushing my thumb down his scar. He leaned into my touch and I tugged him down to meet my lips, before pulling away and forcing lightness to my voice. "So," I began, smiling my most honeyed smile. "Busy day again today? Scribing laws and royal chores?"

He snorted and rolled his shoulders, the movement resembling boulders sliding down a mountain. My hand trembled as I brought it into my lap.

"I have to leave today," he said. At my raised brows he winked. "Not *leaving*, pet, I will be back soon. I am riding north to oversee trade negotiations with Meriden."

Meriden. The Militia base of the nation.

Where Rose was, and the father he and Tor so loathed. Perhaps a futile part of me shone with the knowledge that whoever he was, he'd have to bow and scrape to the prince before me. I nodded, feigning displeasure at the prospect of Taryn being gone. "How long?" I asked earnestly.

"Ten days at the most."

Ten days without him. Ten days to get myself out.

I raised my gaze and bit my lip, nodding as if the prospect upset me. "I will be sorry to see you gone. I'll miss you."

His thumb brushed over my hand. "And I you, lass."

The wrong thing for me to say and do, apparently, for Taryn wanted to ensure I was *properly satisfied* before he left.

For all it was worth, I was satisfied.

Repeatedly.

THOUGH BRUISED AND BATTERED, I was growing strong again. The moment Taryn left in the mornings, I shovelled all the leftover food down my throat before exercising—for hours on end. Peeta visited, bringing me the milk she promised. That, along with another tonic she smuggled in—I stashed the bottles of red liquid under the bed, making sure to take a spoonful day and night. I didn't know what it actually was, nor did Peeta, but the concoction protected from pregnancy. Whilst I could have been poisoning myself from the inside out, I'd rather that than a baby.

Today—today Taryn was leaving. He would not be back tonight.

I'll stay for the day and leave in the night.

No. *I can't be bloody stupid.*

I'd need a plan—a few days without the prince to heal myself.

Heal myself…

The painter had left his canvas behind.

I hadn't used my power since healing Horen. I hadn't dared. I stopped in my tracks, took a deep breath, and searched for my golden light. It felt foreign and faraway like a long lost friend, but as long as *life* lived in this world, my magic would remain. I dredged it up from my core, letting it wash through my blood like summer rain and carry me to a distant place, where the smell of sandalwood and clove swelled. *Gods*, the strength inside me erupted like wildfire and I beamed down at my glowing skin.

I shook the remnants of euphoria away like a wolf shaking wet fur. I'd have to cover myself, throw discoloured powder on my face, or even hit myself a few times so that servants did not notice.

Not that everyone here didn't know I was a magi.

Idiot.

Plans of escape and the pitfalls of each one swept through my mind as I sweated through my exercises. The guards were my first obstacle. I knew from my month of servitude the way to some exits of the castle, but I'd get caught in the grounds.

No, my best chance would be to leg it to the sprawling library—the one Taryn took me to a week ago. There was a grand balcony one level higher than the jagged cliff face. If I could get to that balcony, I could leap onto the cliff, and climb down to brave the waters.

A week. I'd give myself a week to plan and train. And then I'd leave.

That night, alone in bed, I drank the milk to fall into a long, deep sleep, unencumbered by memories or nightmares. When I woke, I spent half the day exercising and the other half trying to plan in my head. The next day, I woke up and did it again.

For six days, I stuck to my routine, and on the last night, I didn't drink the milk.

~

DON'T BE STUPID, *don't be brash.*

I'd have to be smart to pull this off. Strong too, not just physically.

There was no way to tell the time, but once night fell, I counted. To sixty by sixty, at least five times, pacing all the while. I eyed the options from the range of clothes Taryn had bought. I'd mulled over them for days; a tunic for practicality or a dress for disguise.

Assuming everyone in this ruddy castle knew who I was, there was no real disguise, but the tunic would raise questions. My only ruse would be my confidence—my feigned swagger. The dress then. I tugged it on and clasped the fabric to the joint at my shoulders, pulling slippers onto my feet. Out of my small array of footwear, these black silken things were the quietest. I'd tested them all, numerous times. The only thing unaccounted for was a weapon, but with the guards outside the door, I'd kill two birds with one stone.

I brought out the two flagons I'd stowed away, and the remaining ale I'd hidden under the bed from past dinners. Pouring the liquor into both flagons, I added more than a decent shot of the sleeping draught into them. I'd been testing the limits of the ale each night, seeing how much milk I could add without noticing the taste—two shots was the maximum, but I wasn't going to test the guard's palates.

Peeta redid my singular braid this morning, making it tighter than ever before, better for me—out of the way, pretty and practical. I think she'd known, smart as she was. And whenever I caught her eye this week past, it took all my will to not decide to stay just for her.

I couldn't take her with me, too many risks, too many variables. Tor had said a soft heart in this world was courage, but a weak heart could get me killed. It could very well get her killed, too. I slung the long braid over my shoulder and became a picture of sensuality as I strode to the door and opened it slowly, balancing the flagons in one hand through my fingers.

The guards lounged against the walls, one sat on the ground, holding his head in his hands. They were lazy in Taryn's absence. Perfect. They stumbled into position to block my path, reaching for their weapons, their movements clumsy. At least I'd startled the pricks. Schooling a seductive smile, I glanced beneath lowered brows, angling my hips just so.

Three times now since Taryn's departure I'd done this, and I knew for a fact they'd both tipped their ale on the floor the first time I'd shut the door behind me. The second, they told me to join them and drink first. On the third, they drained their ale in seconds.

"I couldn't sleep tonight, again," I said, my voice low and elegant. "I just kept picturing the two of you out here all night with naught to do or drink. Here." I held out the two flagons.

The shorter man actually smiled tonight, bowing his head in thanks as he took one from my hand. The taller guard was meaner. He sneered at my smile, and grumbled as he wrenched the ale away. I smacked my lips together to stop the smile growing, knowing what he wanted to do to me but couldn't. After all, it was his friend's head Taryn shattered against this very wall when he whipped me. The short man was the replacement.

"Will you drink with us tonight, milady?" asked the nicer.

I grinned at him, swaying my hips as I turned. "Of course, sir, allow me to retrieve another flagon for myself," I said, pointing behind me into the chambers.

"No need," came the gruff voice of the other. Thrusting his flagon under my nose. "Drink half of mine."

Nodding sweetly, I grasped his flagon and took a long sip before returning it. It took half a bottle of that milk to put me to sleep nowadays, half a shot was nothing.

After watching me for a moment too long, apparently the bastard was satisfied with my lack of reaction. He brought the ale to his lips and drained it to the dregs. Once done, he smacked his lips and pointed to my door. "Go back inside, *mistress*."

The short man shot me an apologetic grimace.

I smiled back. "I hope you have a pleasant evening, and that I do indeed finally fall asleep. Knock on the door if you'd like further company," I paused a beat, batted my lids, "Or more ale. Till next time, gentleman."

Better to keep their minds occupied with *that* than my attempt at escape.

They returned my pleasantries and I retreated into Taryn's chambers. By the time I counted another sixty by sixty, two distinct snores rumbled from the other side of the door.

CANDLE IN HAND, I beheld the armoured figures slumped haphazardly on the ground. My mouth quirked at my small achievement, but pursed as I looked down the hall. Freedom was still so far away.

Kneeling beside one sleeping guard, I felt for any concealed daggers, finding one under his belt and carefully drawing it from the small sheath. I padded a few steps away, before halting and twisting back.

I should kill them.

But this was cold blood, these men were sleeping. So, damning myself for the few moments wasted, I scurried into the darkened hallway. I knew it careened to the left and went down a stairwell towards the barracks before cutting straight through to the library.

Veering to the left at the end of the hall, I descended the staircase on silent feet. My heart pounded, but I kept my calm. I had to.

It was the middle of the night, but low murmurs of conversation echoed around the walls by the barracks. My feet moved slower in case my footsteps weren't as quiet as I hoped. I held my breath as I passed each door, releasing a silent sob when I met the next staircase unseen.

But when I rounded the corner, I nearly pissed myself.

Two soldiers leaned against the wall, flustered and half-dressed, visible only through my tiny light. They'd seen me, candle in hand, wrenching away any chance of turning back. So, I steeled myself, schooling the swagger a mistress of the prince might have. Lifting my chin, I kept my eyes forward, rolling my hips with each slow descending step, not that it would help me here. The men watched with wide eyes as I walked towards them, letting me continue down the stairs and away.

I convinced myself that I'd caught *them* in the night—let myself believe it. Each step I took sent another tear rolling down my cheek, but I didn't dare lift a hand to wipe them away until I was surrounded by darkness, bar the tiny candle flame in my hand.

Damn this candle, but I was no good blind. I quickened my pace, almost jogging the rest of the way to the library.

The great double doors faded into sight and I loosed another inaudible sigh of joy—no guards stood watch. But my joy and distraction had me miss a woman with long black braids mopping the floor in the dark.

I knew her. She was the one who put the muzzle around my face, the one who'd whispered that strange word into my ear. We stared at each other for a few breaths in the dim firelight and more tears welled at yet another brush with failure. But instead of calling alarm, the woman smiled and tipped her head, continuing her task. As I walked by, I whispered my thanks and strode for the library doors.

I could almost feel the fairy, somewhere beyond that balcony, waiting for me. I could almost smell the trees and the rain and the shaggy hides.

Home.

The doors creaked a little too loudly as I tried to squeeze through the smallest of openings, and in answer...the castle jolted awake.

Shouts echoed through the halls. Clunking footfalls followed. I dove through the doors and shoved them shut. There was no lock, so I lurched for the closest chair, hooking it up and under the doorknob—it was better than nothing.

The guards or the soldiers? Someone saw, someone told. I was on borrowed time. Turning from the door, I made for the balcony.

Only to see the King of Kiliac in the bright moonlight, lounging with his ankles crossed over a table, a book in his lap, watching me with keen amusement.

I swallowed down the heavy lump in my throat.

"A late night stroll, milady?"

I stood, transfixed, while the shouting upstairs grew louder. Horen glanced towards the noise. "Seems you have caused quite a stir, girl." He gestured to the table before him, "Come, show me why my son is so entranced by you, and they will not question a thing."

A blink was the only shock or emotion I let show. "Taryn said it was illegal to touch another man's slave."

The words tasted like bile in my mouth.

Horen chuckled. "I am above law, and above my son." He uncrossed his ankles and straightened. "Besides, I am rather interested to know what bewitching power you have hiding inside your cunt."

I didn't answer.

The king snapped his book shut and tossed it onto the table. So many moments wasted. So many mistakes—my freedom slipped away. Horen rose to his feet. A loud thump crashed into the library doors and he waved nonchalantly towards the noise. "I would suggest you choose quickly, girl."

So I did.

I hurled the small dagger at his face, leaping to the side before running like hell through stacks and shelves. A fury-driven snarl and a deafening crash of doors thundered behind me, but Horen's booming voice cut above everything else. "Find the bitch!"

I pelted from the stacks and ran for the glass doors to the balcony. Footsteps raced behind me. I didn't have the time to stop and open the door.

I'd have this one shot, this one chance.

I just hoped the glass was thin.

I dove, shielding my head and face with my hands. The impact ripped through my skin, but the glass shattered and ocean-kissed air swept around me.

As I landed, rolling over the broken glass, I sprang to leap over the railing. A few heartbeats of free fall, then I bent my knees to take the impact of the rough rocky ground.

The king's bellow fuelled my fire; the soldiers' yells kept me racing. A glint of metal caught and flashed in the moonlight, heavy metallic footsteps fell further and further behind. A maniacal grin stretched over my face—I'd once kept pace with wolves. These men were nothing.

I couldn't scale down the cliffside as I'd planned, not with the guards on my tail, but a slightly higher cliff jutted above the one the castle was built on, careening away from the grounds. The only obstacle was a two meter wide sheer drop between the two cliffs.

Don't think. Jump.

I did.

And I fell towards a brutal death of bone-shattering waves and jagged rocks. My hands just caught the edge of the other side.

Limbs screaming, I dug my fingertips into the soil, not caring if they were breaking bone by bone as I pressed them in deeper. Heaving and sobbing, I kept hold.

My wrists and arms felt like they were about to give out, but my heart and strength soared. At last, I hooked an elbow over the edge, using the leverage to haul the rest of my body up onto the cliff. My sobs of relief echoed through the air.

When my knees scrambled over, I listened for the nearness of the king's bellows, for the sound of his men's shouts. There were none.

Then I realised why.

A cluster of soldiers, weapons drawn, caged me to the edge.

Damning them all to hell, I loosened a shrill wail and twisted to leap off the cliff and into the sea, but was caught roughly around the waist by unyielding arms. An order sounded out, roaring above my frenzied cries. "Take her back to the prince's chamber, chain her. No food until her master returns."

As I writhed and shrieked, I looked out over the ocean awash with starlight. On the horizon, a glimmer of fairy dust faded away into the night.

~

SHACKLED ON EACH LIMB, a collar at my neck, I was chained to the foot of Taryn's bed. Glass raked through my skin, my blood dried and crumbling, but my magic was as far away as that fairy.

They were true to their word, I didn't eat. My muzzle was only removed to pour putrid water down my throat and muzzled servants came each day to remove my filth.

On the third day, Taryn returned.

When I looked at his face, I couldn't discern what I found, whether the shadows were the product of rage, or the bruises blooming on his jaw and eye. He stared at me for a good while from the doorway into the foyer before stalking to one of his locked chests.

I loosened a muffled wail when he turned and I saw a three-pronged whip, each tail ending in a metal claw, grasped tightly in his hand. Fury simmered from him as he prowled towards me. I scampered away, crying, until the chains clanked taut.

I hated this pitiful, helpless, crazed fear.

I pulled against my chains, pleaded through my muzzle, and Taryn's heavy boots pounded the stone floor. I wailed louder when he raised his arm, clutching the whip in his hand—and watched with wide eyes as the whip came flying down.

The metal tips split any skin not already torn from glass.

Searing agony screamed through me. Sharp metal gouged bloody holes, and leather straps burnt tendrils of white-hot pain across my abdomen.

The next blow struck my legs, and red flowed from each place the clawed tails hit.

Taryn threw his weight behind each strike, grunting with each swing of his arm.

Through each of my screams, the whip unfurled again.

It did not stop. Not until every inch of my skin was smeared with blood.

∾

IN THE WEEKS THAT FOLLOWED, Taryn slowly nursed me back to health.

Through the fading of the world, drifting in and out of consciousness, I pieced together the fragments of reality; large hands gently unclasping my collar and washing away blood in warm water, careful fingers pulled out shards of glass, and burnished orange eyes lined with regret and pain as he wrapped each wound.

Since then, Taryn personally changed my dressings each night and spoon fed me broths and teas.

Slowly, through his dogged determination, the hundred or so open wounds closed and healed. Small scars peppered my body—they would fade in time. But three wide ivory snakes across my abdomen and three thick, creeping lines down my right arm where the claws gouged deeper than the rest—those scars wouldn't fade.

Neither would the ones inside.

THE FAIRY WAS WRONG. I couldn't protect anyone.

I learnt to obey, and I savoured the good days—yearned for them. When the shadows lifted from Taryn's features, he came to bed tender. Sometimes, he made me feel cherished. He even began to tell me that he loved me. The bad days—I learned to deal with those, too—learned how to pace myself.

I never saw Peeta again, never asked him where she went.

I was nothing. I was nobody.

I forgot the smell of the forest and the faces of the ones I'd loved before.

Unfortunately for me, Taryn had barred the windows.

CHAPTER 26
MONSTERS

"I believe I have you beat, my love."

He had no idea.

"That you do, clever bastard." The bright voice I'd learned to use as one of my defences trilled out. It was a hideous thing, but Taryn liked it—that was all that mattered.

The prince tipped his head back and laughed.

Play with him, tease him—to a point. There was a line. I never so much as toed it in the recent weeks...months...

I'd discovered a great many things about Taryn's likes and dislikes. How to best pleasure him when his anger began to simmer, which topics to never speak of, and of course—the most important one, to never, ever cry in his presence.

We were playing some form of board game together and I did not know the rules. It didn't matter. Taryn liked to win.

I very rarely left these chambers. Which was fine. At least I could watch each new day dawn upon the world through the thick glass in our bedroom.

His...his bedroom.

I knew the glass was thick, because I'd tried to smash through it. Many times.

When I did leave the chambers, I was escorting Taryn to informal events. Anything official meant I was hidden away—I was his prize, after all. His magi. I'd healed him a great many times now. Whenever he returned from battling bandits and rebels, or supervising a forest raid. Each time my magic reversed into itself a bit more, cowering from my abuse of it.

I didn't heal myself. There was no point.

His hand reached for my face and I relaxed, didn't flinch.

Taryn traced his fingers over the bruises coating my right jaw and cheekbone. Remorse flared in his eyes, but it wouldn't change him. He would be apologetic a few days, tender, tell me over and over that he loved me, then hit me again when his father called him out on one matter or another.

I sometimes found myself wondering what Taryn would have been like if Horen wasn't his father. If the king hadn't created and nurtured a monster.

"Do you hate me?" the Prince of Kiliac whispered.

Yes.

"Never."

A soft smile and a careful kiss—avoiding my split lip. "I have bought you something, lass," he said, brushing a gentle hand over my shoulder as he stood and strode to his dresser. He retrieved a tub of what looked like pale clay and held it out to me, his gaze flickering and shoulders tense. "I believe it was made to cover flaws on a woman's face."

I was at his side instantly, another learned skill. He was giving me makeup to cover what he'd done. *A nice gesture, at least.* I took the tub and looked inside, dabbing in a finger. It did indeed feel like clay...a primitive foundation. I wiped my finger on the back of my hand and smiled dolefully.

"Thank you, my love." Reaching up on my tip toes, I kissed his cheek—ever the sweet, grateful mistress. He beamed, the edges of his eyes crinkling with the movement, and pulled me towards the bathing room. Two muzzled slaves, a boy and a girl, bowed before us. They had brought steaming water, and filled the tub with an assortment of flowers and oils.

Taryn unclasped my dress at the shoulders and let the fabric fall, gesturing me towards the water. I relaxed in the tub, allowing myself to find joy in his sturdy hands while he washed and massaged my hair.

Once finished and dry, Taryn kept up his boyish grin as he led me to the dresser in the bedroom, and out of the bottommost drawer he retrieved a vibrant turquoise gossamer gown.

Turquoise.

I shuddered and closed my eyes. Only for a second. A mere blink.

The neckline plunged down to a golden rope belt at its waist, a way to display my assets to all the men Taryn might want to make jealous tonight. The skirts flowed seamlessly, and would sweep across the ground like wind as I walked. Its sleeves were thin yet elaborate, intricate golden vines patterned across the sheer fabric.

"Do you like it?"

"I have no words."

"You will wear it tonight," he said, puffing out his chest like a peacock. "It is a dress fit for a princess. Fit for you, love."

"Thank you, Taryn. This is a beautiful gift, the second in one day," I quirked a brow. "You're spoiling me."

His cheeks flushed red, like he couldn't contain his pride. "I shall send for the girl to help with your face."

I could do it myself, would rather do it myself. But no was a word my prince didn't favour. "Of course...but first," I planted a well-practised smirk, "I rather think I'd like to thank you properly."

He grinned like a wolf.

ANOTHER PART of this ridiculous life I'd come to enjoy were the times I'd walk hand in hand with the most sought-after man in all of Kiliac into a room full of conniving, snide, horrible women.

Especially wearing a beautiful dress.

I relished their jealous stares and hateful sneers. There was only one person that had the right to hurt me, and he stood right next to me. These women—I was a slave, but I was above them.

I never used to be this way.

But events like this nefarious party made me feel important. Worthy of something more than being thrown around. Here, I was worth jealousy. Here, at least I was worth hating.

My favourite part was when I was nestled in Taryn's lap on the dais and got to watch the women try to approach for a dance. Most of these events were meant to allow the lords and ladies of the court to parade off their daughters for Taryn. The girls tried. Oh, how they tried, to claim a fragment of his time. I loved watching their faces when he would laugh and ask why he'd give them the time of day, when someone like me was in his arms. Sometimes, I would spread my legs and wink at the girls for spite.

I did it for a feeling. Of any kind.

Even shame and self-loathing were foreign.

The king had been absent a while now, in some place south to visit his wife and daughter, whoever they were. I didn't know their names. I never asked because I never cared. Because when Horen was away, Taryn rarely had bad days.

Perched on the prince's lap, I leaned forward to watch the girls dance in the center of the throne room, resting my chin on a fist. Taryn's hand idly stroked my spine as he held conversation with Lord Ulfwren about trade routes with the continent—a boring subject. The women spun on dainty legs between each other, looking at me and sneering with upturned lips. That was usual, but there was one girl tonight, a wickedly curvy blonde in a silver dress, throwing me a look of pure, undiluted hatred. Her blue eyes blazed like an inferno as she glared.

It felt like watching a movie, where some kind of confrontation happened between characters and the drama would be so incredibly enticing, so much fun to watch, that you couldn't look away. It was okay to watch other people despise each other, because you were just an onlooker. Detached. That's what I was now, a character in someone else's story.

I smiled my most vicious smile at the blonde and reached between my legs to stroke Taryn's crotch. His hand on my back halted its path.

Most of the ladies in court gasped, but I kept my eyes locked onto that blonde in the silver dress. Watched her expression turn into an enmity so vicious, I thought she might spontaneously combust. I laughed when anger-ridden tears filled her eyes and she spun on her heels to scurry off through the crowd. Taryn slipped a hand through the plunging fabric at my navel, pressing it flat against my side to pull me closer. Snubbing Lord Ulfwren, he chuckled and leant forward.

"You wicked little creature."

Pressing back, I kissed his cheek. "You should probably dance with at least one of them tonight, my love."

He scoffed. "None are worth my time."

"I don't know," I mused, turning to face the crowd. "There are a great many lovely women here. Perhaps that brunette in the red gown? She is the most beautiful of them all." And she was. I'd watched her throughout the night, dancing freely and laughing with her friends. She reminded me so much of my old mate from Australia, Tahnee... dark skin, chocolate hair, and a smile that could light up the night sky.

He grabbed my chin with a finger to turn my attention back to him, an eager gleam in his eye. "Do you desire her? Shall I bring her to our bed tonight?"

My lips twitched as I cast my stare down, pretending tentativeness to the idea. "No, I desire nothing and no one but you. But," I bit my lip and glanced at her again, "Out of all the snakes in the garden, she is the best choice."

Taryn frowned, looking around my shoulder to find the girl. It didn't take long. After a long moment of surveying her, he looked back with amusement on his face. "You have a good eye, lass." He sighed and nodded, gently grasping my waist to lift me off.

The prince left me sitting on the dais, sauntering down the steps towards the brunette. As he approached her, her cheeks bloomed with colour. She dropped a deep curtsy. Chocolate hair was swept half up in a tight rosette, whilst the rest fell in lustrous waves past her ass. Her blood red gown made her dark skin glow, and it would have been modest with its high neck, if it were not for the split up her right leg ascending to her hip.

She would be a goddess in my modern world.

But here, it was me who was beautiful. Not that I hadn't been before—and some here thought me strange—I didn't look like anyone else, but my vanity and pretension had never been higher. I was, as Taryn told me many times, exquisite.

The prince had not desired me for no small reason, had remained so enraptured by me—so in love with me. Because he did love me in his own twisted way. In the way someone loves something that is theirs.

My chest heated at the sight of him, my gallant prince, bowing and taking the girl's hand in his.

Even now, I couldn't properly discern my feelings for him. Taryn was my worst enemy and my fiercest protector. He was my lover and my jailor. He was my master. I hated him, yet I didn't. I think though, that I might have loved the man he could have been.

Leaning back into the chair, my thoughts meandered, imagining a life away from all this bullshit. Away from his childhood and his shadows.

I rubbed at my eyes.

Enough, Estelle.

I threw the nonchalant mask back across my features, sat straight, and presented the picture of poise. The courtiers watched the prince and his partner spin in graceful circles, but some still glared at me—open resentment distorting their faces now Taryn was no longer able to see. To be frank, I enjoyed this—sitting alone atop the dais in an elegant gown, pretending I truly was above all of these people. A court of barbarians and reprobates indeed.

But then I would catch the eye of another slave, standing like a painted statue around the perimeter of the room. Ready to serve.

Allowing my fantasies to run wild, I imagined roaring a battle cry into the wind so that the entirety of Galdurne would hear. Then I'd unleash my wrath upon the people in this room. Or, I could set the city on fire.

Closing my eyes, I smiled at the image.

"Hello, Estelle."

An oddly familiar voice wrenched me from my thoughts and my eyes jerked open before spearing toward a young man standing before me.

I'd seen him before. I knew him, but couldn't quite place him. Since arriving in Ashbourne, there were so many new faces. So many guards, courtiers, and sons of lords. Rolling my shoulders and sitting taller, I glanced at Taryn, still dancing with the brunette—his attention wholly wrapped in her. As I watched, I realised why I wouldn't have remembered this newcomer's face. Compared to the man I woke up to every day, this one was plain and boring. Forgettable.

"I am afraid I do not know your name, sir."

His stare, first alight with both amusement and hunger, darkened with the flick of a muscle in his jaw. My disregard sent indignance flashing through his features. I did know him—and he looked as if he were a long lost and scorned lover of mine.

"I am Iro," he growled.

My blood stilled, but a blink was the only surprise I let show. I knew better now.

What was he doing here? He was dressed in—well he was dressed like a pompous son of a lord, not the son of a stone mason. But he was here, in Ashbourne, at a royal ball.

Iro smirked, gesturing towards the chair I sat on beside the throne, placing a foot on a step of the dais.

Stupid fool.

"It certainly looks as if you have risen in status."

"Since when did you care for status?" I looked past him and around the room. "Where is Bjorn? Where is your father?"

Iro scowled. "You remember Bjorn, but not me?" His scowl deepened. "It does not matter now, they are both beneath me."

My gaze returned to his face, my brow creasing. "You think fancy clothes make you more of a man?"

Venom coated his voice as he pointed at Taryn's still-dancing figure. "It seems that is the only way to get you to spread your legs. Just like the fancy lad that night in Salem you had doe-eyes for. I tried to be the gentleman." He shook his head with feigned amusement. "But apparently all I had to do to fuck you was wear pretty things."

I thought back to Salem—that night with Rose—Iro had watched, fixated on the two of us. A sour feeling plummeted in my stomach, familiar but distant. As far away as the clouds in the sky that had danced like dragons for two lovers in a clearing.

"I seem to remember, Iro, that you were rife with jealousy that night, too. It mars your features, yet you continue to wear it. Are you really that wanton I should reject you a second time?"

The stupid prick lunged up the stairs so he stood fully upon the dais. He kept his voice low, spitting furiously through his words, splattering my face. "How dare you speak to me like that, you bleedin' whore! Do you have any idea who I am now?"

I crossed my legs and smiled. "You are, and always will be, that desperate little boy who followed me around Salem." I leaned forward, allowing him a full view of my plunging neckline. "And you should know, that the man I spread my legs for, is all you never could be and more. It is his name I scream throughout the night, and it will never be yours."

Iro's mouth fell agape and I welcomed the fury simmering in his eyes. Did he not fear Taryn's wrath? Did he not know exactly where he stood? I flattened out the creases in my skirts, waiting for him to do something, say something, and glanced up to see a lewd expression cross his face.

"What about Tor?"

The air around me went cold.

"Do you scream his name during the night?"

Ice coated my skin, veins of hoarfrost fracturing through my bloodstream. "What did you just say?"

Iro chuckled. "I said, *whore*, that—"

I stood swiftly. Too swiftly and pointedly to pass off as my usual mask of the woman I'd become. "What did you *say?*" I snarled.

The dancers stopped dancing. All turned towards us. I could hear and feel Taryn rushing back, towards the dais Iro stood on. At my features, my expression, the blood vanished from Iro's face like smoke. He stumbled away and I prowled forward with a fury I've never known.

When Taryn's hand appeared on Iro's shoulder, the lad actually squeaked in terror, like he truly didn't expect to be caught in his stupidity. It was only the way Taryn looked at me, that stopped my advance on Iro. Taryn sensed my rage and shadows darkened his eyes.

The prince stepped around the quivering fool, slapping him soundly on the back of the head. He turned to stand beside me, taking my hand in his and squeezing it gently, making soothing strokes with his thumb. "Just because you came to us with this magi's location, it does not entitle you to speak to her. She is the property of your prince, boy. My father made you Lord of Salem. I can take that away."

Whatever was left of my mask fell away in crumbles and a choking sound rendered from me like shattered glass. "He did what?"

Taryn whirled to me, confusion lining his face. "You knew him?"

I didn't answer, I just glared at Iro. He blinked up at me, in the way he used to in Salem. Helplessly, innocently. The bandit attack, Rose's father finding out where he was—the ambush. It was all one in the same.

It was Iro. He'd caused it. All of it.

I let fire and wrath burn in my eyes.

Taryn blanched and stepped away, trying to piece some kind of puzzle together.

"You promised," I breathed. "You bled for that promise."

Iro went as white as a corpse, his gaze darting around he stumbled back another step. Taryn caught his wrist, grasping it tight enough to make him yelp. The prince pulled Iro's arm taut and ripping off his glove, revealing a hand turned wholly black.

Old magic, Tor had once told me. Old magic indeed.

Iro released a strangled sound, tears cascading down his face. The prince looked between us, gauging my fury and pain. A tear fell, just one. Rage twisted Taryn's face as the shadows took over—but it was not directed at me. No one had the right to hurt me.

No one but him.

Taryn loved me. Taryn would protect me.

Taryn would kill for me.

He seethed, red-faced with undiluted anger, but he waited for me —it was my call.

So, I nodded.

Taryn twisted and threw Iro to the stony ground before him. Fury trembled through his limbs, but the prince's voice remained calm, he raised it for all in the room to hear. "You have practised the forbidden arts by committing a blood promise to another. Do you deny this?"

Iro blabbered. Instead of rebuking Taryn's words, all that came out were pitiful pleas of mercy and cries for help.

"Do you deny this?" Taryn asked, louder.

On the ground, Iro rolled towards me and pointed. "She is a magi! She practises forbidden arts—she made me do it! She made me!"

"My healer is not on trial. She has stood under the Maker's eye and has been found worthy of servitude. You." Taryn flung out a finger. "Are not worth the shit stain on a rat's arse." The crowd around us laughed. Bloodlust rose in the eyes of the courtiers. "You have, as evidence claims, performed a blood oath. A magic as dark and ancient as any other. As dangerous as any other."

Many in the crowd nodded and murmured their agreement. Curses shouted, accusations rising—a mob, not a royal court.

"Like my forefathers before me, I will choke out magic's tyrannical place in this world." The mob stamped their feet. "As the firstborn son of King Horen, rat's arse, I sentence you to die."

Two obsidian-armoured guards appeared from the crowd, taking hold of Iro's arms as he screeched and cried. Courtiers scurried back against the walls, turning their noses up at the man on the stones. Taryn came to stand before me, cradling my face in his palm before kissing my brow. "What pain should he feel?"

I was on fire, yet my skin was cold as ice. Iro got my father killed. I looked my Prince in the eye.

"Break his bones."

Taryn dipped his head and stalked to the center of the room.

Taking one of Iro's arms between his hands, Taryn snapped it like a twig. The sound echoed like a gong. Just as quickly—just as violently—Iro's other arm cracked and bent.

It should have horrified me, the sound, the memory. Bones breaking—Kiita screaming. But this felt like a cruel, satisfying kind of justice. For her and for Tor. Each ear-splitting crack of Iro's bones sent a sadistic thrill like an electric shock through my body. His tears could pay me back for all the pain he'd caused.

It still wouldn't be enough.

When Taryn finished shattering Iro's legs with his boots—his screams sharpening to delirious wails—he turned and prowled back to me. I frowned a moment too long at his clear expression, his shadows lifted, before I saw the small knife held out before me in an open palm.

I stepped off the dais, took the offered knife. The offered gift.

All of those crowded in the throne room gasped as Taryn led me by the hand to the broken heap of skin and shattered bone that was Iro. The stone mason's son.

Bjorn's friend.

My friend.

He had told.

He was my friend.

The guards lifted Iro. His head lolled, nonsensical words muttered from his lips. He was too far gone, I realised, to feel any more pain. Taryn stood at Iro's back, cupping his head in his hands and stretching it backwards to expose a pale neck.

Then the Prince of Kiliac bore his eyes into mine.

I stepped forward, once, twice, almost an arm's length away from Iro, I could hear the chanting under his breath. Prayers to the Maker, pleas for mercy, heartbreak and remorse to his father, Bjorn, Kiita, Tor—Estelle.

My palm tightened around the knife.

He was my friend.

I brushed his throat with my fingertips, felt the pulse of his lifeblood. Everything I'd suffered, every pain I endured, was because of this man.

When I closed my eyes, I heard the spear plunge through Tor's neck. Kiita's wrenching scream as blood flooded down her face. Soft spoken words whispered into my head, my heart.

I love you. I have always loved you.

I mouthed the words back to the ghost of a memory. The ghost of a soul.

My eyes flew open, and I plunged the knife to the hilt into Iro's throat. The sound reverberated around the stone walls. Blood warmed my hand, coated it like a second skin and I thought I heard Iro's death pass like the ancient thrumming of archaic drums. But it could have been the sound of my own beating heart.

He was my friend, but he'd betrayed me.

He'd betrayed everyone I loved.

He deserved it.

As Iro's body slumped to the stones, Taryn stepped over it and strode to me, grasping my hand in his, sheathing the knife at his hip. I let him lead me away from the crowd, away from the throne room, and up to his chambers.

Tonight, I met the prince's passion and ferocity entirely.

And I did not fake a goddamned thing.

CHAPTER 27
WICKED GAMES

Today was a bad day for Taryn.

The king returned, calling upon his errant son the moment he'd set foot in the city. Now, the prince paced back and forth in his room, shadows clouding his face in darkness. Perched on the edge of the bed, I waited for him to come to me—one way or another.

Apparently, Taryn's younger sister had come to stay in Ashbourne for a time. He'd tried arguing with the king this morning, earning a broken hand for his insolence. I healed it quickly, made to distract him as best I could, but my efforts went unheard and unnoticed. I was just surprised I hadn't been struck. Yet since the night I killed Iro, Taryn hadn't hit me. Not once.

I never saw Horen these days, which was fine by me. Occasionally, I'd spot him at a party or unofficial feast, but I hadn't interacted with the king since he'd caught me in the library that fateful night. So, I was struck dumb when Horen came barging into Taryn's chambers, stomping into the bedroom with a pretty young girl in toe. My spine slammed into the headboard as I brought my knees to my chest.

The girl lurched from Horen's grasp and ran to Taryn, who grinned broadly and opened his arms, shadows disappearing for his sister. I

266

peeked at Horen over my knees. He watched the scene before him unfold with disdain, as if the phenomena of his children's affection disgusted him. His eyes darted to me, caught me staring.

In a blur of motion, Horen leapt for the bed—I didn't back away an inch, but released a shuddering gasp when I was wrenched off the mattress by my unbound hair. I didn't cry out from the pain, it barely hurt at all, but the girl did, loud and shrill. Horen released me and turned on her. He slapped her across the face whilst she was still in Taryn's arms—the sound echoed off the stones.

We held our breaths until Horen huffed, turned on his heel, and stalked wordlessly from the chambers, wringing his hands at his sides.

When the door clicked shut, Taryn rushed to the bed with his sister pressed against his chest. In his lap he held her close—rocking back and forth—cooing gently as she wailed. Without thinking of the consequences, I crawled on my hands and feet to kneel beside Taryn's legs. The girl raised her eyes to meet mine, sniffed, and reached out a hand to trace the fading bruise on my face. "Same," she whispered through the tears.

Taryn went as still as death.

I ignored him and smiled. "What is your name?"

She sniffed again, scrubbing her face with a balled fist. "Nora."

I spoke in a gentle tone, a real tone. "My name is Estelle Verndari, and I am so happy to have met you, Nora." Ebony hair fell in waves just past her shoulders. "Did you know, in a land faraway from here, Nora comes from a word meaning light? I can see that light in your eyes, Princess."

Her tears waned and she leaned toward me. I wrapped her into my arms. "Close your eyes," I whispered into her hair. "Close your eyes and think of something nice."

Quiet for a time, Nora's shuddering breaths subsided as she raised her head to look at me. "D-does my daddy hit you, too?"

I willed myself, forced myself, to not glance at Taryn, fixing my eyes into hers. They were a brilliant shade of blue, like the open sky on a Kairi day.

"Yes, little light," I said.

I still did not look up, as I heard Taryn begin to cry.

FOR THE FIRST time since I arrived in Ashbourne, I stepped outside the limits of the castle grounds and into the streets of the city. Taryn, Nora, and I were spending the day together, meandering through market stalls and bustling storefronts. The prince bought his sister anything and everything she desired, and purchased a second helping for me.

The princess remained glued to my side throughout the day, as if her life depended on it.

Taryn had not touched me once.

People bowed and moved aside for us, accompanied as we were by no less than ten obsidian guards. Some glared at Taryn with resentment when they thought themselves unnoticed. Many looked at me like people back home would look at a celebrity, and maybe they thought I was a damned princess myself—at least I looked the part. The flowing gown Taryn gave me to wear was modest, and spectacular. Aquamarine gossamer fabric brushed the ground at my feet as I walked, clinging beads and shells serving as a belt.

Nora took one look at me in the dress this morning and clumsily braided more seashells through my hair. Taryn smiled so benevolently that I didn't dare to touch or fix the style. I remained the docile, sweet mistress, even if he did not treat me so today. He treated me with respect.

He treated me the way a man should.

I knew it was because of his sister—knew he was ashamed.

When Nora grew tired of wandering the streets, Taryn took her hand and led us from the bustling district, down to an ocean cove hidden amongst the cliffs. Despite being in Ashbourne for however long, I hadn't touched the sea. I almost had—once. I was almost scared to now. But Nora, bless her, laughed at the top of her lungs, pelting towards the waves the moment her feet hit the sand.

I hoped her soul wouldn't fester like her brother's.

"Go on," Taryn said, carefully, over my shoulder. I wanted to, but I had to remember my place. Remember who I was with.

"Only if you do too, my love."

Taryn blinked for a moment—smiled tightly. "No...I...I want to watch you. Watch you enjoy yourself...play." He rubbed his jaw, tipping his head towards the sea. "Go, join my sister."

Nothing of the Taryn I knew lay in those words, that voice. His hand curled around my shoulder, his thumb brushing a soothing arc against my skin. The man I could have loved. He pressed a kiss to my forehead, before telling me to go again.

I turned again to walk to the sea, glancing over my shoulder. Taryn found a spot on the shore. And so he sat, smiling at me. Looking back at the ocean's expanse, I dug my toes into the sand, allowing myself to feel and enjoy the sensation.

"Elle! Come play with me!"

Nora's bright voice swept across the beach as she nimbly skipped through the shallows. She was carefree and completely happy in the company of the sea. One unbidden tear ran down my cheek, so I made sure not to look back at Taryn as I stepped into the water.

THROUGHOUT THE AFTERNOON, I grew more comfortable in my skin, more enthusiastic to join Nora in her antics. Whether it was playing in the water, swimming through the waves, or just building a sandcastle on the shore. I ran blithely across the sand with her and I let myself laugh.

All the while...Taryn just sat and watched.

When the sky darkened alongside Nora's mood, Taryn got up and dusted off his pants, informing us that we would not be going back to the castle tonight. He led us down the beach towards a jagged cliff-side, ducking into a small cave tucked near the shoreline. The guards remained standing watch at the entrance, but did not enter. I discovered why, when Taryn snapped at one for stepping a foot inside to tell us our dinner was on its way. Nora whispered to me that 'this was Tarry's favourite place in the whole wide world', and that he 'used to come here with Ammy all the time, but then Ammy left.' I flicked my gaze to Taryn, who'd overheard Nora's shoddy attempt at whispering and was grimacing as he worked on setting a fire.

I didn't have time to think on it before Nora told us more about Fayr—the town where she and the Queen lived. About the garden their mother was trying her hardest to rebuild, because whenever the king came to visit he would burn it down. She told us about the children she played with in the ocean, and how the fisherman swore they'd seen merpeople in the sea on a moonless night.

When dinner came, we feasted on fish, fruit and bread, listening to Nora's exuberant stories about her beloved fishing town. As night fell, bringing with it a chilling breeze, Taryn stoked the fire. The princess scrambled toward it like a moth to a flame, and lay down on the bare rock beside it, falling into a deep sleep within minutes—leaving just Taryn and me.

I didn't know what to do, what to make of the Taryn that could have been. We sat in silence a long while, watching the crackling flame, before he spoke—soft as a caress upon my cheek.

"I am sorry, Estelle. I am sorry for everything."

He'd said the words a thousand times, but the way he said them now—I looked up. All the pretences I should have kept, fell into shambles as his eyes filled with more tears.

He brushed a hand through his hair, wiped a tear from his face. "I do love you, you know. More than I have ever loved anyone."

I hadn't stopped staring at him, at his face, usually hard as stone, now open and sincere. I'd never once doubted he spoke the truth when he told me of his love.

"I know."

"But you do not love me."

I shook my head, just a fraction. But an answer, nonetheless.

From the position he was in, squatting with his arms resting over his knees, he rocked forward and crawled the small distance between us, shuffling to sit before me. He lifted his hand. I flinched.

Shit.

He dropped his arm, pain lining his brow.

I used to think I loathed him. I used to be sure that if given the chance or the strength, I'd have killed him in his sleep. But after today, after the night with Iro, I was not so certain. So, perhaps about to damn myself entirely, I responded under my breath. "I do not love you Taryn, but, I don't think I hate you."

The corners of his mouth lifted, slightly, and his burnished eyes glowed. He reached to cup my cheek, brushing his thumb along my jaw. "Well, that is a start, then."

His kiss was soft. Not the claiming, possessing one I'd come to know—but soft and reverent. As if this were our first kiss. *That is a start, then.* Perhaps it was our first kiss. I pulled away, looked into his eyes with an unflinching intensity I thought long forgotten. "Things have to change, you have to change. I will never love you like this."

My face still in his hands, he nodded. "I will never hurt you again."

A real smile bloomed as I leaned forward to meet his lips. When he lifted and carried me into the water, I cherished his kiss and gentle touch.

Entwined under the moonlight kissed ocean, I think my heart finally began to feel again.

NORA STAYED in Ashbourne for five weeks, and I knew five weeks of peace. Five weeks of happiness. Slowly, the prince and princess moulded the remnants of my soul back together, with days full of light and laughter and long nights in the throes of flourishing emotions.

Until the day Horen whipped Nora bloody for giving a flower to a slave girl.

Taryn tried to stop it. He was crazed, bellowing at the top of his lungs, fiercely struggling to get to his squealing sister.

It took five soldiers to hold him back.

It took three to hold me back, too.

Horen sent Nora packing the moment he'd stopped swinging the whip, back to Fayr—not allowing Taryn to say goodbye, nor I the ability to heal her wounds.

It was like a switch.

The moment Nora left the city, the Taryn I knew returned.

And he was more angry than ever before.

CHAPTER 28
ALL THAT YOU KNOW

The agony in my ankle turned into a dull thudding. The bone —I wasn't sure if it was broken or not. Taryn had shackled and chained my leg to a wall and I was trying to crawl to his bed.

Not because I missed him, but because this was the first time he'd brought his betrothed to the bedroom. Before, I'd acted just as I should, waiting on the bed, my back against the post, legs spread just so. But the prince didn't come alone. It was the brunette in the red dress, the one I thought was beautiful, full of life and laughter.

Horen forced this upon Taryn a week past.

At the start of the night, she came in so willingly, touching Taryn all over, pouring herself onto him. But when she noticed I was in the room, she stopped and scowled. "What is that whore doing here?" she'd demanded.

Taryn had unhanded himself from the brunette's grasp, striding to the small table by the window to pour himself some wine. I watched his movements in defence and in the way he liked me to. The prince returned my smile with one of his own, surveying my pose over the brim of his goblet. He'd poured another drink and offered it to me, not glancing at the brunette growing more livid by the second at the dishonour of a slave being offered wine before her.

I'd finished my liquor swiftly, tilting my head to accept Taryn's short but deep kiss. He'd grinned, the faint bruise on his jaw the only remnant of the beating he received from Horen and his knights after Nora left. "Perhaps she is here to teach you the finer art of being my lover? Your atrocious attempts leave me weary."

He'd turned towards the girl, her head dipped low. "Look at me!" As he'd lowered his hand down to me, I took it without hesitation, so he could pull me to stand and fold an arm around my waist. I wanted to warn her—but of course, she didn't so much as glance at me. Instead, she ripped off her clothes. "Prince Taryn, I am yours. Now and forever. Let me show you I can please you better than your whore ever could."

Stupid girl.

"You do not know what pleases me, lass," Taryn teased. While his voice was light, I knew what lay underneath. Today was not a good day. But the girl took it as approval—flirtation and challenge. She sauntered forward, swinging her hips and breasts as much as she could.

Run, you goddamned fool.

She stopped short a meter before me and stretched out her fingers to brush against Taryn's hand splayed on my stomach. "But, if you would like, I could always demonstrate myself in ways I am sure you will enjoy." I couldn't see Taryn from where I stood, but I knew what twisted through his features. Anger at her impudence, anticipation for what was to come and the smallest hint of curiosity at her words. She grabbed my face with one hand and kissed me. Her lips were soft, but her grip was like a vice. She grasped Taryn's hand and pulled it off me, slipping around my hips. She deepened the kiss, exploring my lips and mouth with her tongue. I closed my eyes to fall into the pattern, confused, but curious at her touches. Different than Taryn's.

We were wrenched apart and the girl's piercing scream echoed through the room. Taryn grabbed her hair, dragging her away from me. He pulled her to his chest, tugging her face to meet his. "No one touches her without my leave, you stupid bitch! I do not care if you are going to be my wife, I do not care what you think you are entitled to. Estelle is mine!"

She sobbed through clenched teeth, tears pouring down her face. A stream of apologies and pleas flew out, but nothing she said eased Taryn's wrath.

Shut up. Stop crying.

Taryn's voice simmered softer and crueller. He dropped her hair and let her fall at his feet. "What pleases me are things done *my* way, not yours. Estelle knows this. So too must you learn."

The girl ceased crying just enough to shriek, "Just get the fucking whore out of here!"

So I could not witness her moment of weakness. I doubt she'd let anyone see her cry in quite some time. But that was the third time she'd called me a whore. Taryn usually killed people for uttering it just once. The strike was true and hard, his palm cracked against her face like lightning. Her wail of agony fractured something inside me—I could endure pain, but I couldn't endure this. "Stop! Please Taryn, the girl meant no harm."

His glare cut to me, shadows already marring his features. His eyes held mine as he landed a kick into the girl's stomach, leaving her heaving. I lunged forward, to fight him or heal her, I didn't know. He caught me around the middle, lifted my body over his shoulder, and carried me to the furthest wall, where a chain and manacles had been installed. I pleaded with him to spare the girl, to allow me to calm him, telling him I didn't mean to offend, but he shackled my ankle to the wall and stepped back to smile. "Finally, a new way to make you behave. A new way to make you *change.*"

Darkness consumed the air.

He took his time with the girl. She cried through it all and I tried to get to her, the bone snapping in my ankle as I did. In moments when she could, she turned her face to me and I held onto her stare with my own, passing any kind of comfort I could. But there was none to be had.

Not in this hell we'd both landed in.

CHAPTER 29
SHUTTING DOWN THE LAB

I stood, idle, behind the Prince and the King of Kiliac.

Large tables filled the throne room, transforming the space into a giant mess hall. The court was having an informal celebration to welcome the second prince back from whatever hellhole he'd been sent to.

Straightening the folds of my scanty dress, I winced under my breath at the pain in my right hand. It finally reset itself after being broken—after being shattered. I glared at the back of my master. I was to call him that now. He'd snapped a golden collar around my neck weeks ago to remind me.

He didn't tell me he loved me anymore.

I couldn't count the days, weeks, or months since the princess was brutalised and hauled out of Ashbourne. It was all darkness anyway. None of my ways of surviving, *enduring*, worked now. There was nothing I could do or say to ease my master's wrath. It was never-ending, and he took every scrap of rage out on me. Especially now I couldn't heal him at all. My magic had finally winked out.

I truly was an empty vessel. A ghost.

I was nothing.

The prince and the brunette were to marry soon. She was as

broken as I was, seated to his right at the high table. King Horen's voice boomed through the room, sending a jolt through the girl—my master's fingers dug deep into her thigh.

"Finally! After all this time, we can all celebrate my son's return home from his years of apostasy. *Finally*, Prince Ambrose graces my court with his presence." Horen's voice became pointed, violent. "Hopefully your year in Meriden taught you enough respect and discipline to make you worthy of your birthright, boy."

Prince Taryn's fingertips looked like they were about to puncture the girl's supple skin, but she did not tremble, did not shudder away. At least she'd learned that much. We both knew he'd do worse to her tonight for her moment of weakness, jolting at the king's voice.

The king. His words crept through my mind like snaking vines. Words amongst others, from a distant place. A distant time.

What is it to be then, lad?

Meriden.

I'm not saying goodbye to you.

Ambrose...Ambrose.

Rose.

My gaze lifted from the brunette's leg.

An attractive man with bright turquoise eyes sauntered into the throne room, an outward mask of arrogance and self-importance lining his steps.

The floor crumbled beneath me and my blood turned to ash in my veins as I watched the man I once loved approach the dais.

He hadn't seen me yet.

I don't think he would recognise me.

A year.

He didn't look the same, not entirely. His muscle mass had doubled and he seemed taller, or perhaps I'd become smaller—but it was him. It was Rose.

Ambrose.

Second son of King Horen.

Taryn's brother.

The air around me froze in the same moment the ash inside me did. Icicles fractured over my already broken skin, shattering every-thing. I was screaming. Clawing. Tearing. But no one heard, no one looked. I was nothing. I was no one.

My feet moved on their own, numbly stepping away from the wall I'd hidden against since arriving at this cursed feast—my gaze never leaving that turquoise blue.

Then he saw me.

Neither shock, nor horror, was enough to describe what I saw in him. The flames in his eyes could have incinerated everyone in the room.

Horen was still bellowing—I didn't know what—so everyone's attention was fixed on the king. Everyone's. Except Rose's.

My feet carried me another step before my master reached an arm out behind himself to grasp my waist. He tugged me in and planted a kiss to my exposed side, bit down, and shoved me away again. Only then did I tear my eyes off Rose.

My master once again focused on his betrothed, clamping her thigh in his grasp, so I padded along the wall and off the dais on silent feet. I remained hidden in whatever shadows I could until I reached the closest exit.

Rose's flaming gaze seared my spine the entire way.

When I was free of that room, free of the frozen air inside it, I was finally able to breathe. Then I convulsed. Wracking tremors tore through me. My feet began to run, carrying me towards the only place they could.

But before I could reach my master's chambers, an overwhelming sickness pummelled me from within. It started in my heart, incessant thumping, tendrils of black mist pulsating with every beat, until each limb and blood vessel was filled with it. Until there was nothing left but the darkness.

I fell against something, a wall perhaps, and slid to the ground, clutching my legs to my chest. The metal collar around my neck burnt hot as hellfire itself, but my heart kept pumping black mist and it became all I knew.

All I was.

I opened my mouth to unleash a silent scream, the ones I'd learnt to do. But when I did, the darkness exploded.

Close your eyes and think of something nice.

I squeezed my eyes shut as tightly as I could. When I opened them, every potted plant in the hall had withered and died.

~ AMBROSE ~

IT WAS HER.

After all this time.

Whenever I dreamt of her, she was waiting for me in Tor's cabin, or grinning wildly astride an ash-grey cioraun. Not here. Not in Ashbourne. Not standing behind my father with bruises and scars of all colours, shapes and sizes covering her skin. Her body.

She stared at me with emerald eyes, but they were not hers anymore. Like the death of a forest, the green in her eyes had wasted away—just like the rest of her. Maker, she was no more than skin and bone. The woman I love had become a wraith. An empty shell.

I was going to kill Horen.

His voice still boomed, still pounding off the Maker's forsaken stones, but I did not look. I did not care. She stepped away from the wall and I almost ran to her on pure instinct—until my brother seized her waist and pulled her to him. He kissed her skin. Then he *bit* her.

She did not fight it. She did not pull away from him. She did not even flinch.

Taryn. What have you done?

When he pushed her, *pushed* like she was nothing, she slunk away —keeping to the shadows in the black walls. Once she slipped through one of the smaller exits, disappearing behind it, I was pulled back into myself by Taryn's arms engulfing me.

He smelled like her.

I was going to be sick.

I was going to...going to...I glared at the dais and my blood burned as I saw my father's smirk, his attention pointedly flickering toward the door Estelle vanished behind.

"Brother!" Taryn clamped his hand over my shoulder, shaking roughly. "I never thought I would see the day!" His raised voice dropped to a whisper as he leaned in close. "Though his words are poison, he is glad to have you home as well."

I did not respond, so Taryn shook me again, trying to shrug off my stupor. *Brother.* My brother.

It was not my father who hurt Estelle in ways I...ways I would not imagine.

I could not break. Not yet.

"Taryn!" I roared, forcing my features to return to joy for two old friends, two loving siblings, reunited. I slapped my hand over his forearm. "It is good to see you, still as ugly as ever."

I had to get my brother out of here—I needed time.

Taryn laughed, and I chanced another glance at my father's smug face. He was consorting with some tittering courtier, a pleasure worker leaning atop his shoulder—time was not my friend.

It had to be tonight. It had to be now. Right under their fucking noses.

I looked at my brother with smiling eyes and a concerned bunching of my brows. "Brother, when I rode through the Cliffside Gates, no one was on watch—I do not mean to alarm you, but tonight could be a prime opportunity for any foe to slip in undetected, with three royals in one place."

Taryn's eyes darkened as a strange, unfamiliar shadow fell across his face. He dropped his hand, already striding from the feast. "Tell father where I have gone—we will speak properly when I return."

Yes brother.

We will.

~ ESTELLE ~

SLAMMING SHUT THE DOORS to my master's chambers, I scurried toward the barred windows of the foyer. I couldn't go anywhere else, someone would see me. *Someone would know.*

I was a magi healer, yes, but that power? I didn't know what it was.

Flaming turquoise seared through my mind as I tried to heave against the iron bars. My wrists barked in agony, bones popped and ground together, but I kept pushing—with everything I had. It wasn't much.

The door flew open and I whimpered, my body betraying me. I fell to the stones and backed into the corner like the goddamned rat I'd become.

Don't cry. He'll break another finger.

The burning dried up and my body stilled. Heavy boots rushed forward. *Don't cry. Don't flinch. Don't scream.*

Strong hands grasped my arms and heaved me up. I let myself be, let my body fall limp and submissive, but my eyes landed in turquoise.

The black pumped from my heart and unbidden tears flowed as a voice rang out within the ever-growing shadows.

"Estelle!"

Don't cry, don't scream.

Stop crying.

But I couldn't stop. Darkness devoured me. I cried and wailed and screamed for my mother to save me—for Tor to save me.

"ESTELLE!"

He was yelling now. He was going to punish me.

I tried to scamper away, but he held tight.

"No!" I pleaded. "I'll be good! I'll be good! *I'll be good!*" The black mist reached my throat—I was about to explode, about to succumb to the Maker—the firstborn son of the dark.

Soft hands cupped my face and a warm brow pressed against mine. "Come back to me. I know who you are, and you are not this." That voice? It was not my master's voice.

"Please, lass. *Please.*"

The mist inside me scattered and I opened my eyes to gaze upon a face I'd loved so much—had suffered so much for. "Come back to me," he said again.

I blinked and the shadows vanished as well.

"There you are, wayfarer."

I studied his face, pressed my brow into his. It was Rose. It was my Rose.

No.

His name is Ambrose.

I wrenched my head from his and punched him.

He smiled and relief flared in his eyes. The damned bastard *smiled.* "We have to go—now."

I glanced around the room and trembled—my master's room. If Prince Taryn caught me here with another man, even if it was his brother...Rose was his *brother.* Rose was a prince. Rose was Horen's second son.

I snarled and punched him again. Before I could do it a third time, he caught my hand and pressed it to his face. "I am going to get you out of here."

Words seemed near impossible. "Taryn," I managed to rasp.

The fire in his eyes flared at the name, but Rose did not speak in anger. "I have sent him to the Cliffside Gates, and my father is distracted for the time being, though not unaware I know you are here. We have to make for the Fayr pass. Just the two of us."

"Why?"

For a moment, his face twisted, brows furrowing, but as he studied me, they smoothed out. "What kind of a man would I be, if I do not get you out now?"

I didn't have an answer.

"Listen," his words hurried now, a desperate edge to them. "I need you to help me—I cannot do this alone. I need you to be strong."

So long—for so long I had given up on myself entirely. But Rose had not. He would not. I hadn't tried, hadn't thought to try and get myself out again. My freedom, my salvation, lay in the eyes I hadn't even allowed myself to dream of. His burning gaze kernelled a small fire inside me, so I nodded and was pulled out of the corner and through the threshold of my prison.

WE RACED THROUGH CANDLE-LIT HALLWAYS, keeping to the shadows and holding our breaths lest a rat in the walls might hear. As we rounded a corner and could not avoid the notice of an oncoming patrol, Rose pressed me against a wall and bent to grasp my leg beneath the knee, pulling it up to wrap around his waist. I didn't even think to refuse, that wasn't my choice anymore. But this wasn't Taryn. Though a prince and his brother's whore—it was as good of a disguise as any. He leant in, enveloping me in his warmth and citrus scent and kissed my neck above the collar. Nothing but the stone wall I'd built inside felt the touch.

Before the guards were too close, the softest whisper sounded in my ear. "Forgive me."

I tilted my head, accentuated a sensual gasp, and curled my fingers through his hair. When the guards sniggered and passed out of sight, Rose grasped my hand and we shot off again.

Down the halls we ran in silence and shadows, returning to our farce when others threatened our escape. At some point, the stone wall inside me began to crumble with the caress of his fingers or the brush of his lips, but we shared no words.

He led me to a place I'd never seen before. The distinct smell of horse and hay greeting me as we burst through the door of the castle's stables. Racing past stalls, horses shied and cried out, indignance coursing through them. Tucked into the end of the building, three separate stalls were headed by large golden gates. Behind two, stood enormous black war horses, but behind the third was a familiar and pretty bay mare.

Rose didn't tack the horse, leaping onto her bare back and hauling me up behind. Leaning forward, he pressed his legs into Finn's sides and we hurtled out of the stall past befuddled stable hands, before greeting the dark streets of Ashbourne.

Instead of heading for the front gates of the city, Rose veered Finn to the left, halting her aside a small building close to the castle grounds, housing a forge at the front. Rose slid from the mare, twisting to catch me as I did the same. His quiet yet sharp knock on the door was answered by an older man, short, bald and stocky. He saw me first, eyed widening, before turning them to Rose. "Prince Ambrose," he said in way of greeting.

Rose pushed past him, pulling me inside. "The collar, Farrangar." Any looks of uncertainty or puzzlement erased from the smith's face at the cool command.

"Of course, lad." He rushed to his forge, retrieving a small, thin tool. Apparently, the collar that could only be removed by a slave's owner was removed easily by a few clicks of a well-made pin. "I would have thought you could pick this one yourself, Ambrose," he muttered as the collar slid from my throat and clattered to the ground. "I did not spend those years teaching you the skill for naught."

Eyeing the collar upon the stones, a mighty surge of night-kissed air filled my lungs, bringing with it a faraway smell of cloves and hide.

Rose curtly thanked the smith and made for the door. I brushed my fingertips over bare skin and dropped my hand, stepping forward to follow. Farrangar stopped me with a voice like warm honey. "Here, lass, take these."

When I whirled to face him, the man held out a soft leather knapsack, filled to the brim with finely crafted arrows, the fletching peeking out of the top. I grasped the bag, not daring to refuse an offered gift. He turned and strode to the weapon rack in the corner and pulled down a beautiful white oak bow, extending it out to me, smiling kindly at my blank face. "My sister lives in Salem. You saved her and her daughter. Go with the Maker's grace, child."

I grasped for the words before I found them. "I can't repay you."

Another honeyed smile. "You already have. Twice over." He gestured to Rose, waiting impatiently astride Finn. "Go," the smith urged. To feel the bow in my hands again—my face contorted and Farrangar nodded as if he understood.

Rose stretched a hand down to pull me up behind him again. Farrangar darted from his home, offering a sword up to Rose. "Stay strong, Prince. Take her home."

A hiss in Finn's ear had us galloping through the streets, leaving the blacksmith in plumes of dust, and we almost cleared the city before the shouts rang out and bells began to toll.

Rose dug his heels harder into Finn's side and she widened her stride. People lingering in the streets after dark barely missed being knocked aside as we flew by. It was only when we passed the main mass of clustered buildings and were racing toward a gate in the outer wall of the city that Rose drew the sword.

Between that gate stood two guards. Ready, it seemed, for the horse and its two riders charging them down.

I didn't know if I could do it, but I had to try. My hand felt near shattering, but I leaned around Rose, nocking an arrow and pulling the bowstring taut.

In time with Finn's next bound, I let my arrow fly.

My arrow pierced one man in the chest. Apparently, some things never leave you.

That left the other man for Rose, who made short work of him by making Finn sidestep as he swung his sword in a low arc, and we broke through the blood-soaked gates, leaving Ashbourne in our wake.

WE RODE for a long time over dusty, dead earth, with high cliffs swallowing us on both sides. Finn did not slow, she stayed true, yet I could feel and hear her heavy pants as she galloped. In the far distance, the black mass of a sprawling forest appeared on the horizon.

Home, my wretched soul cried.

Galdurne.

Rose pulled Finn into a halt, hooves skidding along the dirt. I slammed into his back as he flung a leg over her side to dismount and he whirled to me, still mounted. "Go, Estelle."

I stared down at him blankly. "What?"

"You have to—Finn is not fast enough with us both. Get to the forest."

I realised then. I understood.

Rose never planned to escape with me.

Shaking my head, I slid from Finn amidst his groan of protest. Whatever he had done since talking me out of the darkness, however he'd gifted me back my soul, that flake burned deep inside me. And it hurt. Everything hurt.

"Don't do this," I said. "We're not doing this again. We can protect each other." I gulped down my strangled breath and drew my brows in close. "Don't leave me again."

A tear ran down his cheek. "I never left you, lass, and I never will."

The echoes of beating hooves and bellowing orders echoed up the canyon. The time since we said goodbye fell into the dust around us. What I'd done, what I'd endured, and what *he* was—it was all forgotten as I stepped forward and kissed him.

Forgotten, for a moment. Then I allowed the pain, the guilt, and the love I'd felt for him plunge through my lips. He met me there. We stole that moment away from the world, amidst the beating hooves pounding like a war drum.

I did not break away as he wrapped his arms around my waist, lifted and carried me back to Finn. Only when he pushed me up so I could scrabble onto her back did we stop, but I leaned down and grasped his chest, clinging to his tunic. To him.

"It is okay," he said, voice breaking over the words. "You are going to be okay. You are free." I did not let go, so he dropped his face down to kiss my hands, one by one, untangling them from his tunic. He smiled through his tears. "I love you, Estelle Verndari. I have always loved you."

A loosened, dry sob was my only reply, before he lurched forward to hiss into Finn's ear and we left him in a veil of dust. I yelled out, screamed, tried to make her stop, make her go back for him, but whatever Rose trained her to do was firmly instilled. Finn galloped away as fast as her legs could carry us. Swifter now, that over half the weight was gone.

I twisted in my seat to find him, and saw through the haze in my eyes, that Rose was on his knees in the dirt.

~ AMBROSE ~

SHE WAS OUT.

She was free.

I sank to my knees.

She was gone.

The maniacal chase finally caught up and Taryn's raging voice called for them to halt as dirt and rocks spewed up from the ground to shower over me. "We are not going to catch her now on that cursed horse!" my brother roared.

I had never heard such a poisonous voice escape his lips. It seems I did not know my brother at all anymore.

Footsteps crunched on the stones, two black boots trod into my vision. Taryn grabbed me by the arms and hauled me up, shaking me like a wolf with a kill. "Why?" He screamed in my face. "Why would you take her? She is mine! *Mine!*"

I stared at the face of the brother I once knew, but the shadow had fallen over his features again. Something in my own face must have soothed him, though, for the shadows guttered and his eyes became clear.

I could pinpoint the second he figured it out, and have never seen such terror and devastation on the face of a man.

I did not care.

I plunged my sword low into his gut and twisted.

CHAPTER 30
EVERYBODY WANTS TO RULE THE
WORLD

I was free. Away from Ashbourne.

Away from Taryn.

Finn raced beneath me, galloping like she was carried by the wind. I tried pulling on her mane, but I didn't know how Rose trained her to slow, or even how to stop. I guessed she would run until she tired. That did not seem like it would happen anytime soon.

The dark mass that was Galdurne grew larger, like a colossal monster yawning its mouth open wide, swallowing up the sky. I was so close.

Closer.

I didn't think I'd ever see it again.

Every booming stride of Finn's gallop bringing me toward Galdurne sent my heart into another thundering beat. And then it hit me, the smell of the trees. It woke me from the darkness consuming me. Because I hadn't died. I hadn't wasted away into nothing. I was not nothing—not now. I'd just been sleeping.

So had the beast inside me.

It roared as we flew through the tree line.

Finn soared past familiar oak trees, slowing only to leap over an obstacle in her path. She did not falter once.

Then an arrow cleaved the air and plunged into her neck.

The momentum of her speed had us both flailing forward as she plummeted. Her chest struck the ground, hard, but Finn gave a final surge of power to throw me to the side so I wasn't crushed when she rolled. The impact of my body against the hard-packed earth rattled my bones, and with each roll away from the mare, sticks and rocks shredded my skin, tearing bloody ribbons through me.

A black haze engulfed my senses.

I tried and failed to stand. Twice. Three times.

Only the distant rumbles of malevolent laughter shook off the oncoming unconsciousness. Blinking furiously, I could barely make out colours and shapes, my eyes snatching on a brown mass writhing on the ground not two meters away—screaming in pain. Finn. Rose's Finn. His last gift to me. In my stupidity and haste, I'd let Finn run into a slaughter.

Amidst laughter and the harried murmur of deep voices, I crawled on trembling limbs through the dirt towards Rose's horse, wheezing her final breaths. Placing a quivering hand on her twisted neck, my forgotten power surged. Released from behind a floodgate, but the tendrils of light had nothing to grasp onto. No life. Finn was too near death's door.

"Thank you," I whispered through the fire in my throat.

With the sound of my voice, her shuddering breaths calmed and her brown eyes found mine. Shame and guilt plagued my heart as the life inside her eyes faded to black. Taking the mare's head between my hands, I rested my brow into her fur. "I'm so sorry," I said through a strangled breath to her broken corpse.

The laughter behind me grew louder, the sound cackling through the air, tainting it with that poison. I should have been afraid. But I was not.

I was angry.

I didn't have time to stand and heal myself, so I lunged. My limbs were weak, but I scrambled for my fallen bow, swollen fingers grappling with the riser. My hands shook as I reached for an arrow to nock and I twisted up and around to aim.

Too fast. I pushed myself too hard and too fast—I was nowhere near as strong, nor as capable as I was a year past. Now, my frail body finally gave out. Blood rushed to my head and I collapsed to the ground in a heap of bones and flailing limbs, the bow falling from my hands. The soldiers cackled louder as they circled and my anger simmered into desperate, deranged fury. I lurched to grasp for the bow again, but within the red haze my rage created, I couldn't nock an arrow.

Some of the men bent double in hysterics, no doubt eyeing the shimmering black tatters that used to be my dress, or the scrabbling maniac wearing them. I tried to shoot, but the arrow fell to the ground. I reached for another. The second went further, but only implanted itself in the dirt a good five feet away from the nearest man.

It was then my wrist snapped, the sound reverberating through the trees.

I didn't scream from the pain. Pain was something I'd learned to live with. I screamed, because I was not supposed to be so helpless once I left Ashbourne—once I made it home.

When my scream faded into the air, I stood with useless hands dangling at my sides. My power fluttered at my fingertips, but I forced myself to gaze upon the muddy, pock-marked face. Forced myself to stare into his ruddy eyes, his twisted grin. I made myself watch, almost like a slow-motion film, as he drew his arm back—making a fist with his hand, and swung it forward into my face.

My head pounded with the impact, nose crunching, but lunacy thrust to the surface as blood poured from my nose into my mouth. I smiled broadly. Taryn was twice the size of this man, in almost every possible way. Taryn punched twice as hard, too. This man's strike was barely a caress upon my cheek in comparison.

Through rabid adrenaline, or something more primal, my body acted as if possessed. My unbroken arm reached for the soldier's dirk sheathed at his waist, grasped its hilt, and swung it up and through his neck. Slicing through the flesh was easy, and the man's blood flooded my face, entwining with my own, running into my mouth like sour wine.

A second cleaving of the air sounded before a sharp jolt in my forearm had me releasing the dirk.

I glimpsed the arrowhead gorged halfway through my skin as another piercing strike to my hip sent me crashing down to the forest floor once again. Memories crashed into me. *He was walking towards me. I was cowering.*

But beneath my hands were leaves and grass, this wasn't Taryn's bedroom. Those weren't Taryn's boots.

I lifted my glare to the hazel eyes of another man, his face contorted with malice. Hatred darkened his face, hatred at what I'd done to his comrade. Good. I hated him too. My lips pulled back into a snarl as the surge of darkness within me ignited, letting him see the wild beast beneath my skin.

Clammy hands lurched and grabbed my neck and my hair. The forest floated away and spots of white lights winked in and out of existence. I was dying. Some part inside of me knew it. Death pulled at me. Like a thread tugging at my ribcage, death called.

It was all I'd wanted—death. A quick way to wrench me out of this world and back into my old one. But perhaps the stars had heard my wish that night, when I was in the arms of another. Content and happy beyond measure.

Perhaps death would not wake me.

So, for the first time since Tor's life guttered from his eyes, I did not want to die. Not here. Not now.

I wanted to live.

The ironclad hand around my neck felt like a slave-collar, the metal encasing and cutting off air, and the small firelight of my power blew out.

The metal.

I couldn't reach my magic because of the fucking metal.

If I could get out, if I could *breathe*, I could heal myself. I just needed to breathe.

I woke to darkness and pain as my head was slammed into the

ground. My already fog-ridden skull jolted and mud filled my mouth. The hand wrapped in my hair yanked back to lift my face, then a rough shove slammed it back against the ground.

Again and again, my head was battered into the mud.

I felt like I was underground, surrounded wholly by dirt and blood, gasping for air. I was suffocating. The pull towards death intensified, grappling around me, wrenching my soul from inside my bones.

My eyes glazed as my hair was pulled back another time, and the world held its breath. The mud fell away and smoke clouded my fading vision. Smoke from the surrounding camp I'd no doubt been dragged into. And those were cheers that were pounding into my ears. Incessant jeers and bawdy yelling, egging on each thrashing of my face into the ground. I couldn't make out any words.

The tug from inside my ribcage became tumultuous. It built, reinforcing like a bridge.

Or a chain.

Made of gold.

I squinted through the billowing smoke, right towards a colossal dark shape charging through the trees.

A great dappled white stag with a dark face and black legs appeared from the shadows, spearing straight for me. Its antlers were mighty, curved and pointed like dragon wings about to take flight. Iridescent golden eyes lined with molten fury stared into mine before cutting to the soldier flailing the life out of me.

I blinked as Achilles leapt over my head to strike the soldier in the head with his hooves. The resounding crack of bone and tendon reverberated through Galdurne itself.

The soldier didn't have time to scream, but the camp did. The jeers and laughter morphed into shouts of terror and warning as the giant stag dropped to his knees beside me. My face and body were crushed, pulverised to deformity, but the primal instinct of mine returned tenfold, it returned strength to my hands. I grasped my dyr's neck as he thrust it beneath me, and using his might to pull me onto his back, he rose from the mud.

There was no time for joy or relief as I felt Achilles lurch away from the camp, angling toward where I'd fallen with Finn. The stag skidded to a stop, sending a rain of muck upon the body of the soldier I'd killed and the bow I'd dropped.

I didn't squirm or make a sound as I ripped the arrow from my hip and snapped the shaft in my arm in half, wrenching out both ends and tossing them to the ground. Without the ironclad chokehold, my magic resurfaced, barrelling through me with the force of a freight train now that it linked with my dyr. Golden light erupted in my chest, tendrils of liquid gold flowed through my bloodstream, healing wounds internal and external alike. Lingering injuries were erased or fixed, bones reshaped and strengthened.

I was healed and reborn by the time the first line of soldiers broke through from the trees before us. Old blood plastered my face, neck, and chest, and I welcomed it.

Achilles sidestepped and bent so I could reach the bow and arrows, and the feel of the riser in my hands sent an old feeling of confidence and power through me. I was good with a bow and I would not miss again.

The soldiers bellowed their battle cry, officers screaming obscene prices for my head and Achilles's antlers. They continued their blind charge, swords raised and faces full of rage—the fools didn't even hear the deadly growls and snarls coming from the shadows behind me.

But I did.

And I could feel it.

Feel *them*.

The thudding of heavy paws slammed down on the earth beside me and a ferocious roar pierced the air like a thunderclap.

The soldiers halted. All of them—mouths gaping in undiluted terror.

At me, astride my mighty stag, healed with a bow trained on them.

At the ciorauns beside me, crouched low, ready to pounce, snarling mouths dripping with anticipated bloodshed. And at the trees surrounding us, where creatures great and small appeared from the dark.

They had come.

They had come for me as they came for Achilles that day. I roared, releasing a battle cry of my own. Every creature resounded my call. Even the officer's own damned horses, who screamed and threw their riders. Rearing, they brought heavy hooves down upon their throats.

The soldiers formed lines, three parallel ones to push us back, or defend themselves.

A feral grin stretched across my face.

The first line fell from the yaus, ghosting between their legs and swiping razor-sharp claws through the back of their ankles. As the first line crashed down, the wolves and smaller animals swarmed the second. Achilles and I, with the ciorauns at our side, soared over their dying bodies to strike the final line. They fell like stalks of wheat in a hailstorm.

We were the storm. A storm of claws and fangs and fury.

I smelt the soldier's fear. It ran down their legs in turrets of piss and shit.

Arrow after arrow I let fly into the chests, necks, and faces of soldier after soldier.

More creatures flew in from the shadows, descending upon the camp from every direction. Small figures darted into the fray, humanoid but the size of children, carried by flurrying luminescent wings.

Vix.

They shrieked with delight as they plunged into the humans, and I didn't stop long enough to find out why spraying blood marked their path.

With each mighty bound of Achilles' stride, another soldier fell by my arrow or his hard-hitting antlers. Every shot I fired was one I'd practised a thousand times, with a father now gone instructing me how.

We reached the edge of the camp in a matter of seconds, Achilles easily cleared a tent and planted hooves into the mud to skid and twist back. Before we dove into the fight again, a shimmering white mass caught my sight from the trees to the left, and my breath lurched as it stepped out of the tree line. Because it looked for all the world like a dragon.

The beast had four taloned feet and a long serpentine tail. Wings of glimmering moon-white membrane were tucked tightly into its sides and its eyes were wholly black—their depth could not be described. Moon-white scales caught the day's first light through breaks in the canopy, glowing as bright as the white hair of the woman riding it.

No. Not a woman. A female—an elf.

She was terrifying. Beautiful. Lethal.

The female's skin was so dark it shone. Silver feline-like eyes narrowed as she took me in. Her lips twisted in a hiss, four long fangs shooting out. And her ears, they were not rounded and tipped like I would have thought, but thin—jutting out of her head like knives. Her full lips closed over her fangs as she registered me astride Achilles pawing the mud, eager to help end the battle.

The elf's smile was a frightening thing. Terrible. Exquisite.

She drew two slim swords that glistened like glass from her back, winked, and thrusted her hips forward to signal her mount. They leapt into the thickest group of cowering soldiers and guttural screams followed.

Achilles lurched back in, trampling dead and dying men as I resumed my part of the carnage, trying not to marvel at the elf and her mount—at the savage grace with which they slaughtered.

I played my part, finally, after all this time. I helped to wink out the poison from the forest, *my forest*, one by one.

The beast inside me stayed silent.

And that was when I realised—there was no beast inside me at all. There never was.

I was the beast.

As the last scream faded into the cool breeze of dawn, halcyon crept into Galdurne. I turned my attention from the dead bodies and pools of blood, and the creatures stalking and feasting upon it all.

Relief consumed me—I let it. My dyr was never dead, just waiting. Waiting all this time for me to return home. I slid from his back, marvelling at how large he'd grown in my absence. Larger than any horse and certainly larger than the white stags I'd found him with—he would have to be nearly twenty hands high now.

He was here.

His golden eyes followed me when I fell to my knees before him, and his great head dropped as he held my gaze with his own. "I've missed you," I rasped, half-way between a breath and a sob as his antlers encased me, forming a protective barrier between us and the world.

He blinked at my voice, eyes filling with liquid gold.

As one golden tear fell, any stronghold I'd kept inside crumbled. I didn't cry, I wasn't allowed to cry, but I squeezed my eyes shut and leant into him. Let the pain of my year without him consume me so he could feel it too. A mourning of sorts, of the person I was.

Of the father I'd lost.

We shared a moment of grief before an unearthly hiss sounded behind me. Achilles' antlers lifted as I whirled. He stepped into my path, using his forelegs to shield me from the bared teeth of the elf's mount, so I shuffled out from beneath his chest to stand beside him, staring down the creature. It hissed again, the sound enough to bring the bravest to their knees—but I feared beasts less than humans now.

"Hush, Taegu."

I'd expected a clipped, brutal voice at the least—an alien hissing at most. But the female's voice lilted like she was in a dream. It was soft and pleasant, most likely another weapon.

I looked past the creature's maw and saw her smiling down at me, and it was not a terrifying thing anymore.

The female angled her head, studying me before speaking in her lilting voice again. "I suppose it was you the forest sang for. To save." She gestured towards Achilles. "Though I think this one's bellowing could be heard across the land for many leagues. It was him who began the song." Another brilliant smile. "I am glad he found what he was seeking."

Her words were harmonious, like a mother singing a lullaby to her child. I glanced at her mount again, moon-white scales shifting in the morning light, it finally closed its mouth, tucking away those fangs. It rustled its wings, splaying them out wide and shaking them loose like a peacock would his feathers.

The creature reminded me of a dragon, at least, the sort described in Romanian mythology, yet not. Its body was similar to a horse, smaller than Achilles, stocky yet well-defined, but that was where that likeness ended. Its face—the only resemblance I could think of was...dinosaur.

The elf must have read the question in my eyes. "Taegu is a dracolisk. Much prettier than those fire-breathing lizards of the sky." I nodded, reaching an absentminded hand out to stroke the dracolisk's jaw. Taegu leaned into my touch, making a sound similar to a cat's purring.

I almost laughed.

At the elf's sudden gasp, I stole my hand back and snapped my gaze to hers.

"No one but me has ever touched her. Are you an apparition of my mind? Or are you a real human girl who does not shy from a maw full of sharp teeth?"

When I did not reply, Achilles nudged my shoulder with his muzzle. I glared at him. *Busybody.* "I find more comfort in a mouth full of teeth than..." but I didn't finish the sentence, instead I allowed it to drift away. Words seemed like a distant thing now.

So was I, really.

My mind threatened to rupture, so I shook it away and said the only other thing I could think of. "Are you real? I thought you were supposed to be extinct."

A stupid question. I should be punished for stupid questions.

The elf's silver eyes shifted with something I couldn't read as she spoke. "That is an open-ended thing. In the physical sense, my kind still exists in this world."

Right then.

I sucked on my bottom lip, grappling for another appropriate thing to say. Thoughts eddied through my mind, so many things to ask, a curiosity long-since diminished, battering from within. It crackled as if white noise consumed the morning air—too much noise. Too many thoughts. But on the other side was a pit so empty and deep, that if I fell in I'd never get out.

Longer than deemed polite, I remained sucking on my lip. But the elf waited, smiling down at me. "Where did you come from?" I finally asked.

She didn't miss a beat. "A place far from here. I can take you there, if you would like. If there is nowhere else for you to go?" Through the veil of genteel nicety, I sensed something else. She knew. Knew I didn't have anywhere else. I was lost. Free, but lost.

I couldn't go to Salem. Taryn would look there first. I'd probably already put Bjorn and Col and anyone else left alive there in danger by escaping from Ashbourne in the first place, but me being there would make it worse—far worse.

The cabin? I didn't think I could be there without seeing Tor everywhere I looked. Or Rose...*Ambrose.*

I was right all along. He'd played me for a goddamned fool.

All that bullshit he'd spat through the times we'd been together, he'd lied. His *dangerous* father was the fucking king. And Tor, he'd worked for Horen, fought for him. Neither of the men I loved had told me a damned thing, thinking they knew best about how I would take it, what I would think. What I would think of *them.*

But despite it all, I still believed Ambrose loved me.

I knew Tor loved me.

And what Ambrose did for me, only hours ago, letting me go. Again. All for the love he had. The love he'd kept since we parted a year past. I'd given into it, in that canyon. Or perhaps I was just as desperate as ever.

But Ambrose was the brother of the man who had owned me, body and soul, for an entire year. At the sudden maelstrom of bile rising in my throat, I couldn't tell if I was feeling hatred, shame, or betrayal. My living fantasy had turned into a twisted triangle between brothers.

Was that all it was? Some sort of monstrous game within their family?

They were both princes, such people could take and do what they wanted. They were entitled to do so. *And I am an interesting commodity, am I not?* Ambrose told me as much the first time he'd met me. He probably rode back to Ashbourne after every visit, discussing with his brother and father the secrets and technology of my world, the politics he was so bloody interested in—to ensure democracy would never rise in their time. *Estelle, you damned fool.*

I glared at the dead.

The encampment had become a graveyard, or at least, a buffet for the scavengers of the forest.

I could live amongst the animals—find shelter, destroy Ashbourne's legions as they came. Live alone, in a hovel.

There were worse ways to live.

A pointed cough brought me back from the depth of my thoughts. I looked towards the elf and shrank into myself—I'd taken too long to answer.

I should be punished.

Her silver eyes flashed again with that same ire I'd noticed before. Of course she'd be getting impatient, even if I sensed her enmity was not directed at me. Could she sense the bitter resentment pulsating from me in roiling waves? Her words grew softer. "You have been..." At my furrowed brow, she checked herself, shaking the emotion from her face. "I am offering you a place to go, little wildling. Come with me."

My mouth dropped open.

This beautiful, ethereal creature was offering me a home. A place to go. Somewhere far away from Ashbourne. Far away from the prince. *The princes.*

Perhaps where she wanted to take me was dangerous. Maybe more so than Ashbourne itself. Her kind might be crueller than the men I'd known.

No, that could not be true. They were denizens of Galdurne—I knew in my blood the elves would be better. And maybe I should not be alone, not now

Her airy sing-song voice cut through the air. "I am known to others as Nie."

I blinked up as the ghost of a smile threatened to tug at my lips. "Known to others? What are you to yourself?"

Insolence. I should be—

She beamed. "I am the stars, wildling. And you, you are the earth beneath our feet. You are the mountains that stand as tall as an eagle's eye."

I frowned deeper. "Why?"

The silver—the starlight silver—sparked brighter in her eyes. "Because no matter how hard the wind, the sea, and the flames try to bring down the mountains, they do not submit, nor does the earth on which we all stand."

"You don't know anything about me." She was wrong—she was so, so wrong.

Nie slid down from Taegu to stalk forward, and it was then that I noticed the elves were leaner than humans, their limbs longer. And Nie herself, skin of the darkest shade with hair like the moon, sharp cheekbones and full lips, she was the most beautiful thing I'd ever seen.

She came to stand inches before me, her face giving nothing away as her silver eyes stared into mine. "I can see it in your eyes, in the way you cling to the sanctuary of your dyr, yet face death without fear. You were born for greatness and will never again succumb to those unworthy of you. I know this, for it was written in the stars long before you arrived in this world, Estelle Verndari."

Too much noise. Too many thoughts—*too many words.* It took longer than it should, but I echoed what she'd said in my mind...over and over again. So I was not a mistake? It was written—foretold? Perhaps Nie could tell me more, tell me what the hell I was doing in this world. Perhaps she could help me in other ways, too.

As the words finally settled into me, she reached out. An offering —of her world.

I took her hand.

EPILOGUE

This cell, I decided, would be a horrible place to die.

In those long, frozen nights within the barracks of Meriden, I let myself dream about passing on an old man, my hand in Estelle's, with only the stars as witness. But of course, dreams were a ridiculous notion. A deluded man's fantasy.

My thoughts often drifted toward her in these seemingly endless nights beneath Ashbourne—nights of irrevocable darkness. Sometimes, I saw her wild laughter, her hair of wildfire, or felt her soft lips against mine.

Mostly though, I envisioned the way she cowered beneath those windows after trying to break through them, trying to throw herself into the night and death below. Or of how her obscenely scarred arm felt beneath my fingertips, how sallow skin stretched over her bones. After those nightmares, I woke with a start and screamed myself hoarse, trying to rip the pain from my mind, my heart, beating the stone wall until I could no longer feel my hands.

I knew he would come to me.

I knew it from the moment I wrenched that sword from his gut, aware that in the end, I had not aimed to kill. I suspected he had not come before now from fear. Fear of me.

Heavy footfalls proceeded the Heir of Kiliac, and they were altogether different than the ones that thundered toward me in Fayr's pass, driven by rage and fury. I discerned by the disjointed gait that he was anxious—he should be. The last time I saw him, he was a bleedin' mess. I have no doubt that if given the chance, I would run him through again with anything I could find.

I could not think of Taryn without seeing her. The way she recoiled, thinking I was there not to save, but to cause more pain. *The way she screamed at me.* Countless bruises, every bone visible through her sorry excuse of a dress.

Her scent entwined with my brother's.

I got her out. She is free. She is gone.

His footsteps halted before my cell, but I would not turn to him. I kept my feet planted as if they were rooted to the very stones. The black wall of my prison reflected the whirling light of a torch, and I wrung my aching hands together behind my back.

"The guards tell me that you are not eating, brother."

His voice was poison in my veins. I would not turn toward him. Yet my face betrayed me, contorting while my gaze remained locked on the stones.

"Are you feeling unwell, Ambrose? I will find a cook to make salted trout, your favourite. The way mother used to make it for you..." Taryn broke off and chuckled half-heartedly to himself, as if we shared a joke. As if we might exchange brotherly affections.

I should have killed him.

I should have aimed for his heart. Cause his as much pain as he had caused mine. Because my heart...he had beaten and shattered it into a million facets. Her red hair flickered in my mind, the way it swam in the air when she ran through the forest, highlighted by slivers of golden sunlight stealing through the trees. A living flame that kindled my soul. Even in the darkest of my days in the North. It was her, always her.

"Are they treating you well? They report you have not been touched. Have not been hurt."

Hurt.

Hurt?

I could not withhold the savage growl that escaped my lips, nor the shaking in my voice. "The way you hurt her?"

As that black wall swam and writhed in on itself, I squeezed my eyes shut. Two thuds on the ground behind me sounded. I whirled on instinct to see him kneeling.

Taryn's face was gaunt. Hollow. Tears lined his face and he clutched a bloody bandage wrapped around his abdomen with one hand whilst the other gripped a bar of my cell, his knuckles white. "I did not know. Ambrose, that woman from the note, the one he threatened you with Meriden for—I did not know it was Estelle."

"Do not say her name! You have no right!"

Taryn dipped his head. "I...Ambrose, you must know, I never knew, never suspected..."

"Bullshit!"

His face wrenched up, and my brother peered at me with pleading eyes.

I bared my teeth and shook my head. "Why does it matter?"

"It matters because I would never, *never* do anything that caused you pain."

"So inflicting pain to any other woman is alright by your standards?"

Taryn did not answer, but lowered his head and sank into himself. A strangled sob sounded as he pressed his forehead between two bars. Perhaps it was seeing the Prince of Kiliac so broken, so defenceless. Or maybe it was my own damned need to know, to *understand*, but I spoke again in a toneless voice. "Did you force her to..."

His burnished eyes lifted to me. Those damned eyes that used to ground me in the same way Nora's bright laughter or my mother's voice did. His throat bobbed and his mouth fell open before closing again. I knew he would have promised himself to tell me the truth—the whole truth—but it hurt no less when he finally spoke. "No, not... not the first time. She chose to be with me the first time, but she was desperate. Desperate for feeling."

My heart hammered inside my bones as the room fell cold. I stumbled, pressing my back against the wall and sliding to the floor.

The first time...

Taryn answered—I must have said the words aloud. "Yes, brother. But there were many times after, when I did not. Nora came to stay for a time, and it was good. We made love and—"

I could not breathe, could not think. Fire engulfed everything, my blood and bones burned. I grasped the closest thing I could find to throw at him. It took a long while to understand why a large brown patch appeared on Taryn's chest and started to drip down, but when I realised, something close to a chortle ripped from my chest, harsh and cold. "She was trying to survive you. You are a fool to believe it was anything different." I smiled to myself. "She *did* survive you."

"No, that is not true," Taryn rasped. "I love her—"

"SHUT UP!" I stood, pushing myself up with the force of a furnace. Taryn's face contorted, his cheeks flooded with tears. Words stuttered at his lips and I needed this to end. "You know nothing of love!"

Taryn released the bar to hold both hands across his torso and cried the way he had when we were helpless children, cowering under a table whilst our mother fought to keep us safe. "I did...I *do* love her. I just never knew how to do it right."

"It would have been easy. Just to not do any of the shit we saw when we were kids."

A shuddering whimper wracked through him. "I know...I know, Rose, I am so sorry."

Something cold and oily tainted the air around us, rising between us like fogged glass, but it did not lessen how hard each of his words hit me.

"I always thought you were different."

"I am different!" His fists slammed against the iron bars, hammers striking in a forge. "I am not like him! Rose, you must believe, there is something inside me I cannot control. She was good and beautiful and she was mine. I was so scared of being alone, being without her that... Rose, please!"

My gaze fixed on the ceiling, thoughts eddying with memories of Estelle's hair, but the strands leaked the hellish colour of blood and my vision stained crimson like an ichor into my shredded soul.

"She is not yours. She was never yours."

Taryn paused, stumbling over his own words. "I...yes...she was your woman, before—"

"She was never ours to own, you fucking shit!"

The silence that stretched after my bellow was wider than any other. Still, I kept my gaze locked upward, my jaw set.

When Taryn spoke again, it was in a voice that was agonisingly soft and timid. "Of course, I only mean—"

"Leave, Taryn. Do us both a favour and finish what I should have with that sword."

His voice broke over the next words. "You do not mean that."

"Next time, I will not miss your heart."

His quiet sobs filled not just my cell, but the dungeon around us. There was nothing left in my heart for this man, absolutely nothing. Still, when metallic footsteps heralded a small group of people approaching, I kicked Taryn's hand around the bar to alert him to the newcomers.

Horen's twisted face appeared outside my cell and he was positively grinning at his sons' anguish. His cheerful voice filled the void that Taryn's crying left bare, clapping his hands together. "Well, this is fun. I do love family get-togethers." When neither of us answered, he shrugged and set his hands upon his hips, branding Taryn with a scathing glare. "Now, my son, I thought I raised you harder than this. Get off your knees, you look like a ruddy vagabond."

Taryn shook his head slowly, and with more conviction in his voice than I heard all night, he snarled at our father. "I would rather be a vagabond than your son."

Horen simply laughed. "Why? With my help, you got to rut your brother's red-headed whore for a whole year." When I met my father's laughing eyes, I folded into the corner of my cell to blend into the shadows. I knew what this was, and did not want any part of it.

But Taryn's features hardened in a way I rarely saw when in the presence of the king. Through his many whispered words of hatred for Horen, his actions were always an endeavour to please our father. He used the bars to haul himself up. "Enough."

Horen smiled and returned his attention to his first born, but he spoke to me. "Do you not like the details, Ambrose? Would you not care to hear how Taryn loved to make her scream?"

Taryn bared his teeth, but I lifted my gaze to the ceiling, forcing the memory to appear of the day I found Estelle struggling to bathe her infant fawn in the stream. She is free, reunited with Tor and living within the trees...but Tor...if they found Estelle, surely they found him, and he would never have let them take her, unless...an unbidden tear fell down my cheek.

"She was fierce, your bitch." Horen's voice broke through my thoughts like a crack through glass. "If she was of noble stock I may have even been proud, how a blockheaded craven like you could have won her heart." He chuckled to himself. "And a *magi*, nonetheless. I often wondered whether being magi made her taste so divine, but alas, I never found out. You could ask Taryn, though. I know for a fact your brother took her maidenhead, trust you not to know where a cock goes."

I roared. My attempt to summon unsullied visions could not drown out what my father framed inside my head. "That is enough!"

Horen maintained his mocking demeanour, not paying my outburst any mind. "Did you know, my boy, after you had your arse handed to you in Meriden day after day and crawled under your blankets to cry her name, she was crying your brother's name? In pain or passion, one will never know but Estelle."

The bars clattered and I knew Taryn had punched them again. "You do not speak her name!"

Horen snickered louder now. "Are you defending her, Taryn? Oh, well that makes this much more fun. I promised her, you know? When we first met, she tried to defy me as all so often do, so I promised her that I would smile as I watched her break. You should be proud, son, it did not take you long to rut her bloody. It made my promise seem almost childish by comparison."

Fire erupted in my veins. I tore my gaze from the ceiling to blaze at Horen, his mouth twisting in a grotesque version of a smirk as he beheld me.

"SHUT UP! SHUT UP YOU FUCKING BASTARD!"

The king bounced forward, seizing two iron bars and settling his elated face between them. "And what made this all worth it, what really delighted me beyond measure, beyond *reason*, was that look on your deserting, cowardly face when you saw her standing behind Taryn. Bruised and broken, like shattered glass covered in flesh."

A beat of silence ensued, broken only by a sharp intake of air from Taryn. He blubbered and I turned to watch his jaw drop. He stared at Horen like he had never seen him before. Hated him, yes, but he'd never *seen* him as I had. Never known that our father was a monster wearing human skin. Taryn shook his head and whispered, "You did this...you...just to get back at Ambrose for leaving."

Horen's grin stretched from ear to ear. "No, son, you are wrong there. I knew she was Ambrose's woman, but she caught your eye, just as she caught his. Your purchase of her was entirely of your own volition. So, I thought, what better way to punish that deserting rat, then allowing his own brother to rut the girl he no doubt loved. It came together perfectly, really. I gave her to you to play with, and play you surely did. Went a little bit far at times, I admit. I never whipped your mother the way you flayed her that night."

Taryn recoiled as if Horen had struck him. Like a flower wilting on a frozen night, his eyes guttered and fell to the floor. Horen seemed satisfied and turned his attention back to me. So, just to see some semblance of ire from him, I returned an impish smirk of my own. "But she did beat you. She beat both of you."

His relaxed demeanour of contentment faltered, yet the corners of his mouth twitched. Churning blue eyes narrowed. "Are you perhaps as doltish as you look, lad? She—"

"She is free. She made it to Galdurne, and you cannot follow her. She will be stronger now than either of you can imagine."

"If you think she will ever be free from what your brother did—"

"She *is*." My smile softened as I remembered how the kernel of her old self ignited in that canyon, when she clung to me and kissed me with wild ferocity. I would carry that moment with me into the grave. "She is free and I will dance on your bloody corpses when she comes to rip you both apart."

Taryn looked between us, flinching when the realisation of my words sunk into him. Horen twisted to Taryn and crossed his arms. "Listen to how he threatens your throne, Taryn," he sniped, jerking his head to me. "Listen to the feeble words of a craven prince. A disloyal subject. What are you going to do?"

Another test. Always a test with Taryn and our father. Never once had I known Taryn to displease Horen in turn. But, his burnished eyes honed and he turned his lip up at the king. At the look of stilted surprise from Horen, I knew this was the first time Taryn had defied him outright. Perhaps in the past small discrepancies were allowed, but not like this. Not outright insolence from Horen's heir. "Get out. Leave us be, or I will help Estelle to kill you when the day comes."

Horen's clanging laughter was a dreadful thing. An omen. I could not help the sickening cold sweat forming at my nape. Not as his eyes flashed and he spoke in a soulless voice to Taryn, to us both. "Do you truly think it will be me she wants to destroy? Think on it, son."

The Heir of Kiliac crossed the distance between himself and the king and roared in his face. "GET OUT!"

Horen tittered and shrugged, picking at an invisible fleck of dust on his shoulder. "No. As they say, this is my party. And I will not tolerate disrespect from you, or your brother for that matter. Not anymore." He beamed at me. "Guards, get in there, tie Prince Ambrose down. No. On second thought—restrain them both."

I YANKED at the chains digging into my wrists, again and again. But the kingsguard wrapped them so tightly in the beginning I thought they would snap, even before they slammed me onto this marble table. Now, as the sound of Taryn's torture muted out even Horen's perverse laughter, the desire to break my hands to get out was so violent I was blinded to everything but my brother's agonised, inhuman screams.

I did not know what they were doing to him. They had locked him in a separate cell.

In the beginning, I told myself that I did not care. He was getting what he deserved. But somewhere along the line, Taryn's cries leaked through the fissures of my broken heart, first fractured when I laid eyes upon Estelle in the throne room.

My body writhed, muscles screaming, as I tried to wrench myself from the shackles to get to my brother. Nothing else mattered...I needed to make them stop. I yelled to the empty hallways beyond my cell, but my answer was another scream. And another. And another.

I blinked through unyielding tears, my brother's wails beating against my heart like a drum. Through shadows and haze, I wrenched my head to the side as the metal gate of my cell groaned. Horen sauntered in, blood staining his chest and arms, and he hummed merrily as he unsheathed a knife from his hip. I could just discern Taryn's torture continuing in the background. Obviously satisfied, or just keen to get on with me, Horen had left his kingsguard to finish with his heir.

Horen made his way around the table as I struggled beneath my chains. His clammy hand tugged at my hair, shoving my head into the marble. I watched, panting, as my father's face angled above mine, a rancid smile lifting his eyes in jubilant expectation.

His knife flashed in the candlelight as he twisted it through his fingers. "Now this, *this* is a party."

Taryn's screams echoed through the hall, the world, and reverberated into my chest. Horen's smile widened further still, as he leaned in and plunged the knife into my eye.

ACKNOWLEDGMENTS

Writing this book has been the hardest thing I've ever done, though it was never anything less than a work of love.

To the half of my heart throughout this journey, Hailie: from Estelle's conception, to my late night messages excitably updating you on the life of every character within this story, you have been there. This was nothing more than a pipe dream, until you commented on a post from a terrified Australian girl who was way in over her head. Your inspiration, kindness, and friendship has meant the world to me, and this book would have never been finished if it were not for you. Thank you.

To Katie. A, my courage, and my dear friend from across the pond: Without your wisdom, advice and commitment to helping me achieve my dream, I would have thrown the towel in long ago. You have been my supporter, goal-setter, and go-getter. I will never be able to comprehend, nor express my gratitude for what you did for me prior to this release. Thank you for listening to my doubts, my highs and my lows, and for getting me out of a massive reading slump with your incredible stories. Whilst our journeys may differ, our dreams are the same, and I cannot wait to live this life with you as my friend.

To Katie. L: I met you quite late in this journey of mine, though as they say it is the quality of a person rather than the quantity of time they've been in your life that matters. Thank you for all of your effort, guidance and support to help me achieve my goals. Those chaotic three days will never be forgotten.

To Dutch and Dancey: Thank you for being better people than most I've known in this life, even though you are both dogs.

To Shaun, Matthew and Leanne Kanowski, the best family I've ever had: Please skip Chapter 22.

To my cheerleaders—my friends, for encouraging me and filling my heart with all kinds of happy: Annette Willis, Maddy Crispin, Odette Binns, Tracey Ikerd, the blonde lady who read the first page at Office-works when it was printed, Julie Tweedy, and Adina Gunnis.

To the artists who brought my world and my characters to life, and who made me cry with joy: Odette A. Bach, Helena Elias, germancreative, kid-blue, and forest_diver.

And finally, to my amazing, patient, kind fiancé, Daniel: Fuck yes, I did it.

ABOUT THE AUTHOR

Clare Kae has always been a dreamer, finding her place in worlds and characters that seemed more real than what should have been expected. Though, when she's not daydreaming about faraway worlds, she's teaching primary school children in Australia.

Born and raised by a wonderful family and lots of spotty dogs, Clare had innumerable opportunities to see the world and enjoy life the way she wanted to growing up—especially via endless amounts of tea and books. For that, she will be forever grateful. She now lives with her incredible fiancé and two dogs—one spotty and one not.

When daydreaming became something more, and words flowed out of her head like rivers, Daughter of Dreams and Dread was born. Now an indie author, Clare is new to the journey of writing, but an excited soul to say the least.

To follow her on her adventures, feel free to join Clare on any one of her social media platforms, or her website.

www.clarekae.com

facebook.com/clarekaeauthor
instagram.com/clarekae
goodreads.com/ClareKae

CPSIA information can be obtained
at www.ICGtesting.com
Printed in the USA
BVHW080830091120
592851BV00015B/386